GRÆVITY'S
HEIR

SARA BOND

Black Rose Writing | Texas

ISBN: 978-1-68433-421-6
PUBLISHED BY BLACK ROSE WRITING
www.blackrosewriting.com

Printed in the United States of America
Suggested Retail Price (SRP) $19.95

Gravity's Heir is printed in Calluna

*As a planet-friendly publisher, Black Rose Writing does its best to eliminate unnecessary waste to reduce paper usage and energy costs, while never compromising the reading experience. As a result, the final word count vs. page count may not meet common expectations.

To James, my partner, my love, and my best friend. There's no one I would rather be weird with. Thank you for being my biggest fan, my partner in crime, and my truest love.

To Alex and Evie, the lights of my life. It's my privilege to be your mother, and I will gladly spend my nights writing if I can spend my days with you.

To Sarah Sover, my other half. Whether it's dancing, writing, drinking, or raising our kids together, you have been an inspiration, a comfort, and a friend. Thank you.

To Glen Delaney, Kat Harrowick, Stephanie Sauvinet, Sarah Sover, and Angela Super, aka the People What Writes The Space Magic Stuffs. Y'all are the best CPs in the world. I don't know how others manage to write books without their own personal crew of creative mercenaries, but I'm glad I have you.

To my family, the Hinsons, Kratzes, and Germains. My characters always have family problems because it's dramatic. I'm lucky enough to have to make all of it up, because my family is supportive, loving, and a forever comfort. I love you all so much.

Finally, to anyone who has bought this book and enjoyed Lena's journey, thank you for reading. I hope you enjoyed it.

GRÆVITY'S
HEIR

CHAPTER ONE

It was so small. Too small to be this important.

Lena set down her wine glass, picked up the thumb-sized datastick, and turned it over a few times. As if touching it would tell her anything. What sort of state secrets were hidden away in there? Blackmail? Corruption? Boring policy papers? The dull metal rectangle weighed almost nothing.

This was too easy.

She leaned against the unforgiving wood back of the booth and squinted in the darkness of the hotel lobby bar. "And all you want us to do is bring this datastick to Rien?" She hadn't been back to her home planet in seven years, but for the money he was offering, she was willing to make the long trip.

Pierce Mason smiled and took another long sip of his amber-colored whiskey. "Just bring it to Rien. My contacts will take it from there. No need to get you involved with the whole sordid mess of details." He hadn't changed a bit: still smug as he'd been as a teenager. Though with his money, he could afford to be.

"Sounds easy enough," Gael said beside her. Her shipmate shifted to get out of the booth, but Lena subtly shook her head as she lifted her glass to her lips again. She could hear the crowds amassing outside, the sounds of celebration already underway, and she knew how anxious he was to get to the Independence Day parade. It didn't matter. Gael didn't know Mason like she did. There was more here.

"Easy?" Mason's eyes darted around the bar, scanning the empty booths and shadows. "My contact spent months working in Pyrrhen labs getting this data. If they even knew we had it, they wouldn't hesitate to take out the entire city to erase its existence." He swallowed hard, put a hand to his chin, and popped his neck loudly. Lena nearly rolled her eyes. Mason always was dramatic.

"Never mind," he continued. "The less you know, the better. You don't even have to access the data. Better if you don't. Just cryptographic nonsense. Won't even make sense most likely." He sipped his drink again. "But yes. Hard part's done. It's easy from here. Just transport it, and avoid declaring it at customs. I trust the pay is enough for such a job."

"Sure," Lena said evenly. "Small but risky. And some laws are just meant to be broken," she added, invoking her family's motto. She took a sip of her drink and darted a glance at Gael seated next to her. It was dim in the secluded nook of the bar, and Mason had chosen a high-walled booth far from the hotel's reception desks. They had the place to themselves, with everyone else from this part of the moon making their way to the Aegean Independence Day Festival downtown. The dark oak and minimal lighting made the place feel oppressively secretive, which was suitable, given their conversation.

Lena waggled her eyebrows at Gael and gave him a grin. This "easy job" had complications written all over it. Which meant they could demand even more money than the small fortune Pierce had proposed. Gael immediately sat up straighter and mouthed, "No." She smiled wider. Gael might out-rank her on the ship, but this was her deal to make. She ignored him and snapped her head back to Mason.

"We want double what you promised."

Gael sighed loudly. Mason was already offering them enough cash to fuel the *Aspasia*, feed their entire crew of five for a full year, and keep them in wine and whiskey for at least a few months.

But Lena knew what she was doing. Never mind that she hadn't seen Mason since she left home. She knew the kind of money he came into when his parents passed away. Combine that with the salary he received as Rien's ambassador to Aegea, and he had cash to burn. Plus, if he was bragging about the difficulty of getting this datastick and its contents? That made it pretty damn valuable.

She knew he'd pay whatever she asked.

And Mason knew it, too. He smiled as he dropped his gaze and shook his head. "You never change." He brushed a lock of wavy black hair away from his face and turned to Gael. "You ever hear the story of Lena and, what was her name? Violet? Daisy?"

"Poppy." Lena sighed. She reckoned this was part of the payment. Mason was stalling, changing the subject. Reminiscing. Again. It was why their one-hour meeting had turned into a two-hour lunch, followed by drinks and small talk at a dark and nearly empty hotel bar. It had taken this long just to get to the details of the actual job, and now he was dithering on, bringing up the past she was still trying to forget.

"Poppy! That's it. What an insipid little girl." He settled back into the booth with his whiskey, all too ready to reminisce. "We all went to school together. Us and the Mezner boys. All of us too rich society kids, we thought we were everything. The world revolved around us." He jutted his chin out and eyed down his nose at Lena. "Well, worlds really did revolve around some of us, eh LeeLee?"

"Don't call me that," Lena snapped. This was exactly why she'd resisted taking a job from him. Mason knew her too well. At least, he knew the old her. If he was going to bring up things from their school days? It was only a matter of time before he started in on the reason she left. The reason she avoided conversations about her past. She was not ready to deal with that. "The datastick—" she tried again.

Mason waved a hand dismissively at her. "Yes, yes. I'm getting to it." Mason turned his attention to Gael. "So Poppy, little blonde bit of fluff, but she was the bossiest thing you ever did meet. Butted heads with our girl here all the time." He gestured with his whiskey, sloshing the drink at Lena. "Didn't you date her once, too? Before Evan came into the picture, of course."

And there it was. Evan. Lena knew where this conversation was headed, and she wasn't going to have it.

She looked pleadingly at Gael. Before the meeting started, Lena had begged him to help keep things on task, to get their business done with and get them out to the Independence Day Festival. Cedo, their mechanic, was downtown already, and Lena had been looking forward to catching up with his family before they left again.

Gael just shrugged and offered an upright palm. He was right. She had insisted that she was in charge of these negotiations. The deal was hers to make. She had to save herself from death by nostalgia.

"Enough." She reached over, took the whiskey out of Mason's hand, and slammed it down beside the bottle of wine and two other whiskeys, almost all of which Mason had consumed by himself. "We're only on this forsaken moon for another few hours, I want to take in the festivities, and you're stalling." She lifted a hand before he could interject. "We'll take the job. I just have to know who I'm bringing this data to. If you try to waste our time anymore, I'm walking out that door, and you'll have to find someone else crazy enough to transport state secrets across the galaxy."

Mason sobered up as much as he could. He closed his green eyes, nodded a few times as if steeling himself. He looked at her levelly. "Lena, please believe me when I say I wouldn't ask you to do this if I had any other choice. Trust me, I would rather give it to anyone else."

"Gee, thanks?"

"Just listen to me." He reached for a glass. Water, this time. "I trust you. I can't say that about many people. I know it's been years since... since everything happened." He sipped. "But I know you. You haven't changed. When it all comes down to it, you don't let people down."

Lena snorted. "I do my job. And this? It's just a simple drop job. The politics of the issue are just a distraction. Tell me where on Rien to take it, and we'll get it there."

"I hoped you'd say that." He paused. "You're bringing it to Lomasky Corp."

Gael stiffened beside her, but it took Lena a few seconds to process what he said. "Lomasky Corp? *My* Lomasky Corp?" She couldn't help it. She started laughing.

"They're the ones footing the bill," Mason admitted. He let out a deep breath. "This is such a great opportunity for you. You can redeem yourself. Win your way back into society." A wide grin returned to his artfully tanned face as he lifted his glass once again. "I'm glad you're taking this so well. I didn't think you would take the job if you knew who—"

"Oh, I'm not," Lena said, standing. "Thank you for lunch and for the drinks. But you can tell my father he can choke on his money." She reached across the table, took Mason's glass, and tipped it into her mouth, finishing off the whiskey. "And fuck you for wasting my time."

With that, Lena Lomasky slammed the glass down hard enough that she was surprised it didn't shatter all over the polished oak of the table. She turned on her heel and stalked out of the dark hotel bar.

Right into the afternoon sunlight, magnified by the hotel lobby's million panes of glass. It blinded her, and she reeled, blinking, cursing, and lamenting that she had just ruined her perfect storm-out. As she let her eyes adjust, she took in the almost abandoned space. Thick leather couches cut stone tables, and ledges with warm wood tops, marble floors, windows, and skylights everywhere, and not a person to be seen. Everyone on this damn moon was out at the festival. Even the hotel staff. It was just her, blinking in the too-bright space and giving Gael enough time to catch her before she hit the front door.

"What are you doing?" He grabbed her shoulders and reeled her around. "We need this job!"

"The hell we do!" She wheeled on him so fast he flinched. That hurt look in his soft brown eyes caused her to hesitate, but her anger forced her to barrel forward.

He was only the first mate on their ship, not captain, and he could not order her around. Not that she was so happy with Captain Sebastian Raines at the moment either. She threw her hands in the air. "I don't know what I was thinking. How could I let Raines talk me into this? He knows how I feel about people like Pierce fucking Mason." *People from back home*, she added silently. She jabbed a finger into Gael's chest. "And you! You're the sensible one. You should know better than to let me even take a meeting for a job like this. Political intrigue? Spycraft? It's all nuts. You're supposed to be my conscience, remember?" She ignored the fact that she was the one who was seconds away from taking the job and angrily pushed past him, trying to locate the door amongst the labyrinth of leather couches, glass walls, and unidentifiable metals.

"Ms. Lomasky, Ms. Lomasky!" a voice bellowed from the direction of the bar.

"Don't use that name," Lena snarled at the young man who came running up to her.

Gael, ever the diplomat, moved to intercept. "She goes by Loman, these days," he soothed. "Aaron, right? Mason's secretary?" He reached out to shake the man's hand.

"Yes. How kind of you to remember." The young man smiled, revealing a deep dimple in his chin as he gave Gael a thorough once over. The guy was older for a mere assistant, in his late twenties at least. His straight blond hair was shorter than was the fashion, and he was much fairer than most natives to Banika, but his accent placed him firmly as a Banikan. Probably born and raised here to import parents, part of the mining community, then schooled off-world.

After he'd given Gael enough coy looks, he finally turned back to Lena. "Ms. Loman." He didn't even hesitate on the new name. "You forgot your datastick."

"You can tell Pierce—"

Gael snatched the datastick from Aaron's hand as he stepped in front of Lena. "Please tell Mr. Mason that we are thankful for the opportunity, and we will be happy to deliver his data. So long as he can match the price Ms. Loman requested." He looked over at Lena, his eyebrows raised, daring her to challenge him.

Lena merely pursed her lips and crossed her arms in front of her.

Gael continued, "You can wire the funds to *Aspasia* at the Aegean Meridian Docks. Prime Station. Port 472, I believe. We're registered with the Prime dock center."

"Half now. Half when it's delivered." Aaron grasped Gael's hand closely as he shook it, lingering an extra few seconds. "Thank you, Mr. Renard. We appreciate your efforts for our small moon. Truly, this information in the right hands? Well, it could make all the difference. I'll see about arranging an additional bonus if you manage the trip in good time." He retreated back to the bar with no fewer than three backward glances.

Lena grabbed Gael's shoulder and spun him around. "What the hell was that?"

Gael offered a sheepish look and shrugged as he twisted a nub of hair at the back of his head. "I think he has a little crush on me. He's cute. You think I should ask him to the parade with us?"

It took three deep breaths to keep from losing it with him. "Give. Me. The datastick," she said slowly. Dangerously.

"And let you toss it? No." He slipped the stick into the pocket concealed along his waistband. "We need the money, Lena."

"We'll find another way." Any other way, she added silently to herself.

"No. We won't. We're out of fuel. We have nothing lined up but a load of some fish delicacy set for Myrto. While I'm happy to take a job going home, it only pays enough fuel and food to get us there. Then we're back where we started. Lena, we're broke. Raines gave me one job on this trip: Seal the deal no matter what. I'm sorry, but I'm not going to let you get in the way of that." He stormed out of the hotel, and though she rushed after, he'd already slipped into the crowd. She was alone.

CHAPTER TWO

While the inside of the hotel had been as empty as the Levinese islands in hurricane season, the streets were bustling. Every Banikan and plenty of tourists from across Aegea had turned out for the festivities. Young and old, wealthy and poor, the deep bronze skin and bouncing black curls of city natives, and the sun-scorched faces and breaking dry hair of Northern Aegean transplants: everyone was here.

Lena scanned the crowd briefly, looking for Gael's dark head, but there were just too many people. It didn't matter. She knew he was headed for the festival and the Nenads. Cedo would be somewhere off with his brothers by now, but Lena knew Mrs. Nenad would wait for them at the Courthouse as planned. She'd find Gael there.

Then she could kill him, steal the datastick, lose his body in the crowd, and be back on the *Aspasia* before anyone was the wiser.

But then Captain Raines would have her head for killing his best friend, and she'd never hear the end of it from the ship's business manager Cat. And she wouldn't even have Gael to hold her hand and guide her through the fallout.

Lena sighed. Fine. He could live for now. But she was not sharing the whiskey she bought with her share of the commission.

Sparkling gold and blue garlands strung across the streetlights, the iridescent fabric catching the rays as the system's sun peeked around the old downtown buildings. Twinkling lights decorated balconies, and temporary barricades diverted traffic straight to the downtown park where the Independence Day was in full swing.

Lena let the crowd sweep her into its current as she looked around. It was only two years since she'd last been here, but so much had changed. The scars of the Independence War had been painted over, built around, nearly erased. The pockmarks of bullets and mortar shells had been covered over with new stone. Lena could see the exact points where decades-old, weathered bricks met the newer, stronger Haran bricks, sourced locally at the insistence of the community.

The street-level building facades were scrubbed clean, but above, there were still smudges of smoke from the bombs. Old stained-glass and Hachold stone ornamentals along the top floors of the buildings had been replaced by sleek glass fronts and modern, angled-edge finishes.

Still, the bustling city held on to her identity. Glass prisms hung from nearly every window, capturing the bright light of Sinope, their sun, and reflecting it onto the other buildings and the pressing crowds below. Vines and flowers crept out from the crevices between the restaurants and shops, and the office and apartment balconies above featured gardens of natural flora that had been cultivated especially for their brilliant blooms. Everywhere life and color thrived. Lena tilted her head up and watched the blooms falling down the sides of the buildings like still-life waterfalls. Purples, pinks, blues, and reds flowed into one another like rain down an oil painting.

The people, too, seemed in high spirits. Lena nearly had to dive to one side as a group of a half dozen young men ran whooping down the street. *"Banika sloboda! Aegea sloboda! Sloboda!"*

Freedom.

What so many lives had been lost for: freedom from Pyrrhen rule, from what many Aegeans insisted was economic slavery. The moon had fought to be free of her oppressive planet, and five years ago she'd won. Today was Aegea's day for independence, and Lena was glad to be here in the moon's capital to be a part of it.

The stately five and six-story classic Perchete buildings that lined the streets seemed to fall away as Lena emerged at the end of the street and stepped onto the grass of the park. Everywhere, there was open space and people. Hundreds. Thousands.

Voices and music swelled around Lena. Families had spread blankets and set up chairs and tents to claim space early for the fireworks that would come that night. The crowds were thickest here along the edges of the square, as people jostled and squeezed into spots for the parade. Everyone still had time to get into prime viewing position, but only those who got there early enough would see the full spectacle.

So much had changed. Five years ago, before the fighting, the park hadn't even existed. This whole downtown area had been filled with buildings. It was where the occupying colonists from Pyrrhos had made their city center. Built up to the edge of the Caspic Sea, the Pyrrhen buildings had been the pride of the occupying forces. Grand and stately, built of red river stone shipped all the way up from the Hachold River in Pyrrhos's capital.

Those were the first buildings Aegean separatists destroyed. Bombs along the foundations had leveled all but the husks of those grand buildings, as Banikan independents announced to the seven worlds that they were not going to tolerate foreign rule any longer. They wanted freedom, self-rule, independence. As if they had any clue what that meant.

Lena rolled her eyes at the heavy politics of the "independence day" parade, and headed straight for the first tent she found selling drinks and grabbed two glasses of Dornish red. She sipped on the deep burgundy, let it uncoil her stomach and soothe her temper. The politics of the event weren't necessary to appreciate the day. It was enough to be here, to be with people she cared about, and to enjoy the spectacle of it all. She made her way to the only landmark that could be seen in the huge kilometer square park: the Courthouse.

After the war, every single building that had been built at the water's edge, every Pyrrhen landmark, every testament to the occupation had been razed to their foundations. The rubble cleared and the smoke blown away, the townspeople had been left with a question of what to do with the space. They could have built up over the remains, reclaimed the land.

Instead, they planted. Grass, trees, bushes. They turned the old financial and legislative center of the city into a park. Claimed as a monument to the moon and her independence, the park paid tribute to the lives lost in its pursuit.

But there, at the exact middle of the park, stood one tribute: the four grand staircases from the old Pyrrhen courthouse. The once looming courthouse itself was gone, completely destroyed, leaving only an unmarked concrete slab. But at each of the cardinal directions, the great marble steps that had climbed two stories straight up to justice, they still stood sentinel. Leading to nothing.

There was no plaque, no plinth, no memorial of any kind. No words were etched in stone to memorialize those lost in the war, nor statues erected to commemorate their sacrifices. The platform of the courthouse was to be kept clear and unspoiled, the city council had declared, to remind the people that no matter what, Aegea would remain free and strong. So long as her people fought to keep her clean and uncontaminated by those who would seek to claim her.

Even as the rest of the cleared harbor area was celebrated as a park space where local celebrations regularly took place, the courthouse steps remained clear.

It was to those steps that Lena wound her way through the crowd. After only a single circuit around the base, she found Mrs. Nenad.

"Mom!" Lena smiled and offered up a glass of wine as she met eyes with the woman.

At seeing her, the older woman smiled; at seeing the extended wine, she laughed and hurried over. Mrs. Nenad swept Lena into a hug.

She'd lost weight. Mrs. Nenad had never had the plump curves you'd expect of a woman running a bakery, but she was downright skeletal now. Tall, like her sons, and with their thick black curls, twisted up and off her neck, she was a stunning woman. She stepped back to assess Lena and to take one of the glasses of wine.

"You've gotten skinny." Mrs. Nenad shook her head and took a sip of her wine. "Just like my boy. Doesn't anyone on that ship know how to cook? Or do I have to send provisions every few months, so you lot don't starve to death?"

"Hey, we do a pretty good job, considering our limited resupply stops." Lena smiled despite herself. Truth was, though Gael took the helm of most of the meals, even he wasn't that great in the kitchen. He was the only one who ever volunteered to make palatable meals out of the preserved meats, vegetables, and starches they had on board. And Lena thought he had been getting better; she'd stopped having to slather chili sauce on everything to make it palatable. "Besides, you're the one who has lost weight! You know what they say about a skinny baker."

"She spends too much time chasing after wayward sons?" Mrs. Nenad held a laugh in her eyes as she lifted an eyebrow and took another sip. "Come. Let's sit. There's a bench." She gestured to a couple vacating one of the few benches around the base of the Courthouse steps and moved to snag it before someone else could.

The two women sat and sipped at their wines for a moment, taking in the scene.

"You know," Lena said as she gazed up at the near acre of concrete at the top of the courthouse steps, "you could hold one heck of a concert up there. The location is perfect."

Mrs. Nenad looked at her aghast. "To dishonor the dead—"

"The dead are gone," Lena interrupted, anticipating the argument. "They don't care one way or another. But we're still here. I'm not saying you should rent it out to some Pyrrhen pop band or anything. But a tribute concert wouldn't hurt anyone. You could even donate the proceeds to your veterans or a rebuilding project or something. I don't know. It just seems like a waste to have such a prime location and do nothing with it."

"It is not our way," Mrs. Nenad said quietly. "The steps belong to the dead. To celebrate life there would be wrong." She gestured around to the area around them. "But down here, all of this is for the living. Leave the dead their place, and let us enjoy our celebrations fully in ours."

"You see, that's the problem with pilots," Gael said, coming up behind them. "They're always looking up. Even when they should be looking around."

Mrs. Nenad stood and leaning over the back of the bench, threw her arms around Gael. "You sweet boy. Where have you been hiding?"

"Away from her," Gael said, giving Lena a sly look. He knew she hadn't forgotten what had happened, but he also knew that she would die before showing Mrs. Nenad anything that might make her look petty. "Besides, I found someone you might have been looking for."

Gael stepped aside, revealing a tall, solidly-built, black-haired young man. His thick curls hung in his eyes as he held a sheepish grin. "Hi, Mom."

"Cedomir!" Mrs. Nenad took one step on the bench and launched herself over the back toward her eldest son. "You awful, awful child! Why did you not find me sooner?" Throwing her arms around his neck, she swept him into a hug that threatened to cut off his air, but he just laughed.

"Mom, you saw me a few hours ago at the bakery." Lena's mechanic and Mrs. Nenad's too-frequently absent son gave her an affectionate kiss on the forehead as she pulled away.

"Yes, but then you left me to this crowd." Mrs. Nenad pretended to pout as she pulled her son back to take a look at him again. It may have only been a few hours since she'd seen him last, but it had been two years before that. No one could begrudge her a few lingering looks at her oldest child. She ruffled his thick hair until it hung down in his eyes. "Where are your brothers? I assume you were with them?"

Cedo had the good sense to look chastised as he brushed the hair out of his face. "They are at the political tents."

Mrs. Nenad shoved her son away. "Of course, they are. And you had nothing to do with it? Do you expect me to believe you didn't lead your baby brothers to those tents?" She didn't wait for an answer as she took a step back to get better leverage as she slapped at his shoulder. "As hot-headed as your father! You are supposed to be an example. And instead, you encourage them? You send them pamphlets, treatises. Fill their heads with philosophy and politics. They are children. Vaso is only seventeen. Dimitri barely fifteen. They don't know any better. But you? You know better. You lived through the wars. You saw what your father sacrificed."

Cedo met Lena's eyes over his mother's shoulder, looking for assistance. Lena held up her hands while Gael smiled and shrugged his shoulders. He'd find no help from them. "Mom, they're not exposed to anything bad. Fanon was even there."

Fanon, Lena remembered, was Cedomir's favorite local philosopher, an old friend of his father's. She'd read his stuff. Very nationalistic. In his most famous treatise, he'd claimed, "Pyrrhens have long lurked in every crack of our society, every crevice, looking for anything they can scavenge from our hard work, our industry. They are cockroaches, feasting on our captive carcasses. We will not be free until every last one of them is ripped from our mines and sent back to pollute their own filthy planet." All of the man's writings followed that thread: the invader as other, the colonialist as parasite. The only solution, he claimed, was total annihilation.

"Oh!" Mrs. Nenad took a step back in feigned surprise. "Fanon? THE Fanon? The very philosopher-poet I invited into my home and let convince your father to spearhead an assault on the Pyrrhens? THAT Fanon? Oh, please do tell me where I can find him. Please. I would love to tell him one or two things about what happens when philosophy encounters real people's lives."

Lena exchanged a glance with Gael. She was anxious to drop out of this conversation, but there was nowhere to retreat. It was here with her mechanic and his mother, or back to the ship. This wasn't her moon. Lena had no stake in her wars, her fights.

"You know what?" Mrs. Nenad said. "No. Show me where they are. They're going home. Vaso and Dimitri have no place here if they're going to get caught up in something bigger than themselves. You know your brothers. Vaso will lose his temper over something ridiculous, and Dimitri will follow along like it's a good idea. No. They go home."

"Mom," Cedo soothed. "They're just attending a few rallies. They care about their moon. They're not hurting anyone."

"Not hurting anyone? Sure. Until your man Fanon gets his way, and we get another war just to get these Pyrrhen investors and capitalists off our moon. I heard what he's said. 'We will not be free until Aegea is wiped clean of the Pyrrhen stain.' Right? Or am I misquoting?"

"No, Mom," Cedo said as he bowed his head, accepting his mother's anger.

"That man will not be happy until Pyrrhen money is gone from this place. He doesn't care if Pyrrhens pay half my mortgage or prop up our mines while they move to new platforms. It's not enough the military is gone. He doesn't want any of them left."

"It's our moon, Mom. We should be in control of her economy." Cedo didn't ever raise his voice. But he was firm in his words.

"Even if that means starving?" Mrs. Nenad was yelling now, attracting a crowd. "You boys. You don't know what is good for you. Your philosophies, your politics. Until you raise a family of your own and know what it takes to keep people alive, I don't want to hear it."

"Mom, it's okay. We're just talking." Cedo tried to calm her.

"Go, then. You go talk. And when the bloodshed starts, then you come back, and you tell me how sorry you are. We'll see if I'm in the mood to listen then."

With that Mrs. Nenad walked back around the bench to Lena, sat down, drained her entire glass of wine, then snatched the glass from Lena and downed that one, too. Cedo took a deep breath and looked like he wanted to argue with his mother. Instead, he mouthed an apology to Lena and Gael, then turned on his heel and stalked back to the political tents.

Lena pursed her lips as she looked to Gael again. Did he really want to get involved in this mess?

He shook his head. Not now.

Fine. She could wait. She was patient.

She leaned over to whisper in Gael's ear. "The least you can do is get us more wine." She shrugged a shoulder in Mrs. Nenad's direction. Gael raised his eyebrows, but as Lena shooed him away, he conceded.

Lena sank down beside Mrs. Nenad. "You okay?"

Mrs. Nenad lifted her head wearily to meet Lena's eyes. "May you never have children, dear. They will destroy you faster than time, disease, or," she paused dramatically, "war."

"But it's Independence Day. The war's over."

Mrs. Nenad chuckled once as her head dropped. Then the humor seemed to seize control of her as her shoulders heaved until Lena wasn't sure if she was laughing or crying. "Oh, sweet child. I'm only thankful you're taking at least one of my children away from this mess. Want to take on another mechanic or two? Dimitri? There's still hope for him. He's a good boy."

Lena smiled. Dimitri was a good boy. A ceaseless tornado of positive energy, and as clever as he was sweet. But there wasn't room in the ship's budget to take on another mouth, another salary. Though, Lena wasn't going to tell her mechanic's mother about *Aspasia's* financial woes. "It can't be that bad," she said instead.

Mrs. Nenad chuckled again. "No. No, you're right. I'm probably overreacting." She straightened as Gael returned with two glasses of wine. None for himself, Lena noted. "It's just, it feels so similar. I know it's not the same. But the feeling in the air. My boys." She gulped at the wine while Lena sipped at her own. "It all feels the way it did before the last war."

"Well, it's been a long summer," Lena offered.

"Yeah," Mrs. Nenad agreed. "It has. It's been a hot one."

"It's been hard on everyone, I hear," said Gael, sliding onto the bench beside Mrs. Nenad. "I'll tell you what. Let's get some ice cream. There's a great booth a bit that way." He gestured down an alley of tents. "We'll take a walk and get into place for the parade. I hear it's going to be crowded this year."

Mrs. Nenad nodded. "Yes, that sounds nice."

"Lena?" Gael asked.

Lena looked back to the crowd and thought about what they'd been through already that day. "No, I think I'm going to head back to the ship early. Check-in on Raines and Cat and what's-her-name."

"Chandra," Gael filled in.

"Yeah. Her." Lena frowned. It had been a week, and she had yet to warm to the mercenary Raines had insisted they hire on. "Whatever. But you should have fun with Cedo. We don't need him back until oh-eight-hundred. Lots of time for celebrations."

Mrs. Nenad snorted at that. "There will be plenty of those. I bought a few cases of wine for tonight alone." She tilted her head at Lena. "Sure you won't stay?"

"For Dornish wine? Tempting. But no. I won't make good company today, I'm afraid."

"Shame." Mrs. Nenad offered a sly smile. "Good thing I had a full two cases sent to your ship already."

Lena laughed and hugged her. "You know me so well. Do I have to share?"

"All for you. Plus a box of MalKun whiskey. Then, I sent up some Ansaro for Raines and Fiani for you, Gael."

Gael thanked her. "I'll share with Cat and Chandra."

Mrs. Nenad snorted again. "No pressure on you. Everyone has their own treats on board. I heard your new security expert is partial to rum. I sent something for Cedomir, too, of course. You all share only what you want."

"Thank you, Mom." Lena leaned in for a hug, pressing her hands gently against the ribs and vertebrae along Mrs. Nenad's back as she looked for excuses to avoid the festivities. "I'm sorry we can't stay longer. But Cat's shipment is time-sensitive, and—"

"And there's never enough time. I know," Mrs. Nenad said. "Go along. Gael can keep me company."

"Well, I thought Gael might come with me. We have things to discuss." She looked pointedly at Gael, hoping he'd get the message.

"I thought I'd see what the fuss is all about at the political tents," Gael said, smirking.

"But the data—"

"Go on, Helena," Mrs. Nenad said. "Let him have some fun. I'll send him back in one piece, I promise." She stood up and gestured to Lena's glass of wine. "Finish your glass like a good girl. Then you go along."

As Mrs. Nenad tipped the bottom of the glass towards Lena's lips, she had no choice. She sipped the rich red wine back and glared at Gael over the lip of the glass. She could wait. He wasn't getting away from her. And as soon as he brought that datastick back to the ship, he was going to get a full piece of her mind.

"Good girl," Mrs. Nenad said when the glass was empty. "Enjoy your trip back, and I better see you within the year." She reached over for a quick last squeeze and whispered in Lena's ear. "Bring my boy back soon, you hear?"

"I will. Thanks, Mom." To Gael, "See you at home."

"Looking forward to it," Gael said as he patted the hip that held the 'stick.

CHAPTER THREE

Lena was relieved to find the public shuttle back to Meridian Prime Station was nearly empty. Everyone in the city must be out enjoying the celebrations, and few would attempt to leave the surface of the moon until at least the parade was over. Even with the hour and a half long trek across town and the wait for the shuttle, the parade would likely only just be beginning.

She plopped down in a window seat near the back of the shuttle and watched the departure. The thrum of the anti-grav field as it activated settled the uneasiness in the pit of her stomach. The lift as the shuttle pressed away from the magnetic grab of the earth swept over her like a warm blanket. Off world, she was safe. Away from planets, away from moons, away from the political fallout of small men and the large governments that threatened them. She wanted no part of it all.

As the shuttle port dropped away beneath her, she felt her rage at Gael slip away as well. He wasn't the right target for her anger. He never was. She shouldn't let the fallout of her hot temper fall on his head, even if he did offer it with his endless patience and understanding. It wasn't his fault.

She sank down deep into what was left of the well-worn cushion on the public shuttle and hunched down in on herself.

She had behaved terribly, swept up in shame, fear, and, yes, a bit of anger.

You will redeem yourself.

How did Mason have the nerve? That he would use her past against her, just to commit to some political espionage? What could he possibly be hoping to accomplish?

Did he think she was looking for some way back? That she wanted anything to do with the Lomaskys, Rienen society? Her father? She had left all that behind.

Redeem herself? She wanted nothing to do with that life. She didn't want the money, the notoriety, the pressure of living in the public eye. She was happier on *Aspasia*.

She was.

Which is exactly why she didn't want to take this job. She preferred easy transport jobs. She had no illusions about her place in the universe. The easier and more mundane the job, the better.

This whole thing put too much at risk. If anything went wrong, if they were caught, if any of her crew was hurt, it would be her fault.

The datastick had to be tagged. Something this important? Encrypted communications? Ciphers stolen from a secret Pyrrhen lab? There's no way someone wouldn't take the time to tag the 'stick with a simple pinpoint device. Even un-networked, it might activate a signal. Then they could be traced wherever they were. She wondered if it had been activated already.

Surely not. Otherwise, Mason would have already been nabbed.

Maybe it had to be plugged in.

Or maybe it issued a proximity alert.

Or maybe...

She shook her head. It couldn't be tagged. It would never have made it out of the lab in which it was stored. The second it crossed the threshold, authorities would have been alerted that the data was on the move, and Pierce's inside agent would have been caught.

So it was probably safe with Gael. For now.

That small stick was the safest way to transport a message after all. It's why all the most important data was partitioned onto physical media. Electronic waves, networked media, and cloud storage were too easy to hack and monitor. You could set up a satellite net, scan every outgoing message for encrypted materials. Any gov or major company could do it with enough cash and the tech in place. But manually searching every ship? That was near impossible. It took manpower and time, not technology. Once most ships were out of customs, they were free. In the black, you were anonymous. You were no one.

Lena had been flying for seven years, and no one had even managed to find *her*.

If anyone had even been looking.

They'd be fine.

And they'd be looking at the other half of that substantial payday when they delivered it.

Still, we shouldn't take any chances. She planned to plot a course that kept them wide of any possible checkpoints. They had to get to Myrto to deliver Cat's fish. It was already on the schedule. It would draw attention if they deviated from their itinerary. Once they made that delivery, though, they could leave the system. Straight up to the outer reaches, above the rotational pull of Sinope, to the Jump Station. Then jump to Samara and fly to Rien. Easy.

Lena looked at the countdown clock at the front of the shuttle. Plenty of time for a nap. She was all set to slump back into her seat and put everything out of her mind.

Then she saw it. There, sitting across from her, clutched in the hands of a wide-eyed young woman. Its electric blue cover was unmistakable.

Her day hadn't gone badly enough already. She had to run into that book.

Escape Velocity: The Lomasky Drive and the History of Bosonic Fields.

It had sold billions of copies. For several years it was the most popular book in all three star systems. The book claimed to be a history of the discovery and development of tools that made modern space travel possible. It was an explanation of the most famous family in the universe and the story of how they unlocked the potential of gravity.

Everyone knew it was really just a salacious tell-all.

The rise and fall of her generation, how they'd let the family down. Her older brother's notorious parties fueled by drugs and money, followed by a suicide at age sixteen. Her cousins' battles with corruption and incompetence as they squandered the potential of Lomasky Corp and their own inheritances.

And the scandalous highlight of the book, the reason everyone really bought it: a detailed description of the accident that almost cost them everything. Her accident. The hundreds of lives lost. Mariko. Dead.

Lena's fault.

On top of that, it was an "authorized biography" of her family. Authorized by the great patriarch himself: her father, Tadashi Lomasky.

He had sold her out. Probably made millions doing it.

She hated that blue cover.

The wide-eyed young woman who had been greedily turning the pages of the book looked up and caught Lena watching her. It took only a moment. Then she turned those wide brown eyes back to the inside cover of her book.

The cover where a picture of the Lomasky family was.

A picture of Lena.

Damn.

Lena quickly dropped her gaze, but it was too late. The woman nudged her companion and began whispering. She gestured at the picture inside the flap and then back to Lena.

Yeah, it was time to go.

But where do you go on a shuttle in the middle of its flight?

Lena stood quickly and moved a few rows up, but stayed in the aisle seat, alert and ready to move as soon as they landed. She steadied herself with deep breaths and forced herself not to turn around, to meet that young woman's eyes. To turn back and go to her and beg forgiveness.

It wouldn't do any good. She couldn't find forgiveness. The accident happened. There was nothing she could do. It was over. Seven years.

She'd paid her price.

Lena waved down a flight attendant. "Whiskey. Double." She handed over cash for twice the price of the drink. The man nodded and quickly gave her two fingers of the top shelf with a grimace and sympathetic look in his eyes.

Two more drinks later, a genderless voice came into the shuttle. "Ladies and gentlemen, we are on our final approach to Aegea Meridian Prime Station."

"Thank you," Lena whispered to the voice, too willing to dash away into the obscurity of the station.

The voice continued. "We will be disembarking at the moonside docks on the central level. We regret to inform you that the station is on lockdown, and all return flights to Banika and the Gomar province of Aegea have been suspended. Outgoing flights are still permitted. All passengers must disembark as quickly as possible and proceed immediately to their subsequent conveyances. If your ultimate destination is the station itself, please follow directions to the entry gates on the Embassy level where representatives will direct you to your planet or moon's processing center. If you are planning to return to Aegea, please report directly to the shuttle concierge upon exit where you will receive further instructions. We apologize for any inconvenience and hope you will consider visiting again soon."

The announcement ended, and the silence was quickly filled with whispered conversations from the shuttle's few passengers. Unfortunately, the flight attendants had no information to pass along, and as the passengers attempted to access news themselves, they discovered network access had been disabled for all devices. Lena went through the possibilities. Closed access to news and grounded flights? This couldn't have anything to do with the datastick. For one thing, she didn't have it. It was still down on the moon with Gael. Had he been caught?

Surely not. He would have been taken into custody and questioned. No reason to shut down all flights.

Was *Aspasia* anchored then? And what about Gael? Cedo? Were they stuck on the moon?

That would put a delay in Cat's schedule.

Hopefully, Mrs. Nenad's shipment of wine had arrived already. A little Sanga would go a long way to soothing Cat's temper. And everyone wanted the ship's business manager happy. She was the one who signed the checks.

Within a matter of minutes, the shuttle had docked, and the half-dozen passengers quickly disembarked. Lena took a moment to glance at the media stations around the terminal area, but all screens reflected the same instructions they had been given on the shuttle. A quick check of her personal devices revealed that all comms had been disabled here, too.

That was unusual, but it was probably just a normal security precaution.

There was nothing left for her to do but to head back to the *Aspasia* and use the ship's networked capabilities to get an update.

She encountered almost no one on the way to the elevator banks. The docks seemed to be empty, and she arrived at port 472 in record time. The station desk was unmanned and the gangway open. Someone must be on board, then. No one would have left the ship open and unattended like that. Not unless something terrible had happened.

Lena picked up her already hurried pace and dashed through the telescoped gangway, her boot heels clanking on the polished metal. At the end of the passageway, the tight tunnel opened onto the middle two-story cargo area. The space was currently empty except for Cat's oversized freezer crates, sitting along with a few foodstuffs boxes.

"Hello?" Lena called out. Even if no one was immediately nearby, her presence on board should have triggered a chime that would be heard in every common area of the ship. If anyone was on board, they would either come see who it was or open a comm link to the cargo bay.

No one responded

Something was wrong.

Lena ran from the center gangway entrance to the side of the ship. She took the narrow stairs two at a time. Reaching the first level, she turned and dashed for the middle staircase that bisected the kitchen. It would take her up to the bridge. Before she could reach it, Cat appeared at the top, dashing down as fast as she could.

"Where the hell have you been?" Cat said.

"What's wrong? Are Raines and his prize mercenary back?"

"No," she practically toppled Lena down the stairs as she barreled into her for a hug. "No one is here, and no one has their comms on, and I had no idea what to do, and I needed you." She sobbed into Lena's shoulder for only a moment, before pulling herself back up and grabbing Lena's hand. "Everything has gone wrong moonside. They've grounded all station traffic, and I can't pilot the shuttles myself." Lena found herself being dragged down the stairs at breakneck speed, back across the cargo area, and back to the shuttle bays at the rear of the ship. "Wait, what? Cat, what are you talking about? Why would we need the shuttles? I thought traffic was grounded."

Cat scoffed as she struggled to get past the freezer crates, packed too close to the shuttle bay doors. "Because now's the time to start worrying about flight restrictions."

"Are they allowing traffic down to the moon, then? If you're just worried about keeping schedule, and you pull Cedo and Gael before the parade and parties are over, they may not forgive you."

Cat paused with her hand over the shuttle bay key-pad. She turned slowly, her eyes wide. "You don't know."

"Know?" Lena's heart dropped into her stomach with a sickening splash. "What's wrong? Are they okay? Gael?"

Cat closed her eyes and took a steadying breath. "There was an assassination." She paused at Lena's gasp. "Lena, they're saying Cedo did it. Or his brothers. I don't know!" Cat's pitch mounted. "I can't get anyone on comms, but the news. They had pictures of Vaso, Cedo. They had Naomi, Mrs. Nenad. They had her in handcuffs. Screaming." She started to cry. "Lena, I don't know what's happening. You have to get down there. You have to fix this. Get them back. Lena. They're going to kill them."

CHAPTER FOUR

Lena pushed Cat aside and quickly keyed in the code for the shuttle bay. The doors slid open, and she ran inside, tapping in the codes once more to open the shuttle and start pre-flight systems. "Fully fueled? Inspected?"

Cat nodded, wiping at her face. "But the ports are all closed. There's nowhere to land down there."

"Small shuttle. I'll find a place. A park. Something." Lena ducked into the main cabin and toggled on the screens. Black nothingness greeted her as the systems took a few moments to boot up. "Mrs. Nenad arrested, you said. Anyone else in custody?" she called over her shoulder.

"No," Cat called back. "Reports say officials are looking for anyone associated with the Nenad family. But the city is in a panic, and the riots are making it impossible to find anyone."

"Good. Raines will be back any minute. The second he is, you tell him to disengage from the station. Bring *Aspasia* into a lagging orbit from Banika. Hanging back from the city will save power as we bring the shuttle back. Let's see." She tapped at the screen, waiting for it to activate. "Come on. Come on!" At once, the screens came to life, and Lena rapped out a few figures. "Banika is a tropical port. Given rotation? About 5,000 klicks back should be good. We should be able to get back to you easily from there."

"Five thousand, lagging," Cat echoed. "Okay." She paused and poked her head into the shuttle. "Can Raines even do that?"

"The systems are automated. He just has to plug the numbers into the right screens. If he can't do that much, he needs to sign *Aspasia* over to me."

Cat's eyes widened. "Okay. Sure. What else?"

Lena pulled her sleek black hair back into a ponytail. "Don't bother repressurizing the bay when I drop out. Waste of energy. I'll take care of it when we get back. We won't be gone long. Just confirm the seal on the bay doors. I'll be back as fast as I can." The screens powered on, and Lena brought up the nav and comm screens. "And Cat? If you hear from any of them down below? Tell them to hole up somewhere, to stay safe. Tell them I'm coming to get them."

"Good luck," Cat said as she stepped out of the shuttle. The bay doors opened and shut as Cat ran back up to the bridge, leaving Lena completely alone.

She allowed herself one deep breath while she surveyed the shuttle. A short-range vehicle, specially designed for surface drops and small pickups, it was only designed to hold a few passengers and small amounts of cargo. Two seats perched up front behind the pilot and co-pilot with two drop-down seats in the back cargo area. The rest of the shuttle's bulk was designed to hold the vast amount of fuel it would need to break atmo and escape the strong pull of a planet or moon's gravity.

It would serve for a quick extraction.

If that's what this was, she had no idea.

Lena was moving before she had any semblance of a plan.

Well, that had never stopped her before. She tapped in the release code, and the shuttle door on the port side slid closed with a slight hiss of compressed air. She fastened her harness and pulled up the nav screen's preprogrammed locations. She tapped on Aegea, Gomar province, and Cedo's homeport in Banika. The port may be closed, but she could manually reroute as she approached the moon.

Confirm release of boson field before opening the bay doors, this time, she reminded herself. Last shuttle trip she had been in a hurry and had forgotten. Trying to drop out of the open shuttle gate with the field still engaged was like—well, it was like fighting gravity.

The flooring beneath Shuttle 1 slid back into the ship and exposed her to the open vacuum of space. She flicked a switch and released the field that held the antigravity together in the bay. Then, she toggled on the chehon-based push system and with a negative charge carefully nudged against the subtle grav field of the ship.

She checked her nav screen. *Aspasia* was already moon-side of Meridian Prime Station, in geosynchronous orbit with the eastern edge of Risha province. That put her few hundred lateral klicks from Banika. Easy angled descent.

The LIBEL screen showed the gravs of each large interstellar body, including the station, the moon, and the huge planet below them all. A slow escalating neg charge of .768 would give the shuttle enough push to clear the station and get into the stronger gravitational influence of Aegea's lower thermosphere. Then normal gravity should handle the rest, while she fought it the whole way to the surface.

With small finger flicks on the controls and twists against both the graphics of the station and the planet, Lena oriented her shuttle's down position with the moon's surface. That way, when the moon's gravity got its hold on her, she wouldn't have to use even more chehonic power to fight and get herself upright before landing. It was precise work and took years of training to get the feel for the subtle movements, but for Lena, it was second nature.

The distance to the planet decreased rapidly, as the chehonic charge reached its goal.

.7, .725, .75, .76.

Lena switched off the push against the station above her, turned her attention, and engaged a tiny positive pull on the planet. She was already close. No more than .25 gravity, maybe .27 would pull her into the mesosphere, and from there the mass of the planet would pull her in with increasing rapidity. Once she hit the stratosphere, she'd have to counter natural gravity with a push to slow her descent into Banika.

While she waited, she pulled up the imaging for the city of Banika, the closest available ports, and Cedo's family home. She had to find a landing. But where? Where were they? At home? The festival?

The Nenad family lived on the Southside of Banika, near the western bank of the Tralic Sea. The festival on the other side, near the eastern bank of the peninsula. The port to the north was going to be packed with fleeing dignitaries and politicians from the Independence Day celebrations. Travel to and from there would likely be heavily monitored and restricted. She'd never land in that mess.

She scanned for anywhere big enough to accommodate her bulk and remain undetected for a short time. A park, a warehouse rooftop, an empty parking lot.

There.

There was a sporting complex four blocks from Cedo's home and the Nenad bakery. Six different fields. All empty and surrounded by tall buildings. The tayball field would be plenty large enough for a small shuttle-like hers, while the buildings would conceal her approach from most people on the ground.

She targeted the stadium and evaluated her speed. At the stratosphere, she'd need to slow her descent. Maybe a push of .36. Maybe a bit more. Hard to tell.

She had time. A few dozen minutes at this speed. Time enough to get more information on what she was flying into.

Lena pulled up the local news, hoping for anything encouraging. The headlines were anything but.

Beloved Pyrrhen heir killed. Local men wanted in connection with assassination.

Riots shut down Independence Day festivities following political protest.

Authorities pursuing suspected assassin Cedomir Nenad, son of local, beloved baker.

Dominik Domonkos, Peacemaker, dead at the hands of local agitators.

Nenad brothers shoot and kill Pyrrhen heir and leading diplomat, Domonkos. Suspects still at large.

She didn't believe it. Couldn't believe it. Cedo might talk big when it came to hometown politics, but he was ultimately a pacifist. The war that granted his moon independence had torn his world apart. After he lost his father in the final days, he'd renounced the violence that cost him everything.

There was no way he'd do something like this. Not Cedo.

His brother Vaso, though? He was as fiery as Cedo's father had reportedly been. Hot-tempered, proud, and fiercely nationalistic. He might very well have been involved in something this stupid.

A mounting pressure and steady vibration alerted Lena that she was fast approaching the moon's stratosphere.

She hated atmospheric entry. Thrust and propulsion used so much energy, and the whole time you had to fight the craft's desire to plummet to the ground. Plus, all the noise in the atmosphere caused interference. Water vapor. Wind gusts. Clouds. Weather, in general. None of the clean vacuum of space. Much easier to thread a narrow gangway tunnel through an unfamiliar and unguided station port with only meters for error than land a shuttle in a stadium ten times its size.

Atmospheric thrusters engaged, she began the tug of war with inertia, gravity, and her piloting skills to reach the stadium. Her fingers flew over the screen: propulsion forward to center her descent over the stadium. Some reverse thrust combined with enough escalating chehonic force to slow her angled descent, so she didn't go crashing through the center of the tayball boundary lines. All the while, she had to watch her scanners at the flurry of additional aircraft moving quickly from the city center.

From her vantage, she could see the chaos reigning in Banika. Smoke rose from a number of buildings along the bay's eastern edge, and she could see swarms of movement fleeing the fires along the most populated thoroughfares.

Terrestrial vehicles swarmed, while several official aircraft moved between the city's wealthy residential centers and business districts to the east and the main commercial port to the north. It seemed there was a mass exodus. At least for those who could afford it. Luckily, the tayball stadium was near the less affluent residential areas on the southwestern edges of the city, where, thankfully, there was far less air travel. No major vehicle traffic here either.

She reached the stadium without any hails or interference, and touched down softly, careful not to scorch the tended grass with blowback. They could still have a game tomorrow. If the city was still standing.

She powered down the main flight controls and support systems. Activating the shuttle's security system, Lena ran from the stadium and towards Cedo's home. Though she saw no smoke, here, she could smell it wafting from the east. The panicked crowds seemed not to have come this way yet, and for that, she was thankful. She encountered a few scared people running the other way as she neared the bakery. She hoped she was heading in the right direction. If there was no sign of her crew, she thought she might at least leave some sort of message. Some way of letting them know she was moonside.

Rounding the last corner before the bakery, Lena discovered why the streets were so quiet. Police had blocked off the entire block with barricades and yellow tape. Dozens of officers, local and Pyrrhen alike, swarmed in and out of the bakery and apartment above. Officers carried boxes of papers and odds and ends, and she could hear glass and wood breaking inside.

She should have known. The Nenad Bakery wasn't exactly a town secret, and if they had Mrs. Nenad in custody, then they would certainly know about the bakery.

The only good news was that if they were still searching the place, they likely didn't have Cedo in custody yet. He could still be out there. Somewhere. Lena didn't know the city well enough to venture any ideas where he might have holed up. She didn't know of any of his family's friends or extended family, or even where Cedo might have hung out when he was growing up.

She stepped back into the alcove of a neighboring apartment building where she could keep a good view of the activity outside of the bakery without being in direct view of the building itself.

Now what? Cedo and Gael wouldn't be here; they'd be fools to come anywhere near this place. And yet, it was the only place Lena or Raines would know to come to stage any sort of rescue. Maybe she should station somewhere, somewhere with a vantage point, wait to see if they came back. If she spotted them before the authorities, she could stop them, get them out of here.

Lena looked up at the surrounding buildings, all of which looked down on the two-story bakery. She blinked rapidly as a bright reflection in one of the fifth story windows across the street caught her square in the face. Again. And again. A mirror catching the sun.

She smiled. Seemed she wouldn't have to find the boys; they'd found her.

Lena circled back around, cut over a block, and approached the signal building from the back, out of view of anyone monitoring the bakery. She found a door in a back alley open, but not visibly propped, and she silently slipped in. The elevators were out of order, so she took the stairs and found herself presently in an abandoned office space five stories above the bakery.

The floor was quiet, but she could hear arguments coming from down the hall. She followed the voices carefully, mindful that it could be a trap. As she approached, though, a familiar head popped out of a room, a relieved smile on his face.

As Gael rushed to embrace her, Lena noted the blood on his clothes. "Are you all right?"

"I'm fine," he assured her grasping her hands. "The shuttle? Are we clear?"

"At the tayball stadium a few blocks from here. It's clear the whole way. But not for long. There's about a hundred police down there. They're sure to have seen my approach. We have to move fast."

Gael nodded and tried to turn back to the room. "Wait," Lena said, grabbing his arm and tugging him a short distance away. "I have to know what I'm dealing with here. The news is all over the place. What happened?"

"Abridged version: Vaso. He and his friends assassinated Dominik Domonkos, the heir of Pyrrhos."

"Vaso? Cedo's kid brother? Why?"

"You can ask him about it on the ship. He's coming with us."

"What? No! Are you kidding?" She tugged on his hands, bringing them to her chest. "Gae, if he's the one responsible, we need to turn him in."

He dropped her hands, and pulled himself up to his full height, looking down at her. "We're taking him with us. Or I'm not leaving."

He was serious. He was willing to stay here. "Why?"

His face softened, and he closed his eyes. "He's all Cedo has left. They arrested Mrs. Nenad, and they... they killed Dimitri."

The world went cold. "Dimi?" Lena whispered. "Dimi's dead? But. He's just a kid." The floor seemed to fall out from beneath her. "How?"

A tired voice came from the doorway behind Gael, and Cedomir stepped out from the office, his eyes haunted. "He tried to stop them from getting Mom. She got in between the police and Vaso. And Dimitri got between them and her." He stopped. Took a deep breath. "He saved her life. They would have killed her, to get to Vaso." He looked back into the room, and his whole body tensed. When he looked back to Lena, his teeth were clenched and his eyes wide. "He ran. Didn't look back. And I followed him here." He gestured to the room behind him. "He's shot, but I patched him as best I can. Cat can do better if we get him back to the ship."

He disappeared before Lena could agree, emerging moments later with his hand tight around his brother's left bicep. Vaso's right arm hung at his side, a bandage wrapped tight near the shoulder, the sleeve cut away.

"I am not going anywhere." Vaso struggled against his brother's grasp. Lena had never thought they looked much alike. Though they shared the same copper complexion, curly black hair, and small dark eyes, there the resemblance ended. Cedo was muscular and stocky, cool and rational. Vaso was tall and wiry, fiery and intense. That intensity was flaring now as his voice raised. "They shot Dimitri. Those bastards shot my brother. They steal our lands, steal our resources, steal our government, now they steal our lives. I will not leave until every Pyrrhen is dead. They will pay. Dimitri's sacrifice will not be in vain!"

He did not see his brother's hand come around until it slammed into his face and knocked the fight from him. Before Vaso could collect himself, he was thrown up against the wall. Cedo had an arm across Vaso's throat, and he pressed down with each word. "You do not get to say his name. Not yet." He did not raise his voice, but each word was clipped and even. "As far as I see it, you killed Dimitri, and you lost us our mother. You and your temper. I do not know if I will ever forgive you for what you have done." He released his brother and took a step back. "But I also do not know if I could forgive myself for letting the Pyrrhen jackals get their hands on you. That uncertainty is the only thing keeping you alive right now." Without taking his eyes off his brother, he addressed Lena. "Lena, can we get to the shuttle without coming across any authorities?"

Lena swallowed before answering. She had known Cedo for years, but she'd never seen him like this. The eager-to-please, rational mechanic she called her little brother had disappeared, overwhelmed by this man of quiet and righteous anger. His cold fury nearly froze her, and she had to shake herself free before she could answer. "I think so. Most of the police activity seems to be north of here. And around the bakery. If we move quickly, we should get out without any trouble."

"Good," he nodded, his eyes still locked on his brother. "Vaso, you are coming with us. I will not allow my mother to lose another son today."

"I will not!" Vaso objected. "There is a revolution happening here, and I will be a part of it."

"You have done damage enough, little brother. More people will die over this, but not you. Not today." He finally broke eye contact, as he reached down into the waistband of his pants and pulled out a gun. He checked its charge, removed the safety lock, pulled Vaso from the wall, and pressed the muzzle to the small of his brother's back. "Lena, will you lead the way to the shuttle?"

Wide-eyed and scared, Lena complied.

CHAPTER FIVE

The moment *Aspasia*'s shuttle bay doors closed beneath them and the gravity repressurized the bay, Vaso flung open the door and fell into the ship proper.

"Couldn't you have taken it a little easier on the gravity escape?" he gasped as he tried to swallow back the contents of his stomach.

"Oh please," Lena teased, without turning. "We've been free of any inertial pull for over twenty minutes. You're just lucky Raines got *Aspasia* into an anticipatory position." Lena began to power down the flight controls. "Otherwise, we'd have had to fight Aegea's rotation in addition to her gravity."

Vaso clutched his stomach. "I hate you."

"You owe her your life, and you will be respectful." Cedomir stepped over his brother and yanked him none too gently from the floor of the shuttle bay. "I will show Vaso the common areas. Do you know if any of the passenger quarters are prepared for guests?"

"They should be," Lena said. "Cat keeps them ready. Except for the one next to her. She's been using that as her office. Check with her for linens."

"Thank you for everything," Cedo said, his hard look cracking for just a moment as he offered a wavering smile to Lena. The soft skin around his eyes twitched, then with a firm bite to his bottom lip, he steeled himself again. He stalked Vaso out through the shuttle area, out into the cargo bay, and up the ramps to the living quarters.

"You okay?" Gael asked as Lena finished up with the shuttle's controls, turning off the automatic air support and temp controls.

She pointedly ignored him, stopping to make a quick note in the logs that the bay door was a bit slow to open and that it might be sticking. Cedo would have to look at that later. Or not. He was busy.

She added a refuel request to her note as well. She didn't think they'd need to make any further shuttle departures on this trip, but, to be honest, she wasn't quite sure what this next trip was going to look like. Best to prepare.

With that taken care of, Lena hopped out of her chair and started making her way to the bridge. She had to tell Raines that they had to get away from the moon's gravity field ASAP. They were burning unnecessary fuel holding this close orbit. Not to mention, they were sitting in full view of the city's wide-range scanners. Lena wanted to get them out of there and on their way as soon as possible, lest they attract unwanted but completely warranted attention.

"Are you going to talk to me at all about this?" Gael said as he followed her up the stairs of the cargo area.

"Nope."

"Why not?"

"Nothing to talk about. It's done. We're carrying fugitives. My crew is at risk of capture by the Pyrrhens. And to make matters worse, we're also carrying a datastick stolen from, who else? Pyrrhos." She wheeled around at the top of the steps, nearly knocking Gael down. "You do still have it, right?"

He nodded and patted his right pants pocket. "Double checked on the ride up here."

She held out her hand. "Give it to me. I'll hide it on the bridge."

Gael took a quick step back down the stairs. "I don't think that's a good idea. You'll destroy it just to keep everyone safe. But this may have just become the most valuable collection of files in the three systems. No. I think I should keep the stick for now. Until we can get a chance to scan its contents."

"So, we don't know what's really on there?"

Gael cocked his head. "Actually, I was thinking to scan it for tracking codes. Why? Do you think Mason lied about what's on there?"

"Maybe," Lena admitted. Almost definitely, but she kept that part to herself. She didn't trust that Mason had suddenly thought of her after all these years. And the fact that he chose her to deliver something to Lomasky Corp? After everything that happened? He knew she wouldn't be welcomed back there. Besides, what would her father do with stolen communications from Pyrrhos? He wasn't a politician, though Lena was sure he had bought his fair share of elected officials. He wouldn't be able to do anything with Pyrrhen intelligence. She was missing something. "I just don't trust him. Or any of this. And with Vaso and Cedo being hunted, I just want to know what I'm getting us into."

She held out her hand expectantly, prompting Gael to take another step back, his hand hovering protectively over his thigh. "Let's bring it to Raines. He'll know what to do."

Lena smiled. "Sure. I'll bring it to him."

Lena started to take a step down towards Gael when Raines's voice came over the ship comms. "Lena, I don't know what you're doing with that damned shuttle, but I need you on the bridge. Now."

Shit.

Forgetting Gael entirely she turned and sprinted up the remaining two flights of stairs and arrived in under a minute, only slightly out of breath. "What's wrong?"

Gael arrived behind her, panting and bent over at the waist. "Is it the Pyrrhens?"

"What?" Raines turned from the controls, frowning. "No, it's the Aegeans. They're trying to ground us. And I don't know how to pull us out of this orbit with these stupid messages in my way." He gestured at the screens in front of him.

"Move." Lena pushed him out of the pilot's chair and bent over the screens. An all-waves flash was dominating her nav-screens. Even her Large Interstellar Body Estimated Location or LIBEL screens were frozen. The message demanded that all ships in range of the moon and the station dock immediately or risk pursuit. "Did you acknowledge receipt of the message?" She tapped each of the messages, confirming quickly that she had read them, and each one disappeared.

"Damn," Raines said as he peered over her shoulder. "That's it?"

"Not exactly." Lena looked at the fluctuations on the LIBEL screens. No tethers, no grav beams in use. They hadn't enforced the threat yet. Good. If the moon sent out grounding beacons, every ship in close enough proximity could be pulled down into an emergency landing on the moon's surface. The fact that such a move was an excessive waste of energy and could also affect the orbits of vital satellites meant that it was often a last case resort.

Of course, they could just be using the threat to weed out anyone who attempted to run.

She couldn't think about that. She had to do something.

"OK, let's get out of range," Lena said. "The moon's gravity isn't that strong. Get us out of orbit, and into Pyrrhos's pull space." The planet could provide some shelter while they got away.

"They've issued a warning, too."

"Who? Pyrrhos? That's impossible," Lena protested, quickly pulling the notices back up. "They'd have to negotiate overlapping gravity spheres with both moons and all five stations. Are you sure?"

Raines sat down in the chair next to her and turned his attention to Gael back at the door. "Welcome back. Glad you're in one piece. Where's Cedo?"

"With his brother in quarters," Gael said, and he debriefed his captain on the successful rescue mission and its complications. Their ability to prioritize and deal with multiple crises was a holdover from their days in Myrton special forces.

Lena needed better focus to get her job done, so she ignored their conversation as she reviewed the messages she'd dismissed. There. A notice from the official Aegean government with detailed procedures to follow. And sure enough, there were the notices flashing from the Pyrrhen authorities and the Aellan consulate. Each of them overlaid any other communications and demanded acknowledgment before the ship could access its navigation controls.

"Okay, you have my attention," she muttered. She flipped through the detailed notifications on her primary screen a few times before she noticed something. "Wait. That's weird," she said as she pulled all three notices and arrayed them side by side. The word choice. The sentence structure. "That can't be right. They didn't have time."

"What's the matter?" Raines asked, immediately attentive to her again.

"Look at this." The notices that appeared on the screen were automatic translations from their respective languages to Common Standard. Still, there was something remarkable in the translations. "They're the same notice."

"Yeah," Gael acknowledged, stepping up to peer over their shoulders. "What's weird about that?"

"They are exactly the same notice."

"Huh," Raines said.

"I'm missing something." Gael looked between the two of them. "Is someone going to explain or should I leave?"

"They speak different languages," Raines said.

"But the notices would be in Common no matter what, right?"

"They'd be translated," Lena said. "I'd expect a similar notice from the three governments, considering they're responding to the same crisis. But each of these notices is worded almost exactly the same as the others. Setting aside the fact that their languages all have varying syntactical structures, but three LIBs sending out the exact same procedural demands? In almost identical language? How likely is that?" When he didn't answer, she continued her line of thought. "And look at the timestamps. These were sent out almost at the exact same time. When have you ever known any of the major governments to coordinate their demands, let alone these three?"

Raines leaned forward to examine the messages again. "But why would Aegea or Aella coordinate with Pyrrhos? Even for something like this. On Independence Day? They'd make a point of issuing separate notices. Right?"

"Fanon's ethno-nationalist rhetoric is quoted in each of their Constitutions. Of course, they'd keep the messages separate," Lena said, without thinking.

"You've read the Aegean constitution?" Gael asked.

"You know what ethno-nationalism is?" Raines teased.

"Focus, please," Lena snapped. "A Pyrrhen heir was just assassinated, by a kid we're harboring on this very ship. And the government of the moon it happened on is apparently coordinating their response with the offended planet. Now anybody want to help me figure out what to do about this, or shall we talk about my political awareness some more?"

"You're right," said Raines. "It's weird. But right now, it doesn't concern us. Get us the hell out of here, Lee. If they're threatening to ground ships, you can be sure they're forcibly detaining whoever they can. And we can't be stopped with their assassin onboard."

He was right. Get out of here. Keep everyone safe. Worry about the rest later.

"Then you two get off my bridge," Lena said. "I have work to do."

Gael quickly obliged, but Raines lingered for a moment. As soon as they were alone on the bridge, he came over behind her, leaned over and kissed her on top of the head. She almost brushed him aside, but he spoke softly: "Thank you."

"For what?" she asked, not turning.

"For going back for them. For getting Gael back."

Lena bit her tongue. Of course, she went back for Gael. Cedo, too. They were her boys. Her crew. She had a responsibility. "Well," she said. " I wasn't going to lose the only two people who keep this ship running. You and Cat are worthless on this ship."

Raines laughed. "True enough." He spun her chair around, forcing her to look at him. His green eyes were soft and warm and focused completely on her. "You going to be okay getting us out of here?"

She looked down at the hand he placed protectively on her knee. "I'll be fine." She reached down and picked his hand up, removed it, and dropped it into the empty space between them.

"But Dimitri. I know you had become friends with him on our last visit."

She rubbed her hands on her knees, brushing away the warmth of his touch. If he kept touching her, kept comforting her, she would fall apart. "I'm fine." She had work to do.

"Lena," Raines reached for her hand again.

Lena snapped her hand out of reach. "Raines, look, I know. It's sad. We all liked the kid. But we're all dead if we get caught this close to Aegea with the leading suspect for the most politically inopportune death in the past decade. Not to mention what Gael is carrying. I don't know about you, but I have no interest in rotting in some Pyrrhen prison cell. So, if you want to grieve, go sob it up in your room. But get out of my way so I can find a route that will keep us clear of patrols and keep us alive."

She then turned her back on him and switched back to the nav screens. She had to find some route that would keep them free of Pyrrhen satellite posts along the Belt.

She felt him staring at her as she busied herself with a flurry of commands to bring up the LIB screen, the itineraries of their planned drops with the designated cargo, and relevant schedules for the next several months.

Finally, Raines gave up and moved towards the door.

When she heard him finally retreat, she let the tension leak out of her shoulders. She knew she was being cold, that she was pushing Raines away when it was obvious he only wanted to comfort her, to help her. There wasn't time for that, and she really didn't have the heart for it right now. She couldn't let any of it bother her.

Lena had work to do.

She had to keep moving.

CHAPTER SIX

It didn't take long to plot a course. All Lena had to do was keep their current trajectory until they hit the Bellows Belt. The straight shot would avoid major outposts, only a few small fueling stations along the way. Then, bounce back and forth between small asteroids back along the rotational path until they reached the huge gas giant that gave the Belt its name. Bellows was currently only a quarter of the star system behind Pyrrhos and Aegea. Not the shortest trip, but from there, it was a solid, straight shot to Myrto where Cat's fish shipment and their itinerary already said they were going.

No deviations, no suspicions.

It was the only logical destination. On Myrto, Raines's and Gael's homeworld, they had friends, both in the higher echelons of the military and in the darkest reaches of the Myrton underground. They could pass off valuable intel against Pyrrhos for a hefty price and secret away fugitives that they wanted to keep safe.

Aspasia had the fuel to make it without stops, and the funds to cover emergency help if they had to call for it. The advance Mason had wired to the ship covered every necessity for months, and even a handful of expensive emergencies.

Whatever he'd given them on that datastick was valuable, that was certain.

She just didn't trust that it was just some cryptography or government secrets, or whatever Mason had claimed. That sort of information was cheap, easy to pass off to Aegean rebels or Myrton forces. Definitely not something you paid someone to take to Rien or the Lomasky Corp. The cost of jumping to another system ensured that whatever was being transported was profitable, even outside of a regional conflict.

If only she could convince Gael to give her a peek at its contents. She wouldn't destroy the 'stick right away, not if there was something on it she could sell for even more.

But he'd never let her near it now. She'd been too anxious, too angry. Her emotions had gotten the better of her, and now Gael was right to question her motives.

Lena slammed her finger down on the final command to set her course. *Dammit.* She could have finessed it away from him. Sure, she may not have the dimples and easy smile of Mason's secretary, but she knew how Gael felt about her. Everyone knew how he felt about her. The lingering glances, the way he deferred to her over Raines, the special gifts he bought her at every outpost? She'd be a fool to miss it.

And Lena was no fool.

Well, aside from today. If she had just controlled herself at the meeting, held her temper, she could have sweet-talked the stick away from him.

She consulted her route and quickly calculated a schedule. She still had a week to cajole it from him before they reached Myrto.

And with the amount of wine and whiskey on board, I can get it in half the time.

She smiled in a brief moment of triumph before another notice popped up on her screen.

She clicked, and a news alert took over, filled with familiar faces. Vaso, Cedo. Gael.

Dimitri.

Naomi Nenad. Held for questioning.

Lena's vision blurred before she slammed her heels into her eyes to block it all out.

This wasn't something she could deal with. There was nothing she could do. She wanted to scream, to shoot something, to hurt someone. She couldn't do any of that. She was stuck in the middle of space on a ship with people who were counting on her.

So she did the only thing she could do when things got to be too much.

She ran.

Literally.

***

After the bridge and her own bunk, the gym was Lena's safe place on the ship. Here on the treadmill, it was just her, the rotating belt, and the persistent, driving beat of the music she blasted through the room. She had made sure to pick a playlist with no words, so she could just completely lose herself in the repetitive motions of her run. Her legs, lifting and driving down to propel her exactly nowhere. It was a meditation of sorts. She couldn't imagine people running outdoors, on the ground.

There, you ran to get somewhere; here, you ran to get away from yourself.

After a kilometer, her mind was less cluttered. After three, her anger dissipated and grief blunted. She was able to get a handle on her thoughts and really process what had happened. After five klicks, she was done thinking, wrung out, and exhausted.

She finally stepped off the treadmill dripping with sweat and in a much better mental state. She looked at the free weights in the corner. Maybe switch it up? She shook her head. Too slow. Thoughts could overwhelm her there.

She moved back to the treadmill. Another 3 klicks might do it.

Lena ran from her thoughts.

They chased her anyway.

She ran from Dimitri, dead at the hand of Pyrrhen officials. Just fifteen. He was going to go to college. Study history, not be a part of it.

She upped her speed.

She ran from Mrs. Nenad. Naomi. The infinitely generous woman who had served as a surrogate mother to all those who flew with her son. Now in the hands of the people who hunted her sons.

She ran from Vaso's hand in his brother's death. From the senselessness of his politics. Ran from the hunt for the brothers that now engulfed her entire crew. From the datastick in Gael's possession. From the political mess it all made. From the danger facing her family.

And there was nothing she could do about it.

So, she ran.

Until she gasped.

The solitude couldn't last though. Not with, what, six people on board now? Oh, and Chandra, the mercenary Raines hired. Seven. It was a full ship.

It was Raines who interrupted her seclusion.

Of course.

She knew she should apologize for snapping at him earlier, but if she'd wanted to do that, she would have found him in his room, stripped his clothes off, had her way with him, and afterward said she was sorry like a normal person.

Now, she just glared at him and kept running.

Raines didn't seem ready to make nice either.

He hadn't dressed for the gym, still in black slacks and a loose white dress shirt. Still, he came over and sat down on the weight bench directly in front of the treadmill. Giving no indication that he had seen her, he turned his back to her, slowly unbuttoned and removed his pressed white shirt, and revealed a tight-fitting white undershirt over lean hard muscle. He carefully laid his nicer shirt over a set of freehand weights and sat down on the bench with his back still to Lena. He then eased himself onto his back and reached up to the long bar, still set with weights from his last workout.

With a small grunt, he eased the bar off its supports. She watched the careful way he brought the bar all the way down to his chest, touching lightly and lifting it all the way back up. He did an easy ten reps of three before he returned the bar to its rack. He didn't sit up, instead rolled his head back to look at Lena.

"How far are you running?" he asked, his breath even and calm.

"As far as I can get," she huffed.

"Running from anything in particular?" he asked, not really wanting an answer. He cocked an eye at her before he turned his attention back to the weight above him. After another few reps, he finally sat up and turned to look at her directly.

She lowered her speed. A nice slow jog allowed her to keep moving but left her the breath she needed for any argument that inevitably came up.

"You and Chandra have fun at the station?" She couldn't help herself. She was upset, and it was easier to be petty than sad.

He sighed. "We were just collecting supplies and logging our itinerary."

"And you needed her special brand of protection for that? I'm sure she performed admirably."

"Why can't you be nice to her? She likes you, you know."

Lena snorted. Chandra had no reason to like Lena; she had been nothing but nasty to the merc since she got on at Aella. *Aspasia* was no place for a thug like Chandra Nayar, and Lena wouldn't feel comfortable until she left. "She's trouble. We should have left her on Aegea."

"Trouble?" Raines threw his hands up. "She came highly recommended as one of the best personal security agents in the system, and she's been nothing but pleasant the past two weeks. How is she trouble?"

Without waiting for the treadmill to stop, Lena stepped off and walked right up to Raines. He wanted a confrontation? Good. She was in the mood for a fight. "That bitch is a merc, Raines. She's got no loyalty to us, to this ship. And we just brought two fugitives right under her nose as well as a datastick full of Pyrrhen intelligence that Mason claims could change everything for the Sinope system. Do you really trust her to keep our secrets? To keep us safe? Your crew safe? Because that's what's on the line here. Our lives."

Raines turned to steel before her; his eyes narrowed, his entire frame taut and solid. "You ever think of questioning my devotion to this crew or this ship, I will find another pilot. Do you understand?"

Teeth clenched and lips pursed, she swallowed her angry retort and nodded once.

"Good. Now, whether or not you trust her or I trust her, Chandra has a contract with us. If she breaks that by endangering this crew in any way, her company will deal with her."

"And that's good enough assurance? What if the Pyrrhens buy out her contract?"

Raines dropped his chin to his chest. "You're determined to never trust her, aren't you? It doesn't work like that. She's ours until we release her from the contract, or either of us fail to meet its terms. Even then, any information she learns while in our employ cannot be used against us in any way."

"Or her company steps in?"

"They have a reputation to uphold. Violating their contract would—"

"Fine. Whatever." She turned on her heel and slapped the stop button on the still speeding treadmill. "None of it matters." She grabbed the towel, hanging on the arm of the machine and started to mop off her sweat. "Not if Pyrrhos catches us before your pet merc has a chance to turn us in." The exasperated sound that escaped Raines almost made Lena laugh out loud, but she smothered her smirk in the towel. Nothing made it easier to deal with a rough situation quite like picking a fight with Raines. Turn the tension and frustration into something she could deal with, something she could play with. "We've got to get out of range, get us somewhere safe. Then offload our dangerous cargo."

Raines grabbed her hand and yanked away the towel. "You want to sell out Vaso?"

"That's not what I said." she said, yanking her arm away. "Though it would solve a lot of problems." She paused as if considering the option, but it was never a choice. True, getting rid of Vaso would help them immensely. He could take the full blame for the assassination, letting Cedo go free. It might also distract from *Aspasia* having any sort of illicit cargo.

Then, if they could deliver the datastick to someone else, someone who was already heading to Rien, or anyone who wasn't so conspicuous or someone harboring a wanted man or two, then, everything would go a lot more smoothly.

Raines didn't misread the look on her face. "You're not serious!"

"No! Of course not." Not entirely serious.

It didn't matter how easy it made things; she couldn't betray Cedo that way. And she couldn't let Mason down. Everyone was counting on her. Gael was firmly on board with it, too. He had a mission, now. He would see things through, as he always did. And she would follow through if only to avoid disappointing him.

"We need to get free of the Belt," she said, committing to her plan. "Once we're past Bellows, we'll be good." Brushing past Raines, she moved toward the door. She cocked her head at her captain, and he followed her to the kitchen. A fruit juice for herself and water for Raines. He accepted the offered water as he buttoned his shirt back over his undershirt.

She sank down into the chair across from him and took a large gulp. The sugar helped wash away the salty taste of her workout. She took another sip, before settling the bottle in front of her and carefully twisting the cap back on. She then began nervously twisting her towel in her hands.

Reading her perfectly, as usual, Raines spoke. "If you don't want to talk about it you don't have to."

"No, I have to. It affects everyone on board."

"I'm guessing this has to do with whatever the Mason job is? Pyrrhen intelligence, you said?"

Lena frowned. "Gael didn't tell you?"

"Nope. Guess he figured it was your responsibility to fill me in." He took a gulp of his drink, then deliberately held her gaze as he affixed the top to his bottle. "Want to? Fill me in?"

She took a deep breath. "There's going to be a war."

"Gee, you think?"

"Shut up. Even if Vaso's cock-up didn't happen, even if he and his idiot friends never shot anyone, there was going to be a war. Apparently, tensions down there between Aegea and Pyrrhos made it inevitable."

"Lena," Raines said, reaching across the table to pat her hand. "Anyone who has paid attention to the past few years down there could tell you that."

She snatched her hand away. "Will you just listen? Mason said that things were getting tense down there. That Pyrrhos was making alliances, with Levin, Bhata, even Myrto. And that they were just waiting for an excuse to invade and bring Aegea and Aella back under control. That they want the mines and want the moons, both of them, back in Pyrrhen hands. They were already taking steps to make that happen."

"Okay," Raines said, carefully watching his tone. "And what does that have to do with us? Beyond the obvious gadfly on board, that is."

"Mason managed to get some intel that might help undermine any actions Pyrrhos might take. Specifically, he says he got his hands on the ciphers Pyrrhos uses to code their messages. The complete original ciphers."

Raines whistled. "Good for him." He paused. "I assume he gave this information to you, and that's what you're all worked up about."

"Yes," Lena said.

"And what does he expect us to do? Even if we can decrypt every message about this war, we can't do anything about it."

"He wants us to bring it to Rien. To my father."

"So he can sweep in and save the day, I assume? Why him? Why Rien? Why not Naftal? They have a bigger navy. Or hell, why not someone in this system? Someone less than a full jump away? What about Myrto? We're—they're at least already allies with Aegea and Aella. They helped with the original Independence Wars. Wouldn't it make more sense to take it a few worlds away than jumping these all-important ciphers a system away?"

Lena frowned. "I assumed Mason's connections are all in Rien. I don't know." She waved him away. "He wired the details to the ship with the money: where to take the message, who to give it to. I haven't read through it all yet. Why? Do you really think something like this would be better in Myrto?"

"Easy, there," he said with a slow and deliberate sip of his water. "I'm not planning any sort of intrigue here. I just want to know who you've gotten us into bed with"

"Why? Jealous?" She smiled.

"Just trying to keep up with your dalliances, *ma petite*. Old friend from your past. Could be your old flame. Eric was his name?"

"Evan," her smile disappeared. "And you promised you wouldn't ever say his name again."

"You're right. That was unfair." An apology from Raines? Without beating it out of him? He must be taking this seriously. He stood up and began to walk about the kitchen aimlessly. "So we're supposed to carry this data back to your home planet, and what happens then? Your father calls in the Rienen navy to rush in and save two little moons who haven't even had time to adjust to their Independence in any real way? Who's to say Rien would even do anything about this info? Not just pocket it for when they can use it to their own advantage? Your homeworld has no need for resources out here. They have no alliances here. There's nothing for them in any war. And, what about us? What do we care? Aside from Cedo, none of us have any real stake in this. And if you haven't noticed, Cedo's a bit too tangled in things to be much use to anyone in this sector. We all have more important things to worry about."

He was articulating everything Lena had already thought. This wasn't their fight. They didn't want to be involved in any political crises or get their feet muddied in the mess of interplanetary war.

So why not just drop the plans and ciphers off with someone else? She should just get Cedo out of harm's way, take care of her own, and let Aegea and everyone down there deal with things on their own.

Why couldn't they just walk away?

"You're right," she agreed. "It's not our fight. But whether it is or not, we've got the data already. We've also got to get Cedo out of here. Let's at least take the plans as far as we take him and his brother. Maybe not Rien. Let's keep heading to Myrto. We've got enough contacts there, even some Rienen merchants. Like Clara. Maybe Clara could take it home. The *Eurus* usually operates out of Myrto during Yager's summer. She owes me one. We give her the plans, and then we jump to Levin. Take a vacation in the Kyami Islands. My grandmother's people are originally from there. Always wanted to visit. Cedo would love it. And we've not taken some time off in a while."

It wasn't much of a plan, but it's all they needed for the moment. They had some time before they even reached Myrto, so they could easily refine their plan on the way. So long as they had a destination, she could pilot them there.

Raines nodded. "That might work. I'll look up who we know who might be stationed out that way. If the *Eurus* isn't available, there's sure to be someone headed to Samara and Rien. As long as Gael's not committed to some crazy idea of heroics and wanting to do things himself?" He smirked knowingly.

Lena smiled. "I'll talk to him. He has to know we're not the best people for this."

"And you're willing to give up the credits Mason wired us?"

She flinched. She hadn't even mentioned the money involved. But Raines knew the way to her heart. Right through her pocket.

It *was* a lot of money to give up. "Well," she said. "I mean, we can keep some hazard pay, right? After all, we're the ones who are carrying it off Aegea. And in the middle of all this chaos? Surely that warrants keeping part of it, right?" Or most of it.

Raines laughed. "You are awful." He clapped her on the shoulder as he stood. "Talk to Gael. I'm sure you two can reach some agreement on what constitutes a reasonable fee for our valuable services. Then we'll offer the rest to whoever finishes the trip. The easy part."

With that, he turned and left the kitchen.

He was right. It didn't make any sense for them to see the message all the way to Rien. She didn't have to go home. They could pass the data to someone more likely to go undetected. It wasn't about her avoiding Rien. Not really. It was the right thing to do.

So why did she feel so guilty?

CHAPTER SEVEN

She knew she should probably go and check on Cedo and Vaso, let them in on the plan, but Lena couldn't bring herself to get up from the kitchen table. She felt heavy.

Get it together, she chided herself. *Your only job is to keep yourself safe, to keep your crew safe, and keep* Aspasia *in the sky. Beyond that, you don't owe anybody anything. Not Pierce Mason, not the people of Aegea, not even Cedo. If he wants to throw in with the desperate people of his backwater moon, then he can leave and get himself killed on his own. Otherwise, he has no right to force us all to fall in with his doomed nationalist family.*

Thus resolved, she forced herself to her feet and moved for the fridge. A small, dark-skinned woman walked into the kitchen, and both of them came to abrupt stops.

Chandra.

Raines had hired her last month without any consultation from or explanation to his crew. He'd merely said that it was a necessary thing and that the woman would be practically invisible once she was onboard. They would all be safer for it, though.

The mercenary was dressed in simple black fatigues and armed with a pistol in a side holster as well as two knives on either side of her rib cage. She had her thick, black hair pulled back in a severe bun, and her almond eyes narrowed at Lena. "Has Captain Raines been here?"

"No," Lena lied automatically, inflicting the same harmless pettiness she had since the mercenary had gotten on board two weeks ago. She hated having this woman imposing on their space, always lurking, always attentive, always keeping her little secrets. Lena could swear every time she encountered Chandra, that the mercenary was listening to something no one else could hear. So, a little snark, a little cold shoulder was her small way of showing displeasure at having the extra security onboard.

Things had changed, though. This unknown woman could cause them no end of trouble with a single wave to Pyrrhen or Aegean authorities, and since Raines was determined to keep her on the ship despite their new precarious situation, Lena should probably play nice. "I mean, yes. He just left. A few minutes ago." She brushed past the merc, careful to bump her shoulder with a prominently protruding elbow. *Okay, not that nice.* She smiled slightly to herself as she set her barely tasted water bottle back in the fridge.

"Did he say where he was going?" Chandra asked patiently.

Lena turned and considered her for half a second. What exactly did Chandra hope to prove with her pistol and knives out here? She just looked foolish toting them all over the ship. This pretend soldier was nothing more than a drain on resources. "It's not a big ship. I'm sure you can find him. Now, if you'll excuse me, I have work to do." Lena moved toward the door, but Chandra Nayar stepped directly in her path.

"Look," she said. "I get it. You don't want me here. That's fine. But your captain hired me, and it seems like I've suddenly become far more relevant than you would like to admit."

Every vein seemed to frost over. "What do you mean?"

"I'm not stupid. I pay attention. I watch the newscasts. It's my job. It's also my job to keep you safe." Chandra smiled, trying to strike some sort of rapport. "I'm on your side, you know."

"Are you? You don't know us. You aren't one of us," Lena spat. She didn't trust her. This woman had nothing binding her to anyone on this ship other than a useless contract. What about some signed piece of data made her more likely to protect her crew than to turn them all into the Pyrrhens? If you asked Lena, this untested security expert was the biggest security risk on the ship. She couldn't take any chances. Not with her family. "If you want Raines, try his bunk."

Lena tried to push past Chandra, but the smaller woman seemed to dominate the space. There was no way to walk around without shoving right through her. "I get it," Chandra said. You're not the first to put a stone wall in front of me. But whether you like me or not, I'm here to do a job. That job means I'm on your side, no matter what. I've got your back; I fight your battles. I keep your secrets. All of them."

"All of them?"

"Yes. All. Whether you're running from the past or the present, I keep your identities secret, Ms. Lomasky."

At the invocation of her real name, Lena took an involuntary step back, but Chandra's expression didn't change. She was pure ice. Lena swallowed and pulled herself up to her full height. "Good. That's good." She stood over the smaller woman and looked down her nose. "As long as you don't expect us to be friends, we should work together fine."

Chandra laughed. "Friends? I will be impressed if you manage civil. But sure. Friends. Let's go with that."

Lena managed an awkward half-smile. "Yes. Let's," she said before turning on her heel and fleeing the kitchen. She had hoped for confident and imposing in their latest confrontation, but she wasn't sure she'd even managed competent or sane.

Ugh, everything about having that woman on board unnerved her. The way Raines refused to say how he'd found her. Or who exactly her employer was. Her unverifiable credentials. How she knew things she shouldn't.

The sooner they could get out of this system, get rid of the plans, and hide Cedo away, the better. The whole thing was messy, and Lena hated mess.

Lena dropped by her room to grab some clean clothes and then headed down to the showers on the passenger level to rinse off the sweat of her run. She turned the water as hot as it would go and let it scald and wash away any lingering anxieties. One foot in front of the other. One day after the next. It's what she'd done for seven years. She could do it for a few more yet.

After twisting her dripping black hair up into a clip, she threw on a black tank top and some loose pants and headed back to the bridge.

Gael was waiting for her in the co-pilot's chair. He spun around as he heard her feet on the steps. "What did he say?"

Lena slipped into her seat and automatically pulled up her LIB and nav guides. "What did who say?"

"The Prime Minister of Levin. Who do you think? Raines. What did he say about our mission?"

"Our mission?" She hated how that sounded. It made the simple fly-and-drop delivery feel more important, more immediate. Exactly how Gael liked things. But she didn't want to have any moral imperative attached to Mason's job. It was just a job.

"It's just a job. Raines thinks we should take it as far as Myrto. He thinks—and I agree—that there's no real need to take these ciphers all the way to Rien just because Mason has his contacts there. The info can be put to better use here in the Sinope system, not jumped away to Samara. Not that it's really my place to say what should be done with it. It's just a delivery job. But still, we have some responsibility, right? Anyway, we agreed it should probably be dealt with by people who have some stake in the present conflict. Myrto is already an ally of Aegea and Aella. They're better positioned to make use of the ciphers. So we can just drop it off there, on Myrto, when we deliver Cedo and Vaso."

She toggled on and off a few screens while she babbled, but she paid no attention to what she was doing. "Besides, we have more contacts in Myrto than we do Rien these days. Maybe we can deliver it to some of your military friends there. They can handle this sort of thing. A jump to Rien? Waste of fuel, really. This will get the Aegeans all the help they need." Lena stopped as she realized Gael was waiting for her to take a breath.

"Are you quite done? Or do you need to justify yourself some more?"

Lena didn't trust herself to answer.

"Are you really that scared to go home?"

"Rien is not my home," she said.

Gael sighed. He wasn't going to argue the point with her again. He didn't have to.

"I'm not hiding," Lena insisted. "I just don't have any obligation to go back."

"Yes, you do! You literally just signed off on a job with someone who apparently trusts you more than he even trusts his own people."

"Mason doesn't trust me. He's just using me," she insisted, still avoiding his eyes. "And I'm not saying we betray him and hand the info over to the Pyrrhens. I'm just saying we don't need to go out of our way to —WHAT? Why are you looking at me like that?"

He sat silently for a few moments before closing his eyes and turning away from her. "Lena, I don't understand you sometimes. You are so desperate to hide from your own reflection, you never see what other people see."

"I don't need you to analyze my character flaws, Gael. I'm plenty good at it myself."

"I'm not talking about your flaws! I'm talking about the virtues you are so determined to bury underneath your self-loathing. Mason trusts you to bring his information to his contacts on Rien when no one else in his entire bureaucracy or personal network can be trusted. Cedo trusts to you to keep him and his brother safe when an entire empire is poised to fall down on top of them. Raines and Cat and I all trust you to do the right thing because that's what you do. And here you are determined to prove us wrong and compromise your word and just dump your friends and your responsibilities in the laps of some military contacts on Myrto?"

Lena's brows knit under the weight of his scrutiny, but she wasn't going to back down. "We can refund part of the fee."

Gael's head fell backward as he sighed. "It's not about the money, and you know it, Lena."

She closed her mouth. She had nothing more to add.

Gael stood. "If you and Raines are in agreement, then there's little I can say to change your minds. I'll see who is best for this in Myrto's military. There may be someone in the hierarchy we can trust with this." With that, he turned and left.

In the empty space he left behind, Lena realized she was clenching her jaw, and it was beginning to give her a headache. She took a deep breath to clear herself of any lingering guilt or anger or whatever it was clawing away at the inside of her skull.

The decision was made. Myrto. She just had to get them to Myrto. Then she could let all of this go.

Work now.

She turned her full attention to her LIB map. They were making solid progress away from Aegea and her current political struggles. Another day or so and Lena wanted to move to a pull on the Belt instead of this lagging push on the waning moon. There wasn't a large enough body to pull on until that point, so they'd have to ride out their initial push.

She typed up a quick message to Cat asking her to work with Gael and iron out the details of their trip to Myrto. They wouldn't be staying long, and Lena would want to get their business done as quickly as possible to avoid attracting attention. Cat would see the message and get straight to work, lining up a few side transport jobs that would supplement a course they'd already chosen and keep them flying for months longer. With Cat on the case, Lena could expect a detailed itinerary within a few hours.

Next, the Aegean, Pyrrhen, and Myrton authorities would all need to know their itinerary to keep *Aspasia*'s registers clean. Lena logged the trip across the channels, noting their legal delivery of the Gomar Kinf—some rare fish Cat had picked up that was highly prized and highly paid for in Myrto—and the stated aim of picking up new cargo for transport. Cat would take care of specifying exactly what cargo that would be and syncing it with the individual border checks. The Myrto ports would coordinate their arrival, register the available docks at the appropriate stations, and help them avoid any major collisions with other approaching or departing ships.

The sky was big, but there were too many occasions when major ships could come too close to one another's grav fields, especially when around any of the major ports. It usually wasn't a big deal to the bigger ships, but smaller ships could find their courses radically altered if they drifted too close. The enhanced boson emissions of massive bodies had a tendency to gum up the works on smaller ships. If the interfering ship was big enough, the smaller ship could even be brought into involuntary pulls if they got close. When an especially large ship like those of military size got into range, there could be a collision before anyone had a chance to act.

A military ship like the one that popped up into Lena's Vicinity Alert System.

As a loud alarm started on the bridge, Lena opened a comms channel to the whole ship.

"Um, Raines. Gael. We have a situation. Please come to the bridge immediately. Cedo, too."

She shut off the comms and turned to her bosonic emissions screen. So long as the bigger ship hadn't directed any pull on them, they should be able to direct a quick pull on the moon and planet behind them to drag them back and out of the way until the bigger ship passed. Otherwise, they were going to drift directly into the larger vessel's path.

"What's going on?" Raines was the first to arrive, and he immediately rushed to Lena's side. With a hand on her shoulder, he leaned over to look at the screen. "What the hell is that? Why weren't we alerted to a ship that size in our vicinity?"

"Because she was just floating there," Lena responded, agitated. "She wasn't giving off any bosonic readings. Until a few seconds ago, she wasn't reading anything more than her mass produces. Like an asteroid. But as soon as we came upon her, there she was. I— I think she was lying in wait." She began increasing her subtle pull against the distant Aegea and Pyrrhos behind her, trying to avoid any push against the now obvious and much closer field around the large warship. Such a long distance maneuver would take a few minutes to begin to affect *Aspasia's* velocity.

"And how did our VAS not see her?" Raines demanded, leaning on her and squeezing Lena's shoulder slightly.

"Without an active field, our Vicinity Alert System may have read her as debris or an asteroid. Easy to move around with our automatic systems. Nothing to worry about."

"Lena, what's wrong?" Gael came rushing in, slightly out of breath.

"Looks like a warship," Raines answered as Lena concentrated on upping the pulls she had established. None of her controls seemed to be reacting the way they should.

"Cedo, I thought you fixed this," she shouted as he, too, arrived on the bridge.

"The L-drive? I did! Controls were all responding before we docked yesterday." He had his toolbox at the ready, but it was already too late for that. She needed the controls. He couldn't fiddle with them now.

Lena upped the chehon concentration to get a stronger pull on the planet behind her. She really hoped she wasn't wasting vital fuel on this. If they used too much, they might get stuck in the new trajectory and start to drift right back where they came from, and they'd waste even more fuel as she tried to reverse it.

Unfortunately, that did not seem like it was going to be the problem.

"Lena, you're drifting too close. They'll notice us." Gael said. The ship was looming closer and closer, no matter what Lena did.

"It's too late." Lena realized what the problem was as she stopped trying to fight it. "They've already got us."

CHAPTER EIGHT

Lena hesitated and looked back at Cedo behind her. It was just a second, and though Cedo was focused on the screens in front of them, she knew both Raines and Gael noticed. She hesitated and hated herself for it. Then she hit the comms button. "Everyone, we have a situation. Be on notice and be ready to act soon." Behind her, Raines and Gael were already trading looks. "That's a Pyrrhen warship, guys, and it's got us good. What do we do?"

"Ion propulsion?" Raines suggested.

"First thing I'd disable," Gael said.

"Hard burn?"

"Only scorch their hull."

"Jump?"

"We're inside the Belt. Even you are not stupid enough to try a tesseract this close to a star."

"I'm just throwing out ideas." Raines protested.

"Well, try harder," Cedo interrupted their rapid-fire dialogue. "A Pyrrhen ship means my brother and I are both dead."

There was a moment of sobriety. Then Lena reached over and gave Cedo's hand a squeeze. "We're not letting anything happen to you. They'll figure something out." She was sure she sounded more confident than she felt.

Cedo squeezed back, but Lena could see a light sheen of sweat beginning to break out on his forehead.

"Their mass dwarfs ours," Gael insisted. "Chehon, hard burn, it doesn't matter. If they've got us, we don't have enough fuel to force even a 30-second burn against that big a ship!"

"What about trying a Beechum?"

"We can't pull off a Beechum."

"Why not? Gael insisted. "We're small enough to seem insignificant. They could decide we're not worth the energy."

Raines kept his mouth shut for half a second as he seemed to consider his options. "And what do you propose we use as our trump? The Lomasky heir or the wanted Aegean assassins? I'm pretty sure both baits end with us all in chains."

Gael actually seemed to be evaluating whatever the hell a Beechum was.

Lena interrupted and looked up from the screens she was scanning through. "Guys. Fun as that sounds, we only have a few seconds here. What is happening?"

The two men exchanged looks before Raines stepped forward. *"Ma petite*, I don't think we have a move. Without external weapons and with our tiny mass, we're completely at their mercy. The safest thing we can do is contact them and follow their orders and hope they don't have any special interest in finding out who our passengers are." He avoided any glance at Cedo.

"Okay," Lena said. "So, what are those orders likely to be? Are they going to disable *Aspasia*? Board us? What?"

"They'll board us for sure," Gael said. "Survey the contents of the ship, interview the crew, the normal docking procedures with any civilian encounter. The question is, why they're forcing an encounter at all. Did they follow us?"

"It's probably nothing to do with us specifically. Just enforcement of the latest embargoes," Raines reasoned. "The chatter at the Prime Station was that random stops have been happening pretty regularly inside the Belt. They probably want to review our cargo and confirm our manifests."

"What do we do, then?" Cedo asked. "We cannot hide Vaso or myself. They will do a life-signs check and know how many we have on board."

"And they'll confirm that against our manifest," Raines said. "Damn. I logged us at Aegea because I couldn't disengage from the Meridian Station without uploading something. But I didn't account for Vaso."

"So, we're only off by one?" Lena said, thinking quickly. "That's good. That's fine. Everything was in such a state when we left Aegea, we can claim that the discrepancy is just a mistake. We took on an extra passenger or something. Tried to help someone stranded in the groundings."

"That's good," Raines said. "Good thinking."

She basked in his praise for a second before Gael spoke. "But what about the waves? Cedo and Vaso? Their faces are everywhere."

Raines leaned forward and hit the comms button and broadcast to the whole ship. "Chandra. Get into civvies, or as far from work clothes as you have. Borrow from Cat if you have to. Cat, help her. Vaso, sit tight."

"How about not?"

Vaso's voice from the back of the bridge caused them all to turn. He was standing in the door with a gun leveled directly at the assorted crew. No. It was aimed at Lena. "Turn us around."

Lena reflexively put her hands in the air and slowly stood. The others likewise turned and gave Vaso their full attention.

"That's a Pyrrhen warship." He gestured to the now looming ship in the near distance of their windows. "I will not be given to the Aegeans or the Pyrrhens or anyone. Turn us around."

"Can't do it," Lena said. "We're caught in a bosonic pull. I don't have the power or the mass to get us away."

"Then you have to hide me. I won't go down like this. Not to them."

"I can't just hide you. Standard protocol is to scan us for life signs. They'll know you're here and where you are the second we dock." Lena said.

"Then don't dock! Keep us sealed," Vaso insisted.

"Can't. They'd overpower our systems in a heartbeat. Or else they'll just tow us to someone that can." As she kept talking, Gael began inching forward, while Raines kept inching around to Vaso's left, both trying to be unobtrusive.

"Then we have to get out of here." Vaso turned to face Raines. "And don't think I don't see you. You keep moving this way, I will shoot your pilot."

"No, you will not." Cedo ignored the subtle movements of his crew and walked directly toward his brother. "You idiot, that gun's not even loaded. And your safety is on."

As Vaso looked down and regarded the gun, Raines dashed forward, grabbed the weapon from him, and removed the obviously loaded magazine. He shot a look at Cedo who shrugged and smiled.

Gael took a deep breath of relief, and only after he got a nod from Raines did he step away from shielding Lena. She hadn't even realized he'd moved between Vaso and herself.

"We're not giving you up," Raines said to the disarmed and chagrined Vaso. He looked to Cedo. "Either of you."

"So, what is the plan?" Cedo asked. "The only way we hoped to get out of this was to stay under the radar and away from anyone official. Now that plan is sort of blown. You know if anyone gets their hands on us, they're going to hand us over to the Pyrrhens. They'd be crazy not to."

"Only if they know who you are," Raines said.

He handed back the stolen gun and full magazine back to Cedo, who promptly put them back together, engaged the safety, and tucked the gun in his back waistband. He lingered at his brother's side, though safely out of reach. Raines returned to Lena and leaned beside her, as always on the edge of the console.

"I logged our passenger count but didn't log names. With the chaos that happened when we disembarked, we can try to bluff. Now, if these guys are on the lookout for you or your brother, they'll know that you live on the *Aspasia*, but they don't know for sure that you're on board. Last anyone knew you were somewhere on the moon. If we disguise you and your brother, we can sell you as our newest security detail, and Chandra is some additional passenger we picked up at the station."

Cedo paced back and forth as he listened to Raines's idea. He stopped and looked to Lena. "You think they will go for that?"

"Maybe," Raines said, ignoring that the question wasn't posed to him. "We're going on a couple of assumptions. First, that no one noticed Lena's off-the-books landing moonside. Things were a bit hectic, so a shuttle might have gone unnoticed, or at least unlogged. Also, we can assume they didn't keep reliable records of who used their own shuttles as things got shut down. They can't be sure who did and didn't leave the moon and who got off the station or who is still there. Things were a mess, and we can use that to our advantage."

"But there are pictures of Vaso and Cedo circulating around the entire system by now," Lena said. "Do we really think they won't recognize either of them?"

"Good point," Raines said.

"I have an idea about that," Gael said. "May I?" He looked to Raines who nodded once, trusting him without any question. Gael quickly disappeared from the bridge.

Raines continued as if he'd never been interrupted. "Cedo, you have lots of black clothes. Anything that fits Vaso?"

Cedo looked his brother up and down. While Cedo was solid and muscled, Vaso was much lankier, and a good deal taller.

"I've got some," he said. "Pants might be a bit short on him, but you shouldn't be able to tell once he has boots on."

"Good," Raines said. "Then all I need you to do is keep your mouths shut. Your accents would give you away in a minute. Vaso, can you manage that?"

Vaso looked to the crew. "You are not going to give me up?"

"Of course not," Lena said.

"Even if it would help protect Cedomir?"

Well, in that case, Lena wanted to say, but Raines interrupted.

"There's no guarantee they wouldn't take you both anyway. If anybody asks us about you, we'll all disavow you and your whole family. Hopefully, they release us without too many questions. Then we get you as far as we can from Aegea and Pyrrhos and this whole mess." He lifted his hands. "It's the only play we've got."

Cedo spoke up. "Thank you." He grabbed Vaso's arm. "We do not want to put you in any danger. Any of you. If there is any indication that things are going badly, do not hesitate to give us up. We would rather go down alone than take you with us."

"That's not happening," Lena said with as much confidence as she could muster. Cedo managed a weak smile, and he took Vaso by the arm, steering him off the bridge.

Lena stood up to follow and see how she could help, but as she stood to get up, Raines put a hand on her shoulder. "Wait. Sit. I need to know. How did this happen?"

"What do you mean?" Lena said, sitting back down.

"Did they follow us? Do they know who we are? We can't pull this off if they followed us all the way from Aegea."

Lena turned to her screens. "I don't think they did. I would have noticed." Tracking back through the LIB readouts of the last few hours, she scanned quickly. "I should have noticed this. See here?" She pointed to a small blip on the screen. "That's the ship that has us now. It's active now, but up until a few minutes ago, it was reading as an insignificant body. It was giving off no fields, no grav disturbances. It must have been just drifting, using support services, but no navigational power. It's called a halcyon state. It's rare, but I've used it once or twice to get us past sentries when we didn't need the scrutiny. To my LIB scans before, it looked like a piece of debris or a small asteroid. It wasn't until we fell in range that it came to life. Now look at this." She pulled back on the screen to show multiple such bodies in the area. "Here, here, here. They all look like dead rocks, right? But that was a few hours ago," she scanned back. "And now they're all active. This one," she pointed to an inert body. "It was active back on the other screen. It's obviously a ship, too. And if we go further back, we can see," she pointed to the screen. "There. It was dead, but another ship approached and brought it to life."

Raines leaned over her to scan back further. He entered in a quick command to identify all bodies in the surrounding areas that might be ship sized. The screen came to life with hundreds, some operating with full services, but many more seemingly lifeless. Lena immediately recognized a pattern, a predictable distance between the bodies.

"It's a net," Lena said as she scanned back further and further than she thought she should. "And it goes back several hours. From before the assassination." She turned to look at him. "This isn't a normal stop, Raines, but I don't think it's related to Cedo."

He looked at her and then back at the screens. "Have they hailed us?"

"Not yet. But we're not going anywhere, so they're not in any rush."

"They're probably reviewing our manifests," Raines volunteered. "Seeing where we've been, who we've docked with lately, who we've done business with. They're probably checking our cargo history. It's okay. Everything is standard."

"Standard?" Lena snorted. "They've snagged my ship right out of the sky. There's nothing standard about any of this."

"My ship. And it's going to be okay. It's a legal check. It's inconvenient and a bit dangerous considering our passengers, but we're going to get through this." He put a hand over hers on the console. "I'm going to get us out of here. Cedo and Vaso are going to be fine." He gave her a quick kiss on the forehead and left the bridge.

"My hero," she said to his disappearing back. He wasn't taking her concerns seriously. He was too focused on the immediate issue of Cedo and Vaso. He was right. That was what they should focus on. But this wasn't right. Nothing about this was.

At that, a ping signaled an incoming transmission. Waiting message from the *Bayern*. She assumed that was the ship that had seized them.

"Ship *Aspasia*, you have entered the controlled territories of the Sinopean system. Without proper dispensation from the Central Powers, all travelers may be subject to random searches and questioning under the proper authorities. We ask that you submit to these searches so that we may allow you to progress without further sanction. Any resistance will be taken as an act of aggression and will be met with due force. We thank you for your lawful submission."

The transmission cut out, and Lena felt the cold knot of fear settling down into the pit of her stomach.

Controlled territories? Central Powers?

The words didn't mean anything to her, but it didn't matter. She had a job to do. She had to protect her crew.

With that thought, she opened up the communication channel to respond to the Pyrrhen warship.

CHAPTER NINE

Nearly two dozen Pyrrhen soldiers swarmed *Aspasia.* As ordered, everyone aboard the ship lined up along the gangway, and Lena could do nothing but grit her teeth as her beloved home suffered the indignity of invasion.

Vaso and Cedo, quickly shaved bald and dressed in nearly matching black short-sleeved shirts and thick canvas pants, stood shoulder to shoulder alongside Raines. A visible gun sat in Cedo's shoulder harness, its unloaded twin in Vaso's. Cat stood on the other side of the brothers, trying to control her shaking as soldiers walked past.

Lena wanted nothing more than to go to her friend and hug her and assure her that everything was okay. But it wasn't okay. Nothing about this was okay.

So, she seethed beside Gael, and beside him was Chandra dressed in borrowed casual clothing from Cat. If things had been different, Lena would have laughed to see Chandra in Cat's sundress. The mercenary tugged at the hem of the too-short gingham dress and shifted her weight in the too-small heeled sandals. If she was forced to move, Lena was certain Chandra would fall right over.

There was no way they'd pull this off.

Heavily armed and with no regard for her ship, the Pyrrhen soldiers blustered about, opening storage crates, spoiling food and drinks, and destroying the carefully maintained order of the bay.

Lena opened her mouth to voice an objection as one of the soldiers broken into her cache of Dornish red wines, but Gael quickly jabbed an elbow into her side. She only managed to get out a single breath of protest. Raines instead stepped forward to assure the soldiers of their full compliance and welcomed them to the ship as if he were a cruise director.

They ignored him, and Lena could only watch in horror as another half-dozen soldiers clanked through the gangway and up the stairs up to the multiple levels, no doubt to ransack the bedrooms. And her bridge. They were in her bridge. Her skin began to crawl. Were they going through the logs? Adjusting her nav controls? *Aspasia* was a finely tuned instrument; were they messing with her settings? She could probably fix it in a matter of moments, but it was the principle.

She was stripped raw, her secrets exposed, and she was left naked and vulnerable. Lena could feel them from the hairs on her arms to the nerves in her twitching calves. They were inside her, and she wanted to fly at them, force them out.

Little by little, reports came through the soldiers' comms, and a commander with a checklist confirmed the cargo, layout of the ship, and more.

As a call came through about the nav logs being code-locked came down, she knew the next step. They'd ask for the codes or break through with brute force.

She stepped out of the line despite Gael's late attempt to grab her. "Stop."

Each of her crew, from Raines down to Vaso in his borrowed clothes, turned to her in fear.

"Stop?" The commander in the cargo hold looked to his checklist and then walked towards Lena. "You? You are this ship's pilot, yes?"

Lena tried to swallow but found her throat dry. She hadn't thought to speak, but she hadn't been able to help herself. "Yes," she croaked. She licked her lips and tried again. "Yes. I am the pilot of *Aspasia*. And this is unacceptable treatment for a legal transporter in neutral space."

The commander stepped forward to look at Lena's face. He got so close she could see the flecks of amber in his green eyes and the white hairs amongst his blond. "There is no such thing as neutral space. You are subject to evaluation by any authority in this area. As your contents have been flagged, you are subject to further scrutiny."

"Our contents?" Raines stepped towards them. "We have nothing but legal goods here and have registered each and every delivery manifest with the appropriate transnational organizations. You have no right to hold us."

The commander looked back to another soldier who stood at the ready with a databoard. The soldier stepped forward and spoke in the commander's ear as he navigated through multiple screens. The commander nodded and pulled up a specific screen. He then looked up to Raines and

Lena and smiled. "I'm afraid that is not entirely true. Though you have logged every docking, delivery, and pickup, it seems you were incomplete in your registers."

Lena felt a lump form in her throat. But he wasn't talking about the manifest. Something was wrong here. Something didn't line up. "Incomplete? That's not possible. Our records are flawless."

"Then would you care to explain why you have an undocumented crate of Callahan rifles in your cargo hold?"

Raines started. "What?"

"A crate of—" he consulted his chart— "Callahan Full-bore Auto-lock rifles. Customized triggers, double cartridge thorough gauges. Quite the weapons for a legal transport ship to carry. And not a word about it here in your, um, cargo register. You do claim a crate of Gomar Kinf that there is no evidence of in your hold. Bound for Myrto? I have to wonder what your Myrto buyer could want with 40 of these very expensive weapons."

Raines turned to look at Cat. "Did you confirm the fish were in the crate?"

Cat's face drained of color. "No," she gasped while shaking her head. "The Kinf was for a new client, but, but she was recommended by a trusted source. I was told not to open the crate so it could maintain consistent temperatures. F-f-for the fish. Kinf. It goes bad."

The commander smirked. "And you expect us to buy that?" He turned to the soldier standing in front of her. "Take her into custody."

"What? No!" Cat protested as the soldier took hold of her arm and began putting her into handcuffs. "I didn't know anything about guns! Please," Cat sobbed. "You have to believe me." Gael grabbed Lena before she could move, and Vaso did the same for Cedomir.

No one could stop Raines. As a soldier attempted to guide Cat up the gangway, Raines reached out and grabbed the soldier's free arm. "You will release her." The soldier reacted instinctively by wrenching his arm back and reaching for his gun. Instantly, no fewer than seven rifles were trained on Raines. He let go of the soldier and threw his hands up in a defensive pose before addressing the commander. "I trust Cat completely. She didn't know anything. Catherine Sanders is the most by-the-book person I know. There's no way she would have knowingly taken illegal weapons on board."

"And who is to say you all didn't know about it?" The commander sneered.

"Show me the guns!" Raines yelled. "You can't! This is ridiculous. There's no way we have illegal weapons on board. Show me the inside of that crate."

The commander ignored him. "Take the girl. In fact, take them all. We'll get to the bottom of this. And someone bring that crate on board. I want them cataloged and sourced in the next hour."

The crew of the *Aspasia* loudly protested as the Pyrrhen soldiers approached, but quickly succumbed when they raised their weapons. The soldiers took special care to disarm Cedo and Vaso, but, thankfully, they didn't seem to notice the lack of weight in Vaso's unloaded weapon. Even more importantly, they didn't seem to recognize either of the brothers. Raines briefly struggled as the soldiers attempted to secure his wrists with plastic ties, but a quick wrench of Lena's arms and her sharp gasp of pain, and he was as obliging as a beaten puppy.

"Separate them, and prep them for questioning," the commander said. "I'll start with the 'by-the-book' book-keeper. Bring the pilot to Prince."

And with that, the crew members were marched from the *Aspasia* and onto the Pyrrhen warship.

CHAPTER TEN

The *Bayern* was huge.

Onboarding, Lena and her crewmates were directed down a series of long hallways to an elevator that took them up some unknown number of floors, up several more hallways, and then up another set of stairs. Then, Lena and Cat were dragged off away from their friends by their own pair of escorts and separated into two rooms.

The room Lena was put in was featureless aside from a single empty table and two chairs set across from each other. Her armed escort directed her to sit in the chair opposite the door, and they secured her already bound hands to a metal loop built into the table.

Her escorts left her.

She had to laugh. How dangerous did they think she was? She was on a military ship, separated from her crew, her hands bound, and with no idea of where she was on this maze of a ship.

The thought of escape didn't even enter her mind, but a dismayed resignation did. She and everyone she knew and cared about were under armed guard for nebulous charges none of them could answer for. She wasn't even sure the commander's claims of hidden weapons were real. Not that it mattered; they weren't exactly going to give her a chance to inspect the goods for herself.

And those thugs still had full run of her ship. They could tear *Aspasia* apart, and there was nothing Lena could do to defend her.

She wanted to cry, but things were beyond that. Somewhere on her ship, hidden on a small datastick, that was Gael-only-knew-where, was a cypher and stolen plans that could make the difference in what looked to be a serious international incident.

If only she had looked at what was on it. If only she had some idea of what they were dealing with, she might feel better. Or worse.

Of course, it might not even be hidden. Gael had not bothered to tell her where he had stashed the datastick. For all she knew, he still had it on him. Or there was a very obvious datastick sitting in the middle of his desk with a big sign that said: "Secret Encryption Codes for Pyrrhen War Plans Here." All she could do was trust that Gael had had the good sense to set it aside in a discrete location.

She wondered if she'd get a chance to ask him.

Where was he? Where was Raines? Cedo, Vaso? Cat? Was she in an identical room down the hall? How long had it been? Fifteen minutes? Thirty?

It didn't matter. There was nothing she could do. Her friends were trapped, she was trapped. It was a matter of time before the soldiers scanned everyone and realized who Vaso and Cedo really were. How had Gael thought shaving their heads and disguising them would make a difference?

She rolled her shoulders back and stretched her neck. Wiggling, she tried to scoot her chair forward, but it was bolted to the ground. She sat on the edge of the chair, and skewing her elbows akimbo, she managed to rest her head on the table. It wasn't the most comfortable position, but maybe she could take a nap while she waited. It wasn't like there was much use in her staying alert and worried.

The tension had just begun to seep from her shoulders when the door in front of her opened. A young man of medium height entered the room. He had short dark brown hair and a close-cut, if somewhat patchy, beard. He lifted his gaze up to meet hers and smiled, showing rounded cheeks that were seemingly comfortable with genuine smiles.

"So sorry to keep you waiting," the man said. He extended his hand to shake hers but quickly noticed that she was still tied to the table. "Oh," he frowned. He turned back to the door and spoke to the guard who was standing directly outside. "Who ordered this? Do you really think she's going to storm the *Bayern* without any weapons? Are you that frightened? Get in here and take off these restraints." He stood in the doorway as an abashed soldier came in and cut her loose from the plastic handcuffs. The soldier mumbled a quick apology and quickly disappeared. "I am so sorry. That was completely unnecessary. They're a bit on edge, lately. You understand."

Lena rubbed her chafed wrists, mostly for show, but thankful for the release, even if it was symbolic. She was still a prisoner on this massive warship. "Actually, no. I don't. I don't understand at all. What the hell is going on? Why are you holding my ship?"

"You haven't heard? It's been all over the waves. Seems there was an assassination on Aegea. The heir. Dominik. Nice kid. He was the leading advocate for continued peace between Pyrrhos and Aegea, you know? Shot in the head by some hooligan gang member. Never should have visited the moon, you ask me. Such a shame." He sighed as he sank into the chair opposite Lena. "Nice fella. Domonkos, not the assassin. I met him once or twice at some social events back on Pyrrhos. His wife was lovely, too. Older woman. But they were so in love..." He waved his hand as if to sweep away the memories. "Neither here nor there. He was the heir to the Pyrrhen throne. Only one to preach the peace between the moons and Pyrrhos. And some gang of kids killed him in cold blood." He stopped and cocked his head at her. "I'm surprised you didn't hear anything. I know there was a vicinity notice that required authorization to dismiss. It seems strange that a pilot could have missed it."

Damn, Lena thought. "Of course I read about it," she said. "Notices came from several governments in the area. I just don't understand what that has to do with a Pyrrhen warship stopping my perfectly legal travel." *Good. Stay on the defensive. Let him do the talking.*

"Ah, well, there are a few reasons," the young man said. He looked down to the sheet computer he held. Then he stopped, looked up at her with a quizzical look, and gave her a half-smile. "I am so sorry. Where are my manners? Captain Lieutenant Richard Prince." He extended his hand.

Lena tentatively reached out but met his wrist in an equal grasp. "Lena Loman."

He shook his head. "Ms. Lomasky, we know who you are. No need to dissemble amongst friends."

She gritted her teeth. That wouldn't make things easy. "My family disowned me. Out here I go by Loman."

"Naturally," he spread his hands. "No one can begrudge you seeking a bit of anonymity."

"That's not — Yes. Thank you."

"Of course, since we do know who you are, I do have to ask what you're doing with this particular band of— individuals. One would think, with your pedigree, you could command any piloting job in the systems." He paused and winced. "You haven't found your accident to cause undue hardships, have you?"

Lena took a deep breath. *Easy, now. He's trying to unnerve you. He only has as much power as you grant him. Aside from the multiple guns and entire warship at his back, he can't hurt you unless you let him.* "No, I chose the *Aspasia* as much as she chose me."

"Oh, good," he said, bringing his hands together. "I'm glad someone of your legacy was not reduced to a compromising position just because of a few mistakes in her youth." He offered her that charming smile again, transforming his face and lending him a youthful, laughing appearance.

He's trying to gain your trust, Lena reminded herself. *He is not your friend. He has his soldiers crawling all over your ship. Remember that.*

"I appreciate your concern," she said out loud. "It still doesn't tell me why you've stolen my ship out of the sky."

"Stolen?" He set down his sheet. "No, no. You misunderstand our intent. We are merely attending to the security of our territory. The Central Powers have agreed that in light of certain recent events, stricter measures are necessary to assure our people of the security they have come to expect."

There it was again: the invocation of "Central Powers." He was talking in riddles. She took a stronger offense: "Stricter measures? Seizing random ships in neutral space is considered stricter measures? I'd call it an act of war."

A scowl came over Prince's face before he caught it and smiled again. "War?" he said. "No one is declaring something so drastic."

"Of course not," Lena said. "That would be impolitic. But this 'Central Powers' thing? That sounds pretty damn political, doesn't it?"

Prince leaned forward. "A marriage of convenience between Pyrrhos and a few lesser moons in this sector of the system. But it's unimportant given your circumstances." He looked down at as computer and swiped across a few screens. "It seems, according to my reports, your ship was conveying unauthorized arms across our territories. Is that true?"

"As Cat, er, our business manager told you, we have no knowledge of weapons on *Aspasia*. Every weapon that we have onboard has been registered with the proper authorities. We have licenses for every single one. If there is a crate of anything, we had nothing to do with it."

"Nothing? Hmm. You would attest to the legal state of your cargo then?"

"I would attest to the innocence of anyone on board my ship." She crossed her arms and settled into her chair. As far as she was concerned, she had nothing to hide.

"That so? Even," he consulted his files, "Cedomir Nenad? Son of Nadia and Jovan Nenad?"

Lena's heart froze, and her eyes closed. *Of course.* If they knew who she was, they knew Cedo. They would know who the brothers were in a second. Dammit. "Of course," she forced a smile, doing her best to scramble back from the precipice. "Cedo had been with the *Aspasia* as long as I have. But he went home. Back in Banika. On Aegea." *Stupid. He knows where Banika is.* "As far as I know, he's still there with his family. What could he possibly have to do with anything?"

"Ms. Lomasky," he said, disappointed. "Let's not play games. I'm not an idiot, and I'm a little offended that you think I am. You received the information about the assassination, you know who did it, and you know that we know your mechanic and first officer were both at the scene. Do you want to keep playing dumb, or do you want to just concede the truth and plead for a lesser sentence?"

Lena sat up and gripped the edge of the table; it was all that was keeping her from leaping over and strangling this smug bastard. "The truth is Cedomir did not kill Dominik Domonkos, and I will stand by that truth to my dying breath. He may object to the illegal occupation of Aegean territories and may have philosophical objections to the ongoing hostilities between Pyrrhos and her moons, but he would never, ever take the life of another human being." *Unless that human being happened to be threatening him or his family.* But Lena left that unsaid.

"And yet you do not deny that he was at the scene of the murder," Prince pointed out. "Along with Gael Renard?"

It kept getting worse.

"I don't deny they were on Aegea, no. But they had nothing to do with any of this."

"I see," he replied, obviously unconvinced as he consulted his data. "And are you aware that several members of the Nenad family have already been identified and been taken into custody in direct connection with the incident? A brother, Dimitri, was killed at the scene, and his mother and several of her employees were captured. There is also substantial evidence that a second brother, Vaso? He also managed to escape. Do you have any information on his current whereabouts?" He set his screen down to gauge her reaction.

She steeled her face as she had to see her original lie through his questioning. "I do not. As far as I know, he's still back on Aegea with Cedo. Either way, my crew had nothing to do with this."

The man nodded slowly. "I see." He closed the folder in front of him and clasped his hands on the table in front of him. "I'm afraid, then, Ms. Lomasky, that you are under arrest."

"What?" She stood. "Why?"

"In addition to the concealed weapons your crew are illegally transporting to Myrto in clear violation of Central Law, you stand accused of knowingly harboring a pair of fugitives and political criminals. We have already ascertained the presence of Vaso and Cedomir Nenad on your ship, haircuts notwithstanding. The fugitives will be extradited to Aegea for immediate public execution, and you and your crew will be transported to a secure facility on Pyrrhos. I'm sorry, Ms. Lomasky. I had hoped you would cooperate. It might have lessened your sentence. Because you refused to give me the truth, though, I am forced to pursue the full punishment under the law. Good luck, and I hope things go well for you."

He rose in one smooth motion, moved to the now open door, and let in a pair of soldiers who handcuffed Lena once more. He gave her one final pout. "I'm afraid there's nothing more I can do for you. I only hope your crew is more cooperative."

CHAPTER ELEVEN

The secure holding facility in the warship's underbelly was spare and cold: two unlined mattresses on metal cots bolted to the floor, a single toilet, and a sink, with a long glass wall along the outside. Lena paced the mostly empty space as she watched a pair of guards chatting and laughing on the other side.

She didn't wait alone for long. Within the hour, she was joined by both Raines and Chandra. An invisible panel in the glass wall dropped away into the floor, and they were ushered into the cell. The moment they were shoved in, the panel instantly raised, and the wall once again appeared seamless. Once closed, the sounds of the outside world were silenced. Still, the visible comm units in the topmost corners of the room made it clear that any sound they made would be heard.

With that in mind, the three stayed quiet. After the immediate questions of each other's health and well-being, they mostly avoided talking. Lena was scared to ask about the others, whether they knew anything. Any concern for Gael, Cedo or even Cat might be misconstrued or used as evidence for complicity of guilt. Best to keep quiet and see how things played out.

But even with everything else going on, Lena loathed being locked in a room with Chandra.

Chandra took up residence on one of the cots, sat down, leaned her back against the wall, crossed her legs, and closed her eyes. Within minutes, her breathing had deepened, and a reasonable person might think her to be asleep. But seeing as her head never dropped, nor her posture slackened, Lena had a hard time believing the mercenary was anything but fully alert.

While Chandra sat there being unnerving and Raines took the other bunk for a quick cat nap, Lena could do nothing but pace. She was too restless to relax. She was in a cage, a jail cell, on a military ship. How did something like this happen?

She eyed the guards that came in and out of the room outside, watching for any sign. Of what, she didn't know. A restlessness, an urgent bit of news, anything that might let her know that something was happening outside of this cell, that her friends were okay or not. From time to time, she could see a bit of news pass between the guards as shifts changed, but nothing told her whether it had anything to do with her or her crew or even her ship.

If they put a single scratch in her hull, Lena was going to buff those scratches with Pyrrhen blood.

Fed up, she walked right up to the glass and pounded quickly against it, careful not to linger in case it was charged to shock unruly inmates. The middle-aged guard on duty looked up from his desk down at the other end of the room, stood, and begrudgingly walked over to a small comm unit beside the cell.

He reached over and pressed a button. His heavily accented voice piped through, bored and unimpressed. "*Ja?* What do you want?"

"I want to know how much longer you think to hold us without giving us access to a proper defense representative. These are trumped-up charges with completely fabricated evidence, and I demand to speak to someone."

The grizzled guard looked back to his desk and the novel he had abandoned on its surface. "I'm just told to watch you and make sure you don't hurt yourselves or each other. I don't know anything about charges."

Lena threw up her hands and turned her back on him. "Of course not!" She paced to the back of the cell. Her stamping woke up Raines, who rolled over to look at her as she paced back to the glass. She glared at the guard before collecting herself, squeezing her eyes shut, taking a deep breath, and then opening them again, smiling in a way she hoped was beatific. She was the picture of dignified calm. "Is there someone else I can talk to? Someone who may have some authority over the illegal handling of civilian guests?"

The guard shifted his gaze to the door, hoping someone was coming to relieve him soon. "I don't know, *fraulein*. I'm just a grunt. I could call my superior, but I don't know if he can help you, either."

Lena smiled broadly. "Could you be a dear and call him?"

He looked skeptical. "Um..."

"Lena, give it a rest." Raines was apparently awake now. He sat up and looked to the guard. "It's okay. We're fine. Thank you."

The guard muttered something incomprehensible in Pyrrhen and cut the communication link between the outer and inner rooms.

"What the hell, Raines?" Lena turned on her captain. "We need to get to a higher up. This isn't right!"

He stood up and walked to Lena. He only stood a few centimeters taller than she did, but he managed to make her feel small right then. "You don't think everything that is happening is sanctioned by a higher-up? We were unfortunate to get caught in their net, but the moment we got pinched, and they realized they had caught a big fish, we were passed up to the highest authorities. Lena, that blockade was set up for something like us, and we delivered Vaso and Cedo like obedient drones."

"So we just sit here and rot?"

Raines laughed. "Rot? We've been here less than two hours, *ma petite*. We haven't even begun to ripen."

"But we're not doing anything," Lena growled. "There has to be something we can do. They're going to execute Cedo. Maybe even Gael. For something they didn't do. We can't let that happen!" She felt every muscle in her body tense up. She just wanted to hit something or scream or run.

"Hey," Raines grabbed her arms and gave her a quick shake. "Stop. This is not your fault."

"But if I could have avoided the ship. If I could have gotten us out of range." She felt herself losing control.

"You did everything right, *ma belle*; I promise. Sometimes, though, we get caught in things that are bigger than us." He pulled her into a tight embrace. "There's nothing you can do, right now."

"You could shut up," Chandra said from her cot.

Lena could feel the muscles in Raines's arms tense up as he released her and turned to the mercenary. "What the hell did you say?"

Chandra didn't respond but jerked her head towards the glass front of the cell.

The guards were changing watches. A new young soldier came in and shook hands with the older man who had been on duty. They extended their respective handhelds and entered in their personal identification codes. The older soldier mouthed a few words while nodding towards Lena and then disappeared. The younger guard settled down at the desk facing the prisoners but stopped halfway down into the chair. A smile spread across his face, and he walked over to the glass. He pressed the button as he squinted into the cell. "Nayar? That you?"

Chandra unfolded from her position on the cot and walked over to the glass. "Armin, it's been a minute."

The young soldier laughed. "A minute? It's been a lifetime! What the hell are you doing on that side of the glass? Especially on the *Bayern*?"

Chandra grimaced. "Just a mix-up that I hope will be resolved before too long. I hate cramped spaces."

"I hear you." The guard looked down at his handheld computer. "I got nothing for you on here. But then you know they don't give us details about this sort of thing. Just do as you're told. Keep your head down."

"Oh yeah, I remember," Chandra said. "Who you serving under?"

"Well, they've got a new guy overseeing my unit. Some Prince? His name, not his birthright," he laughed again.

"Oh yeah? I heard of him a few years back. I'm surprised he moved up so quickly. Must have graduated from some cushy officer school."

They shared another laugh.

"I hear you. He's a bit overzealous, you ask me. Gotta do everything himself, and everything is a capital offense. Probably why you got nabbed. Seems he's pushing for something to make his name. Lucky he has to answer to Commander Reimbold. If something isn't good for Pyrrhos, she won't do it."

"Homeland first, huh?" Chandra said. "I can appreciate that. But still, it might be embarrassing for her if this Prince keeps us penned. You've got a Lomasky in here."

"No shit!" The soldier looked to Raines. "Rienen royalty, eh?"

Raines put his hands up to ward off the accusation. "Not me, friend." He cocked his head at Lena. "Look to the lady."

Lena looked over at Chandra. What the hell was she doing? Drawing this kind of attention wasn't going to help matters.

Armin looked Lena over from head to toe, suddenly interested in her presence. "You a Lomasky princess, sweet?" the soldier was practically leering at Lena now.

"Rien doesn't have an aristocracy," she said. "We're a democracy."

"I'm not an idiot," the soldier scoffed. "I know you're just some rich capitalist. But," he considered, "that much money, you might as well be able to buy a title."

"Exactly," Chandra said. "Why do you think I'm working for her?"

"Nice gig!" Armin said, all smiles again. "Personal security? Man, I can't wait until my term's up, and I can start charging. Think I can hit you up for a recommendation in another year?"

"You can try, but it won't do either of us any good by then," Chandra said. "When word gets out that Pyrrhen forces are randomly holding Rienen heiresses for no good reason, no one will hire any of us again."

The soldier frowned. "Eh? You think so?"

"We'll all be out of jobs. I'll be lucky to get out of this gig with a single credit to my name. I'm supposed to provide security and then in my first few weeks on contract, we get nabbed by my old fleet for some political bullshit? I'm screwed." She stopped and suddenly smiled as if an idea had occurred to her. "Wait. Maybe you can help."

"Me?" Armin said. "How? It's not like I can break you guys out. We're in the middle of deep space."

"But we won't be for long. They're going to have to transport us back to a base at some point."

He shifted his weight uncomfortably. "Nayar, I like you, but I am not putting my career on the line to break you and some rich bitch loose."

Chandra shook her head. "Wouldn't ask you to. Besides, you probably wouldn't be our escort. Shifts being what they are. All I want is information. If you could find out where we're headed, maybe let me know who is escorting us, that sort of thing, I could see about setting you up somewhere nice when this is all over?"

"You'd do that for me? Really? Because I have dreams of owning my own place off the coast. Maybe in Levin."

"Hell, man, you help me save my job and get this girl back home, I'll buy you a place myself. A nice beach bungalow. You can bring your girl. Mia, right?"

"You remembered!" Armin broke into a big smile, but he faltered as he thought about the situation. "Wait, how would any information help you? You'll still be under guard, and our bases are as secure as any ship. Nowhere to run."

Chandra nodded. "Yeah, but you leave it up to me. I'll find a way around it."

"If anyone could, I'd believe you'd do it. All right," the young soldier said. "I'll do what I can. But I want a nice house. Ocean views."

"You got it," Chandra said.

Armin looked back to his desk. "I guess I should get back to work. But I'll try and find what I can."

"Thanks, man. I appreciate it."

"Sure, thing. Anything for you. Man, the way you saved our asses back on — Right," he said as Chandra shook her head. "Info." And Armin cut off the comms and retreated back to his desk.

Chandra walked back to her cot and resumed her previous position, the back of her head resting firmly against the wall. Raines and Lena meanwhile turned their backs on the glass to gape at the mercenary.

She opened a single eye as she realized their gaze was focused on her.

"What the hell just happened?" Raines asked.

Chandra smiled at her cellmates. "That was one of my former *kinderkadetts*. Trained him. One of the younger recruits elevated to junior officer status. He had less than a year with my unit. But he seemed to attach himself to me. When I saw him, I thought I might find a way to help. I apologize. I am improvising at this point."

Lena looked to Raines and back to Chandra. "So, you didn't mean what you said? About being in this for the money?"

"Hell," Chandra said. "I meant every word. If I don't save your ass, I don't get a credit. And if I don't get paid, what the hell am I sacrificing myself for?"

"The right thing?" Lena said, indignant.

"Doesn't pay as well."

Lena wanted to be shocked by the statement, but she felt the truth of the words. They had to be practical. No one could afford to be governed by lofty ideals of right or wrong, moral or immoral. They were faced with a single question: imprisonment or freedom, and they had to make their choices according to that reality. If Lena was going to get back to the freedom that *Aspasia* represented, then she might have to make some compromises along the way. Still, it didn't sit right. "What happens if your kadett helps us and gets caught?"

"Honestly, I doubt anything he says or does will help us in any real way at this point. But if he gives us some useful information, and it gets back to anyone that he had something to do with it?" Chandra shrugged. "Typical response is capital."

"They'll KILL him?" Lena said.

Chandra straightened. "Princess? Settle down. You want out of this, someone has to pay the price."

Lena stalked over to the seated merc and loomed over her. "Stop calling me princess. I am not my family. I have no claim to my father's protection. And if I die out here, in the farthest corners of the universe, he will probably throw a parade. Do you understand?"

Chandra shut her eyes and leaned back again. "I know. I did my research. Luckily, my friend out there didn't. He probably doesn't know that your family cut you off. That you are destitute and living off the wages you make from day to day on some barge of a ship. Tell me, Ms. Lomasky," she said as she stifled a yawn. "Do you think it would be better for ignorant people to think you're worth a fortune or that you are the biggest pariah in the Samaran system?"

Lena's breath hitched, and she turned away. The truth hurt.

Despite the tell-all book, most people still thought the Lomasky name was worth something. And so long as the name attached to it wasn't Helena, they were right. Whatever accident had happened, the Lomasky name was still one to make starships move and governments stand at attention. Whatever details were involved, whatever scandal had rocked Samaran social circles, here in the Sinopean system, where monarchies and dynasties had been rising and falling for millennia, such intersystem gossip merely confirmed everyone's opinion: a weak democratic pedigree and a bit of money was no substitute for a true aristocratic legacy.

"It doesn't matter," Lena said. "If he even contacts the nearest Lomasky rental agency, he'll find that my father won't pay a dime for my safe return."

"You might be surprised." Chandra almost smiled, but there was no joy in it. "You're the only heir he has left. Your father might be willing to forgive a lot at this point."

"You know nothing of—" Lena began to protest before Raines stepped to her and put a hand to her chest.

"Lee." He pulled her to the side and whispered to her. "You need to get a hold of yourself. If using your father's name is the only way to get us out of this, we're going to use it." He stopped her before she could protest. "I know. I know how you feel about it. But we don't have a lot of options here. What would your father do in this case? He'd use every resource at his disposal to get out and keep moving. Right now, that's his— your name. And Chandra's connections, apparently. She seems to have made an impression on at least one person on this ship."

Chandra snorted. "Probably more than that." She straightened but didn't leave her cot. "I trained *kadetts* at Baltus on Gaiar. Probably half the nuggets in this fleet. We're just lucky one of the weakest got assigned to security on the *Bayern*."

Raines didn't miss a beat. "That's why we stand a chance. Chan's got the right of it. We can't do anything here or on any base. But we get control of whatever transport they put us on, we could get out of here."

"You don't give up, do you?" Lena asked. "We're in a holding cell, separated from the majority of our crew, held captive on a Pyrrhen warship at the intersection of nothing and nowhere, and you're going to hold on to this thug's crazy hope that we might possibly be transported to a Pyrrhen BASE so that we have an easier chance of escape?" She threw up her hands. "You are both insane." She began pacing again.

Raines ignored her and went to sit down on the bunk where Chandra was sitting. They began talking in hushed tones. Presumably establishing plans for when they were transferred from their heavily armed military ship, escorted by an armed escort, and confined to a more stable and secure unit like a military base. Sure. There was a hole in that schematic they could exploit. Right.

It didn't matter. Let them plot an escape plan. It gave them something to hold on to. They could have it. As far as she could figure, though, the only thing that could save them was a pardon or trade from an interested military party.

What were the chances of them securing any sort of pardon?

Despite what any ill-informed solider-recruit might think, her family was never going to come to their rescue. They'd probably be glad to be fully rid of their wayward daughter. She'd be a late footnote in the next version of *Escape Velocity*. Lena Lomasky, imprisoned and executed in a Sinopean political skirmish. Clean and easy disposal of the family disgrace.

What was more likely was these charges would be dropped when it became clear that the majority of the crew of the *Aspasia* had nothing to do with the assassination, and the guns were an obvious mistake.

In the short term, though? They were trapped on this horrible ship while horrible soldiers destroyed her ship, and Vaso and Cedo were going to be transported to Aegea where they would likely be executed, and Cat was probably going to prison for smuggling guns, and there was nothing any of them could do about it.

She could really use a drink.

"Helena Lomasky?"

The voice came through the speaker, and it took several moments for Lena to realize that it was addressing her.

She looked up and saw a crowd of armed soldiers and a pair of uniformed officers all standing and looking at her on the other side of the glass. The shortest officer addressed her. "Helena Lomasky, you are required to report to a private interrogation. All occupants of the cell align along the right wall and place your hands in the designated circles." He pressed a button and the seemingly empty wall to the right displayed six circles at chest height, each shoulder-width apart.

Chandra and Raines had apparently experienced this drill before as they both got up without question and lined up against the wall with Chandra claiming the back two circles, Raines the middle, leaving the two circles closest to the glass for Lena. Everyone watched as she slowly walked forward. Before she placed her hands, she turned to Raines.

"Anything happens to me in this," she whispered. "I'm going to come for you first."

Raines smiled. "I should hope so."

"That was a threat. Not a promise."

"Same thing, *ma petite*."

Lena turned and placed her own hands in the final two circles.

When she made contact with the wall, the glass panel at the front of the cell slid down from the ceiling. Three armed guards walked forward and trained their guns on the prisoners. The short soldier with a sheet computer stepped to the side. "Helena Lomasky, step forward."

She looked to Raines for assurance and immediately regretted it. It made her appear weak, and she hated to look like she needed her captain to back her up.

Still, the move made, she waited for him to respond.

He turned to survey each of the guards individually, looking them over from head to toe. He gave some skeptical looks, presumably when he saw a lace or button out of place, and each guard, in turn, squirmed under the scrutiny. He landed, finally, on the small man who had made the demands. Everything he saw on the short officer seemed to inspire disgust or amusement. Raines smirked at scuffed shoes, pants that had grown frayed around the edges, shiny knees, an off-kilter belt, dull buttons, and a tie that had come askew. By the time Raines turned back to Lena with a nod, the guard was completely unnerved. But Raines smiled at his pilot. He spoke as if she was headed into a fair fight instead of as a prisoner on a warship. "Go get 'em."

It was exactly the encouragement she needed. She adopted a shark's smile and turned to the waiting soldiers with a hungry grin. "Show me to your master."

CHAPTER TWELVE

An armed escort led a handcuffed Lena down what seemed miles of corridors into what she assumed was the center of the ship. While the original interrogation chambers had been near the fringes of the ship, this room was buried deep within caverns of hallways and blank rooms.

As they passed through the long corridors and walked by dozens of open doors, the stark military atmosphere of the warship gave way to something else. Austere offices, classrooms, and training spaces turned into warmer rooms filled with papers, books, whiteboards, and equipment. White coats replaced uniforms, while work tablets and spare parts replaced sidearms and salutes.

Inside workrooms and laboratories, men and women fiddled with electronics, soldered equipment, and scribbled notes. A stab of homesickness grabbed Lena by the stomach, and her chest hitched. It was so familiar. She was in the development sector of the warship: the place where technologies were conceived and birthed. The place where innovation happened.

Where soldiers found new and more efficient ways to kill each other.

It was ironic to Lena, that no matter how advanced society grew, no matter how far their science reached or how deep their philosophies delved, mankind always came back to the most rudimentary means of ending disagreements. In the end, death on a mass scale always seemed to help men of politics reach some sort of resolution.

Thus, weapons development was still key to deciding the most pressing conflicts of the day. Most planets devoted huge portions of their vast tax resources to the design and production of more specialized weapons, more exact ways of cutting down those who opposed them. It was simple; any conflict could be easily be solved by simply wearing down the opposition with casualties until they eventually recognized that resistance was just too costly. Lasers and ballistic missiles, massive bombs, nuclear weapons that could transform thriving cities into radioactive wastelands in a matter of seconds: civilization had become quite proficient at destroying itself. Modern man wasn't entirely callous. Deaths in the thousands, the millions, those might just be statistics to the average viewer back home, but no one wanted to watch people suffer. It was why nearly every planet and moon and inhabited asteroid in the three systems had outlawed chemical and biological weapons. Sure, such were efficient in wiping out a population and leaving a city intact. But to watch skin peeling off the bodies of still-living children, to see the agonizing asphyxiation of elderly populations left behind in bombed cities, to witness the slow radiation poisoning of nearby populations? That was just too much.

Left with the importance of the appearance of empathy and the limitations of war, engineers had to find new ways to kill each other. Precision, range, efficiency, all could be improved with the next generation of weapon, and each planet, moon, and principality was willing to spend billions to have the best new toys. It was into this world that Lena had been escorted.

The soldiers accessed a door and brought her to a small office off one of the labs. The room was full of books, writing boards, and computer screens. Every wall was filled, drawn on, crammed with information, everything covered in data and figures. Bookshelves were packed solid, white screens were so covered in notes they had almost zero white space left, and nearly every available surface was covered in paper. And yet, the room was immaculate. Every book was shelved with the spines aligned just so; the boards were wiped clean of all stray marks, left only with exact equations; and the screens showed no signs of dust. Even the stacks of paper on the shelves and tables and chairs were stacked perfectly with corners lined up with the edges of desks.

Lena's escorts roughly shoved her into a chair in the middle of the room across from a large desk.

They then, to her surprise, reached over and removed her handcuffs and filed out of the doors without a word, two to the lab off to her left, and the two other soldiers to the door behind her at the opposite end of the room.

She was suddenly alone.

Maybe they were letting her go. Maybe they were going to ransom her back to her family. Maybe they realized this was all some big mistake, and they'd brought her to their highest ambassador to deal with the political fallout of holding someone like her.

But then why was she in the office of a scientist and not some bureaucrat's cubby? She should be dealing with someone important.

She sat in her chair for a good fifteen to twenty minutes before she lost patience for the waiting game. If she was going to be stuck here, she might as well look around. She briefly skimmed over a board of formulas and drawings of circuitry or something, but very little of it made any sense to her; never was much for hardware. She walked over to one of the bookshelves. One of the most efficient ways of knowing someone was to see what books they kept. She scanned a shelf that had some of the most worn spines, the most oft-read books. This would be where she found her ammunition.

The Fundamental Concepts of Bosonic Forces. Making a Proper Bosonic Drive. The Key to a Future Metaphysic. Energy Fields Today. Reaching for the Stars: History of the Lomasky Family. The Lomasky Drive and the History of Bosonic Fields. Fields, Gravity, and Untestable Motions. Obviously a scientist or engineer in bosonic pull/push systems. Not unusual on a warship. All ships, planes, and transport craft used bosonic fields in flight, and entire teams would be needed to monitor and maintain the equipment that controlled gravitational pulls internally and externally. It made sense to have someone on board who understood the underlying principles.

There were shelves and shelves on the nuances of her family's work. All natural. All expected. Then she got to the final shelves. Not about the Lomasky Drive. These were about the family itself.

Lomaskys, Driven.
Loren Lomasky: His Life and Universe.
Lomasky Meets Thrace: Lomasky's First Discoveries.
Defying Gravity: The Story of the Lomasky Dynasty.
The Lost Daughter: A Thesis on Helena.
Lena's Lament: Lomasky's Loss.

Great. That explained why she had been brought here.

The scientist was a fan. Someone who thought she could offer an inside look and wanted to pick her brain on her family's work. Wanted to know the latest innovation or development in bosonic field theory or artificial field generation.

Or worse. Someone who was obsessed with her family. Or her story. Or her.

The office door behind her slid open.

It wasn't a fan.

Lena swallowed hard against a lump of grief in her throat.

His hair had grown out. He had always worn it short before. Now it was wavy and thick. Lighter brown, too, than she remembered, with a hint of red when the light hit it. It hung low about his face but was pushed back out of his eyes, as if he had spent all day running his hand through it, trying to tuck its length behind an ear but failed. It made him look somehow less lean, though she could see he had lost a great deal of weight.

His eyes were still as blue as ever. Piercing. Square jaw, marked by a day's stubble.

The right side of his mouth quirked up for a half-second before a full grin emerged. Then his cheeks overwhelmed his eyes as the smile filled his face.

He dropped the files he was carrying and ran to her, wrapped his arms around her and held her in a tight but intimate embrace. "Lena! Oh, my Lena. Oh, my darling, I can't believe it's really you. They said it, but I didn't believe it. It's you." He continued to murmur endearments as she tried to find her bearing.

Evan Thomas.

Her Evan.

The love of her life.

Former love of her life.

The man she had spent nine years with. Loving, caring for, being cared for.

The man she had almost married.

Evan.

He was here.

It was too much.

Lena felt her knees start to turn to jelly, but she refused to fall.

Instead, she threw her arms back around her ex-fiancé, returned his embrace, and let her head drop to his shoulders to hide her tears.

She hadn't thought seeing him would be like this. It felt good in his arms. Safe. Familiar.

Strange, though.

She should shove him away, scream, yell. Anything but this clinging desperation.

His arms were warm about her, busy on her back, soothing away the fears and anxieties of everything that had happened in the past several hours. He took her tension, the trembling that started in her knees and found its way to her lower lip. He was here.

They remained wrapped about each other until Lena grabbed a tenuous hold on her senses. She lifted and shook her head and pushed away from Evan. He looked hurt for half a second until she spoke.

"How?" One word. It was all she needed.

His eyes clouded and brows knit as he nodded. "A fair question. You're right. I owe you answers. Forgive me. I saw you, and I just..." He stepped back, walked over to his desk, and gestured to the chair. "Will you sit?"

Lena complied without a thought.

Still, she found herself tapping her foot as she waited for him to walk around his desk, settle himself down in his own chair, and return her gaze. As soon as she realized she was fidgeting, she forced herself to stop, to remain calm and listen.

He smiled at her. "Would you like a drink? Coffee? Tea? Pure ethanol?"

She couldn't bring herself to so much as smile.

"Right. Too soon," Evan said, dropping his grin. She noticed his foot tapping, as well. He followed her gaze and stopped tapping. "Got it from you." He smiled again. "Sorry." Dropped it. "Well. How? Right." He stopped himself and took a deep breath. Started again. "After the accident, after the whole thing fell apart on Rien, well, there was nothing holding me there. I mean I could stay. Your father assured me I still had my job with him, that nothing had changed as far as that was concerned, that just because you were ... gone. It didn't mean I had to leave. But I did. Of course, I did. If you weren't there, I had nothing. Nothing but my work. So I left. I went back home. I returned to my family and resumed my research on my own. Turns out my little brother—you met him that time? Emmet. He had entered the Pyrrhen fleet. Had made captain in no time—always so smart— and he recommended me for a research position. Well, they offered me my own lab, as many assistants as I needed, and all the freedom to continue my research at will. And I've been here ever since. You won't believe the tools I have access to, Lee."

She flinched at the familiarity. "Don't call me that."

Evan's face fell, but he nodded. "You're right. I'm sorry. I got caught up. But seeing you. It's like you never left."

"I left?" She snapped. "*I* left? Where the hell were you? When my family fed me to the wolves, where were you? In some lab? Headed home to your brother and promotion? When my world came crashing down around me, where were you? You never came. You never even wrote!" She stood, knocking her chair to the ground behind her, but she hardly noticed as she gasped for breath. "I needed you, and you weren't there."

He stood as well. "I tried to be! I came to your home every day. Your family said you wouldn't see me. Wouldn't see anyone. And immediately after the press conference, you were gone. No one knew where you went. I didn't know if you were alive or dead. It wasn't until years later that I had any idea what had happened to you. You left. Without a word. Without a letter. Without a goodbye."

She turned away from him, tried to process what he was saying. She found herself in front of the bookshelf with all the books about her family. *The Lost Daughter.* She pulled it out and held it, looking at her picture on the cover—graduation picture. She was twenty then?—before dropping it to the floor. "You came? To my house? After what happened, you still came?"

She heard him approach, felt him inches behind her back, his warmth, right there. But she refused to turn around. "Of course, I came. Lena, it wasn't your fault. It was an accident."

Lena felt a lump climb up into her throat. Another book. *Helena Lin Lomasky: A Disgrace.* It wasn't even a good picture of her. Dropped behind her. *The Tragedy at Larissan Yards.* Dropped. "All those people."

"It wasn't your fault."

Another. *Passengers of the Nereid.* Floor.

"I was at the helm."

His reached a hand to touch her on the shoulder. "It wasn't your fault."

The Nereid Tragedy. Floor.

"It was *all* my fault."

Evan grabbed her other shoulder and slowly but forcefully turned her to face him. "Lena." He lifted her chin and kissed her softly. "It wasn't your fault."

The kiss hit her like cold water to the face. Less than a second, but sense memories overwhelmed her thoughts. His lips on hers, just like a million times before. Him reaching out to her. His hand, right, comfortable, on her waist. The warmth of his body so close. She wasn't ready.

She didn't want to be ready.

Not again.

Not now.

Not yet.

She shoved him away and staggered backward, managing to knock a shelf loose. An entire shelf of books on her family went crashing to the floor. She stumbled as she reeled away. "What the hell was that?"

Evan had the good sense to look abashed. "I'm sorry. I thought... You looked like you needed comfort."

"If I do, I don't need it from you," she spat. "Not anymore." She stepped over the books and stalked back to the chair in front of his desk. She righted it and sat down, refusing to look at him. "That was a long time ago. And we're a long way from Rien." She crossed her arms and waited for him to retreat back behind his desk.

She waited while he stepped gingerly around the fallen books and took his time circling the enormous desk. Finally, he sat down in his soft leather chair.

She steeled herself. "Now, tell me what you're going to do about this whole captive thing I've got going on."

Evan looked shocked for half a second and shook his head. "Oh! Right. That."

"Yeah, that," Lena said, forcing as much ice into her voice as she could manage. He might be able to forget this wasn't some romantic reconnection, but she wasn't about to.

He flushed, and his eyes began to drop to his papers. He bit his lip. His soft lip that had just touched hers. He grimaced briefly, and even that was endearing. Damn him. "I don't know if there's anything I can do," he admitted, his eyebrows and lips turning down in tandem in a perfect display of bewilderment and loss. "You were in restricted space with illegal cargo."

"Restricted space?" Lena exploded. "There's no such thing!"

"There is when a war is going on."

"There is no war."

"There is now." He reached down and pulled out a tablet. The screen behind him instantly displayed the front page of the Bolken Herald, a premiere news site on Pyrrhos. *Pyrrhos Has Chosen War: Mediation Rejected*, the headline read. He flipped to another site; this one from Kraynak, Pyrrhos's capital city. *Pyrrhos Mourns Favorite Son: Vows Vengeance*. "Domonkos was the leading voice for peace between Pyrrhos and Aegea. With him gone, there's no voice for restraint." Another from a major news source in Aella: *Where Pyrrhos Goes, So Goes Aella*. An Aegean source: *War Declared: Aella Vows It Will Defend Pyrrhos*. As if the planet needed help from that little moon.

"So Pyrrhos just decided that it would unilaterally close down interplanetary space because it has a little tiff with its moon?"

"This is more than a little tiff. Domonkos was visiting on Independence Day as a gesture of goodwill. He was there to discuss mining leases and as an ally of Aegea, an advocate. That he was shot by an Aegean nationalist is a declaration of war."

"So your grief is with Aegea. Set up a blockade or something. What have the rest of us out here got to do with it?"

"If war is to happen, we must secure our space. Pyrrhos can't have Aegea's allies in Myrto coming to prolong this argument. It's an inconvenience, but a necessary one."

"Inconvenience?" Lena scoffed. "You are stopping random ships in the middle of deep space. I think we've moved beyond inconvenience. You are violating international laws."

Evan shrugged again. "It's necessary. And frankly, it's unlikely anyone is going to interfere with what we are doing here. No one can really match the might of the Pyrrhen navy in this sector. They'll let us take care of the situation here and resolve it on our own terms. And we'll bring resolution to our moons as quickly as possible."

Lena could not believe what she was hearing. He spoke as if Pyrrhos ran the entire Sinopean system.

Granted, if Pyrrhos already had warships spread out all along the inside of the Belt, they truly did. They would have complete control of the inner planets and moons. Anatolia, Aella, Aegea, all relied on trade to keep their mining populations thriving. By restricting that trade, Pyrrhos could easily secure most of the major economic chains and the majority of the chehon reserves in the system. That would leave only Iphito and Myrto on the outskirts of the system, trade-rich and resource-poor. While heavily populated and armed, they were both small moons, and couldn't stand up to the combined might of the central LIBs. Without help from Judan or Levin in the Pandian system or Rien or Naftal in Samara, Myrto and Iphito would quickly fall. The entire Sinopean system could be controlled by a single power within a few years, maybe months.

The systems of Pandia and Samara would have to know immediately what was happening, raise their own armies, and arrive in the system to stop the inevitable expansion. And they would have to know exactly how to combat these so-called Central Powers. What their plans were. How to translate messages. How to combat their movements. Decode communications. It could take a year; even if they got the message tomorrow.

And the message they needed was stuck on *Aspasia*.

Lena tried to keep these thoughts from her face as she glowered at her once, former, ex, whatever-fiancé. "I don't care. I don't care what your 'people' have planned for system-wide domination or whatever this whole mess is. All I want to know is what you're going to do about me? What about my crew and my ship?" Lena demanded.

"Right," he said as he shuffled through his papers. "Well, like I said, you were in restricted space with wanted criminals. The *Bayern* has been authorized by our alliance with Pyrrhos to detain the Nenad brothers and any who aided them. Their lives are forfeit to Pyrrhen justice." He looked up, his eyebrows creased and lips pursed. "I'm sorry. I really am. I don't think I can do anything for them." He smiled then. "But I may be able to do something to help you."

"My crew," Lena said quickly. "I'm not leaving without them. What about the rest?" She'd figure out what to do about Cedo and Vaso later. If she got the rest out of here, she could come back. She'd figure it out. She wasn't giving up.

He shook his head. "Lena, someone must go down for this. I can't save you all. But," he paused, tapping the file as something occurred to him. "I may be able to convince my superiors that you knew nothing of what was happening. Maybe your secretary, what was her name? The one who was smuggling weapons."

"Cat would never—"

"Yes, her. Cat Sanders. We can say that she smuggled the boys aboard along with the guns. She's been a sympathizer all along. You and your captain knew nothing about it. You were the victims here."

"But that wasn't what happened. I—"

"No! Don't tell me. As far as I'm concerned, you weren't involved." He stood and began pacing as he worked out the details. "I'll arrange it so that they transport you to Kannenberg for sentencing. I know the head Justice there. Lachner. Owes me a favor. We'll plead your case there. Don't worry. I'll take care of this."

"But Cedo. Gael, Cat, they're my crew..." Lena protested.

"Forget them. They're as good as dead." He knelt before her chair and grasped her hands. "Lena, I don't care about them. It's you I care about. Forget them. At best, my people will take the rest of your crew back to Pyrrhos for sentencing. There could be a long trial as they make a spectacle of things. But you? Lena, you can be saved now. Please, Lena, let me save you." He grabbed her hands. "I lost you once. I'm not losing you again."

The way he kept saying her name, invoking it, it pulled at something buried deep inside her. She stared at him. This man who once seemed so familiar to her, who once held every inch of her heart. His blue eyes pleaded as if he was the one in danger on this ship. She smiled weakly. His eyebrows had gone bushy. He needed sleep; the furrows under his eyes were deep. That single dimple on the right side of his mouth that you could only see when he bit the inside of his cheek emerged as he waited for her to speak. Dammit. "I'm not yours to lose." She forced the words out of her mouth.

He closed his eyes and took a deep breath. "I know. I know. Everything got screwed up. Before. That was before. Now. We have another chance. If I can save you, if I can get you through this, maybe we can start over. I can earn your trust again. I can show you what life is like beyond Rien. Beyond your family. I can give you a life, Lena. A real life."

She had a real life. On *Aspasia*.

But he was right. If she couldn't get out of this, that life was gone forever anyway. The first thing was to survive.

She had to get off this ship. Get Raines off. Then she and Raines could get their crew back. She could get her ship back. And she could get back to the sky. They could do this. But, she had to get free.

"Okay," she whispered.

"What?" he said back. "Okay? Did you say okay?"

"Yes. Do what you can. But Raines. I need Raines and Gael. And I'm not leaving without Cat. Can you do that?"

He stood, still holding her hands and dragging her to her feet. "I will." He kissed her hands. "Of course, I will." He kissed them again. "Oh, Lena. You'll see. We'll get through this. It can be like it was. Better! We can build our own life. You don't need your family. I can give you everything they could and then some. You'll love Pyrrhos."

"Whoa, Evan, stop." She pulled her hands back, gently but forcefully. "First, we have to get my crew free. Then, we can talk about what follows. But I'm not the person you knew before. So much has happened. I...I'm going to need some time, first."

"Of course! Anything you need." He ran over to his desk and hit a button. "Get me Commander Reimbold," he said in an officious voice. "We have a matter to discuss." He released the button, looked to Lena, and pressed the button again. "And get a private room for Ms. Lomasky. She's a guest on this ship. Set her up in civilian quarters. With a private bathroom." He released the button and smiled at her.

Lena gaped. "You can get me transferred? Just like that?"

"Well, no," Evan laughed. "Technically, you're still a prisoner. Armed guards are on every level. But they can give you a private room, at the very least. You're not likely to go anywhere. There's nowhere to go! But give it time. I should be able to get a comfortable shuttle for us—"

"And my crew."

"And some of your crew, yes. I'll accompany you to Kannenberg myself. Then the whole thing can be settled. What is it your family always said? 'Some laws are meant to be broken.'" He looked down to his desk screen and started. "Whoops. I have to go attend a meeting. The gentlemen outside can escort you to your new quarters." He gestured toward the door. "I'd love to treat you to dinner this evening, but I already have a packed schedule for the next day or so. I'll send word for you when we leave, though, and I will see you soon." He escorted her all the way to the door, a hand settled comfortably on the small of her back. "Lena, I can't tell you what it means to have you back." He kissed her softly on the cheek as the door slid open to reveal the guards standing in wait. "You'll see. Everything will be all right now."

"Thank you." She forced a weak smile. "I ... I will find some way to repay you."

He laughed. "Of that, I have no doubt."

And he passed her off to the armed guards like the prisoner she was.

CHAPTER THIRTEEN

Lena was escorted to a private room two levels up from the labs.

It had a plush bed, a small desk with a few popular novels, a private bathroom, and a heavy-duty lock that could only be opened from the outside.

She wanted to sleep, to shut everything out for a while, but no matter how comfortable the bed was, she couldn't rest.

What was it she had told Cedo? "Evan was the love of my life. Until he wasn't." He had always been there. The good friend. The man who knew the real her, who had seen past the party girl of the tabloids and the society princess her friends all knew. Evan had always seen her eager mind and passion for flight. He'd encouraged her when she wanted to get her pilot's license. He'd stood beside her when she told her father that she didn't want to study business; that she wanted to be a real part of her family's legacy and not just another person to manage it.

"And what does Evan do?" Cedo had asked her.

"He," Lena had faltered. How did she describe him? "He's brilliant. Cedo, you've never met a more brilliant man. The way you have an instinct for machines? He has that instinct for physics. He understands forces the way, the way my grandfather understood them. He just knows how things fit together, how they dance, how they fight, how they work."

"Sounds like you miss him."

"No," she had insisted. "That's done. That life is gone. He's gone. He abandoned me."

"But have you abandoned him?" Cedo smiled. "You talk about your fiancé the way Vaso talks of Aegea. His potential, his glory, everything that makes him special."

"Isn't that how you see your home?" Lena had been eager to turn the conversation.

Cedo sighed but took the bait. "I see Aegea's potential. Sure. But I see her struggles. It is not enough to have the potential for greatness. You must also have the avenues for exploring it, the freedom to realize it. People and places do not always have the opportunities for such. They must seize them or make them out of nothing. And that often means struggle, hardship."

That Cedo or anyone aboard *Aspasia* would bear Aegea's hardships personally had never occurred to either of them. Would he speak so eloquently of Aegea's freedom now? Was he willing to serve as his moon's human sacrifice if it would ensure her freedom?

Not that it made any difference. His moon would fall to Pyrrhos control again, and he'd die if she didn't do something.

If Evan didn't do something, she corrected. She was still powerless.

Lena Lomasky did not do powerless.

When Evan finally called for her again, she was ready. A short nap, a shower, and a change of clothes had steeled her resolve. She was going to get her crew off this ship, back on *Aspasia*, and damn the rest. Evan was going to find a way to get all of them or none of them. And if that meant promising Mason's datastick, then so be it. Not that she had it. Or knew where it was. Whatever. She'd find a way.

A new set of guards appeared to usher Lena once again to Evan's office, though it seemed her danger level had been downgraded; this time they let her walk without restraints. They walked in silence the short distance to the elevator and to the science wing of the ship. Every person they passed avoided Lena's gaze and seemed unaffected by the heavy arms of the soldiers.

One of the soldiers keyed open Evan's door with a lengthy numerical passcode and walked her inside.

It had only been a few hours, but the office had changed. The entirety of the room was in disarray. Papers lay scattered about on the desk, chairs, and side tables. Large and small pieces of metal and electronics peppered the chaos in piles. Two large touch boards loomed over either side of Evan's desk, filled with sketches and equations that had yet to be downloaded to his desk unit and wiped. More papers spread across Evan's desk with notes scribbled in the margins and across the data sets.

Even Evan himself seemed to be in disarray. He looked as if he hadn't left the office since she was taken away last night. His eyes were bruised with exhaustion. His jacket was flung carelessly over several stacks of pages, his shirt untucked, and his blond hair slicked back with sweat and oil. He was currently running his hands through it as he paced and barked into his personal comm piece.

"It has to be there! Did you check everywhere?"

Lena's guards pushed her just barely into the room and quickly retreated before they could attract Evan's attention. Lena stood awkwardly as the door closed, not sure if she should approach.

"I want that office torn apart. Check inside the furniture and go through every page of every book. We know he had it." He paused as he listened to the response. "I don't care how long it takes. You will find those plans. If they fall into the wrong hands... Just find them. Or I'll hold you personally responsible for every life that is lost." He slammed the unit to his desk so hard Lena was afraid he had cracked the desk screen.

Standing, he leaned over his hands on the desk and let his head fall. He took a deep breath and lifted his head to meet her gaze. "I'm sorry. I know you just got here, but I'm running a little late because I've been dealing with a ... complication."

"Is everything all right?" Lena asked, scared to hear his answer.

"To be honest, no. But don't worry. It's not your problem." He noticed that she had yet to approach and laughed a bit. "Relax, Lena. It's a war issue. Nothing to do with you. Come sit down." He gestured to the chair in front of his desk before realizing it was covered in a stack of papers. He quickly rushed around his desk, picked the pile up, and moved them to an empty spot on the floor beside his desk. "I'm making progress on your front, actually. In fact, that is what I'm late to. Would you mind if I left you here for a while? I shouldn't be too long, and I should have good news for you when I get back."

"Of course," Lena said, finally moving into the office. "Take all the time you need. Should I go back to my cell, er, room?" She smiled to let him know the slip wasn't an accident.

He forced a wan smile. "I'm sorry. I know. I'd call off the guards if I could. But it's still a secure ship. We have protocols, and we can't have civilians running around unattended. But you're free to stay here. Here, use my personal notebook." He picked up a tablet computer and handed it to her. "Get on the waves and catch up. A lot has happened since you left Aegea."

I bet. She accepted the offered computer. "Thanks. I'll do that."

He reached over and gave her a quick kiss on the cheek. "I won't be long. Lena." He left her then in the silence of the cool and cluttered office.

She stood for a moment, unsure of what to do. She had the computer and could easily look up the news and see if she could find any information on her situation or what was happening back on Aegea.

But she was alone in a very messy office full of unattended documents belonging to her ex-fiancé.

She set the tablet down and made her way to Evan's desk. Flipping through some of the stacks around the edges, she quickly dismissed most of the documents. Most pages were full of equations, some memos with innocuous interdepartmental messages. She moved one of the stacks to get at some of the bigger pages underneath.

Designs, blueprints, electric grids, and diagrams. Gibberish.

She wasn't an engineer or a technician and didn't understand the intricacies at work in the machines she operated. She didn't have to. She knew how to work them. The ways they moved, the ways they responded to her commands. Ships, planes, they were her dance partners; they might not speak the same language, but they moved in the same rhythms. Still, she'd seen enough diagrams of engines and bosonic devices to recognize that these 'prints were similar. Not an engine, though. The propulsive device wasn't there. This had a different structure. No way to divert the forces generated. But a bosonic device for sure. There was the containment, and there the energy units. And the field generator for the radioactivity.

But where was the mechanism for expulsion? Gravitons had to be focused in order to generate force in one direction or the other, either push or pull. The radiated bosons needed somewhere to go: either to generate the gravitational field or to provide pulses against other large gravitational forces.

Lena flipped through the diagrams. The expulsion was definitely missing.

Okay, so not an engine. Or at least not one with which she was familiar. Odd.

What was Evan working on?

She moved the blueprints aside and looked to the pages of equations. Numbers, symbols, and letters swam through the pages with notations confounding her.

There! That was familiar. A notation about spins. One of the foundations of the Lomasky drive was a manipulation of the spins of gravitons. This notation was about altering those spins: the foundations for push and pull principles. And then something else, "Non-renormalizable."

Meaning, the energies of gravitons could not be accurately calculated or quantified because of their peculiar nature.

That was what had made the Lomasky drive so revolutionary. Her grandfather had used the unique properties of chehon radiation, used the element's responsiveness to radioactive stimulation and discovered that at high exposure, gravitons could be separated and manipulated like electrons. And when focused in large quantities, gravitons could generate fields that mimicked propulsion, regardless of the accepted equations or their normalizability. By ignoring the accepted physics, he'd made it work. Lena still didn't understand how, but, to be honest, almost no one in the known universe did. Maybe a handful of scientists.

And Evan Thomas was one of them.

It wouldn't be surprising if he had found a way to put that knowledge to further use. But what had he built? A new drive? No, these blueprints, they were for something much smaller than a Lomasky drive. And though they were clearly chehonic in nature, there was no expulsion mechanism for the resulting gravitons. Were they contained? That wouldn't work. If they were completely contained, the gravitons would exponentially replicate until the mechanism collapsed under its own, well, gravity.

So, the device was missing a component. She shuffled the pages to look at the next blueprint. Something was missing here, too.

The containment element, the formulas for the fuel.

And the next print, question marks dotting the margins.

All of these blueprints were incomplete.

Then a page caught her attention.

She scanned: *The Lomasky weapon ... millions of lives ... unacceptable losses ... must be eliminated ... no means of defense ... uncover the plans and eliminate. We must stop them.*

She froze as the words seemed to fall down inside her and nestle into the empty space of her belly. She read the page several times, but no matter how she tried, she couldn't focus. Every few sentences, there it was. Her name. Her family. Her company. It made no sense. Not in this context.

Evan's work was in bosonic field generation.

Not. Weapons?

The words didn't make sense. Lomasky tech didn't work that way. It repelled. It pushed or pulled. Even if was used to project ballistics, the aim would be so horrible as to make most weapons useless.

Lomasky tech couldn't be used as a weapon.

Could it?

Lomasky weapon.

The she realized. The lack of containment. Imminent mechanism collapse.

No. Not collapse. Implosion. On a massive scale.

She shuffled through more papers. The notes became harder to decipher. *Lomasky weapon more concentrated. Single point of contact. Wider distribution.* The notes contradicted each other.

She started to move about the room. Each pile was a different set of notes, diagrams, memos.

Then a handwritten note.

Evan's handwriting.

She sat down and began to read.

I came across the experiments by mistake. I was visiting a colleague in another sector. I never thought they were capable of something like this. I always had the utmost confidence in my department if not the whole company. (See personal notes.)

The project was classified under "Stabilizing Flight Controls" and was conducted in a private lab in the commercial flight division. Cursory review of the components revealed an explosive weapon with multiple effects. Further observances revealed a single device capable of using bosonic fields to target a single locale more precisely than any previous weapon with fewer aftereffects. Exact mechanisms unknown. Exact parameters unknown. Exact delivery methods and effects unknown.

Was dismissed soon after and was unable to capture any records or images.

Goals: replicate weapon

Test

Develop countermeasures

Produce defensive weapons

Note: A number of prominent people were on the project or brought in to consult and could offer means to uncovering more exact plans. Surveillance of each if possible: Harper Alfano, Willam Kasprzyk, Daniel Menkes, Laura Alfano, Michael Bailey, Briana Ward, and Pierce Mason.

Mason?

Her family's company was developing weapons, and *Mason* was involved? He didn't know anything about engineering and couldn't understand the principles of bosonic manipulation if he had spent his entire life studying it.

And yet there it was.

Pierce Mason had helped her family develop weapons. And Evan, the Pyrrhens knew about it. So, Pierce *was* being monitored after all. No wonder he needed her to deliver his messages.

Dammit. Oh, damn him. The 'stick. It was never about cryptography. Damn him.

That meant they knew of her meeting with him. They might even know of the plans he had given her. That was why the *Aspasia* had been stopped. It was to get at her. To get at Mason's message.

That's what this was all about.

Lena's heart dropped. This was never about Cedo or Vaso.

The Pyrrhens were after her.

CHAPTER FOURTEEN

When Evan returned, he found Lena sitting behind his desk, in his chair. She had cleared the desk of all the papers and tablets, which were now in a pile on the floor in the middle of the room. If she had had matches, it would have been a blazing fire. She was feeling dramatic like that.

"Oh," Evan said.

"Yeah. You could say that." She gestured to the empty chair across from her. She was holding court now. "Sit."

He looked confused for a minute, but then offered her a small smile and acquiesced. "You found the papers."

"I'm not an idiot, Evan. You wouldn't have left them here if you didn't want me to see them."

He nodded. "It was the coward's way out, I know. But I didn't know how else to tell you."

"That you pulled my ship out of the sky because you think I know something about this device my father's company built? That you put me and my crew's lives at risk in pursuit of something I didn't know existed until today? That you lied to me and thought to play off our chance meeting in the middle of space as a coincidence? Do you think me that stupid, Evan?"

He winced. "I don't think you're stupid. I just." He lifted his hands up in a helpless gesture. "I couldn't let you slip through my fingers again, Lee."

"Do not call me that. Don't you ever call me that again. You lost the right." She glared, holding on to her anger. "Have you been following me all this time?"

"No. Not until you scheduled your meeting with Mason. He was our target. We've been monitoring him for months. We were hoping he would pass someone information we could use. I never imagined it would be you."

Lena pursed her lips and schooled her face to impassivity. She couldn't confirm she had it. Not yet.

"We've been hoping for a break of any kind, some way to get at him, some way to get him to talk. We know he's still in touch with your company back on Rien."

"It's not my company. It never was." It had always been her father who called the shots. Did her father know about this? That was silly. Of course, he had to. He knew everything that happened at Lomasky Corp. But this? This didn't seem like him. "What the hell is all of this, Evan? My father's company has never developed weapons."

He sank back in his chair, a curious look on his face as he studied her. "You really didn't know, did you?"

"Know what? I still don't know what this is all about! Bosonic weapons? It's impossible. The tech doesn't work like that."

He gave a small snort that sounded both amused and surprised. "Well, this complicates things."

"What?" She slammed her hand down on the desk, shocking herself as well as him. "What the hell is going on?"

He stood, gesturing for her to stay seated. "Lena, I am sorry. It seems we are in a situation due to my own miscalculations." He began to pace before her, as he explained. "I always thought you knew. You had to have known. You were in line to take over Lomasky Corp as soon as your first official flight was completed. You had sat on the board. I figured you knew it all: major contracts, product lines, everything. You must have at least known who you worked for." He waved her down as she started to stand indignantly. She slowly sat back down, and he continued. "I see now that I was wrong. It's unfortunate, truly. I could have used your help stopping this."

Lena closed her eyes, took a slow breath, and spoke very deliberately. "Evan. I am going to ask one more time, and then I'm going to go back to my cell. What are you talking about?"

He stopped pacing. He slowly turned back to his chair and settled himself in before looking her in the eye. "Lena, your family has been working with the Rienen military for years. Developing military ships, convoys, everything. A few years back, they moved into more serious research. Shielding, defense stuff. Some of this filtered to the general production lines, but the rest? When they got into serious weapons?"

He waited for a moment, and she took the opportunity. "Evan, what are those plans for? What is that device?"

He looked at the pile. "They're incomplete mockups for a weapon I discovered right before I left."

"But there's no projectile function, no ammunition. There's no component that is explosive. I looked. As far as I can tell, it's a containment device for chehon-generated bosonic energy."

"Good for you. You're right." She twisted at his patronizing tone but stayed quiet. "Presumably it uses bosonic fields in a charged burst or eruption of some kind, but the fields just don't work in a way that would cause damage. Not enough to be a weapon. You can create concussive waves, small sudden field generations pushing outward, and those have been used in previous Lomasky weapons, but this doesn't seem to have that expulsive capability. There's no way to direct bosonic fields on a small enough scale. Our designs are incomplete, and though we've spent years trying to build something similar, we can't do it."

"You're trying to recreate the weapon?"

"Only so we can develop countermeasures. Lena, if you had seen the level of security surrounding this thing. Nothing was allowed in or out of the labs. No one was allowed to converse with those working on the project. Even then, all of the scientists and engineers working on it had to be escorted to and from the premises, and they were being housed on the Lomasky campus."

"But somehow you got access."

"Yes."

"And you want me to help you figure out, what exactly? How the plans work? What this weapon does? How to build it? Even if I knew the first thing about this weapon, which I don't, why would I help you?"

"Because someone has to stop your family."

"And you think that someone is me?" Lena scoffed. "I have nothing to do with any of this. I don't know anything, I don't have any background in weapons development, and if you haven't noticed, I'm currently your prisoner on a fucking Pyrrhen warship. So unless you have some plan to get me and my crew off this thing, then we are done." She folded her arms, stared levelly at him, and tried desperately not to think about the datastick. Never mind that it was on her captured ship. She'd get it back. Then she'd have something to bargain with.

Evan walked around the desk and knelt beside her. He turned the chair until she was facing him, looking down at his upturned face. "What if I can get you out of here?"

"I'm listening."

He reached for her hands. She thought about pulling them back, but in the last moment, she allowed him to take them. His grasp was soft but strong, familiar but strange to her all at once. Even as she wanted to hate him, to let all her resentments and fears settle on him, just this small touch made her heart beat loudly in her throat. He was still Evan. Her Evan.

"I might be able to get some of you out of here. I've spoken to my judge on Kannenberg, where you're supposed to go for processing. He owes me a favor and can get you and some members of your crew off on a technicality. The charges of smuggling can be dropped, and you can be on your way."

"What do you mean some members?"

"Sebastien Raines, Chandra Nayar, Catherine Sanders, and you will all be processed independently on some lesser charges. But your friends, the Nenad brothers? There's nothing I can do there. They killed Domonkos. There were too many witnesses. I'm sorry. They will have to pay for the crime."

She yanked her hands away and stood in outrage. "Cedo didn't do anything! It was Vaso who—"

He grabbed her hands and pulled her back down. "I believe you. But the fact remains that the brothers were both there. And one of them pulled the trigger. They will have to be transferred to Aegea to stand trial with their co-conspirators, a group of rebels back on the moon."

"And Gael?"

"Someone has to answer for the brothers' escape from the moon. He was seen with them. We have multiple photos of him at the parade with them before the incident. He's the easiest to blame. I'm sorry. If I could save your whole crew, I would. But knowingly aiding and abetting the Nenad brothers in their escape... well, someone has to pay, and I'll be damned if it's you." He squeezed her hands and looked up at her. "I won't lose you again. I can't." He stood and pulled her to her feet as well. "Lee." He stopped himself. "Lena. I failed you once. I wasn't there. I should have tried harder to come to you when you needed me. I should have ignored your family and been there, no matter what. I am so sorry you had to face everything alone. But I'm here now. I can make things up to you. I can make things right. If you give me a chance, Lena, I will spend the rest of my life making it up to you and proving that I can be the man you need."

Her mind raced as she looked into Evan's tear-filled eyes. This man who she had once loved, who claimed to love her still, could she trust him?

He said he could get her out of here. If he could truly manage to get her free, get her and any of her crew off this ship, then she would find a way to save Gael and Cedo, and yes, even Vaso.

Right now, Evan was all she had.

"You get us out of here, and then what? You said you want to stop my family? How? What do you want from me?"

Her cold reply had an effect. Evan released her hands and pursed his lips as he regarded her. "I need you to go back to Aegea and get something from Mason."

The datastick. "You think he can help you get your weapon working?"

"If he has the information I need, he can help us destroy this weapon. Develop countermeasures."

"And you think I can get it from him?"

Evan laughed dryly. "I think you could get anything you wanted out of him. He had a soft spot for you. He's always trusted you."

You have no idea how much, Lena thought. It didn't matter, really, what she agreed to at this point. All that mattered was getting off this ship and saving her crew. "All right," she said aloud, smiling and taking Evan's hand a final time. "We have a deal."

CHAPTER FIFTEEN

Several hours later found Lena crammed between Raines and Chandra on the backbench of a short-distance personnel shuttle. Cat sat on the bench in front of them with a guard, while Evan sat just ahead of her with another guard. At the front of the shuttle were the pilot and yet another soldier. The four prisoners had their hands bound in the standard plastic maglock cuffs, and any attempts to converse were shut down with a pointed look from the heavy-browed, armed man seated next to Cat.

It certainly didn't feel like a rescue.

Lena attempted to nap as best she could in the upright position. She rested her head on Raines's shoulder, settling into the crook of the arm that he managed to extend slightly in her direction. The warm, familiar smell of him settled her, allowing her to relax and rest. She took comfort in his half embrace, forgetting, for a moment, who was sitting in front of them and what was to come.

Raised and angry voices soon reminded her she was on a cramped shuttle in deep space.

She struggled to an upright position as Raines shook his head at her, warning her to be quiet.

"What do you mean a transfer?" Evan said. "I was assured I would be with them the entire trip to Kannenberg. Commander Reimbold told me personally." He was standing up and looming over the pilot while the security guards nervously fingered their guns.

"I'm sorry, sir. Reimbold gives commands aboard her own ship. But out here, if an order comes in from a higher authority, I have to follow."

"This is unacceptable. I will continue with the prisoners," Evan insisted.

"I'm afraid I have orders to detain you and return you to the *Bayern*, sir." The pilot was not backing down, but with his gaze continuously darting to the soldiers behind Evan, it was clear he wasn't prepared to defend his orders either.

"I'm not some soldier to be ordered about by some mid-rank pilot. I am a scientist with a commendation from the Leader himself. I will not be told by some petty soldier what I will or will not do."

"Sir, I am an officer of the Pyrrhen fleet, and…"

"I don't care if you're the Rear Admiral! I am not leaving my fiancée to some prison warden on a decrepit way station. Now you get your superior officer on comms, and you tell him that I'm not leaving her side."

Raines nudged Lena before she could deny being his fiancée, and he cautioned her with another shake of his head. He was right. Nothing she could say would make a difference right now. Instead, Lena did one of the things that came least naturally to her: she held her tongue and waited.

"Sir, I have to ask you to sit down. The decision is made, and I will follow my orders. If you have issue with the General's orders, feel free to take those issues up with her. In the meantime, I will do my job. Now sit down and be quiet, or my soldiers will tie you to your chair."

Evan sputtered for a few moments, but at the unmistakable sound of energy currents beginning to circulate through the guards' weapons, he quieted and slunk back to his chair. He didn't yield completely, though. He immediately began to punch messages into his communications unit, though Lena was unsure he could manage a connection without tapping into the shuttle's long-range waves. They hadn't docked yet, and it seemed unlikely the pilot would open his wave up to any of the passengers' personal units.

As the soldiers settled back down, Lena turned to Raines and whispered softly in his ear. "What did I miss?"

Raines scanned the soldiers to make sure no one was paying attention to them before he responded. "Looks like we're not headed to Pyrrhos. They're handing us over to another crew at the *Scharnhorst* instead. And your *boyfriend* isn't coming with us." Lena didn't fail to miss the edge in Raines's voice.

"Do you think they're up to something?" She asked, focusing on what really mattered.

"They're Pyrrhen."

Chandra shifted perceptibly, letting them know everyone could still hear them while Cat began to side-eye them from her seat ahead. The four prisoners rode in silence for the rest of the trip.

CHAPTER SIXTEEN

The *Scharnhorst* was easily twice the size of the *Bayern*. A warship with hundreds of individual ports for shuttles, fighters, and transports, it was a fully armed city traveling in between the Bellows Belt and Pyrrhos's orbital path. No one could mistake this ship for anything other than what it was: a threat to the enemies of Pyrrhos.

The shuttle docked, and the security officers and Evan quickly disembarked, leaving the door open on the four prisoners restrained in the back. The pilot took his time toggling open the appropriate hatches for the fuel, air, and waste. The deck crew on the *Scharnhorst* would take care of hooking up the refueling lines and the removal of spent chehon that could later be either disposed or further refined and recycled.

After a few minutes of waiting patiently, the prisoners began to feel restless. Cat squirmed in her seat and turned to look back at the rest of them. Her still bound hands clasped the top of the leather seat back, and she dangled her legs out the side into the wide aisle toward the door. "So, they been treating you guys well?"

"Shut up back there," the pilot said, not even bothering to look up from his controls.

"Oh, we're not hurting anyone," Cat shot back. "We're still locked up and got no place to go. Some small talk won't hurt anyone." She talked big, but her hands were clasped so tight her knuckles turned white.

The pilot grumbled to himself but didn't protest further. Cat smiled and turned back again. "What do you think? They going to line us up against a bulkhead and shoot us all or send us out of an airlock?"

"Well, at least Cat's having fun," Raines said, looking to Lena.

"This is all a misunderstanding, isn't it?" Cat's voice thinned with growing panic. "By now they've opened the crates and ruined my fish. They'll see it's all a mistake. We'll all be on our way soon, right?"

Lena sat up. "Sweetie, I don't think they were ever interested in guns. They've got Cedo and Vaso on charges of assassination, and Gael for aiding their escape."

"Wait. They're...what are they going to do to Gae? Cedo?"

Lena pursed her lips as she and Raines sat straighter simultaneously.

"What?" Realization dawned. "No!"

"Hey!" The pilot shouted back. "I don't care if you talk, but keep it down, or I'll bring the guards back."

Cat nodded and lowered her voice. "Lena, they can't execute them. Cedo didn't do anything. And Gael? He had nothing to do with any of it."

"I know. I know, sweetie. We're going to get them back. Evan is going —"

"Evan," Cat interrupted. "Wait. That was him? *The* Evan? Your Evan?"

"He's not my anything," Lena said as Raines stiffened. Suddenly the large shuttle seemed cramped. She shrank back into the seat, unconsciously making herself as small as possible.

"Honey, I'm so sorry. I didn't know. I was wondering what he was prattling on about." Cat looked like she wanted to dive over the back of her bench and hug her friend. "Oh, I could kill him."

"Don't kill him yet," Raines said. "It looks like he's the one who's getting us out of here." He nodded to the open entrance as Evan's voice floated in.

"I don't give a radiated damn what your commander says." Evan's voice came through. She could hear his sturdy footsteps followed by a dozen feet that were clearly used to marching, not the scurrying they were doing now. "I'm going to say my goodbye. I never got it before, and I'll be damned if I miss out this time." The footsteps stopped as Evan's voice approached the vessel. "You tell your commander or general or whatever that if they want me to touch a single ounce of chehon going forward, they'll back off. I am going to say goodbye to the love of my life, and you're going to have to shoot me to stop me."

All attention in the shuttle shifted involuntarily toward her. Even the pilot had given up on what he was doing to look back at her.

The shuttle port was silent as everyone waited.

Finally, an officious voice responded. "Very well. Talen?"

The pilot's head shot up, surprised. He made his way to the shuttle door in the space between the second and third passenger benches and poked his head out. "Sir?"

"Can we give them a bit of privacy?"

The pilot turned his head to look back at the four prisoners. "But sir," he called back. "I can't leave—"

"Talen, they're not going anywhere. There are only two exits from this port. One is through us. The other is into space. Exactly where do you think they're going to go?"

"But sir..." Talen protested.

"Get your ass out here. You need to let them fuel you anyway."

With that, the pilot stumbled out of the front of the shuttle and down the ramp to the waiting soldiers. Each of them could be heard to take a few respectful steps back, but it was clear they had not left the shuttle bay.

Evan, meanwhile, walked purposefully up the ramp, entered the shuttle, and took a step or two towards the back where Lena, Raines, and Chandra were seated.

Lena stood and shuffled past Chandra to the open aisle along the side of the shuttle. With her hands still bound before her in the magnetically secured plastic cuffs, she met his eyes and was suddenly profoundly aware that she had been a prisoner for nearly two days already. She was at his mercy, unable to meet him on equal footing. It made her resent him even more.

If he was trying to win her over, he'd have to start trying harder.

"What." It wasn't a question.

Evan walked up to her, grabbed her shoulders, and leaned over to kiss her forehead. "Forgive me. I have to leave you for a bit."

"So it would seem." Lean didn't give him any warmth, standing rigid and hard.

"This was not what I planned. But it isn't over."

"Oh?"

"Stop that. I don't deserve it, and you know it."

"We're being sent in chains to a strange planet with no clue as to our fate. Forgive me if I'm not too happy about it." It might not be fair, but she wasn't letting up.

"Fine. Sulk. I'll just tell the rest of you," he looked to the three other prisoners. "They lied to me. The Pyrrhens have no intention of giving you up, of letting you go free. Not such high profile prisoners. They're going to take you to our capital city, and they're going to kill you in a public execution."

Cat gasped, and Lena couldn't promise she didn't have her own audible reaction.

"I'm so sorry. There's nothing I can do. Turns out this order comes from the Leader's own office. All of our generals follow him lockstep these days. They're going to use Lena's notoriety to galvanize the troops. They think if they show that they won't bow down to any capitalist system," he looked to Lena, "the influence of our fellow nations," he looked to Raines, "or our own checkered alliances," and he turned his gaze on Chandra, "then they can prove that we are truly free to pursue the glory our people are entitled to."

"We're symbolic," Raines said as Chandra cursed.

Lena felt her knees grow a bit weak underneath her. Evan, who was still holding on to one of her arms, felt her quaver. He held tighter and guided her to the front bench where Cat was seated. Lena sat down hard, embarrassed, and scared. She stared out the open doorway at the waiting and expectant soldiers. She should stand strong, shouldn't show weakness, but her hope was fading fast. "What do we do, Evan? What *can* we do?" She hated herself for it, but she looked to him. She met his gaze and saw into his piercing blue eyes. She had forgotten how clear they were, deep lagoons of aquamarine. She softened as she whispered, "We can't give up."

His eyes filled for half a second before he blinked the emotion away. "I would never expect you to." He pressed her hands together, and then his wrist contorted. He reached down through her palm and back along his opposite wrist, under his sleeve. "Don't react. They can't see me, but they can see your face."

Lena darted a quick look to the soldiers waiting, and it was true. They had positioned themselves so they could see their interaction perfectly. Well, not perfectly.

In only a fraction of a moment, Evan had brought his hand into his sleeve and back out into her waiting hands. He wrapped her fingers around a soft piece of plastic. "It's a key. There's a special magnet on the end. It fits into each of your cuffs and will release the bolt on contact. I slipped it from your guard hours ago. I just didn't have a chance to get it to you."

Lena lowered her head, trying to portray sorrow at their parting as she bumped her brow to his, further obscuring their hands. Meanwhile, she slipped the piece of plastic deeper into her palm as he clasped his hands around her fist. "When the hell am I supposed to use this? We have guns trained on us every second."

Evan nodded just enough for her to feel it. "I know. But when they switch to your transit crew, they're going to go down to only two guards and the pilot. Apparently, the heavy guard was for me, not you. They don't trust me, can you believe? One of your new guards is favorable to your merc friend. He trained under her. He will, at the very least, hesitate to shoot you. If you are all free by the time you get in the air, he may give you enough time to recover the weapon from the second guard. If you can get either gun, you can take control of the ship. Then, get out of here. Get back to *Aspasia*. She's been towed to the Pyrrhen Halten. It's an outpost along our orbit. Trailing by a few day's journey. It's one of our ship graveyards. There's minimal security there, so you should have no trouble getting her out."

"The rest of my crew?" Lena whispered in his ear, careful to make it look like a stolen endearment. "Cedo? Gael?"

"Still headed to Aegea as far as I know. Forget them. Please." He squeezed her and kissed her cheek sending a warm thrill through her. "Please, my love. Things are only going to get more complicated from here. Please. Get free. Take your ship. Get out of here. Go home to Rien. Anywhere but here. I'll find you wherever you go. I won't lose you in this war."

"Come with us," Lena said on a whim. They could use his influence, and she could figure out if there was anything left between them. If they could go over the datastick together, they could figure out what to do. If there was a "they".

He chuckled. "Oh, my dear." He wrapped his arms around her tightly, pulling her close. "I wish there was another way. I really do. But someone has to distract them while you get away." He pushed her back to look at her face. "Hey. You'll get through this."

"What about you?" Lena said.

He laughed, though. "They can't hurt me. They still need me. Trust me. I'm the most brilliant mind they have right now." He never did lack for confidence.

He looked over his shoulder at the waiting soldiers with their weapons not currently pointed at the shuttle but ready to at a moment's notice. "Promise me that you won't take any unnecessary risks. Please tell me you will do what you can to survive what is coming. Don't go back for your friends."

Lena shook her head. "I can't promise that. I can't leave—"

"That's enough." The officer behind them began to approach the shuttle. "You're done."

Raines looked back and nodded before turning back to her with a stern look on his face. "Then, I'm sorry, Lena. If you won't renounce your crew," his voice broke in a staged way as his eyes held steady on hers, "there's nothing I can do for you. I ... I'm sorry. I only wish you were still the girl I knew. Goodbye." He took a dramatic step back. Still, with his eyes locked, he mouthed the words "I love you" and he turned to walk down the ramp back to the soldiers that were waiting.

Lena, playing her part, dropped her head, and brought her hands to her stomach as if their parting brought her physical pain. Instead, she let her fingers play at her waistband to hide the piece of plastic at the seam. Evan had handed her the keys to freedom, and as she watched him stalk away and disappear through the door into the *Scharnhorst* proper, she realized she hadn't thanked him.

That's when the missile hit.

CHAPTER SEVENTEEN

The entire station shook as klaxons began to blare throughout the ship.

The remaining officer and soldiers in the shuttle bay staggered momentarily before finding their feet and flying into motion.

They ran immediately toward the inner bay door, disappearing, leaving the bewildered pilot to rush back to his shuttle and contemplate the words that came over the internal comms system.

"Action stations. Actions stations. All hands. The *Scharnhorst* is under attack. I repeat. We are under attack. The Myrtons have begun a full missile launch against our hull. Active combat soldiers to weapons' posts. All inactive soldiers to release capsules. All shuttles to release ports. Other active personnel prepare for evacuation."

As the soldiers scattered, the pilot threw himself into his chair and began powering up the shuttle's engines. "Everyone back to your seats. A guard will be back in a second, and then we're out of here."

"What is happening?" Cat demanded.

"You heard it. We're under attack."

"So? Why doesn't the ship just switch on gravity shields and repel anything that attempts to approach?"

"Are you out of your mind?" The pilot turned to gape at her for half a second. Then he was a flurry of action at the controls while calling back over his shoulder. "This is not some tiny cruise ship. The *Scharnhorst* is the size and mass of a small moon. The use of shields would be an extraordinary waste of chehon. A full shielding could last only a few hours before our fuel ran out, and then we'd be exactly where we were before, but adrift instead of able to maneuver. No one would be stupid enough to waste fuel that way."

He was ranting as he checked fuel lines, waste levels, and everything that had yet to be addressed by the deck crew.

"What do we do?" Cat asked, a shrill note entering her words.

"We get the hell out of here, that's what. Let the warships fight it out. Now everyone sit down." The pilot turned back to his controls. "Dammit. We haven't been fueled yet. We don't have enough to get to the next way-station." He stood and faced the group, all now sitting obediently and looking at him with blank faces. "Do any of you know how to hook up the fuel to a standard long-range shuttle?"

None of them responded, though at least two of them definitely knew how.

"Stay here and don't move," he commanded, pointedly patting the gun at his hip as he moved to the door again. "I'll be right back."

As he exited the shuttle, another explosion rocked the station, sending him sprawling into the empty port. He scrambled to his feet, sputtering, and dashed to the fueling station on the opposite side of the large shuttle.

The moment he disappeared from view, Lena pulled the plastic key from her waistband and found the hole in the cuffs at each of her wrists. She slid the metal magnetic edge of the key into the holes and felt the pressure on her wrists release.

By the time the pilot came running back around the side of the shuttle, the prisoners had freed themselves and returned to their seats. Chandra lurked just inside the door, out of sight. The pilot stumbled back into the shuttle as yet another shock rumbled the port. His inattention made it easy for the mercenary to slip behind him and grab the gun out of its holster and train it on the hapless man.

"All fueled?" she asked the pilot.

He nodded slowly, grasping the situation immediately.

"Good. Have a seat." Chandra gestured to the seat directly behind the pilot's chair, which the pilot took without question. She joined him. "Ms. Lomasky, if you would be so kind."

Lena jumped into the pilot's chair while Raines slid in next to her. She flipped the switches to close the fuel and waste ports on the shuttle and closed the shuttle door. Then she turned on the control screens and brought up the bay commands.

"Code?" she asked the pilot, fingers poised over the screen.

"Are you insane? You can't open that door! We're under attack. We don't have any weapons."

Chandra lifted her gun toward the pilot. "I have one. Code?" she repeated.

"J583HK," he mumbled.

Lena entered it in, closed the internal port doors, sealing them off from the rest of the station and entered in a command to open the external doors. Instantly the screen went red, flashing a warning at her.

Raines leaned over to see her screen. "What's going on?"

"I don't know," she admitted, tapping on the warning message. "Damn. The port door is locked down. Probably damaged from the attack. It won't open."

"What do you mean it won't open?" Cat demanded from the back of the shuttle.

"I mean," Lena said, slamming commands into the shuttle's now unresponsive computer, "that whatever is happening out there has engaged a failsafe. The computer has shut us down, and won't let us out with this shuttle."

"You mean we're trapped here?" Cat was beginning to panic.

"No," Raines said, seizing hold of the situation. "There's no visible buckling. It probably just means there's an air leak in the port bay. And we just need to find some way to override the failsafe. Get it to open despite any damages."

Lena turned to the pilot. "You, what do I call you?"

He crossed his arms obstinately. "Like hell. You and your friends can sit right here and wait for those soldiers to get back."

Chandra jammed the pistol under the pilot's chin and forced the small man to look her in the eyes. "I'm going to get tired of threatening you in a minute. The lady asked you a question. Answer it."

"Karl," the pilot choked out. "Karl Talen."

"Well, Karl," Lena said. "Is there a way to override the safety mechanism from inside this shuttle?"

Karl's eyes darted to Chandra, but he answered. "No. Overrides must come through the port's control panel."

"And do you have the codes to authorize it?" Lena asked patiently.

He gritted his teeth. "Yes."

"Good." Lena turned to Raines. "We need to go out there and take care of this."

"Agreed," Raines nodded. "But we only have the one weapon, and we don't know when or if those soldiers are coming back." He turned to Chandra. "You got this here?"

Chandra's smile spread like a bruise across her face. She flipped the gun over and handed it grip first to Raines. "I think I can handle our friend without bullets."

Karl had never looked more terrified.

Raines took the gun. "Cat, stay put. We'll be back in no time."

"Sure, sure. I'll wait here." Cat sat back but kept her eyes on Chandra and the pilot.

Lena, ever the fastidious pilot made sure to go through the entire docking procedure—her landing gear was all in place, the doors were secured, air was stable, grav was stable—as Raines tapped his foot. "Can we do this?"

Lena scowled at him but didn't stop her checks. "One of these days you're going to realize that I'm the only reason you're still alive."

"And on that day, I'll be sure to thank you properly. But today, *ma petite*, time is of the essence." He reached over her and flipped the switch for the shuttle door. A hiss startled her as the airtight seal released, and the door lifted. Raines poked his head out and gave an exaggerated look around the bay. "Looks safe to me," and without waiting for the ramp to re-extend he jumped down and ran toward the port control room door.

Lena reached under the shuttle console and grabbed one of the remote comm devices, which would allow her to contact the shuttle from outside. She pointed at Karl in what she hoped was a menacing manner. "Have those codes ready when I call." She ducked past Chandra. "Can you manage to keep him quiet? We don't need him getting anyone's attention until we get this resolved."

Chandra grinned again at Karl who looked so miserable, Lena almost felt sorry for him. Almost.

She ducked out of the shuttle and was immediately aware of the whistling of oxygen at the port doors. It was damaged after all. And it had to be a big hole to make noise like that. She dashed after Raines, who was already tapping on the panel beside the port's inside door. "Door code?" Lena called into the comm device before she even slowed down.

Chandra responded with the code that Karl told him, and Lena called it out to Raines so that the door was opening by the time she made it there. The two of them slipped into the control booth, and while Raines double-checked that the door out into the station proper was locked, Lena looked over the expanse of panels, switches, knobs, and buttons set before her. It was a sea of control mechanisms, and she had no idea where to start. "Damn," she muttered under her breath.

"Problem?" Raines asked, suddenly behind her.

"No. No problem." *Only a million of them*, she thought. *Okay. Think. If you activate the wrong switches, you open up the wrong door and show the entire station that we're still here. Or you vent us out into space. So, avoid doing either of those things.* Instead she stopped thinking and followed her instincts. She avoided the controls nearest the door that led into the station, assuming those would interact with the station. Also, they were the farthest away from where she was currently standing, so she'd have to reach over Raines. She instead tapped a screen closest to the door they had just entered through. Nothing. No response. Damn. Powered down. That red button above it? The screen came to life.

Lena let out a sigh of relief.

"Lucky guess," Raines said.

"Shut up."

Prominent on the screen was the warning about the damaged door. Acknowledge, pull up details.

"Huh," she said.

"Fixable?" Raines asked.

"Pretty damaged. But not really our problem. We just need to override the failsafe. We can then operate from inside the shuttle." She pointed at the screen. "See there? Something knocked one of the sensors loose. The computer can't confirm that the door is sealed anymore. I can disengage it so we can open the door. Of course, if we open it up, it could damage it further, and they would have a pretty significant air leak. But as long as they keep the control booth doors and inner bay doors sealed, they shouldn't have a problem."

"Glad you're worried about the safety of our captors. So, we're good to override and open them?"

"Looks like." She pulled up commands to override the safety measures. "Chandra, need the override codes," she called over the comm.

Before she could respond, though, Lena heard beeps at the other end of the booth. Someone was trying to get in from the space station.

Raines had locked the booth, but the far panel came to life with a warning message on it as someone tried to override that command. Raines ran down to check it and began frantically attempting to deny entry.

"Um, Lena? We have a problem."

"Shit," she said as she dashed over. "Wait." She read the scrolling messages across that panel. "Ha! That's some helpful irony." She pointed to the screen. "The same safety measure that's preventing us from opening the outer door is keeping them from coming in here. If there's an air leak and the outer door to the booth is open to the port, they risk putting the entire outer hallway at risk." Then she noticed something else. "Shit," she said again.

"Problem?" If he said that one more time, she might start screaming.

"Yes," she hissed. "The second we override the lockdown information, the safety protocols are also overridden. They'll be free to open the booth door or the main shuttle bay door. The question is, which of us can move faster?" She pulled up the safety measures and began individually overriding what she could and finding workarounds for what she couldn't. "We're going to get shot, aren't we?" Lena asked, much more calmly than she felt.

"Most like."

"This is not my best day ever."

"Aw, chin up, darling," he said cheerfully through his teeth. "At least you're not locked in a cell because your pilot's ex-fiancé is a traitorous scab of a man whose people are going to murder everyone you care about in the universe." He smiled at her as if he'd just handed her a gift and couldn't wait for her to open it.

She stared at him in shock. "Evan had nothing to do with—"

"With the fact that his people are waging an illegal war and are starting with our completely innocent mechanic? Maybe not, but he didn't exactly try to stop them, did he?"

"He—"

He dropped his smile and gestured to the control panel with his gun. "Do you wanna do your job and let these guys in to shoot us, or do you want to go chase after your boyfriend? I'm sure he'll be happy to hand the rest of us over for execution if you run away with him." He reached over and snatched the comm unit out of her hand. "Chandra. Codes. Now."

He then dropped the unit onto the panel, lifted his stolen gun up, and took a stance between her and the station door, ready to shoot anything that came through.

Lena gaped at him. *Now? He brings up his stupid jealousy now?* If they got through this without getting shot, she was going to have serious words with him. But she was dragged back to her task by a tight voice relaying a rapid series of numbers and letters. She hurriedly entered them into the command line and picked up the comm. "Stay on the shuttle and stay out of sight. We're about to have company." She turned to Raines. "You ready?"

"Ready," he said, not turning to look at her.

"You are unbelievable. We get through this—"

"You got it," he spat back.

"Ugh!" She slammed her hand on the enter button.

CHAPTER EIGHTEEN

Lena sprinted for the shuttle with Raines on her heels. Behind him, she could hear a tone sounding through the booth as the override went through, and the frantic beeps from the other side of the booth ceased as the door began to open. She could hear confused voices as the soldiers registered the pair of figures now dashing away across the shuttle bay.

Sharp reports sounded as the soldiers sprang into action, cleared the booth, and opened fire. Lena saw sparks as several bullets struck the outside of the shuttle. Looks like they didn't care to take them alive this time.

Clearing the door as another shot rang out beside her head, she leapt over the ramp, past the benches, and dove toward the controls. She heard as Raines fell in behind her, and she slammed the switch up to close the door. As the door began slowly closing, she pulled up the controls for the bay door.

"Fast! Before they realize what we're doing," Raines yelled as he attempted to return fire between the gaps of the closing door.

"Not helping!" She screamed back. She could barely hear him over the shouts of the soldiers and the hysterical screams from the back of the shuttle. "Cat! Shut up!" The door finally slid shut with a quiet hiss, and the sounds of gunfire disappeared.

Lena's hands flew across the screens in front of her. She had to get the bay door open. Luckily, the override had worked. The safety warning was gone. The shuttle bay door would open on command, and Lena gave it willingly.

That was bad news for the six soldiers standing outside the control booth.

In a matter of seconds, they realized what was happening. A warning light in the bay started flashing red, and Lena could see as the control booth doors began to shut automatically. Realization dawned on the faces of the soldiers, and they all lost interest in the shuttle. They sprinted to the control booth, and when the door wouldn't respond to the open button, they attempted to break in through the glass. She could see them shouting while two technicians in the booth attempted to stop the bay doors from sliding open.

They were too late. A strong wind swirled around the soldiers as the huge doors behind them slid open, venting the oxygen in the shuttle bay into the cold emptiness of space. Several of the doomed soldiers attempted to grab hold of anything solid, anything bolted down. Grating, support beams, control panels. One even managed to grab the end of the fuel hose as it whipped wildly back and forth in the maelstrom. The man spun directly in front of the shuttle for a moment, frozen for half a second, suspended before her. Lena could see the brilliant green of his eyes, open wide in terror. He clung as hard as he could to that hose, and she watched as he screamed.

All was silent.

All was struggle.

All was in vain. The pull picked up as the doors opened further, and one by one, the soldiers were sucked past the floating shuttle.

Lena couldn't see any other faces as they were ripped away, spinning, sliding, dying, but she knew they were all screaming silent screams.

Echoes of before. It was the same. Nothing would help.

The two technicians in the booth were a flurry of motion. The woman was yelling and pounding at the inside door, trying to get out and save the lost soldiers, while the other was doing everything he could to reverse the motion of the bay doors.

There was nothing they could do. The soldiers were gone.

"Um, Lena? Can we leave now?"

Lena turned her tear-streaked face to Raines. "Those people. Just like before."

"I know," he said softly. "I know. I'm sorry. But. We have to go. Before they figure out how to shut the door on us again."

"Right," Lena whispered. "Right." She grabbed hold of the shuttle's landing controls. The gravity in the bay had automaticaclly been released as the door slid open, so it only took a small bit of thrust against the station to push them gently out of the shuttle bay.

They drifted out, past explosions and flashes, past dangers and threats. Drifted, inching outward and away.

In minutes they were several kilometers from the station, but moving slowly, floating on that initial push from the ship.

The urgency of their escape had fled Lena's thoughts, and she couldn't bring herself to do more.

She kept seeing that poor soldier's face. His silent screams. The look of terror. His spinning limbs as he was sucked out into space.

The brilliant green of his eyes.

I did that, she thought horrified. *I killed him. Them. I killed those poor men. Again.*

She clutched the landing controls as if they would anchor her to the shuttle. She knew at any moment she too would feel the cold rush, that she would be ripped from this life and sent spinning into oblivion.

She felt a hand softly pry her clutched fingers away from the controls. She looked up. Raines was kneeling in front of her. She had no idea how long he had been trying to talk to her, but gauging by their distance from the station, they'd been floating for a good fifteen, twenty minutes.

"Lena," he said softly. "I know what you are feeling right now. Trust me. I do." He grasped her hand in between both of his as he looked imploringly at her. "But I need you to pull it together. No one else here can pilot this ship, and there's a warship shooting shuttles out of the black."

Lena blinked at him. *Warship?*

Right. The reason they had gotten away. The *Scharnhorst* was under attack. They were under attack. No, not them. They were free. Spinning in space.

She looked back behind her in the shuttle. Chandra stared back, seemingly unaffected, while Cat sobbed behind her. Karl, the other pilot, was apparently unconscious beside Chandra.

She absently wondered what had happened to him.

She looked back at Raines.

"Lee? You're the only one that can pilot this shuttle where we need to go. Can you do this?"

Lena swallowed. Could she? Terrified faces swam before her. Cat. Raines. Cedo. Gael. Each being swept out into the vacuum. She shook her head, trying to clear them away. She couldn't fall apart. They had to get out of here. She had to get to her friends. They still needed her. She nodded. She could do this.

Lena took a deep breath and turned back to the controls.

Okay. Hard push. Avoid the warship without getting shot out of the sky. Find *Aspasia*. Find her crew.

No problem.

She swallowed as she realized she was developing an increasingly delusional mantra.

CHAPTER NINETEEN

Avoiding the attacking warship was easier than she expected. The ship was using almost exclusively ballistic and propulsive missiles and, despite Raines's claims, only targeting the one thing large enough to hit at extended range—the other warship. The *Scharnhorst* seemed to be holding steady against the barrage and was already returning fire. The rapidly fleeing transport shuttles, fighter ships, and personnel carriers were simultaneously of less interest to the warship and presented much more difficult targets. The only ships that got hit were the ones that got in the way of the shots being traded back and forth.

Their tiny stolen shuttle was easily overlooked as they sped away from the battle.

Lena didn't really have a plan. She didn't have a destination. She just ran away.

She was good at that.

But they had limited fuel, and if she kept up a constant push against an object that was steadily receding from them, they would soon find themselves stranded, adrift in the space between this station and Aegea. She had to decide where they were going and how they were going to make this right.

Make it right? How could this ever be right?

Lena blinked furiously as she tried to block the thoughts. Not now.

Not now.

Focus on the task. Do the work.

Not now.

She dropped the push vector, letting them drift on their inertia for a few minutes. She reviewed the extended LIBEL scanner and made note of any small bodies that could be ships lurking in their Halcyon states. Most of those small bodies could just as easily be debris or asteroids, but she'd rather not take any chances. A few adjustments to their trajectory and she managed to plot a short-term flight where they could easily slip between any LIBs, unnoticed and able to maneuver away should any of them spring to life. She set a proximity alert at a very large distance so she could have time to react if that happened.

Then she turned to look at her passengers.

Soldiers' eyes. Mouths open in silent screams.

No.

Not now.

Push it down. Push it away.

Cat was huddled on the backbench, wiping away at the tears that stained her pink cheeks. No help coming from there.

Sitting next to a still unconscious Karl Talen on the middle bench sat Chandra. She looked relaxed with her arm along the back of the bench, and her legs crossed languidly on a low table in front of her. She seemed content to wait around until she was next called to action.

And in the co-pilot's chair beside her sat Raines, cool and unreadable. He reviewed the LIB screen after Lena set a course, taking note of her proximity alerts and nodding in agreement at the path she had set. As she turned to him, though, he looked up from the screens and met her gaze.

He turned his chair and reached out for her hands. He didn't react when she snatched them away. He just continued to watch her.

"Don't," she warned.

"I didn't say anything," Raines said softly.

"Just don't. I can't. Not now." She closed her eyes as if to block him out, but all that did was allow the faces to come back. Her head started to reel, and she gripped the armrests of the chair and opened her eyes to reorient herself.

"Okay." That was all he said.

They sat in silence for several minutes, just drifting.

She knew he wouldn't push, lest she retreat further. He'd leave things up to her. Let her make the call she needed to make. And he would support her.

She had to focus. Make a decision. Set a course.

Run.

Or go back? *Aspasia*, her ship, her home. The datastick, and the plans Evan was so desperate to get and Mason so desperate to hide? If she was right, that datastick could hold the key to her family's legacy as well as their shame. It was up to her to do something about that.

Or go back to Aegea? Save her friends. Cedomir. Gael. She looked at Raines and back at Cat. Her true family.

She closed her eyes again. This time her crews' faces replaced the horrified faces of the soldiers she had let slip out that airlock. Cedomir's dark eyes shadowed under heavy brows, his small mouth in a surprised "o" of terror. Cat, her long blonde hair streaming back as she desperately reached out to Raines who was ripped away from her, screaming. And Gael, his dark face and his soft brown eyes locked undeniably on hers. Reaching for her, even as he slipped away into the black.

The plans would have to wait. *Aspasia* would wait.

She turned to the console and pulled up a bulletin service for Aegea and began a search for relevant terms. Execution, exhibition, public event, assassination.

Raines noticed the change in her posture. "You made a decision? Where are we going?"

She smiled and looked askance at him. "You have to ask?"

He returned her smile. "Not really." He turned back to the console as well and pulled up the information he had apparently already queued up while she plotted their course. "They're being transported to Banika. Execution is set for the steps of the Courthouse."

"Of course," Lena nodded. "The untouchable Steps. How symbolic." She pulled up a stored map of Banika. "We're going to need to find a good route in. I have no doubt the ports are going to be heavily monitored, but we might be able to get in using our current transponder."

"Right, we're on a Pyrrhen ship."

"Shuttle," Lena said. "This thing is hardly bigger than an atmo-plane."

"Well, your derision suggests your snark is back in business," Raines said. "Does that mean you're going to be okay?"

"Okay?" Lena stopped. The faces that haunted her. Those silent screams. The fire. Wait. There hadn't been any fire this time.

Had there?

She noticed her hand begin to tremble and felt a shake beginning at the base of her neck and spreading down her back. She grabbed hold of her console and took a deep, steadying breath.

No. There hadn't been a fire this time.

She studied the map she pulled up. She had no way of knowing what waited for them on the surface of Banika, whether the war Mason feared had truly begun, whether they would be able to save anyone. Whether she would ever see Gael again. Whether she was going to be responsible for more death. Okay? "Ask me again when we've got Gael." She was proud of how steady her voice was.

A shadow passed over Raines's face, but it was gone before she could respond to it. He pursed his lips and nodded. "You can get us an easy, straight shot to Aegea, right? How long will it take?"

"That's a good question," she pulled up the schematics. She was pretty sure it had only been a few days since they had left Banika for the Bellows Belt. It was a short trip back if you had speed on your side. Sadly, they weren't close enough to any major bodies to get a strong initial acceleration without expending some serious chehon. That meant fairly slow going until they were within push range of a station or a large enough asteroid passing through their path.

Lena adjusted her screens to highlight anything larger than 100km before remembering she was in a shuttle much smaller than the *Aspasia* and corrected to any larger than 50km. They were close enough to the Belt; there were some rocks this far out. She found a few within a few thousand kilometers of their path, close enough to use even their small masses to gain a little momentum.

She mapped out a path that would use the asteroids' trajectories and a scoping push field to keep them on a relatively direct path to Aegea. She'd do intense initial pushes —enough to probably knock a small asteroid off its current path, like billiard balls on collision courses— followed by a few less intense pushes. That should give them sufficient speed in the initial moments to ride through until they could begin to approach Pyrrhos and her moons. The route was fairly easy to plot, but they would be cutting it short on fuel. The initial small pushes cost a lot of energy, but time was of the essence, and they didn't have any larger bodies along the way to give them later boosts to their speed. She had to rely on her initial estimates and hope for the best.

Plus, she still had to make sure they had enough fuel to decelerate when they arrived at the moon. At the speeds she hoped to reach, they'd have to start decelerating almost as soon as they came within grav range and she was able to switch to a small push back against their velocity. That combination of approach and deceleration would cost them a lot more chehon on the back end. This shuttle was not designed for such long-range trips.

Her tiny fuel reserves and insufficient software made it an incredibly difficult course to plot, and she threw herself into it, eager for the work. Too much time had passed by the time she looked up from her equations and diagrams and remembered where she was. Raines had fallen asleep sitting up beside her, his mouth opened slightly as his brows furrowed over his dreams. She turned around to find that Cat was also completely passed out in the backbench, and Karl still had yet to regain consciousness. Only Chandra was still awake and alert.

Great.

"Not tired?" Lena asked quietly, turning her pilot's chair all the way around to face the mercenary.

Chandra gave her a half-smile. "I was asleep. Heard you finally move."

Lena crossed her arms and cocked her head. "You sleep that lightly?"

"Useful talent, my line of work."

She laughed quietly. "I bet it is." She looked at her sleeping friends. "I'm sure you will be able to keep track of all your charges out here on the edge of space."

Chandra's eyes narrowed. "You're free, aren't you? I don't see you on an enemy ship anymore."

"Yup. All thanks to you. Good job." But it was true. The mercenary had done her part to free them. She'd worked almost like she was part of the team. It didn't mean Lena had to make nice.

"Guess we should make the most of our freedom, huh?" Lena smiled. She then stood and moved to the back of the ship.

Personnel shuttles served multiple purposes, carrying officers and dignitaries in addition to prisoners. They usually carried some stores. Lena slipped into the open area behind the backbench, careful not to wake Cat. A small kitchenette lined the back of the space with a cabinet of dry goods and snacks, a refrigerator, and, yes, a fully stocked bar. Excellent.

Lena grabbed two rocks glasses, a bag of ice, and the closest whiskey from atop the bar. She turned and lifted up one of the glasses in offer to Chandra.

The merc simply stared impassively for a few moments, seeming to study Lena's face, looking for something that would warrant a response. Her brows furrowed and then arched before she shook her head once. She then turned away from Lena, settled back into her seat, crossed her arms, and closed her eyes.

Well, then.

More for Lena.

She tipped some ice into her cup, topped it off with whiskey, and returned back to her chair at the front of the cabin. She considered bringing the whiskey with her but wisely left it behind.

Settled into her chair, she stared out at the black before her, sipping her drink. Finally, there was no more work to distract her. Nothing to lose herself in. Nowhere to run from herself. She could settle and rest.

It all came rushing at once.

The faces.

Not the ones on the *Scharnhorst*.

The others. The ones with the flames.

CHAPTER TWENTY

What had they called it? *The Tragedy at Larissan Yards. Lena's Lament. The Nereid Tragedy.*

All her fault.

Her fault.

The shocked, bloodshot eyes as people were sucked out through the wreckage of the loading arm. Bodies spinning into nothingness. The silent screams she could see as the flames licked up the viewing dock.

I did that.

The fire erupted and spread rapidly through the docking station and then was just as rapidly distinguished as the oxygen fled the entirety of the level. Wiped away as if it never existed. Leaving only the bodies.

I did that.

The bloated corpses they had recovered. Her mentor Professor Donnelly. Her old girlfriend Poppy Donovan.

Mariko.

Her little sister Mariko.

Dead.

All because she miscalculated.

She failed. She killed them all.

With a stupid, careless mistake.

She had pulled when she should have pushed. Seven years of training, and she had never made a mistake. Seven years of perfect flight. Jumps, interplanetary trips, small course navigation. Lena had excelled at everything. She had a gift, her teachers all said. A natural hand for flying. Not a single mistake. But in her big moment, the moment she had taken the helm at the launch of the Lomasky Luxury Liner, the big moment when she was brought into the family business, brought into the fold, and heralded the new age of the company they had built, she had failed.

She had failed them all.

With cold and numb fingers in the present, she lifted her glass and took a big sip of her whiskey. Cold peat and fire fell down her throat and warmed her from the inside.

She had always been so careful, so mindful. The flight had gone perfectly until that moment. She had brought the ship from the shipyard where tireless crews had spent years perfecting the *Nereid*, the shining jewel of her family's fleet. The luxury cruise liner was to be the symbol of a new era of flight. The ship that brought in the press, the passengers, the prestige. And she, the Lomasky princess, would pilot it. The departure was perfect. The short flight to the Larissan Yards had been flawless. Her approach was textbook.

She should have just glided into place and let the loading arm come out to her, let the automated dock reach out to her while she held the ship steady. But she had to show off. Had to bring the *Nereid* just a little closer. After all, her family was all there. Mother, father, the camera crews. Mariko, her little sister waiting on the docking arm. They were all ready to show her off, so she had to give them something to be proud of.

She had to deliver the ship perfectly. She couldn't rely on the automated systems. It had to be her, or it wouldn't count, right?

She should have glided in. It was what she had planned to do. A slow glide. Perfect approach. But the dock arm wasn't approaching properly. It had stalled. It was out too far. If she glided in, the approach would be off. The dock arm would have to maneuver out to her, adjusting height, distance, tiny piecemeal movements that stuttered to completion. But the angle was right. If she could just push a tiny bit against the moon behind her, with a subtle counter push against the station, she could angle herself just right. She'd done it a thousand times. She was good at it. These subtle, intuitive moves were what made her such a good pilot. Automatic systems could anticipate a lot, but they were constantly correcting themselves. Adjusting. It looked sloppy. Inelegant. Piloting should be elegant. So, she pushed at the moon and grabbed hold of the distinct gravity field at the center of the dock.

She must have miscalculated. Used the pull on the station that was meant for the push on the moon. Or the other way around. Instead of the elegant dip into the path of the arm, she overshot.

It was a half-second mistake.

Just half a second before she realized what she'd done.

That's all it took.

The *Nereid* lurched toward the dock at incredible speed. Into the arm where the expectant crowds were waiting to welcome the crew ashore. Waiting to congratulate her on a perfect flight. Waiting to send her into the next wave of Lomasky success.

All those people.

Mariko.

Reporters, dock workers, relatives of the honorary passengers, stockholders. People she knew. People she didn't. Hundreds. Watching, waiting.

Some had died in the initial impact. The force of the massive liner crashing into the loading arm collapsed the structure, crunched it in like a paper cup, ready for the trash. Then the holes where the structure was exposed to the vacuum of space began to widen and leak out the people still inside. Then the fire from the fueling lines spread into the adjoining wing. The departure gate. The voyage hospitality room. The control booth.

She saw it all, and there was nothing she could do to stop it.

Her fault.

A stupid mistake.

Her fault.

Lena shook herself, stood, and made her way to the back of the shuttle. She reached for the liquor shelf again.

"Need help finishing that bottle?" Cat asked gently from behind her.

Lena turned to find her friend sitting up and looking at her. Lena let out a small laugh that sounded almost like a sob. "Probably should let you help. I have to do some actual flying in another few hours."

Cat nodded but wisely didn't say anything.

"Have a good nap?" Lena walked back to the bar, grabbed an additional rocks glass, and slipped in beside Cat on the bench, offering her the glass.

Cat accepted and held it steady as Lena tipped in a fingerful. She'd forgotten ice. She stood to get it, but Cat motioned her back down. "I don't need any." She sipped her drink and grimaced a little as she swallowed. "You know, you should probably try and take a nap yourself. You look tired."

Lena laughed bitterly and took a swallow of her own refreshed glass. "You could just come out and say I look like shit."

"You look fine. Just, I'm sure this has all been hard on you, especially. I mean, it can't be easy seeing Evan after all this time."

Lena lost her forced smile. "Yeah. I hope he's all right." She had a feeling he was well-protected on that station, despite the chaos they had left it in.

"It seems like he was doing just fine for himself," Cat assured her.

"Hm?"

"Great connections, people who listen to him and follow his orders. Looks like the Pyrrhens are treating him pretty well."

Lena frowned. It was true. Evan now had everything he'd always wanted when he was a lowly research assistant at Lomasky Corp: a private lab, unlimited research funds, subordinates, respect, power. And he had the chance to work on some very serious research.

The weapon.

She still had a hard time believing her father's company had created something like that. The Lomasky Corporation built ships. They were explorers, scientists, and travelers, not arms dealers.

How had they gotten involved in weapons development? How had Mason gotten involved? What was Evan doing with those plans? And just what did the weapon do?

She had nothing but questions, and no way and no time to find the answers.

Lena realized Cat had been quiet for a few minutes and was now staring at her, worry lines creasing her brow.

"Sorry," Lena said. "What did you say?"

Cat reached out and took the empty glass from Lena. Lena didn't remember finishing that latest drink, but she didn't stop Cat from pouring her another. "I said, 'I can't imagine what's going through your head right now.' But we'll be home soon. I'll make you some red curry, let you take a long shower. You'll feel better soon."

Lena knocked back her drink and had to stop herself from pouring another. "We're not going home. Not yet."

Cat sputtered. "Where else would we go?"

"Aegea," Lena said softly.

Cat balked, her face turning red. "But they're in the middle of a war! Why the hell would we—?" She caught herself. "Gael."

"And Cedo."

"Bullshit. I know you care about both of them, but this is about Gael. You think you're going to be some great hero and swoop in and save the day, don't you? Save the man who loves you. You are out of your mind! Lena, he's dead."

"He's not," Lena said, her voice level and quiet.

"If he isn't now, he will be soon. Sweetie, I love you. I love Gael. But we just barely escaped with our own lives. You saw that warship. If there are already firefights out here, then this is big. This is bigger than us. And Cedo and Gael now are back there in the thick of it." Cat's voice rose with each sentence, panic pitching her higher and higher. The rest of the crew were awake now and watching the arguing women with increasing concern. "You can't make the decision alone. This isn't about you and Gael. Raines and Chandra and I are here, too. We get a say."

Lena stood calmly and looked down on the small blonde, forcing Cat to tilt her head at an awkward angle. Then in a dangerous, low tone, Lena spoke. "No, you don't. We're talking about our crew and our home, and it's not up for debate. Right now, this is my shuttle, just as *Aspasia* is my ship. None of you know how to fly her, how to keep her in the air. That means that right now, I make the decisions. And we're going back to Aegea. Half of my crew is down there in the hands of those that would kill them. I am going to get them out, and anybody who disagrees with that plan can find alternative transport when we land. Unless you'd rather try and hitch a ride from here. I'll be happy to open the waste hatch."

Cat's eyes went wide as she sank down onto the bench and shut her mouth.

Lena turned to the rest of the watching and listening passengers, including a suddenly awake and still terrified Karl Talen. "Anybody else want to question my decision?"

Raines smiled and shook his head softly. Chandra remained passive, and Karl began visibly shaking.

"Good. We have several hours before we reach grav range of Aegea. We have three people waiting on their execution, and we have no plan for getting them out. I hope you all get some ideas soon because I'm just concentrating on getting us there. But I will tell you that I'm not leaving without them. So, you better come up with something." With that, she crossed her arms and stared them down. She was desperate to keep her anger boiling. If she stayed angry, if she stayed moving, pushing forward with a plan, then she wouldn't think about faces disappearing into the black. She wouldn't see her brilliant sister's blackened, burned body, lying there in the morgue. Hear her mother's anguished cries as they covered Mariko with a sheet. See her father's eyes fill with tears of grief and hate as he denounced her, as he disowned his last living child in front of the whole galaxy.

"Well?" she prompted.

"Okay, well," Raines began as he took a step back toward her, "I think we can safely assume the Pyrrhens are running the show. They are the ones who caught us, and —"

"I don't care. You figure it out." Lena brushed past Raines and sank into her pilot's chair. She couldn't deal with this right now. Let them figure out how to save the day. She'd done enough. More than enough. She folded her arms around her and tried to find a way to lean back in the chair and grab hold of the warmth the whiskey kindled inside her. She was tired. She needed to just rest.

But if she closed her eyes again ...

She pushed the thoughts aside. *Concentrate on the warmth. The sensation of falling. Focus on your body, not your thoughts. Don't think.*

As she started to drift off, Cat came up from behind her and offered her the bottle of whiskey. "It's the last of it. Thought you might want it." Lena knew she should turn it down, should try to keep a straight head, but at this point, she just needed a bit of the oblivion that way too much whiskey could offer. She took the bottle.

"Thanks," Lena sighed, gesturing for Cat to take the co-pilot's seat. She could feel the edge of her anger fade as the last of the whiskey slid down her throat, her resolve weakening.

"I didn't mean to doubt you," Cat said, hesitantly. "It's just, are you sure about this?" She gestured to Raines and Chandra now heatedly discussing plans in the middle of the shuttle. "I don't think we have any idea what we're getting into. And I want to save Gael and Cedo as much as anyone, but do you think it's even possible? Isn't this just a suicide mission? The same kind you would mock Gael for attempting?"

Lena wasn't sure. It did seem impossible. There were just four of them on this shuttle, plus a hostage. One gun, no resources, and no hope against an army of guards. How could they save anyone? And if they did, how would they get away again? They should just count themselves lucky they had gotten away once, get *Aspasia,* and run.

This time, though, she couldn't. She couldn't run from this. "We have to try, Cat."

"I admire you then. I really do. Because I can't see how we're going to pull this off."

Lena handed Cat the empty bottle. Was she putting everyone in danger? Would it all be her fault if they got captured again just because she wouldn't give up on her friends?

But as she watched Raines and Chandra leaning over a datapad they found in one of the cabinets, she realized she wasn't the only one who wouldn't give up. They were both former military. They wouldn't leave anyone behind if there was any hope they could get them out. If there was any chance at all, those two would figure it out. Raines was clever and resourceful, and though she didn't really know Chandra, she recognized and begrudgingly respected the grit and determination that could pull them through this.

There was a chance. And they were going to take it.

"They'll figure something out. And we'll get back to our ship soon."

They would. They had to.

CHAPTER TWENTY-ONE

Chandra and Raines had argued for nearly three hours, trying to decide whether they would stand a better chance at breaking their friends free at the holding cells or the execution site. The problem was, they weren't entirely sure where the holding cells were. Any number of buildings near Petrovka Square were suitable holding sites, or the prisoners could be brought in from a further location and staged at the execution site. Without a chance to scout the city, they couldn't narrow it down with enough time to act.

The execution site, though, was heavily publicized with an exact time and place for movement. If they attacked then, they'd have to spring an escape in front of thousands with only a small window of opportunity.

Not ideal.

With some small input from Cat and Lena, Chandra and Raines drew up diagrams based on what they all could remember about Petrovka Square and the area around the Courthouse steps. The very public location of the execution could work in their favor. Since the park was cleared of all buildings and cover, the Pyrrhen forces would either have to escort their prisoners across a long expanse of exposed park land or erect a temporary holding area near the steps.

If the security forces opted to transport the prisoners in, they would likely use some sort of caravan of vehicles. Lena and the others could attack anywhere along the transport route. Most of the escorts would be armed, but they would, no doubt, be outnumbered by the crowds of people ordered to attend the execution. The crowds could be used as the crew's primary weapon. If they could set off some sort of bomb, the resulting mob would create enough confusion to allow Lena and Raines to get their friends free from their escorts and disappear into the crowd cover.

If the prisoners were held instead in a temporary enclosure, their window of opportunity would be smaller. They'd have to deploy a diversion between the enclosure and the Courthouse steps. The minimal window of opportunity meant they'd need a backup for preventing the execution. In that case, they could rely on Chandra's unique set of skills. Chandra had trained briefly as a sniper and would be able to take out several members of any shooting squad in a matter of seconds, given the right tools and vantage point.

Unfortunately, they were severely lacking in both. The only gun they had was the pilot's pistol, which was mostly useless long range. Plus, the Courthouse was located near the center of the park, nearly a quarter-mile from the closest building. Chandra would have to find one of the stationed snipers watching the procedures, dispatch the gunman, and get herself into position to take out any threats on the Courthouse steps. She'd have to do this in a small enough window so that the original sniper's support team didn't realize the disruption. Then, Chandra would have to take out the execution squad after they left the prisoners' enclosure but before they could execute any of their prisoners. The margin for error was infinitesimally small.

Until they arrived on Aegea, though, they had no way of knowing which scenario they would be facing and how to proceed. So, they planned for both. The whole crew would get to the site early enough to place small bombs Chandra and Raines cobbled together with equipment and old comms units from the shuttle's weapons cache. Then, Lena and Raines would be on the ground, in the crowd, as close to the steps as they could get, ready to move at a moment's notice to get as many of their crew free as possible. Chandra would find a sniper to subdue and obtain the needed weapon to take out as many guards as she could. And Cat would stay behind with their hostage, ready to force him, at gunpoint, to move the shuttle from the roof of the school if they were discovered. At the most opportune time, Raines would deploy the synced bombs, and in the ensuing chaos, they would free their friends, and rendezvous in the Old Fourth Ward, near the bakery, before heading back to the shuttle.

It wasn't a great plan. But it was the best they could do.

Lena wished she could have patched into the Pyrrhen network to get a satellite feed of the location, to give them a better idea of the forces they'd be facing, but with a ship as small as the shuttle, she just didn't have the comms power. She would have had to relay a network signal off a larger ship or station. They might as well set off a beacon advertising their location, and the plan depended on the fact that no one would see them coming.

So, they went in blind, and Lena found herself pushing through the thick crowd of spectators as unobtrusively as possible, to make her way as close to the Steps as she could get.

There. A tented structure. Surrounded by guards. Damn. She was really hoping for the caravan.

That meant that their plan relied on Chandra. She would have to take out the guards after the crew was escorted from the tent, but before they ascended the steps. Then, Raines would set off the bombs by opening a single channel between the comms unit triggers he'd devised. They would all go off at once, and Chandra would take out anyone who tried to interfere as Lena and Raines rushed the steps from opposite directions in the riot that would hopefully follow.

Lena managed to work her way all the way to the south foot of the steps, angled to get a good view of the makeshift stage at the top and the tented structure where her friends were being held. She looked about the crowd, trying to find a glimpse of Raines, to know that he was where he needed to be. There were too many people. She had to assume he was on the north end of the steps, near the lake but as close to the tented structure as he could get, despite the police cordons and the armed guards stationed all around it.

She turned to glance over her shoulder, back at the city skyline. The buildings seemed so far away. She couldn't imagine that Chandra would be able to get a shot off accurately enough to do them any good. However, both Raines and Chandra had insisted that long-range snipers were more than capable. She just had to trust in the mercenary's marksmanship skills.

Just as she began to get nervous about the plan and its viability, the guards in front of the tent began clearing a path to the steps. It was happening. Already. She wasn't ready.

Lena steeled herself, ready for the shots that would ring out above her head. She had to stop herself from looking over her shoulder. Chandra would do her job.

As soldiers and police forced the crowd back to form a small pathway from the tent, the flaps pulled back, and a contingent of troops marched out. All were armed and walked in lockstep as they made their way to the steps. Two, four, six, there were at least twenty guards marching toward her.

A pair of officials, stern and rigid came after the first dozen. Dressed in Pyrrhen military dress, they stared straight ahead, refusing to look at the people as they passed. The first, a fair, wiry man with a sharp face and hooked nose frowned as if the crowds had an unpleasant odor. The second man, shorter and darker, clutched papers to his heavily ornamented chest as he marched forward beside his partner. Both were haughty, assured, despite the rumblings of the crowd.

Then Lena saw them. The first of the prisoners.

At first, all she could see was a shaved head, disappearing and reappearing between the shoulders of the soldiers in front. Then his face.

Cedomir.

His face was bruised, and his lips bloody. They had beaten him.

She would kill them.

His head was bowed as he shuffled forward. His hands and feet bound in iron shackles that clanked in the quiet crowd. How old fashioned. How symbolic. He stumbled every now and then but was quickly pushed forward by the guards immediately behind him. As he made it to the steps, he had to be physically helped up. He was limping terribly. What had they done to him?

Then behind him, Vaso. Also heavily battered. His left eye was nearly swollen shut, and his face was distorted with bruises and open cuts. Lena could barely look at him. She heard the intakes of breath on either side of her as others caught a glimpse of Vaso's face. A woman to her right cowered and buried her head in her companion's shoulder, refusing to look.

Lena could hardly bring herself to look beyond, but as row on row of paired guards followed the brothers, there seemed to be no other prisoners. She stood up on her toes, scanning the crowd, but the guards stopped coming. There was no one else.

Gael wasn't here. That made things more complicated. Lena spared a quick glance around, trying once again to find Raines. Every face she saw was following the procession up the steps. It was nearly impossible to differentiate between one person and the next, but she was sure that Raines was not where he was supposed to be. Had he seen? Did he know that only Cedo and Vaso were up there? Did that change the plan? Was he trying to locate Gael?

She dared not use her comm device to contact him or Chandra.

She could only watch as the soldiers marched the brothers up the steps.

There were too many guards. Why were there so many for just the two of them? A half dozen, even a dozen soldiers, they could probably handle. Chandra had been confident in her abilities. But twenty? More? How would they take so many guards out and still get Cedo free? And where was Gael?

Lena looked back to the tent. He could still be inside. Was he shaking as he waited to hear the shot that would end Cedo's life?

A microphone coming to life brought her attention back to the stage. The two Pyrrhen officials had taken their places, facing out to the south end of the steps, looking out toward the city, toward her. Behind them, Cedo and Vaso had been forced to their knees, a half dozen guards on each, guns trained on them. Vaso was mumbling something to himself, a prayer of some kind, but Cedo was still, silent.

Lena tried to move closer, but at the foot of the steps were more guards, keeping people back from the sacred marble stairs. She couldn't get closer, couldn't get close enough. This wasn't going to work. She darted a glance back over her shoulder, knowing she wouldn't see anything but more expectant faces watching the steps, waiting to see what happened.

Something was wrong. Chandra should have begun firing as the guards emerged from the tent, as soon as she saw and identified the prisoners. But here they were, all amassed on the top of the steps. Making their speeches. All was calm, orderly. Where was the riot? Where were the shots? Where was Chandra?

Where was Raines? Was he holding off on the bombs until Chandra took a shot? Should he? Should he blow them early? A riot might stop what was happening up on the steps in front of everyone.

The shorter, heavily ornamented official was talking, but Lena could hardly concentrate on his high, thin voice. Key words filtered down. "Domonkos." "Beloved son." "Terrorists." "Violation of interplanetary law." "Criminal acts." Try as she might, Lena couldn't piece together the phrases.

This farce shouldn't be allowed to continue. She looked back again to the city buildings trying to pick out which building Chandra was on.

"Sentenced by a council of Aegean citizens and Pyrrhen officials." She looked to the other side of the steps. Surely Raines had built the bombs correctly. The explosions would happen any minute. A riot would stop things. A single shot. Anything.

"No question of their guilt." There had to be something she could do.

"The Nenad brothers have a long history of agitation."

She had no gun. No bombs.

"And they finally crossed a line."

She looked about her. Guards in front of her. She could grab one. Create a disturbance of her own.

"Their actions have irreparably damaged the agreement between Pyrrhos and her moons. We can no longer trust that our uneasy peace will be kept."

She had no combat skills. She would just get herself killed.

"For the crime of the assassination of a beloved son of Pyrrhos, the punishment, on both Aegea and Pyrrhos, is death."

No. No. This couldn't be happening. She looked over her shoulder. Where? Where was Chandra?!

"And to ensure that something like this never happens again, to keep our worlds and our governments safe from unjust and illegal actions, we must take action."

Raines. He had to stop this. The bombs. He had the detonator. He would stop this.

"Cedomir and Vaso Nenad, the judgment is final. You have been judged guilty of terrorist acts in the assassination of Dominik Domonkos. Your rights as citizens have been revoked. By the powers granted me by the Central Powers, I declare your lives forfeit." Both officials stepped away from the microphone as an ornamented guard stepped up and cleared his voice.

"Under the Pyrrhen codes 12-45-96 and Aegean legislation House Resolution 534-16, your execution is authorized."

This wasn't happening.

Six guards aligned themselves down a single step as the officials and the ornamented guard stepped down further. The remaining guards fanned out, moving down toward the crowd and stopping just a few paces above them. Cedo and Vaso were facing the north crowd at the top of the Steps, facing Lena. Vaso lowered his head further as his voice was caught by the still-live microphone. "... in this world and the next. Preserve my soul and hold me close, oh Lord, in this world and the next. Keep me safe, oh Lord, in this world and the next. Remember my life and my deeds, oh Lord, in this world and the next."

Beside him, Cedo said nothing. He simply lifted his head, clear-eyed, as he looked to the guards standing below him.

"On my mark," the ornamented guard said.

"No," Lena whispered.

"Ready."

"No!" she said, louder, her voice stark in the silence of the square.

At that moment, Cedo looked down toward her voice. He scanned the crowd, and then, for a brief moment, he saw her. His brows creased and his mouth quirked in a small smile as his eyes filled. Then he pursed his lips as his head fell to his chest.

"FIRE!"

Shots rang out, drowning Lena's scream, as Vaso and Cedo fell to the marble before the amassed crowds of Banika.

CHAPTER TWENTY-TWO

Lena's world shrank down to the trickle of blood coming down the top edge of the steps.

It was thicker than she thought it would be. It didn't drip so much as creep, falling softly and disappearing over the lip of the next step.

Cedo and Vaso had fallen out of her line of sight. Several guards climbed the stairs to retrieve the bodies and then descended on the opposite side. She couldn't even get one last glance at her friend. He was gone, leaving behind only that dwindling seep of blood on the marble steps. If it was his blood.

Cedo was gone.

It was all she could do to keep breathing. Deep inhales filling her chest, slipping from her lips in small sobs. She hardly noticed when her knees gave out beneath her, and she sank down into the crowd. Nothing but the press of bodies around her as she forced herself to keep breathing.

He was gone. Her smiling, laughing friend was cold and dead and gone. That passionate, kind, brilliant young man. Everything they had done to get back here, to save him, was pointless. They should have turned and run. He was dead.

Her breaths started to run ragged, catching in her throat, stumbling on tears that she tried to swallow back.

Suddenly, there was someone beside her. A young woman. A stranger who dropped down next to her and grabbed her hand. Squeezed. "Shh," she murmured. "Shh. You're okay. You're okay." Lena turned to look at her, tried to place her face. She was young, with thick dark hair and soft brown eyes. Did she know this woman?

The struggle to identify her was enough to distract Lena from her breathing. She frowned, ready to ask her who she was, but the woman spoke. "You need to stand up now. You can't draw attention to yourself. Stand up." And she got to her own feet and pulled Lena up beside her, still holding tight to her hand. As Lena stumbled upright, the woman squeezed her hand again. "Good girl," she whispered. "Good girl. You're okay. Just a little longer. Just get through this. Just a little longer. Just face forward. That's it. You're okay."

Lena dutifully looked forward and drew strength from the hand of this kind stranger. She had almost forgotten where she was: in a dangerous crowd, just inches away from armed soldiers. They were actively looking for signs of sedition, and here she was marking herself as a sympathizer, a friend of the executed. What was she thinking? She wasn't safe. None of them were.

She finally responded to the woman beside her, squeezing back. "Thank you," she whispered. "Thank you. I'm okay."

Out of the corner of her eye, Lena could see the woman nodding, as they both looked forward at the ornamented officers ascending the now clean stairs. She saw no sign of Cedo or Vaso. Even the trickle of blood had been wiped clean. It was as if nothing had happened.

But the tension in the crowd belied that. No one spoke, but the rigid postures, the clenched fists, the pursed lips, and narrowed eyes told Lena that the people were barely holding back a tide of anger. If she had to guess, only the armed soldiers were keeping things calm.

The sensitive microphone picked up the short officer's light cough as he cleared his throat and reclaimed his place at the top of the steps. "Let the events of this day stand as a message to all who would threaten the peace of the Central Powers. We will not stand for sedition, for treason, for terror of the kind perpetuated by men like Cedomir and Vaso Nenad. Those who would threaten our peace will be dealt with swiftly and appropriately. The coming days will bring many changes to this city and others across Aegea and Aella. As Pyrrhos resumes rightful control of the mines at the Risha deposits and establishes a command center in the old Pitolsch Ward, there will be limited access to these areas. The ports along the Caspic Sea will be outfitted with new security measures for your protection. Also, a curfew will be instituted for all Banikans as of this evening. Unless you have business with the Pyrrhen government or have prior approval, all Banikan citizens must be in their homes within an hour of sunset."

At that final pronouncement, the crowd finally began to stir. Silence gave way to furtive whispers as angry Banikans realized they'd be confined almost 15 hours a day. People began scuffing their feet, elbowing their neighbors, and angrily murmuring to one another. The soldiers along the edges of the square and throughout the crowd shifted their grips on their guns.

The officer cleared his throat loudly, the speakers around the crowd echoing with his coughs. "Failure to comply with this new curfew will result in immediate detention and potential further penalties." He consulted his notes once more. "Further, media outlets will –" He never finished that pronouncement. The microphone in front of him exploded, and a blossom of red began spreading over his jacket. He clutched his chest and stumbled backward. Before anyone could respond, the other ornamented officer beside him reeled back as a shot took him in the head.

Chandra.

Screams erupted from the crowd as soldiers dashed up the steps with their weapons trained on the crowd, searching for the source of the gunshots. That put them directly in Chandra's sights. Three more soldiers fell to the sniper before they realized they were perfect targets on the steps. They rushed into the crowd, guns still aimed at the people. The people ran in fear, pushing against each other in a frantic attempt to get away. As bodies began to shove against one another, the crowd got more and more desperate.

Lena felt herself torn from the kind woman's hand as the crowd tossed her this way and that. She tried to follow the woman as she ran but soon was lost as the press of people carried her away from the steps, back towards the city. An elbow caught her in the ribs, and as she folded over in pain someone else's shoulder jammed into her cheekbone. A foot found her toes. A shoulder barely missed her eyes.

I have to get out of here.

An explosion ripped through the air behind her as a blast of heated air assaulted the back of her neck. The bombs. She had forgotten about the bombs. The air filled with screams. She knew the screams were mostly fear; the bombs were not packed with anything that could hurt anyone. There would be a flash, a loud bang, and lots of smoke, but there was nothing inside to generate shrapnel.

Still, that was little comfort. Fear was the true weapon in a crowd. As planned, the terrified Banikans were thrown into panic, and the stampede Lena feared and wanted, became a reality. The press of the crowd formed a vise as the people behind her crushed against the people in front of her. It didn't matter which direction she wanted to go; she was heading back into the city.

Behind were more bangs as more of the bombs were set off. Raines apparently had his bombs widely spaced around the park as each concussive sound seemed to come from a different direction. BOOM! BOOM! BOOM! Four, five, six. How many had they made? BOOM! Seven.

BOOM! Off to her right.

That wasn't right. They hadn't enough supplies to make more than five, maybe six at the most.

BOOM!

Another, just behind her. And they had all been designed to go off at the same time. She turned to look.

BOOM!

Heat surged against her face and brought her to a halt. Ahead of her, a dozen people were engulfed in a huge explosion of flame, as others around her fell, bloodied and broken. Lena staggered to try to stop, but she was shoved violently in the back. She lost her footing. She sprawled, trying to catch herself, and the skin ripped, burned from her palms. Still, the press of people continued. Someone stamped on her leg, and another one stepped on her raw hand. She screamed and struggled to get back up, but someone fell across her, pinning her chest to the smoking street.

"Help," she cried into the roar of the chaos around her. She tried to push the person off her and get up, but he was too heavy. "Help!" She screamed again.

She was going to die here, choked with smoke and trampled beneath the feet of a panicked city.

No. She couldn't accept that. She'd come too far. She had too much to lose.

She put her hands beneath her and shoved with everything she had, feeling the asphalt of the street digging into the exposed scrapes of her palms and staggering beneath the weight of the man on top of her. She wiggled her hips to shake herself loose, feeling a pain in her knee shooting up her leg. One final push she was free of the body.

And it was a body. His face was half gone, singed black, his chest a ruin of blood.

She darted a look around. Everywhere she looked, the injured writhed while burned and trampled bodies peppered the pavement.

These weren't the bombs her team had set. Their explosives weren't this powerful. This wasn't their doing.

Someone else had set these off.

It didn't matter. She had to get out of there.

She pushed herself to her feet, and as soon as she cleared the immediate blast area around the bomb, she was again pulled into the inescapable tide of people. She had no control over the direction she was headed or the speed at which she moved; the multitude was all there was.

She struggled to keep up with the panic-set pace, but her leg slowed her down. Each step shot pain through her body, and it was all she could do to keep moving forward. She had no choice. Keep moving, or die here.

Forward. Into the city. Into the main streets and thoroughfares of the economic center of Banika.

If she could just get to the edge of the crowd, she could find shelter, get herself out of this madness. But the press inward was as undeniable as the push forward. She could feel the bodies suffocating her as they pulled her along. Elbows, shoulders, backs, everything was pure pressure against her.

Then, a different touch. A lighter touch.

That whisper of a contact was more insistent than all the force of the mob. Lena looked to her left.

There, running beside her was the kind stranger.

The woman made eye contact with Lena and nodded firmly. Then the insistent whisper of her fingers interlaced with Lena's own, grasping her hand.

With the woman's guidance, Lena was able to wind her way through the throng, over to the edge of the street, up on the sidewalk. Before Lena knew it, the two women had slipped away from the masses and down an alleyway.

Lena staggered as the press of the bodies dissipated, and they were alone.

The alley was nothing but a space between buildings, no more than a few feet across. Lena would have never found it on her own. Even now, she looked out at the hordes rushing past the opening and wondered how the woman had navigated them so perfectly into the small space.

"Are you all right?" the woman asked, looking Lena over.

"Yeah," Lena gasped. "I think so." She watched as the initial rush of people began to thin already.

It had been only minutes since the first bombs had exploded, but Lena felt like she had been running for hours.

"Can you walk a little farther?" The woman gestured to Lena's injured leg, frowning.

Lena tested it gingerly. "I don't think it's broken. But we had probably better get somewhere safe before my adrenaline wears off."

The woman nodded, turned down the alley, and began walking away from the crowd. Lena limped after her. "Thank you," Lena managed between gasps.

The woman nodded without turning around.

"I mean it. I don't know what would have happened if you hadn't helped me back there."

The woman turned slightly, revealing a crooked smile. "Which time?"

"Either," Lena admitted. "I shouldn't have lost it at the steps. That was dangerous."

"You had just lost your friend. It was understandable."

Lena slowed. "Wait. How do you know he was my friend? Do you know me?"

She didn't slow, and Lena had to quicken her pace to catch up as she turned a corner down another narrow alley between buildings. "Only indirectly. I was a friend of Vaso."

"Oh," Lena said, unsure what else she could say "I'm sorry for your loss."

"He knew the price," the woman said.

"Price?"

The woman nodded as she continued walking. "There is always a price for freedom. I am sorry they had to be the first ones to pay it, but they will not pay it alone. Not for long."

"What are—" Lena began, but the woman stopped as they reached the dead end of the alley. She stood before an unmarked, nondescript door. She rapped on it quickly twice, paused, and then twice more. The door opened, and the woman stepped in and disappeared as it closed silently behind her, leaving Lena alone in the alley.

Seconds later, the door opened again, and the woman popped her head out. "Well?" she asked before disappearing again, leaving the door ajar this time.

Lena looked around at the empty alley. She could still hear the screaming crowds muffled in the distance behind her. They'd moved east, away from the riots. Sirens had begun to whine, and she could just make out the sound of air support coming in from the ports to the west.

Raines was back there somewhere. He could have escaped the mob, gotten somewhere to safety. Or he could be injured, dying in the street, trampled by the panicked crowds. Or he could have been arrested. He could be anywhere, and they had no comms to get in touch.

Lena cursed. She didn't have any other options. She couldn't go back. Not until things settled down. The only way was forward. She swallowed her doubts and followed the woman into the dark doorway.

The door slid shut behind her, leaving them in total blackness for a few seconds. Then a solitary lightbulb slowly came to life above them, revealing a small hallway leading to a staircase headed down.

The woman confidently made her way down the hallway and down the staircase, evidently expecting Lena to follow again. Committed to this path, whatever it was, Lena hobbled down the stairs after her, wincing with each step.

CHAPTER TWENTY-THREE

Down and down they went, passing through hallways and narrow stairwells until Lena had no idea what building they were under or how they'd ever get back up to the surface. For one accustomed to the sky, the pressure of deep underground gravity was claustrophobic.

Finally, the woman came to a single long hallway. She walked to the last door on the left and knocked three times. To Lena's surprise, she then ignored the door, turned around, and opened the last door on the right. Bewildered, Lena followed.

A pair of armed guards trained their guns on the women as they walked in. Lena instinctively raised her hands.

"State your business," the guard on the right said gruffly, his face hidden behind his helmet's faceplate.

"Villim," the woman sighed. "Put the gun down. You saw it was me before I reached the first stairway." She turned to Lena. "He's just posturing. Come on. There is someone who would like to see you." With that, she pushed past the two men, with a murmured greeting to the other guard.

Lena eyed the guards warily but obeyed without protest. As they passed the initial armed barrier, the room opened up into a huge warehouse-like space that was buzzing with energy. Dozens of young men and women moved about, frenzied but purposeful. To her right, amongst cots and sleeping bags, several injured individuals were being tended to. To the left, there was a small group gathered around a table, arguing and jabbing at what looked to be a map between them. Deeper in, others were speaking hurriedly into comms units or working on tablets and terminal screens. Several people were grabbing scribbled notes from the comms center and dashing in and out of the large doorway at the opposite end of the cavernous space.

While she saw the occasional gray hair or lined face amongst the scattered and busy, most everywhere Lena looked, she saw determined, hard set looks on impossibly young faces. Most of them couldn't be much older than Dimitri, and nearly everyone seemed to be younger than Lena herself. These were university-aged, people who should be just venturing out into the world and discovering who and what they wanted out of life. They were kids!

A few looked up as Lena, and her escort walked by, but most of them were engrossed in their tasks and paid the women no heed.

Lena had no idea what she had stumbled onto.

"This was one of the headquarters of the resistance in the war. The secret of its existence was passed along from our parents, and we kept it in good order for such a day as this. As you can imagine, things are a bit more interesting here just now." The woman smiled, obviously proud of the scene. "This is just the beginning. We have a long way to go."

"Go where?" Lena stopped. "What is all of this? Who the hell are you?"

The woman finally stopped her tireless march forward and turned to assess her. Seeing the bewildered look on Lena's face, she frowned. "You were Cedomir's shipmate, yes? The pilot? Lena Lomasky?"

"Yes, but—"

"You brought him home, yes? On Independence Day?"

"Yes, but—"

"For the assassination?"

"What? No!" Lena shook her head. "No, Cedo was not a part of that. That was Vaso. Cedo would never—"

"Of course he would. Any of us would."

"Not Cedo," Lena insisted. She had seen the anger, the anguish after Dimitri had been shot, the desperation with which he tried to save Vaso and get him off world. "He didn't know about any of this. Cedo was not a murderer. You don't — didn't know him." Lena choked on the words.

"I did know Cedomir. Longer than you ever did. And I know exactly what he was. He was a patriot. A hero. And we will honor his sacrifice by continuing what he and his brothers started." She gestured around her. "This is where the resistance begins anew. We are the Black Hand," she smiled as if introducing her college sorority, "and we have been working for Aegea's freedom for years. The Aegean people will not suffer under the shackles of Pyrrhen slavery for much longer. We will have independence, no matter the cost. The assassination of Domonkos was the start. But it was just a taste. Today, though. Today was the beginning of what is to come."

Lena's eyes widened as she realized. "The bombs. That was you."

"There will be more," the woman said, confirming.

Lena was horrified. "But those were your own people down there! You bombed the crowd!"

"Our operatives targeted Pyrrhen soldiers."

"Who were in the middle of your own people!"

The woman shifted her weight uncomfortably. "Some casualties couldn't be avoided. It is what happens in war." She shook her head. "We didn't want any of this. But we will not stand by and let our moon be taken again. We can't." Her voice grew strained, desperate. "We can't do it again, Lena. If we let them take our moon, if we let them back here, back into our lives, again, there will be nothing left." She reached out and grabbed Lena's arms, digging her fingers into the flesh of her biceps. "We can't lose ourselves. Not again. Not to them. We can't. We can't!"

Lena looked at this desperate woman. Her words rang with familiarity. They were Fanon's ideas. They were Vaso's words, the words Cedo had decried even as he agreed. Was this how they all felt? Were these the thoughts that drove Vaso to kill in cold blood? To drag his family and everyone he knew into this madness?

People around the two women had begun to stare, and in each look, just beneath the surface of their industry and buzzing activity, Lena could see the same desperation. These were people so willing to remain free that they would kill and even die if it would force the Pyrrhens out. They were not blind to the harm and destruction they had caused. They knew there was more to come, and the shadows of that future bruised each face. It settled under their hollowed eyes, pursed their angry lips, and steeled their steadfast spines.

They were only beginning to fight.

And for now, at least, it seemed Lena was with them. Or at least among them.

"Okay," Lena said.

"Okay?" the woman was confused.

"Okay, I'm with you."

The woman dropped Lena's arms and took a step back. "You are?"

"I don't know what I can do to help. I'm no soldier, and I won't be any good on any front lines, but I won't do anything to stop you. Some laws are meant to be broken, right? So as much as I can be, I'm with you," Lena said.

The woman's face lit up, and she moved as if to hug Lena, but Lena stepped back and held up a hand in protest. "Wait. This is not my war. I have no place in it, and I won't go putting my family in danger for your ideals. I still want to get my crew and my ship as far from this mess as I can. But if you want to get anyone off world, if you want to send word out to any outposts or get through the blockade, well, I'm already involved enough, so I'll do my best to help you. But I'm not risking me and mine any more than that for this. This is your fight. But I won't get in your way."

The woman nodded soberly. "I understand. That's all I could expect, I guess. And there might be a way you can help."

That was sadly unsurprising. "Oh?"

A voice behind her answered. "It's true. And you already have agreed to it."

CHAPTER TWENTY-FOUR

Lena turned to find a young man with light brown hair and a lightly lined brow. He smiled, revealing a prominent dimple in his chin which lent him a boyish charm.

"I know you," Lena said.

"Yes, I'm sorry to see you again under such circumstances, but I'm glad you made it here, nonetheless." He smiled again as she tilted her head, obviously trying to place him. "Aaron Meyer, Ambassador Mason's personal secretary. I brought you to his meeting at the Hotel Moskva."

"Oh, that's right. You gave me the datastick," Lena said, unable to come up with anything more meaningful to say in response. "Is Pierce here?"

Aaron lost his smile and shook his head. "No, I'm afraid not." He abruptly turned to the woman. "Have you filled her in?"

"Not much. Just the basics," the woman admitted. She shuffled and looked down at her feet, looking suddenly years younger.

Aaron nodded. "Okay, I'll take it from here. Thank you." He suddenly reached over and gave her a hug. "I'm glad you're safe. Now, go get some rest. You're going to need it."

The woman rolled her eyes over Aaron's shoulder at Lena. "Yeah, yeah." She pulled back and smiled. "I'll be fine." Then she turned and walked away.

Lena smiled at their easy familiarity. "Girlfriend?"

Aaron visibly shuddered. "No! She is my little sister. Senka. And I tend to prefer partners more like your friend Gael. Tall, dark, and gorgeous." He pointedly looked behind her. "Any chance he's with you?"

"No," Lena said, a bit put off by the casual small talk, considering their circumstances. "He's... I don't know where Gael is." Had he been left back in the tent beyond the Steps? She'd never gotten close enough to see. There had been all those soldiers; surely they couldn't have just been there for the Nenad brothers.

"The Pyrrhens. They have him. I think." She looked around at the operation surrounding them. These kids weren't soldiers. They were hardly even what she'd call an organization. But they were a force of sorts, and today's demonstration showed that they had some power behind their ideals. Maybe they could help. "We came here to get them—him back. I need to get him back." She looked to this young man she barely knew. "Can ..." She could barely get the words out. "I need your help."

Aaron looked at her carefully. He knew who she was, and how little she had to offer him at this point. Still, he gave her a small smile. "We might be able to work something out. Follow me." He turned on his heel and began making his way across the warehouse. Lena had no choice but to follow him, hobbling as she favored her still wounded knee. He led her to a secluded corner in the back of the warehouse space. It was shielded by sheets hung along makeshift scaffolding. She slipped inside the edge of the tattered fabric that Aaron held back and discovered an office of sorts.

There was a wide, long board set on two stacks of boxes, obviously serving as a desk, which was covered in papers and maps. There was a single chair and a few sturdy wooden crates. He gestured to the chair. "Please, sit. I know you've been through a lot. I'll go get us some coffee and see if I can get some information on your friends." With that, he swept back out behind the bedsheet curtain, leaving her behind in the muffled quiet of his crude office space.

She was alone.

Lena gratefully sank into the chair. The chair creaked, and she was sure the backrest was going to collapse against her weight, but it held her up for the moment. It was enough.

She slumped over the desk, bowed her head, and closed her eyes, letting the full weight of the past few hours gather in the space between her shoulder blades. What had they been thinking? She and Raines and Cat had tossed their hard-fought freedom away, to rush into, what? An ill-conceived mission to save their crew? To save Cedo and Vaso? The brothers were gone. And she had no idea what had happened to Gael. He might not even be on this forsaken moon. He could be on some prison transport ship, bound for Pyrrhos. Or he could already be dead. Now, she had even lost the friends she had when she landed here. Cat was hopefully still safe in the shuttle they had stolen from the Pyrrhens, but she couldn't know how long that would last. Someone was bound to discover her and the prisoner she had no real hope of holding. And where was Raines? Or Chandra for that matter? They could have been discovered, taken by the militant Pyrrhens or trampled to death in the riot. She couldn't check in with them. They had no comms, wasting them on bombs that were utterly irrelevant in the face of the Black Hand's actions. Their rendezvous in the Old Fourth Ward was undoubtedly compromised.

Lena was utterly and hopelessly alone.

She wanted to stop and cry. It wouldn't matter. No one could hear her. Not with all the noise. With her head bowed and eyes closed, she could have let it all drown her and disappear into sleep.

If it wasn't for the noise.

Out beyond the curtain, voices raised, panicked and distraught. She could hear anger and tears, whispers, and frantic conversations alike. Someone was barking out orders as other voices rose to argue against them. Another group seemed to be arguing about whether it was better to stay put or get out there and "do something." Someone yelled for help—maybe it was from the sickbay — and she heard boots running away into the distance.

The atmosphere was one of chaos, of panic, of confusion, of anger, and of loss. It was overwhelming. This, Lena realized, was what war was like on the other side of the history books. No generals were here crafting clever strategies and planning tactical moves to suppress or subdue uprisings. No carefully coordinated drones were sent in to "deal with" the threat of the other side. No troops were coming in from the reserves when things got too heated on the ground.

These were just people determined to do something, anything, and acting in a semi-organized chaos. These were young, untrained individuals who had nothing but their determination and their impromptu incendiary devices. Their best weapons were their intimate working knowledge of the city and a desperation that would spur them to fight when the odds were stacked against them.

It seemed foolish to Lena, but who was she to criticize their methods? Aegeans had fought in just this way before, and they had gained their independence, then. Who was she to tell them they couldn't do the same again?

Still, she wanted nothing to do with it. She wanted Gael. She wanted Raines. She wanted her crew. She wanted her thrice-damned ship.

From somewhere, Lena heard shouting grow louder. A lone hysterical voice rose above the others. "You can't keep me here! I have to get back. Let go of me. I'm not one of you."

Lena stood. She knew that voice.

She threw aside the curtain and looked toward where she had come in. There. Held down by three strong young men.

"Raines!" She rushed to him. "Let him go." She began pulling at the men piled on top of him. "He's with me. Get off."

"Lena!" Raines exclaimed in relief. "You're okay." He stopped struggling, which let the men relax their hold on him. They pulled him to his feet none too gently, and he let them. "I thought I lost you. I saw you fall, and—" He pulled out of their grasp as Lena fell into his arms.

She let herself mold into him, feeling the warmth of him and drinking in his smell. "You're here. You're here," she murmured into his shoulder. Never had she been so relieved to see him. She was safe. If he was here, she was safe. He'd know what to do. Raines would have a plan. He always had a plan.

"I take it this is another friend of yours," Aaron said behind her. "You do find the attractive ones."

Lena left the comfort of Raines's arms to find Aaron flanked by his sister and six men with guns aimed directly at Raines.

"Yes. Yes!" Lena said, holding her arms in front of her and stepping between the guards and Raines. The gesture was purely symbolic as she noticed another half dozen guards plus the three big guys on the other side of Raines. They were completely surrounded, and the men were eyeing Raines distrustfully. "He's with me. He's on our side. Stand down." She chose the "our" purposefully, hoping that it would mean something.

The guards kept their stance, though, until after an interminable minute, Aaron finally nodded once. At that, the guards turned and dispersed back out into the warehouse, supposedly to resume their posts.

"My apologies," Aaron said, sounding not-at-all contrite. "We are a little on edge. Especially when people manage to skirt our security systems and walk through the back door."

It was Raines's turn to lift his hands in defense. "I was following Lena and this one," he gestured to Senka. "But I got carried off with the riot. Couldn't make it down the alley in time. I had to double back, but by the time I got there, they were gone. I tried every door in the alley, but they were all locked."

"Then how did you manage to get through our door?" Aaron demanded.

"Some sneaky looking guy came along. I hid behind some trash cans and watched him go straight to the last door. Knock a code and then disappear. So, I followed."

"Sneaky looking guy?" Aaron turned to his sister.

She narrowed her eyes. "Mikel. I'll talk to him." But she stood her ground, glaring at Raines.

Aaron simply nodded again and turned his attention back to Raines and Lena. "You understand, our security is the only thing that keeps our operation safe at the moment. It's a precarious time. We can't compromise our location."

"What even is this place?" Raines asked, looking around as if he had only just noticed where they were. He gestured to the crates behind the sickbay, which Lena now realized held munitions and explosive components. "I take it you are the ones responsible for what's happening outside?"

"No," Aaron said. "What you've seen has been the direct long-term result of generations of oppression and subjugation and the immediate result of the murders of Cedo and Vaso Nenad. But if you want someone to take responsibility for setting off the bombs, then yes, that was us. Though," Aaron frowned, "killing the executioners was not specifically part of my plans."

"Oh," Lena said, a bit sheepishly. "That was us."

Aaron raised his eyebrows as the corners of his lip quirked. "Indeed?"

"We were going to... I mean we were trying to save..." Lena couldn't finish her sentence.

Aaron's wry smile vanished. He turned to his sister once again. He leaned down and whispered in her ear. She nodded, shot the two interlopers a glance, and left. "Senka will get us that coffee I promised." He gestured back to his office magnanimously, as if he were inviting them to a state dinner rather than an impromptu war room carved out of some basement storage space. "We should talk."

Lena looked to Raines who took the lead as if he had made the invitation himself. Lena followed, and Aaron fell in behind them. As they settled themselves onto chairs, boxes, or whatever served for seats, Senka entered with three mismatched mugs of steaming coffee and passed them out before retreating once again.

Lena took a cautious sip. It was surprisingly decent: a deep rich roasted taste with caramel undertones. In an instant, she felt some of the tension in her back release as she let the hot liquid coat her insides and settle into her empty stomach.

"We have some food on the way," Aaron said, reading her mind. "It's not much, but it'll help us get through the next little bit."

"Ever attentive, aren't you?" Lena said, meaning it as a compliment, though she worried it came across differently.

Aaron didn't seem to mind. "I have a head for details and a heart for my people. In this endeavor, they come together."

"And this being?" Raines asked.

"We are the Aegean Resistance. Her Black Hand" Aaron said, giving each word its capital letter. "We are the ones who will stand up to the Pyrrhens and their Pyrrhen servants. We are the ones who will expel our occupiers and restore Aegea to her people once again. This Pyrrhen occupation is a full declaration of war, and we intend to answer the call."

"Quite the manifesto," Raines said. "And just who are you to face down the Pyrrhens?"

"Who am I?" Aaron said. "I am no one."

"Bullshit," Raines said. "I'm not a fan of false modesty, and you don't exactly wear it well. Now let's try that again. You're obviously the man in charge here. At least everyone looks to you before they make a move. Who are you? And why do you think you can face down the largest military force in this system?"

Aaron looked at Raines as if he hadn't really seen him until now. He assessed the mob-tattered clothing that had once held a stylish cut. He took in the careful physique of someone who took the time to maintain his body. He evaluated the light brown hair in its slightly overgrown military cut, the hard cheekbones, and steely grey eyes, and he nodded his approval. "All right, yes, I am currently in charge here. But that is a matter of unhappy circumstance more than it is any testament to my leadership abilities. I was Pierce Mason's personal assistant before he was killed."

Lena couldn't control the gasp that escaped her lips. "Pierce is dead?"

Aaron turned a sympathetic look to her. "Not long after you left, I'm afraid. The Pyrrhens had been watching him for months. They knew he had intel and were scared he was going to get it to the wrong—or right— people. Arrested him in his office and charged him with conspiracy against this so-called Central Powers entity. And for inciting the assassination of Domonkos. Executed him for treason the next day. No trial, nothing. He was dead the second they got a hold of him."

Lena felt sick. *Pierce, too. Gone?*

"I'm only glad," Aaron continued, "that he got the plans to you, first." He leaned forward, his arms pressed hard against the desk. "Tell me you still have them."

Lena swallowed the coffee and bile that threatened to come up. "I... well, that is... they're..." As far as she knew, they were still on board the *Aspasia*. But where her ship was, was another question. Her stomach roiled again at the thought of her ship in Pyrrhen hands. "They're safe."

Aaron stared at her. "So, you don't have them?"

She got defensive. "On me? No. I'm not stupid. I wouldn't bring them back here. They're somewhere safe. Where the Pyrrhens won't find them."

"Are you sure?" His voice was full of desperation.

"Yes," Lena said. They *were* safe. As long as they were still on *Aspasia*. And the Pyrrhens didn't search the ship. And as long as they could get back to the ship. And then get to Myrto in one piece. "But I don't know if we can get it anywhere to make a difference. I mean, aren't we too late? The war has started. State secrets and intrigue don't matter if war is breaking out. Our mission failed."

Aaron averted his gaze for only half a second, but it was enough to signal to both Lena and Raines that he was hiding something. "Not necessarily."

That confirmed it. "It's not just plans on there, is it? It's something else."

"What do you mean?" Raines frowned. "I thought it was just intercepted intel, Pyrrhos's plans for an invasion, some cryptography. What else?"

"Wouldn't that be enough?" Aaron said. "Bases? Supply lines? If we could anticipate where they would strike? If we can intercept their plans and know what they're going to do, then we could—"

"But that's not what's on there." Lena knew. Evan had been right. "It's the weapon. The Lomasky Weapon, isn't it?"

Aaron nodded as Raines turned to gape at her. "Lomasky Weapon? What the hell is that?"

Lena ignored him.

"How much do you know about it?" Aaron asked.

"Almost nothing. But the Pyrrhens know quite a bit. And they're looking for it as desperately as you apparently are."

Aaron's gaze narrowed. "That's because it's not just some weapon. This thing could change what warfare means. It has the potential for mass destruction on a scale we've not seen before. It could be used to wipe out entire cities. Total and complete annihilation in a matter of seconds with no lingering radiation or fallout of any kind. It makes nuclear warfare look primitive and messy."

"And we have that thing on my ship?!"

"Not the weapon itself, Raines," Lena said patiently. "Sit down. So far as I know, it's just the plans. The blueprints and equations for a bosonic weapon. And it seems they may be the only complete plans out there." She realized something else. "Pierce didn't steal them from the Pyrrhens, did he?"

"No," Aaron admitted. "He's had them since he stole them from your father's company. And he destroyed all other copies and evidence back on Rien before he came here. He thought the plans might be safe if no one else knew they existed."

"But that's ridiculous," Lena said. "Of course, people knew they existed. Whoever developed the weapon. There had to be teams of scientists working on this thing. Engineers. Testers."

"All dead. Or missing. Or locked away in some Lomasky prison somewhere." Aaron shook his head as Lena opened her mouth to protest. "Mr. Mason knew they had to be taken somewhere safe because members of his team began to disappear. Just a few at first. But as more began to have bad luck, ill-timed heart attacks, car accidents, he recognized what was happening. And why. Someone didn't want anyone knowing this weapon existed. He did what he could to keep it out of their hands. He and a few members of his team erased and destroyed files, equipment, paperwork. They were very thorough. But in case they weren't, they made a few copies of the data for themselves. In case someone tried to recreate the research, to build the weapon. The hope was that they could find some way to defend against the weapon. But each of those members dropped out of contact over the past few months. And with everything that started happening here, Mr. Mason knew the plans he had weren't safe anymore."

"So why take them back to Rien? Why take them back to Lomasky Corp? If that's where the trouble started." Raines was on the edge of his chair.

"Because we had come to think the Pyrrhens might have one of the other copies of the plans and were planning to unleash it on our people. The Lomaskys may be our only chance of building a counter-weapon."

That surprised Lena. The way Evan had been acting, his desperation for Lena's help, his incomplete files and blueprints. But that had all been staged. Evan had all but admitted that. He had wanted her to ask questions to get involved. He clearly had some version of the plans already. He was probably hoping she would help him find the missing piece.

Evan could be telling the truth, though. He may have discovered the Aegeans had the plans and were worried that this so-called Black Hand was willing to use it on the Pyrrhens. Aaron, their supposed leader, had all but admitted to that much. They all wanted the weapon for themselves. To use it, to use to build a counter-weapon? In the end, the why didn't matter. The owner of those plans could turn this war.

None of that mattered, though. Right now, she was stuck on this forsaken moon, her crew scattered. If Lena had any hope of getting those plans to anyone, she needed her crew back. "If you want us to get those plans back," Lena said, "then we need your help. We need Gael and our mercenary back, and then we need to get back to our shuttle and get off of this rock."

Aaron stood and walked to the flap of the office. He peeked around, whispered a quick conference with someone standing out there, and then came back in. "We think your friend, Gael, is being held at the Palata Beograd. That is where Cedo and Vaso were being held before the executions. It's one of our most famous buildings. Troops have been stationed there since the Pyrrhen forces arrived."

"Is there any good way in?" Raines asked.

"A few. Our best bet would be to use the underground tunnels."

Raines grinned and eyed his surroundings. "I'm guessing you have access to them from here."

Aaron returned the smile. "It's why we have our base here."

Raines nodded to himself. Lena could see the thoughts flying and the plans building behind his eyes. "Good, good. I need to talk to anyone here who might have a good idea of the layout. Anyone who worked in the building?"

"I think we can find someone," Aaron said. "We have a strong idea of where in the building they were holding the Nenad brothers. They'd probably have any other prisoners near there. And if you need backup..."

Raines broke into a wide grin. "Oh, I think we could definitely use some backup."

CHAPTER TWENTY-FIVE

"What do you mean?" Lena demanded. "I'm going with you!"

Raines crossed his arms. "You're not, and there's no argument. You don't know the first thing about close-quarter raids. You don't have military training. You'd just be in the way."

"I can help!" It wasn't fair. She felt like a child begging to be taken along to her parents' outing. It wasn't just that she felt left out; she already felt useless in this hideout, like a burden, like a silly socialite in the middle of something she couldn't possibly understand. And now Raines was going to leave her while he rescued their friends without her? No. "I could serve as a lookout or help get people out."

"No, Lena. You're staying here with Senka." His look softened, and he raised his hand as if to reach out to her before he stopped himself. He took a deep breath and balled his fists at his side. "I can't risk it. I can't risk you."

"Like I'm so much safer here! Like I was safer out there? At the Courthouse? Setting off bombs?"

"Exactly!" He threw up his hands. "Exactly! Lena, I could have lost you out there in that mob. I thought I had. When you went down near that bomb." He closed his eyes, reliving it. "I couldn't get to you, Lee. I couldn't get through fast enough." He opened his eyes and looked at her. "I'm not debating this. I'm not risking you again. I'm going to get our man, and then we're all going to get that damn shuttle and get our ship back. But you have to stay safe, or none of that matters." He did reach for her then. He took her hand and squeezed. "Please, Lena? Will you stay safe for me?"

It was the question that did her in. If he had told her to stay again, if he had commanded it, she would have fought him. But he asked. She sighed. "All right."

His look of relief almost revived her defiance, but she held her tongue as he leaned in and gently kissed her cheek. "Thank you," he whispered.

"You better bring him back," she said firmly, returning the squeeze of his hand.

"I will." He had no doubt, so neither did she.

He tried to pull away, but she held tight to his hand and brought him back to her again. "You come back, too." She kissed him then with a fervency and desperation that seemed to come as much from the air around her as from inside her. She was lightheaded when she finally let him go. "I don't want to find another captain for my ship."

He laughed with a breathlessness that matched hers. "My ship, *ma petite.*"

"I love you, too."

And with a smile, he left her alone amongst the Aegeans.

For an hour, she did little but sit and wait. She allowed a nice young man to bandage and wrap her injured knee and spray some foul-smelling stuff on her raw, scraped hands. He had braces, bandages, and splints of all kinds scattered about and wrapped her knee with great care and a smile. She wondered how long his smiles would last when things progressed beyond a few minor scrapes and bruises. When bodies began piling up. When people he knew came in and couldn't be saved.

She managed to find someone with a secure comms unit, and she radioed back to the shuttle. Cat answered, relieved to hear her voice. Chandra had made it back with an additional arsenal of weapons that she had taken from the snipers she had subdued, and she was currently making Cat and the pilot Karl very uncomfortable.

"Please," Cat whispered. "Come back soon. Chandra won't say anything about what happened. She just keeps cycling through the weapons. Taking pieces apart, mumbling to herself, targeting things out the door. No one's found us yet, but it's only a matter of time before Chandra starts shooting. Lena, she'll bring the whole Pyrrhen army down on us."

"Just sit tight," Lena said, attempting to convey calm and confidence even if she felt none. "We'll be there soon."

"You promise?" Cat sounded like a little girl, small and afraid. "She keeps looking at me."

"I will do everything I can," Lena promised, trying to sound like Raines. "We're going home. All of us."

She didn't have the heart to tell Cat that "all of us" no longer included Cedo. She couldn't bring herself to say it out loud. Not yet.

Cat agreed to stay put, but Lena didn't hold out hope that she would last too much longer. Cat Sanders was not made for high-stress situations like this.

Not that Lena was facing all that much stress at the moment. She wondered where the action was, where the intense battle meetings happened. Weren't the rebels supposed to be full of action planning their next big move? Shouldn't they be rallying the troops, getting ready to take back their moon?

Instead, it seemed everyone had had their fill of excitement for the day. Most of the people in the bunker were resting, recovering, tending their wounds. Those that were all in one piece were sitting in pairs and small groups, talking softly. Some were organizing weapons. Others were re-packaging medical supplies. Senka sat with a group, rolling up bandages, loading magazines for the weapons cache, and laughing as they worked.

Having nothing better to do, Lena made her way over to join them.

As she approached, everyone stopped talking. Senka rolled her eyes. "It's fine. She's here, isn't she?" That was enough for the group. They quickly resumed where they left off.

"Here," Senka offered, scooting aside on the crate where she was perched. "You can help me." Lena gratefully sat down beside her as Senka passed her a magazine and a handful of lead bullets. "You know how to load, don't you?"

Lena did, but she was surprised at the primitive nature of the weaponry. Lead slugs backed by gun powder. All these years of advanced technology, and they were still fighting each other with nothing more than bits of metal slag fired at high velocity. Then again, what more was needed? All it took to kill a person was opening them up a little. Expose a vital organ, an artery to the outside, tear up the insides a tiny bit, and instantly, no more person. Warfare was easy.

She slowly used her thumb to force the bullets into the spring-loaded magazine. One on top of the other. Each one, each flick of her fingers, a bullet that someone here hoped would pierce the skin of a Pyrrhen. Each one designed to kill, to rip someone's body open and expose blood to the hungry air.

Only halfway through her second magazine, Lena stopped. She couldn't do this. She couldn't help these people kill. Not even to defend their homeland. If that's what they were doing. After all, they were the ones who had antagonized the Pyrrhens. It wasn't really about freedom. About sovereignty. It seemed to really be about who controlled the resources of the Aegean mines. In the end, it was what all wars were about: money.

She looked up at these people who were so intent on war that they couldn't wait for their moon's military to mobilize, for the troops to do their jobs. They were taking things into their own hands, fighting on their own terms. Senka was a young, pretty thing. She could have been a college student studying art or philosophy. The young woman next to her, someone's charismatic young mother. She would likely have dozens of friends with children of their own. The young man shooting glances at her and rolling bandages, her equally charismatic husband. An architect rebuilding Banika in the Aegean cultural tradition. The friend to his left, an aspiring politician, making her way up through the local government. The young man beside her, a struggling artist.

Each of them could have lives. Instead, they were preparing for war and talking guerrilla tactics and strategies.

"We need to get them bottlenecked near the Square. Come at them from both sides. Target the higher-ups," the aspiring politician said, her eyes flashing with the firebrand energy Lena knew would take her far.

"More assassinations?" The artist picked up a new set of loose bandages and began rolling. "That will just make them angrier. Get them organized. No. We need to keep things random. Target places we know they're at but keep them guessing. Make them nervous! Then wait for the troops to clean up."

"And how long will that take?" the young husband asked, taking his share of the new bandages. "Our troops have supposedly been organizing for a week, and we have yet to see a single Aegean uniform. They've written off Banika already. Probably focusing their efforts on the smaller cities, where they can actually get supplies brought in."

"Pasic is right," Senka said. "Banika is too symbolically important to the Pyrrhens right now. It's why they hit us first. They've got too many forces already in the city. We can't rely on the troops to back us up. It's up to us to take back our city."

"How?" Lena blurted before she could think to stop herself. Every face turned to look at her. She shook her head. If only she could keep her mouth shut. Too late now. She set down the bullets and the magazine. "I understand wanting to take back your city, but why can't you just for one second think of all the lives you're ruining with all of this?" She gestured back to the ersatz sickbay. "Your own people are going to suffer, to die! What's so bad about some rich Pyrrhen owning the mines versus some rich

Aegean? Some distant Pyrrhen politician running the city versus some Aegean businessman? It's all the same in the end. You'll still lead almost identical lives on your little moon. Focus on what you do have, and stop letting wealthy chess players keep using you as pawns in their struggles for power."

The group of them seemed stunned to silence. But Senka narrowed her eyes. "Is that what we are to you, Ms. Lomasky?" She stood, stepped toward Lena, and menaced over her. "Are we pawns to people like you?"

Lena gulped. She should have kept her mouth shut. Senka knew who Lena was. Or at least, Senka thought she knew, and that was enough. She couldn't know how living in the black, living without resources, without a family, without ground under her feet could change anyone. "I'm not who you think I am," she protested weakly.

"You are. You're no one," Senka spat. She grabbed Lena by the front of her shirt and yanked her to her feet. "You belong to no one. You have no home. You have no people. You don't know what it is to have a place that is yours, that is your family's, your people's. You could have no idea what it is to fight for that. To fight for not just ideals, not just philosophies. Fuck. We could care less about that. We are fighting for us. For our heritage and for the heritage, we will pass on to those that come after us." She shoved Lena back off the crate, sending her tumbling onto her back. Lena's head hit the concrete of the basement floor, and she blinked away stars as Senka approached, looming over her sprawled form. "The only thing that matters here, the only thing that will keep you alive on our 'little moon' is whether you are useful to our cause." She placed a foot on Lena's injured knee and put just the smallest amount of pressure. That light touch was enough to send bolts of pain up Lena's legs, threatening spasms in her lower back. "What do you say, Ms. Lomasky? Are you useful to us?"

Lena let out a whimper of pain, and Senka lifted her foot. Lena gasped for air for half a second. "Dammit, I already said—"

Before she could finish her thought, a commotion at the back entrance turned Senka's head.

About three dozen injured came stumbling in through, some carrying people, some supporting others, still more limping to safety before collapsing inside the doors. Senka and the rest jumped and ran to help in any way they could, leaving Lena forgotten on the floor.

Lena choked down her pain as she sat up. To a person, every one of the people coming in the door was covered in blood and soot. More bombs. These stupid people. But Lena couldn't dwell on how it happened. She pushed herself to her feet and hobbled forward to see how she could help. As she approached the medical cots, a man grabbed her by the arm.

"You? Any medical experience?" he demanded.

"No."

"Then get back," and he pushed her back away from the center of activity. She stumbled back and looked on with dismay. One young man was screaming as four people attempted to hold him down. His leg had been blown off below the knee, and they were trying to stop the flow of blood. Another was sobbing, tears mingling with the blood that trickled from a head wound. He was clutching a young woman who was not moving, her face a mess of blood and tissue beneath a curtain of blood-soaked hair.

All around her, people were dying, screaming, bleeding, and there was nothing she could do.

A small touch against the back of her leg startled her, and Lena spun around. A young man was lying on one of the cots. He was not screaming or sobbing, but his face held no color, and the mess of bloody bandages on his stomach told her that he was severely injured, if not dying. Lena frantically looked around. There was no one to help him. They were all already doing everything they could.

She knelt down beside him. "I'll find someone to help you," she promised and stood. Before she could move, though, he reached out with surprising strength and grabbed her hand.

"No," he said, his voice steady and calm. "Please. Stay with me. You have a familiar face."

She bent over him, carefully avoiding looking at his stomach. The smell was overwhelming; blood and offal and death. She almost gagged, but she steadied her eyes on his. "I can't help you. I don't know anything about this. I—"

"It's okay," he smiled weakly. "It's too late for that. I just, I don't want to be alone."

"Don't say that. I'll find someone—"

"Please." His voice broke. "Please, don't leave me."

Lena stopped and returned the grip on his hand. He was dying. Just like Cedo. But she could be here with him. Cedo had been alone, but she could be here. Her eyes welled with tears. "Okay," she agreed.

She knelt down beside him. She looked briefly for a pillow, a blanket, anything to make him comfortable, but there was nothing in the utilitarian space. So she offered up the only warmth she could. She smiled at him. "My name is Lena. Helena, really, but I go by Lena."

"Dejan. But my friends call me Dej." He returned the smile. "Thank you for staying."

"It is my pleasure, Dej. I wish I could do more. But as you can see," she gestured around, "the spa is currently overbooked."

He started to laugh. It wasn't funny. None of it was funny, but there was a desperation in it. You could cling a little bit to sanity with laughter in the face of tragedy. Lena laughed, too.

"I'll have to make an appointment to come back some later time," Dej said. "When you're not so busy."

"Please do. We'd love to see you again."

"You have a beautiful smile," he said, his words growing thin. His eyes were growing dark, and his color was getting worse.

"Hey, stop that." Lena said. "You're saying goodbye, and we just met. You're going to be okay."

He laughed again, carefully as every movement caused his stomach to shift and the bandages to grow wetter. "I'm not. I wish I was. But I know what's happening to me." He smiled at her. "I was a med student."

"Are. You **are** a med student. And you're going to graduate and be a wonderful doctor."

"Not going to be a doctor."

"Yes, you are!" Lena insisted.

"No," he chuckled weakly. "Not doctor. I'm studying to be a nurse. Labor and delivery."

"Oh." Lena could feel the tears falling down her cheeks. "Oh, that's wonderful."

"It really is," he agreed. "It lets me make a difference. I help life come into the world. It's..." he trailed off as his head lolled to the side. He watched as frantic teams of people worked on the other injured. "It's not much use here."

"You shouldn't even be here," Lena said. He was too young. He had too much potential. She looked down and could see that blood was pooling beneath him, slowing dripping down, soaking through the cot, and landing in a small puddle on the floor.

"Where else should I be?" He was sincere as he looked at her. "Aegea is my home."

Lena wanted to say what she really thought of that. That home is wherever you wanted it to be. That you didn't have to wed yourself to a piece of land, to a history, to a people. That this war was stupid and a waste of good lives, of lost potential. That his death was a waste.

Nothing she could say would help. So, she kept her mouth shut.

"Besides," he continued, "the revolution means that future births will happen in a free Banika."

"But what if you lose?" Lena couldn't help the words from escaping her mouth.

He chuckled again, but it soon collapsed into a cough. "We won't — we can't lose." He began coughing again. Lena tried to sit him up, to clear his lungs, but he cried out in pain before falling into more coughs. The sound was wet and desperate. She looked for some sort of water, some sort of assistance, but Dej managed to get himself under control. He continued. "We won't lose, Lena. We won't stop fighting. We will be free. Or we will die. Those— those are our only options."

Then he closed his eyes. He seemed to concentrate on his breathing. Lena waited.

When Dej opened his eyes, they were wet with tears, and he looked weaker. "Thank you."

"For what?"

He tried to squeeze her hand, but his fingers barely twitched in her grasp. She squeezed his instead. "You stayed." He closed his eyes as he took another long, slow, wet breath. "I didn't... I didn't want to be alone."

Lena started to cry.

"Please don't," he whispered. "It's okay." His fingers twitched in hers again as he tried to squeeze. He was trying to comfort her.

Lena wrapped her other hand around his and leaned in over his head. She kissed his forehead to hide her tears. "Yeah, it's okay." She touched her forehead to his and stayed like that as his breathing slowed. She could feel as it caught on each intake, hitching on some irregularity inside of him. Then it seemed to sigh as it left his body. She wasn't sure when he lost consciousness, but she knew his last breath. He labored to take in a deep lung full, letting his chest expand and lift. Then, he seemed to hold it in for the longest time. She held hers as if she could hold on to him with it.

Then with surprising ease, he let it go.

And another life was gone too soon.

CHAPTER TWENTY-SIX

Lena refused to leave Dejan's side until they came to take his body away.

Someone discovered them sitting together, silent in the midst of everything else that was going on and found Dejan already going cold. Lena just sat there, holding onto his hand. She knew he was gone, but she couldn't leave him.

He'd asked her to stay.

So she stayed.

She stayed as one of the resistance doctors came over to check his pulse. She stayed as the woman motioned someone over to take him away. She stayed as they covered him with a sheet and carefully lifted his body and moved him to a corner of the room with the others who hadn't made it through the latest bombing.

She stayed.

She was still kneeling beside the empty cot when her crew returned.

It should have been a joyous reunion. She should have run, crying into Gael's arms. She should have kissed Raines for bringing them both back in one piece. She should have tearfully thanked the rest of the rescue team for bringing her men back to her.

But that isn't what happened.

Her boys returned with some cuts and bruises, some new twitches and sensitivities she'd have to learn, shadows in their eyes that she would know better than to ask about, but they came back. And they found Lena, silent, kneeling beside an empty blood-stained cot, Dejan long since removed. Still, she stayed.

Raines and Gael, without a word between them, ignored their own hurts from the past few hours and went to Lena. On either side of her, they helped her to her feet and guided her to a chair. They settled her down and took turns trying to break through, trying to talk through her haze. Raines got her tea and water while Gael sat and held her hand in silence. Only when she was seated again somewhere away from the cot, after tea and silence and time, did she finally recognize the faces in front of her.

Seeing her friends, finally recognizing them, she let herself cry. Tears filled her brown eyes as relief, regret, exhaustion, and grief finally welled up in her. Lena bit her lip as she tried to hold it all in, but Gael swept her into a silent embrace, and she let it all fall out. She clung to him, and he held her, understanding.

They didn't need words. Not yet. It was enough that they were together.

CHAPTER TWENTY-SEVEN

Lena had never felt so relieved to feel flight controls in her hands. The second her hands grasped the throttle and pitch wheel of the stolen Pyrrhen shuttle, her heart steadied. Breathing was easier, her head stilled, and all was right and good. Even these uncalibrated, unfamiliar controls could make things right.

She rested her right hand on the pitch wheel, while her left gently caressed the control screen primary buttons. This was where she belonged. Not hidden underground. Not in the middle of something she couldn't comprehend. She needed precision and control. She needed to translate her desires and needs into subtle movements that would give her exactly the forward motion she wanted. She needed to fly.

Now, she just needed her own ship.

And the plans. She had a promise to keep.

She'd promised Aaron and Senka that if they released her and her crew and helped them get back to their shuttle, she would not rest until she got the plans Gael had hidden on-board *Aspasia*. She would remove those plans from Pyrrhen control by any means necessary, even if it meant destroying her own ship. Beyond that, neither she nor Raines or Gael were willing to commit to what they would do with the plans. The could agree to remove them from Pyrrhen access, but whether that meant bringing them to the Aegean resistance, bringing them back to the Lomasky Corporation, or destroying them completely, none of them knew what they would do.

It was enough for the Black Hand. They had a trade in the meantime.

Lena let Raines and Gael handle the delivery of Karl Talen to the Banikan rebels. The Pyrrhen shuttle pilot would make a decent hostage, and give the Banikans some starting point for return of their own combatants.

Cat was more than ready to get rid of him. "He has done nothing but cry and complain since we got him. You'd think a Pyrrhen hostage would be more, I don't know, stoic. Principled? But he wasn't at all. He was insufferable. Even Chandra got annoyed, and nothing bothers her."

Chandra didn't seem bothered one way or the other, but she looked amused at Cat's complaints.

Raines ignored them both and opted to check out, taking up the empty middle bench and a well-earned nap, while Cat and Chandra sat together on the backbench, their knees touching as they talked quietly.

That left Gael to sit beside Lena in the co-pilot's chair. Bandaged and bruised, he seemed to still be in one piece, but some part of him felt removed, distant.

As she pushed the shuttle away from the surface of Aegea and past the moon's gravitational pull, she tried to swallow past her grief. Cedo's absence sat in her throat, just behind her tongue and weighed down into the upper reaches of her chest, threatening to cut off her air. He should have been here, advocating for his moon's cause, condemning the riots and bombs, agreeing with the bloodshed. Anything. He should have been here.

Lena looked from the empty space on the middle bench to Gael, who sat staring straight ahead as they moved beyond the atmosphere and back out into space. Had anyone told him exactly what happened?

She didn't know if she needed to. Cedo wasn't with them. That was enough. She didn't have to give it voice.

As the moon began to curve away, as the clouds of the northern storms became fractal designs, and the oceans became inkblot puddles beneath them, Lena took a deep breath in through her nose.

Gael's gaze darted toward her, startled at her intake of breath. "Don't."

Lena sputtered. "Wh—what?"

"Don't say it," Gael said, his blackened and bruised eyes already closed. He shook his head and buried his chin in his chest. "I know you think you need to say something, but don't." He took a deep breath and staggered on the exhale. "I've been through enough the past few days, Lee. I don't need to hear that he's gone."

Lena didn't say it, but she watched the tears fall beneath Gael's closed lashes. "I'm sorry," she whispered.

Gael nodded slowly. "He believed in this." Gael opened his eyes and looked at the fading horizon through the front glass of the shuttle. "Cedo believed in this moon." Shadows crossed across his face as they crossed over the oceans below. "Was he wrong?" He gripped the inoperable controls of the copilot's seat. "Was he wrong about this place? Was it worth —" he swept his arm across their view. "Was he worth this broken city? This doomed moon?"

Lena considered it, and Gael granted her the silence she needed. She watched as the city, then the coastline, then the continent drifted from them. They were headed back following the moon's rotation, and the city and coastline obscured far before the horizon did. Beneath them were millions of people. People who believed in what they fought for. People who got caught up in the excitement. People who disagreed, and still more who wanted just to live their lives and ignore the rest. People like Dejan and Senka and poor Mrs. Nenad, executed just days before her sons.

Lena watched the city fade away, and she answered carefully. "I think he was," she struggled to say. She wanted to cry, but she smiled instead, the twitching corners of her mouth fighting her the whole way. "I think he was worth it. I think the whole damned city was worthy of his sacrifice."

Gael didn't look at her. He stared straight ahead at the diminishing curve of the moon. But he nodded and reached to grab her hand on the push controls. He gave her fingers a firm squeeze. "How do we help them? How do we make this right?"

And that was the crux of it. She wasn't doing anything just for Cedo, or Mason, or Dejan or anyone else. She was trying to make things right, to make up for everything she'd failed to do before, to make up for those she failed before. If Aaron was to be believed, she had the plans for a weapon of untold power on her ship. And it was her responsibility to get that weapon to someone that could make use of it, could defend this beleaguered moon, defend all those who might suffer if the wrong people got their hands on it. She had to help bring reinforcements. "First thing is to get back to *Aspasia*. We can't get very far on this shuttle, and we need to recover those plans."

Gael nodded and smiled at her. "It wouldn't hurt to be home if we're going to be in the middle of this."

Lena returned his smile. "We can get some clean clothes. And I wouldn't mind a run." She turned her attention back to her screens. Mostly clear of the moon's gravitational pull, she now only had to clear them of the stronger pull of the planet Pyrrhos below it. They were already far enough away that it wasn't difficult to give just a bit more power to the shuttle's bosonic fields and lightly direct them against the planet's subtle, but undeniable pull.

The directionality of this small shuttle's bosonic field generator was slightly off. And there, just as she guessed, a breach alert. The hull's field containment must be damaged. Even more reason to get back home. While the hull itself would keep out any radiation from the bosonic fields for a time, the constant bombardment would weaken it. Given enough time, they could cause a more material breach and expose them to contamination or empty space.

But that would take weeks. Days, at least.

She thought.

Best to get home.

"So, where is she?"

"*Aspasia?*" Lena asked, searching the unfamiliar screen menus to find some sort of containment analysis or hull field assessment. "According to Evan, she's being held by the Pyrrhens at their Halten Station in a trailing orbit. I figure we can take the—"

"Wait, according to who?" Gael was staring. "I thought you just said Evan."

Lena's eyes grew round. She hadn't told him. Of course, she hadn't told him. She squeezed the bridge of her nose as she avoided Gael's gaze. Why was she embarrassed? It wasn't like it was planned. But there it was. "Evan Thomas was on the *Bayern*. He was sort of their lead scientist. And he found out I was on board, and we sort of..." She waved her hand back and forth in a noncommittal way. She wanted to move on, but she should have known it wouldn't be that easy.

"Sort of what?" Gael demanded. "Lena, that's not something that just happens. You don't just happen to run into your ex-fiancé in the middle of space. Lena, that's more than just a coincidence that can be dismissed by a handwave. How were you not suspicious of that?"

"I'm not an idiot, Gael. Of course, I was suspicious. And it wasn't a coincidence. In fact," she winced as she remembered the conversation with Evan. "I'm the reason Cedo and Vaso got caught at all. The Pyrrhens weren't tracking them. They were tracking me. Us. They were tracking anyone who met with Pierce Mason, and when they saw that it was me, well, he just had to stop us. They weren't after Cedo, at all." She paused and then shook her head. Guilt wouldn't help her right now. "The Pyrrhens know about the datastick. Or rather, they know what's on that 'stick."

"The crytopgraphy?" Gael asked. "Doesn't that render it fairly obsolete? If they know we have the encryption codes, then they'll just change the codes. The Banikans won't be able to use it at all."

"There's something else on there. Blueprints, or equations, or something. It's the plans for a weapon. A weapon of such scale that it could take out a city like Banika in a matter of seconds."

"Like a bomb?" Gael looked skeptical. "We've had big enough bombs to take out entire continents for years. They render the place uninhabitable for generations. What good would that do anyone?"

"No, not like a bomb. Or, yeah, but not like what we've seen before." Lena waved her hand again. "I don't know exactly how it works, but it could wipe out a city and leave no radiation, debris, anything behind. It's a clean bomb. I think."

Gael was quiet for a minute. Then, "And your friend Pierce had the plans for this?"

"Yeah."

"And he got it from the Pyrrhens?"

"Um, maybe not from them?"

Gael let out a breath. "That's a tiny relief. Okay. Who did he get these plans from?"

Lena bit her lip and grimaced. "He... He may have gotten them from the Lomasky Corporation."

The air seemed to rush from the shuttle so suddenly that Lena started to check the oxygen levels.

"The Lomasky Corp?" Gael repeated. "Developing weapons?"

Lena didn't answer. She didn't have any answers. He was right to be skeptical. Lomasky Corp didn't deal in weapons. They were a physitech company. They dedicated themselves to innovations, to travel, to progress: to easier ways of living, not dying.

It all made it that much worse. If there was any chance at all that Evan was telling the truth, that the Aegeans' fears were right, then Lena had a responsibility. She had to stop this thing from getting out into the universe. She had to get her hands on that datastick.

"You do manage to keep things interesting. Kannenberg, you say?" Gael reached down and pulled up the nav screen in front of him. "Gotta get outside the belt, but the station's on an in-swing this time of year, right? Three days if we burn hard?"

"I think I can do it in two and a half," Lena confessed. "We were lucky Chandra was able to get the shuttle fueled right before coming to your sorry rescue." She jabbed him a little too enthusiastically. She didn't want to talk about what happened back on the *Bayern* or the *Scharnhorst*.

"I never doubted you'd come for me." He paused just a beat too long. Then, "And Raines, of course. Okay. We get our ship. Then what?"

"That's a good question. I don't know."

"The original plan was to take the 'stick to Myrto, right?"

"Right," Lena said.

"So Myrto. Then? Does Raines want to head to Levin? The Kyami beaches are incredible, and you could do with a bit of sun."

Myrto and then Levin? If she could still pass the 'stick off, if she could avoid going home to Rien, she'd take it. But it all depended on getting to *Aspasia* first. After could be decided later.

Not ready to think about it, Lena sat back and put her feet up on the edge of his chair. Her course was set for Pyrrhos, and she wouldn't have to make adjustments until they neared the Belt in a few hours. "Did I ever tell you, the Lomaskys are originally from Levin?"

Gael followed her lead and leaned back in his chair, propping his legs up on the edge of her seat. She could feel the side of his boots pressing firmly along the outside edge of her thigh. "I didn't know that. Though I guess I could have guessed. You have some Levinese features. Your eyes mostly."

"I always thought I took after my mom," Lena said. "But definitely got the Levinese hair. Never could get my hair to take a curl."

"Oh the struggles of perfect, sleek, shiny hair," he teased as he tugged on his thick, tight coils.

She rolled her eyes and shoved his feet off her chair. His heavy boots fell with a thud on the metal floor of the shuttle. Raines was suddenly awake, while Cat and Chandra barely looked up from their conversation.

"Everything okay?" Raines said, rolling his head around to work out the kinks of his nap.

"Sorry," Lena laughed. "Didn't mean to wake you. We were just talking about retreating to Levin after we get *Aspasia* back."

Raines moved up behind them, standing right over Gael's shoulder. It was a tight squeeze with so many up in the front of the shuttle. These close quarters were going to wear on them after another day or so.

"That could work," Raines said. "We can dock briefly in the islands after Myrto. Stock up and float a bit. Kyami, maybe? Get some alone time on a beach?" He raised his eyebrows at Lena.

"Just what we were thinking," Lena said.

Raines put a hand on her shoulder. "We'll figure it out. Don't worry." He leaned over to give her a quick peck on the cheek. She welcomed the kiss, but she looked past him to see the frown lingering on Gael's face. It was gone before Raines stood back up, replaced by his normal, easy smile.

"Then that's that," Gael said. "Let's go home." He looked expectantly, hopefully at Lena.

"Yeah," she said. "Let's go home."

CHAPTER TWENTY-EIGHT

Home was under siege.

Even across the far distance from which the crew viewed the shipyard, it was clear that they were not going to board the *Aspasia* any time soon. The Halten Station buzzed with fighters and shuttles. Small carriers shone lights at her ship, and Lena just knew they were crawling around inside her baby.

"They're swarming all around her, the filthy bottom feeders," Lena fumed, her knuckles turning white as she gripped the flight controls. She could hardly bear to think of them infesting her home, rifling through her as they looked for the datastick that was hidden in a secret compartment in the frame of Gael's bed.

The only consolation that Lena had was that if they were still searching the ship, they hadn't yet found the plans.

"They're probably taking her apart, piece by piece," Lena moaned as she blinked away tears. Her home. Her sanctuary. Defiled. Invaded. And there was nothing she could do about it.

"Hey," Gael reached over and squeezed Lena's hand. "It going to be all right. We're going to get her back." He squeezed her again and offered a weak smile as she made eye contact.

"He's right," Raines said as he leaned over her and smirked at the screen. "This isn't over. We're about to make them pay."

Raines, Gael, and Cat stood around her, watching the scene play out in front of them. Each of them had to be as torn up as she was. To varying degrees, *Aspasia* had meant the same thing to each of them: freedom, independence, escape.

For Lena, *Aspasia* was an escape from her notoriety on Rien and a safe space to heal her wounds.

For Raines and Gael, *Aspasia* embodied freedom from the obscurity and boredom of military retirement. After they had both been discharged from the Myrto military, they could have easily retired on their pensions and lived quiet tedious lives. But Raines had other plans. He had bought the *Aspasia* with his inheritance (and a few high-interest loans) and convinced his best friend to set off for adventure and trouble, or at least something (anything) other than retirement. Gael couldn't let Raines have all the fun, so he joined as first mate.

And for Cat, *Aspasia* was an independence she would have never known otherwise. As the sixth child of working-class parents, Cat had no promise of an easy life. She was doomed to toil for some major corporation on Rien, another peon in the capitalist ocean, a worker bee in the hive of mediocrity as she fulfilled her daily duties and went home to a minuscule apartment in the city.

Aspasia allowed her to be something more, to control her own destiny. As the business side of the crew, Cat set up every job, collected payments, and kept them fed and moving from LIB to LIB. She was the backbone of the crew.

Aspasia was more than a ship; she was everything. And there she was. The symbol of their freedom and independence, their home; and she was overrun by the enemy.

Funny how Lena had already come to think in those terms. She had wanted no part of this war, and yet she had been swept into it all the same. First the Pyrrhens had seized her ship, held her prisoner. Then the deaths of Cedo, Vaso, and even Dejan made it more than personal. She was already thinking of the Aegeans and the Pyrrhens as "us" and "them." And seeing "them" surrounding and swarming her ship cemented it. They were the enemy.

And they have to be stopped, thought the illegal pilot of an unarmed Pyrrhen shuttle up against multiple fighter ships and an armed shipyard. Just what did she think she was going to do? Blast through them all with a few handguns and rifles?

"Okay, Smart Guy," Lena said, turning on Raines. She was angry, and she knew it unfair to snap at him, but she couldn't help herself. "Just how do we make them pay? My ship is crawling with Pyrrhens. I have no weapons and no way of getting through undetected. What exactly is your plan?"

Raines smiled. Of course, he had a plan. He always had a plan.

"Look more closely, Lee." He drew up a long-range scan of the shipyard. "What do you see?"

"Nothing," Lena replied automatically. "Nothing but a swarm of Pyrrhens surrounding my ship." The scan showed the large structure of the space station as well as the many ships attached to and drifting around it. Each ship was a point of light, and the screen looked like the trading posts over Maritown on Rien. The sky crawled with constant movement, with small ships that seemed to be transports and shuttles as well as much larger ships floating beyond the edges of the station.

"Wait," Lena said, zooming in on some of the large ships. "Those are far too large for this shipyard. They have nowhere to dock. They're just floating nearby. What are they?"

"My best guess?" Raines ventured. "Warships. The whole place is crawling with military transports, warships, and fighter planes. This is a full-on military operation, and the station is completely overwhelmed. They can't handle all that traffic. Now, the way I see it, we have two options here. Since we have a Pyrrhen shuttle, we can hope this particular stolen ship hasn't been flagged in any way, we use its transponder to dock casually near *Aspasia*, sneak onto the station, hope no one is on board or scanning the area immediately surrounding *Aspasia*, get on board, and then hope no one notices as we, oh so carefully, slip our huge transport out without anyone noticing."

"There's a lot of hope in that scenario," Cat said. "And I'm clean out of that right now, so I hope you have a better idea."

Raines grinned and turned to his first mate. "Gae, we have an outpost near here, yeah?"

Gael raised his eyebrows and cocked his head. "We?"

"Myrto. Our military. We have something stationed in Pyrrhos's trailing orbit. Right?"

"Oh." Gael frowned and then nodded. "Yeah. Survey outpost. Mostly for diplomatic purposes, but some armed transports and a warship or two." He turned to the others. "The Calvais outpost is where our envoys would land, so they had a safe space when negotiating with Pyrrhos after the accords in—"

"No need for a history lesson," Raines interrupted. "No one cares. I just need to know, is it close enough and stocked enough to man any sort of attack?"

Gael's eyes widened, and he crossed his arms in front of him, bringing his shoulders up as his chin dropped to his chest. "Damn. That's how you want to go with this?"

Raines's eyes glittered. He was actually having fun. "Well, we have something they want."

"We do?" Cat asked.

Lena stood, forcing Raines back a step. "No."

"You wanted to get rid of it as soon as possible, right?" He leaned forward, reclaiming his space.

"But giving the datastick to the Myrton military?"

"It's a weapon, isn't it?"

Cat squeezed herself in between them. "What the hell are you talking about?" Cat faced Lena, her back to Raines.

Chandra stepped up beside Cat and faced Raines. "What are you not telling us?"

"Okay, everyone out of the cockpit," Gael said, standing up and forcing the crowd back into the larger areas of the shuttle. "Raines is right. Lena and I received some information that may be of value to Myrto's military."

"And Pyrrhos' and Rien's and every damn government in the three systems!" Lena shook her head. "No. We're not giving a super-weapon to the military."

"Super-weapon?" Cat's voice grew shrill.

Chandra smiled and turned to Cat. "Hey, turns out you were shipping weapons after all."

"You are *not* helping," Cat snapped. "Why is this the first I've heard about this?" She looked to Lena first, and then wheeled on Raines. "We're a crew. You don't keep secrets like this."

"Well," Lena said, glaring over Cat's head at Raines. "There haven't been a whole bunch of opportunities for chit chat lately. Besides," she pointed to her ship, far below them. "It's not like we have our hands on the plans right now. They're down there. On *Aspasia.*"

"And the Myrtons don't know that," Raines said looking at no one but Lena. "Which means we can still use them as a bargaining chip in negotiations to get our ship back." He smiled that dangerous smile again and lifted a single eyebrow. "Do you trust me?"

Everyone's attention shifted to Lena. She hated him for half a second. But she did trust him. If anyone was going to save them, he was. She nodded.

It was all he needed. Raines turned to Gael. "Gae, do you still keep up with Royer?"

CHAPTER TWENTY-NINE

The Myrton military station was certainly more than just a "survey outpost." The structure was practically its own moon with at least three dozen docks for mid-size ships. *Aspasia* could have docked outright without needing to send out shuttles. Inside, the station was just as imposing. The crew were met by a pair of uniformed escorts and guided far into the upper levels of the station. Long, echoing hallways led to cavernous rooms and more hallways. There had been no efforts to soften the industrial edges of the place. Their footsteps pounded out ahead and behind them, surrounding them with a barrage of clanks and clangs. It was all suitably militaristic.

Ironic, if the Myrtons were claiming to maintain a simple diplomatic and scientific outpost this close to Pyrrhos.

The guards pressed them into walking in pairs down the hall, pushing them forward with their authoritative presence. "Um, are we in trouble?" Cat attempted levity, but the fear in her voice made the question real.

"It's fine," Gael reassured, seeming at perfect ease as he walked beside Raines. "Protocol."

Cat whispered to Lena as they followed close—too close—behind their captain and first mate. "Why does that not reassure me?" she whispered.

"Breathe easy, dove," Chandra said, alone at the back. "I've got you." She was still armed with her borrowed guns from the Banikans. The guns looked small, though, compared to those of their escort.

Lena reached over and squeezed Cat's hand. "It's okay. Raines wouldn't have brought us here if it wasn't safe."

Cat accepted the warm assurances from Lena's touch but was still skeptical. "Raines gets us into plenty of trouble, so forgive me if I stay a little on edge."

Lena could see Raines smiling, even if he didn't turn his head to acknowledge them.

The lead soldier pressed a button on a keypad in front of a nondescript door. They all waited a few seconds before a female voice came from a hidden speaker by the door. "How many?"

"Five," the soldier responded. "Two formers, two civilians, and a merc."

"Let them in," the voice responded. "Code 2013."

The soldier keyed in the code, and the door slid open. He entered without a backward glance as if expecting them all to follow without complaint. Gael and Raines obliged immediately. Lena and Cat exchanged a glance and a shrug, respectively, and followed as well. Chandra though required a prod from the back escort, but she, too, followed after a moment.

They were led down a short, slightly less industrial hallway. This one, Lena noted, had at least some soft, insulating paneling along the walls, and an actual ceiling instead of exposed pipes and conduits. *Almost homey. There might be actual human beings here instead of just soldiers*, Lena thought.

Still, she clung to Cat's hand as they followed the soldiers, Raines, and Gael into a well-appointed sitting room.

Instead of the grey and black industrial setting like the rest of what they'd seen, the open space was simple and restrained. The walls were saturated with a rich teal while white accents and minimalist, geometric artwork stood out on the walls. Nestled at the direct center of the room was a seating area with white chairs and tables, all designed with simple lines. A rug of golden yellow stretched out under the chairs, pulling everything together into an intimate moment.

The soldiers stepped back as the group filed into the room. As Chandra stepped in, the soldiers slipped out and closed the door behind them. It slid into place with a decisive click, which was echoed by a secure beep.

"Locked in," Chandra confirmed as she tried to open the door. She smiled as she looked at the rest of them. "Shall we sit? Chairs look comfy." And she sank into one of the white, cushioned seats, her arms spread over the backs of the two on either side of her.

Lena looked to Gael who looked to Raines who shrugged and sat beside Chandra, almost nestling into the crook of her arm. He cocked his head and gave Chandra a satisfied smile. "Maybe they'll have refreshments. I could do with a snack. Anyone else?" He looked at the others and gestured to the chairs.

One by one, they each took a seat. Cat on the other side of Chandra, with Lena directly across Raines, Gael beside her. They only had a moment to stare at each other before the door slid open.

Without thinking, Raines, Gael, and Chandra came to their feet and stood at military ease. Lena and Cat scrambled to their feet a moment later, if only because being the only ones seated at that point felt silly. The former military members all kept their stiff "easy" positions, but Lena and Cat, having had no training in protocol or procedures, or whatever they wanted to call it, both leaned forward to see who came in the door.

Lena was unsurprised to see a stiff-postured colonel enter first, with a steely gaze and near-snarl on her face. Behind her, though, was a civilian. He was nearly as sharply and stiffly attired, but he had an ease about him that clearly marked him as non-military. As the colonel entered and stopped just inside the door, the civilian breezed past her with a big smile.

"You boys come to re-enlist? We could sure use the help!" He clasped his hands with glee as he looked to Raines and Gael, who instantly broke into smiles, though their posture held.

"Oh, you can relax," the man insisted. "Colonel Liviani is just here to make things legitimate in the chain of command." The woman's eyes narrowed, but otherwise, she didn't move. "Oh, please, everyone sit, sit. Refreshments are on the way."

Cat laughed. "Well, thank goodness. We're starved." She sat and pulled Chandra down beside her. The colonel leaned over to the short man and snarled something in his ear. The man listened with a smile on his face, nodding along. Liviani then stood, sneered at the room again, and stalked to the chair on the far side of the room.

The man, unaffected by his colonel, just broke out in a wider smile and walked toward Raines and Gael who rushed over to embrace him. They had an easy familiarity with each other and traded gibes and punches alike before each taking their seats.

"Royer, I'm guessing?" Lena said. Raines and Gael wouldn't have such an easy rapport with just anyone.

"Oh, sorry," Raines said, still smiling like a fool. "Lena, Cat, everyone, this is Jules Royer. We sort of worked together when we served Myrto."

"Reunions for everyone this trip," Chandra muttered loud enough for everyone to hear.

"The universe is an awfully small place sometimes," Lena said in full voice. Then she smiled at Royer. "So, you're the famous engineer we've heard so much about. You're taller than I thought you'd be."

"Aw, you guys talk about me?" He beamed at Gael and Raines.

"I've never said anything good," Raines insisted.

"I'm sure. The four of us never had anything but awful times in the trenches, after all," Royer joked.

"Four?" Cat asked. "Who's the fourth?"

The tone lightened only slightly as the three men's goofy grins faded into nostalgic, if sad, smiles.

"Lucas," Gael answered. "Better than the three of us combined."

Raines and Royer nodded.

Lena knew the story. His name was Lucas Palomer. He and Gael and Raines had known each other before the wars in Myrto.

It was Lucas who convinced Raines and Gael to sign up for the Myrton military. He joined the military, trying to impress a girl and had turned to his friends to back him up. Raines and Gael had never entertained the idea of military service, but with their best friend involved, there had been little other choice. Someone had to keep him out of trouble, and to do so, they would have to be within arms' reach.

It wasn't such a far stretch for Raines and Gael to join the military, either. Raines had always been hot-headed, and he had a family history of service. Gael had needed the service to excuse the loans that had enabled him to join the charter school where he'd met Raines and Lucas in the first place. A short military engagement over territorial disputes with Naftal seemed the perfect solution for their needs. Lucas would get the girl—er, girls; Raines would justify his excessive braggadocio, and Gael would enter his future career debt-free.

They all met Royer in their first month of training. He was the junior engineer assigned to training them on the advanced propulsion weaponry. Poor Royer's job was to teach them how to aim and fire weapons that mostly relied on advanced targeting technology and rendered soldiers moot. Even Royer thought his job fairly pointless.

But it was his training that saved their lives in a small village outside of Platons. The Naftish had established a settlement there, and they were attempting to spread inward through the continent toward a major Myrton settlement. The unit Raines, Gael, and Lucas belonged to was commissioned with a full evacuation of civilians in the area. All was going well in their defense of the local population, when an EMP took out their targeting technology, leaving them open to an ambush.

Thankfully, Lucas and Gael had remembered the seemingly pointless manual weapons training Royer had given them, and they covered Raines while he got the last of the civilians to safety. When they returned to camp without a single casualty, they had all three ambushed Royer with contraband champagne, and the group were inseparable until the end.

Lena had heard all the stories. Of Royer keeping watch while the other three rerouted the comms feeds to bring the finals of the Myrton Cup to every bunk in camp. Of Gael trying in vain to keep Raines and Lucas from sneaking Royer out for his first taste of blue wine in a nearby tavern. Of Lucas smuggling in Naftish cigars after a long week of ditch-digging and latrine duty. Of Royer finding a way to keep them off such duty for the rest of the engagement. They had never found out how Royer managed that one; he wasn't high up enough to have access to assignments, but still he had shifted things around enough that not a single one of them had ever dug another latrine ditch.

Lucas was ever the mastermind. He had schemes, and he found ways to achieve them, no matter what the obstacles. "Rules are meant to be broken," he always said. For that, Lena could respect him.

And then, in the last days of the war, as the Naftish took the last holdings of Harnier and Myrto worked out a deal to relinquish claims to the outer moons of the star system, Lucas was shot through the stomach in a small skirmish and bled out in Raines's arms while Gael held the Naftish off from their position.

That was the end of the war and their group. While Royer accepted a high paying civilian job with the Myrton military, Raines and Gael accepted honorable discharges and parted ways. Then a few years later, Raines called Gael up and asked him to join him running transport between the systems. He had used an unexpected inheritance combined with a few high-interest loans to purchase a ship. All he needed was for Gael to join the team.

Gael had been only too happy to jump on board. He knew how much Raines needed to get away from everything on Myrto that reminded him of Lucas. And Gael was looking for an escape of his own. Heading out with Raines, striking out for the stars and the many planets of the systems he'd never had a chance to see, well, it sounded like a better idea than sticking around home.

This may have been the first time all three were back together after Lucas died. They were all happy to trade war-stories.

"But of course, Raines had been out on patrol all day, had just arrived back, sweating his ass off and dead tired," Royer was saying. "So, the sirens are going off, Gael is yelling for him to get out of there or he'd die. And he just comes to the door, calm as you please and yells, 'Fuck all of you. I'm dying in the air conditioning.' And just slams the door!"

Raines laughed with the rest of them. "I hadn't had any sleep in over thirty-something hours. At that point, getting hit by a missile seemed the better option. At least I'd be comfortable when I blew up!"

The colonel loudly cleared her throat, and every eye turned to her. "Are we quite done?" Colonel Liviani's lips were pursed, her cheeks inflamed, and her eyes narrowed.

"Thank you," Chandra whispered audibly. Cat gave her a look, but she merely shrugged and swept her hand to offer the colonel the floor.

The colonel stood to take command of the room. "The reason you are all here is not as a friendly rendezvous, though the fact that you are familiar with one of our employees gives us a much more compatible starting point for negotiations."

Lena wasn't sure how such negotiations like this usually went, but she was sure that signposting one of your strategies wasn't necessarily the best idea. Unless it was the weakest of your assets.

This might not go so well.

"From your initial message, Mr. Raines, I am led to understand you want something from us, and you are willing to exchange important information on the recent Pyrrhen military actions and possible cryptography for their communications." Raines nodded, and the colonel continued. "While we are certainly eager to receive any information you may have for us, we are naturally reticent to offer anything substantial in trade. We are in a precarious place here near the Halten Station, and are reluctant to take any actions that might undermine our delicate position with our system's sovereign planets and moons."

"We haven't even asked you for anything yet," Cat pointed out. "How can you shoot us down without knowing what we want?"

The colonel gave a half-smile. "You are offering us information in exchange for a favor. You came to this outpost specifically, avoiding Pyrrhos and her outposts and satellites which are in abundance here, despite the fact that you arrived on a Pyrrhen military shuttle. That means that the shuttle is most likely stolen, and you are attempting to skirt their surveillance over this area. You could need supplies or medical assistance, but if that were the case, your captain would not have asked for a meeting with the highest-ranking officer on this ship willing to meet with him. That means you want something that only I can authorize, which means you want troops of some sort to either escort you somewhere I imagine you are not supposed to be, or you want to engage in hostilities of some sort, which you are unable to accomplish on an unarmed convoy shuttle. If that is the case, then I can go ahead and tell you that we are unable to help. Any aggressive movement from us in this quadrant could signify greater things to the Pyrrhen government than our government is willing to signify at this time."

Lena was impressed by her assessment of the situation, but Raines just scoffed. "So, you have to stay quiet unless you want to risk an international incident."

"In rough terms, yes," the colonel agreed. "Our outpost is ostensibly here only for diplomatic and scientific purposes, and any aggressive movements would undermine our purpose and any inroads we have made in the past several years with the Pyrrhen government. I am sure I don't need to explain how difficult it has been to establish even a rudimentary diplomatic relationship with the Pyrrhens after we struck an alliance with Judan in the Pandia System. Things here are too unstable for us to move against them or be seen to aid their enemies in any way. We must remain neutral."

Gael leaned forward. "That isn't an option. Forgive me, Colonel ... er, what was your name again?"

"Liviani. Colonel Renee Liviani," she replied. "And I do not believe you are in any place to tell me my options, Captain Renard."

Gael straightened. "Former captain. And forgive the impertinence, Colonel, but you don't understand the situation."

"I beg your pardon?" The colonel narrowed her gaze. Lena felt sure she would have withered under it, but Gael stood firm.

"You are afraid that movement by your troops will instigate further conflict with Pyrrhos. But I'm telling you, it's too late. You're in conflict."

"Our diplomatic ties are strong, Mister Renard." She leaned hard on the change of address.

"No, they aren't," he replied calmly, not rising to her bait. "You have no fewer than five warships in the vicinity of this outpost, and your station is outfitted to equip more than a dozen more. You claim to be diplomatic, but your entire operation is run by military personnel. You may have a defensive posture here so close to Pyrrhos herself, but this station is clearly designed to be an operations post for any military engagements against Pyrrhos. With military activity increasing between Pyrrhos and her moons, you no doubt have more warships on the way here. So, forgive me if we don't buy into your claims of pacifism."

Liviani smirked. "As you say, our posture is defensive. We pose no threat to Pyrrhos, and we will not compromise our standing by making an aggressive move. As far as we are concerned, recent activities are nothing more than a territorial dispute with regards to Pyrrhos and her moons. The Pyrrhens are no threat to us so long as they are merely reclaiming Aegea and Aella. It is a local issue. We will tend to our own interests."

"But Aegea is your ally!" Lena said. "Are you not obligated to help her defend her people?"

"Our original alliance, Ms. Lomasky, is with Judan, a whole system away. It is only their alliance with Aegea that gives us any interest in this mess in the first place. Judan does not seem interested in mobilizing in this system over territorial disputes. And further, their alliance, and by extension, our alliance, is only with Aegea's government, not her people. All our reports indicate that the government is acceding to Pyrrhen actions on her surface while they sort out their political disagreements. Let them do what they wish. We are under no obligation but to defend any but our own."

Gael sank back, defeated.

"Permission to speak?" Unexpectedly, Chandra was sitting upright and watching the colonel with a level gaze.

"Granted," Liviani said.

Chandra stood in one fluid motion, standing at ease before the colonel. She held her head erect, with her hands clasped behind her back, and her steely brown eyes narrowed directly at Liviani as she delivered her statement. "Ma'am, forgive my impertinence, but you are either stupid or lying. And given your rank and otherwise intelligent demeanor, I am inclined to believe you are lying. Your people are directly threatened by any aggressive actions by Pyrrhos against her moons, given your planet's proximity to the inner orbits of this system. Plus, your government has recently taken very blatant and obvious steps to highlight your alliance with Judan in obviously-meant-to-be intercepted correspondences, despite that empire's rare entrance into this system, and frequent missives cite their own alliance with Aegea and Aella. Your government's insecurity in those alliances means you want assurances that if you make a move, Judan will be able and willing to defend that position. It currently seems unlikely, unless Judan has unreported ships lurking on the outskirts of the system. We've checked. They haven't been here in months. In addition, as my employer has noted, in the past week you personally have already mobilized several warships to this outpost which provides optimal staging for any military engagement in this area. In addition to the five war carriers, you have two destroyers lurking in the Bellows Belt, at least a dozen frigates at a secret base not a day from here, and a squadron of fighters masquerading as transports doing frequent manual surveys inside the Belt. More than that, in the past three days your people, on just the other side of the Belt, have released an additional dozen carriers with some 400 hundred fighters each on board, and they are headed in this immediate direction with another three-headed toward Pyrrhos."

Lena gaped at the woman Raines had hired. Lena had been scanning comms for three days and didn't know any of this. How could Chandra, who had not so much as touched a terminal or access point in nearly a week, know the inner workings of the Myrton deployment directives?

Still, the information seemed to be accurate. The color drained from Liviani's face, and the left corner of her lip began to twitch upward. "The Myrton government will not engage this conflict," she repeated uselessly, "until its other players regretfully decide to engage us. And to suggest otherwise is to imply aggression on our part. A claim that is utterly untrue."

"I beg your pardon, Colonel," Chandra smiled, "but an act of aggressive defense at this stage is indistinguishable from an act of offense."

"Especially in the paranoid eyes of the Pyrrhen government," Raines piped up from his seat. He spoke confidently, but at a direct look from Liviani, he quickly shut his mouth again.

"In the eyes of anyone, really," Chandra corrected, undeterred. She kept her gaze on the Colonel. "Your increased presence here makes you a part of the war, whether you attack first or not. You and your outpost are a threat to Pyrrhos's security, and whether Judan gets involved or not, as Judan's ally, you are obligated to defend Aegea and Aella if they are threatened. The only question is whether you will act to your benefit now while you have the advantage, or will you wait until Pyrrhos brings the fight to you?"

The room was silent. Everyone held their breath as the Colonel continued to glare at Chandra. The dark-eyed mercenary simply stood there, letting the moment extend as long as it needed to.

The Colonel stood, suddenly, her chair skidding back behind her. Lena was proud of herself for not jumping, but she saw Cat grab for Chandra's hand.

No one else moved.

The edge of Liviani's lips twitched in a wry smile. "You've got us well-mapped, then?"

Chandra smiled herself. "Yes, ma'am. Warships and fighters to a one."

"Director Fournier?"

"He's the one."

Liviani chuckled then, a sound that Lena would never describe as warm or amused. "Yoddha defends its name, then. I hadn't realized you had declared either way. I really hope your company is on the right side."

"We're on the side of whoever pays, ma'am," Chandra said.

Liviani's smile got wider. "Then why are you with this lot?"

Chandra's own smile dropped away to Liviani's further amusement.

The Colonel laughed again. "All right. Keep that secret. We might be able to help you. But we cannot be seen to make the first aggressive move. I trust you have a way around that?"

Raines spoke up. "We do."

"Very well," Liviani said, turning toward the door. "Let Royer here know what's what, and we'll do what we can. And I want that intel you promised immediately." With that, Colonel Liviani turned on her heel and marched from the room. The door slid shut behind her with a whir and a decisive click before most of them could release the breath that they had all collectively been holding.

Cat turned on Chandra. "Yoddha?! You're a Yoddhan mercenary?"

Lena was surprised as well. Though it explained a lot about Chandra's access to intel and incredible dedication to secrecy, she hadn't thought Raines could afford to buy a mercenary from the most elite company of warriors, soldiers, and assassins for hire.

"I am," Chandra said softly, steadily holding Cat's gaze. For the first time, Lena thought she saw a chink in the merc's armor.

The Yoddha company was notorious for their ruthless methods and their nondiscriminatory contracts. If you had the money, Yoddha agents would kill, steal, and lie for you across the galaxy, often in that order. Based out of Bharat on the dark side of Judan's second moon Ganara, they had no allegiances to anyone—not to their own Bhatan government, not Judan, not anyone. They were company people through and through until they were hired out. Then, once under contract, they were utterly and completely devoted to the letter of their contract until it was either filled, they were killed, or the money ran out, often in that order.

The question Lena had was where the money had come from to hire them in the first place. Raines wasn't exactly flush.

"It was the right call. Chan's been invaluable to us," Raines said.

"But they're evil! The whole company is full of soulless monsters!" Cat shouted at him.

"I am inclined to take offense," Chandra said softly. "Some of our agents are less rigidly moralistic than others, but more of us have stricter codes than any of your average traders, transporters, or smugglers." She looked pointedly at Cat. "We have skills that are needed in extreme circumstances. And you've not complained about how we've used them on this trip so far, dove."

Cat had the good sense to blush and look ashamed, but not enough sense to stop talking. "But your contracts ..."

"Are signed at our own discretion," Chandra said. "Agents choose their own assignments. And we are careful about the ones we dedicate ourselves to. Some of our agents don't like to kill, or they are at least more particular about who they put down in the line of duty."

"And others?" Cat pushed.

"Would break the necks of those who continue to ask questions."

With a small whimper, Cat shut up and sank back down into her chair. Chandra turned to Royer who was grinning; he'd obviously enjoyed the show. "If we deliver the aggression you require, can your people deliver an appropriate response?"

"You seem to know our formations better than I do. You tell me?" Royer joked.

Chandra did not smile.

"She asked you a question," Gael said sadly, still seated.

"Yeah, we can deliver a response." Royer looked to Raines for some backup, but he just shrugged.

Chandra turned to Raines and Gael. "One of you needs to borrow a pilot and a transport shuttle, nothing official, something that could be easily overlooked and can dock at the shipyards. So, no diplomatic vehicles. A supply shuttle of some sort should work. And it needs to have a walk-out. Bring your suits."

"Wait, I can fly a transport shuttle," Lena said. "Why do they need another pilot?"

"Because you are coming with me," Chandra said. "We have an attack to launch."

CHAPTER THIRTY

"Any resistance?" Chandra was looming over Lena's shoulder as they neared the Halten docks. Lena could feel hot breath on the back of her neck.

"Back off," Lena said calmly, despite her desire to scream at the woman. "If they try to stop us, I promise you'll know."

"Nayar," Gael said calmly from his spot on the bench behind them. "She's got this."

They were on the stolen Pyrrhen shuttle again, with its executive starkness and stiff, unyielding controls. Lena couldn't wait until she was back on her own bridge with her own beautifully delicate, responsive controls. *Aspasia* listened to her as much as she listened to the ship. They had a relationship, an understanding, and every minute she piloted this inferior machine, she died a little inside. It was time to go home.

But that wasn't where she was headed, apparently. Not yet.

Chandra begrudgingly sank back into the co-pilot seat, which was not nearly far enough away for Lena.

"Okay," Lena said, pulling up a side screen that showed the available ports along the docks' small transport section. "We have a few options. Along here," she indicated a small portion of the docks, "we have several spots available for civilian transports. It's only a few landings away from the *Aspasia*, which is right here. But that's not—"

"That's not where we're going," Chandra interrupted.

"That's not where we're going," Lena finished, an edge creeping into her voice. "Thank you. I'm aware. However, it is the least patrolled area of the docks with only a few security on each landing. So, it's the place we can most likely slip in unnoticed, and our manifest won't be reviewed until we're gone again."

"We need to be closer to the fighters, though," Chandra said, leaning over and taking control of the screen. She navigated right to the docks where the military ships were located. Clearly, she knew the Halten docks better than Lena did. Probably better than the soldiers who manned it did, given Yoddha's reputation. Lena bristled but held her tongue. "Put in here. This is a military transport and will have pre-clearance."

"Unless it's been revoked," Lena said.

"It hasn't."

"How can you be so sure? We made quite an exit from the *Scharnhorst.* I would be shocked if they hadn't managed to flag this shuttle by now. It's been a few days."

"Then prepare to be shocked. They have not flagged any ships or shuttles from the *Scharnhorst.*"

Lena was exasperated. "How do you even know that?"

Chandra just smirked. "I am a professional, Ms. Lomasky. I confirmed every part of this plan before we departed the Myrton outpost."

"How?!" Lena exclaimed. "You haven't touched a screen in days. How do you possibly know more about the system than anyone else?"

Chandra ignored her and continued to monopolize the screen in front of them. Lena turned to Gael for backup. He gave a one-shoulder shrug. He didn't seem bothered. "If it's accurate information, then why question how she got it?"

"Because it doesn't make sense." Lena said. "It's like she has a computer in her head that's feeding her information about the whole damned three systems at regular intervals."

"I do," Chandra confirmed, not bothering to look up. "Here." She pointed to a section of the docks, highlighting a specific port and bringing up the docking commands. "Right here. It's only one landing down from the fighter we need, and there's a gap in the scheduling that will allow us time to commandeer one."

"That's not possible," Lena said.

"I assure you, the schedule has enough of a gap between pilots and the patrol rotation—"

"Not that! A computer in your head. You can't have anything like that. The technology doesn't exist."

"It does," Chandra said, undisturbed by Lena's outbursts. "Yoddha agents have been using it for years."

"How has no one ever heard of it then? You can't just keep something that technologically advanced secret from the rest of the systems."

"We can," Chandra said, leveling her gaze. "The same way your company kept secret their advances in bosonic weapons and gravity bombs."

"Bitch." Lena regretted it the second it slipped out of her mouth, but she wasn't about to reel it back. She meant it. She meant a lot worse, but Chandra was still armed, and Lena, well, wasn't.

"It's not like it is a well-kept secret," Chandra continued, unwavering. "Well, except from you, apparently. Let's see, the Aegeans know the weapon exists, the Pyrrhens know, the Rienens who commissioned it, the Myrtons most likely."

"Great! The whole damn universe knows my family trades in death. Do they all know that I've got the plans, too, or is that still at least partly a secret?"

"Enough know. Which is why we've got to get your ship back."

"Why? So, you can get your hands on it and sell it to your company? I'm sure Yoddha would love to wield power like that."

Chandra still seemed unaffected by Lena's words. "We have no interest in wiping out entire cities or their populations. Should one of our clients ask us to obtain the plans, build the weapon, and use it, then our agents will face the choice of whether to assist in such an endeavor and will establish a fee for such services at that time. Until then, it pays to know where the plans are, and how we can secure them should it become, as you say, lucrative."

"You are disgusting," Lena said.

Finally. Something seemed to affect her. Chandra's eyes narrowed, and her nostrils flared as her lip curled slightly. Then she frowned before smirking. It all happened so quickly, Lena couldn't believe she'd seen so much emotion pass over the merc's face.

"My hands have not been dirtied by this affair, Ms. Lomasky, whereas you seem to have quite a bit of blood on yours. Your family developed this weapon with help from your childhood sweetheart and your very own fiancé. You managed to obtain these plans and then lose them when you lost your ship to Pyrrhen control. Your old friend and your own crewmate were both executed in an attempt to draw you out to locate the plans. And your so-called 'escape' on the *Scharnhorst* cost multiple innocent lives, even though the whole affair was orchestrated by Pyrrhen higher-ups to let you get away and lead them to the plans. So please tell me how disgusting I am again because you seem to have an interesting perspective on morality."

Everything stopped, and the universe fell through a hole in Lena's stomach as she pieced together all Chandra had said. "What?" Lena whispered.

Chandra sighed, then, shaking her head. "You are a sad, lost little girl, and I'm doing all I can to help you clean up the mess you've made. But unless you wake up and start paying attention, you're going to ruin the lives of everyone you've ever met."

"Enough." Gael stood, then, and Chandra looked up expectantly. "You've made your point, Nayar."

Chandra opened her mouth to say something, but at a look from Gael, she stopped and nodded.

"No," Lena said. "No, I want to know. What do you mean the escape from the *Scharnhorst* was orchestrated?"

Chandra looked to Gael for permission. "May I?"

Gael closed his eyes and hung his head. "She has a right to know." He sat down and refused to look at Lena.

"Know what? Gael? What do you know?"

"I didn't know for sure. Or I didn't until Chandra just confirmed. But I suspected."

"What?" Lena pleaded. She looked from Gael to Chandra and back again. Chandra simply watched Gael. "Dammit. This shuttle will not move until I get some answers. Now, somebody start talking."

Gael nodded, then, and Chandra finally acknowledged Lena. "Your fiancé planned the whole escape. You and the plans were the entire reason *Aspasia* was stopped. The capture of Cedo and Vaso Nenad were just a lucky coincidence for the Pyrrhens. You were the original target."

"I know," Lena said, her eyes filled with angry tears. "I know that. Evan basically told me that himself. He thought I might know something about the plans."

"He wanted the blueprints," Chandra confirmed, "and he knew outright that you had them. He assumed you would have saved them to your ship's network, or at least stored them in an obvious place. When the Pyrrhens didn't find them immediately, they arranged for you to lead them to their location. Your fiancé—"

"Ex," Lena said. She couldn't stand to hear Evan called that anymore.

"Your fiancé," Chandra continued, "orchestrated an escape opportunity for you aboard the *Scharnhorst*. You were supposed to take advantage of the chaos of the alleged attack, escape directly back to your ship on this stolen and monitored shuttle, and deliver the plans to the Pyrrhens."

"But the warship, I saw it attack," she protested.

"We all saw what we were meant to see. A warship attacking the *Scharnhorst*. But there were no warships stationed there beyond the

Pyrrhens' own. The Myrtons weren't involved. Colonel Liviani has already confirmed that they have not moved against the Pyrrhens, nor do they plan to. It was staged."

Staged? But that ship had been shooting at them. She'd seen it. The flashes. The explosions. There was even damage to this very shuttle. Wasn't there?

She checked the ship status screens. The hull damage alerts. They were all there on the primary screen. Look deeper. Lena pulled up the raw data reports, looking for evidence. Oxygen, containment, radiation. Nothing. Everything was normal. Nothing wrong with the field containment. No fluctuations in the radiation. No breach.

Lena couldn't believe she had been so stupid.

And Evan was behind it all. Her Evan. Who had known about the weapon from the start. He had used her and manipulated her to get to the plans. He had seized her ship to get at them. And he had fed Cedo to a hungry mob below. He had killed her Cedo, used his and his brother's deaths to launch a war, and all to get his hands on the damned weapon. He had been prepared to offer up Gael and anyone else connected to her just to get at these plans. She had been such a fool. She had played right into his hands every step of the way.

She felt fire beneath the tiny capillaries of her skin and just needed a direction to point herself. "Then why are we doing exactly what they want, now?" Lena demanded. "We're headed right into their trap. We're in their shuttle, heading straight to them."

Chandra smiled. "But we're not going to your ship, or to the plans. We're going to get this war properly started."

CHAPTER THIRTY-ONE

"Are you sure you can do this?" Gael asked Lena as they pulled into the port Chandra had chosen.

Chandra had been right about the security. With their Pyrrhen military shuttle's transponder, plus the likely orders from Evan to stand down and let them approach *Aspasia*, no one tried to impede their docking. They were cleared instantly and without question to dock on the military side of the shipyard, on the same level but several dozen landings away from *Aspasia*.

Lena was going to be sorry to disappoint the welcoming crew no doubt waiting for them aboard her beloved ship. Truth be told, she wouldn't have minded trading a few barbs and shots with Evan.

Oh well. At least she wouldn't have to mop up that particular mess.

"Yeah," Lena said with more confidence than she felt. "I can do it."

"I can take point on this, you know. I can do it for you." Gael reached a hand to her shoulder.

Chandra rolled her eyes. "No, you can't. I need you on cover with me. You've got the aim and experience. She'll be fine. A toddler could handle those guns, as long as she doesn't choke."

Lena clenched her teeth as she shrugged off the warmth of Gael's touch. "I won't miss."

"Reassuring," Chandra snorted. "Ease up on the controls, there. We've docked." Lena released the controls she hadn't realized she'd been clutching. She was starting to hope Chandra would fall out an airlock. Or maybe Lena could use the mercenary as a body shield. Make her earn her pay. Chandra continued: "Just see that you get out as soon as you pull the trigger. Don't wait to see if you made contact. A blast of that size should stir up all the fight we need."

As the bay doors of their port fell shut and the bay repressurized, a ding sounded in the shuttle, and the All Clear light came on just in view of the shuttle's window. "All clear," Lena said, though she knew they had all seen the light.

This was it. There was no going back now.

Chandra's face lit up. She'd never seen the mercenary so spirited. Either she truly lived for her job, or she loved the adrenaline of rushing headfirst into danger.

Lena figured it was the latter.

"You know where you're going," Chandra said as she stood, adjusting the guns holstered beneath her arms. If she needed to draw either of those weapons, though, Lena knew that the mission would have failed. "You know what hinges on your success and what results from your failure." She trained her eyes on Lena. "You know what you have to do."

Lena did. With everything she had learned about her family, about her past, about herself, she knew exactly what she had to do.

"Good luck," she said, as Chandra smirked and disappeared out the open shuttle door.

Gael stood a beat longer evaluating Lena, who sat there, staring at him evenly, gathering her resolve. Whatever he sought in her eyes, he apparently found, because he leaned forward and kissed her gently on the mouth.

She hadn't expected that. It was a Raines move, but totally unexpected from Gael. She almost flinched away, but she knew what he was trying to communicate. He wasn't a man of many words. She knew what it took for him to lean in like that, to bridge the unspoken gap between them. He was saying goodbye. In case. In case they failed. In case they succeeded. Either way, it might be his last chance. She leaned into him as well.

She could feel his surprise as she deepened the kiss. She didn't mean him to read more into it, but in that moment, she didn't care if he did. He had stood there behind her. Always there. Always at her side. No matter what happened. No matter what was revealed about her or her mistakes or what she had cost them. He was there, and she was thankful.

So, she kissed him back.

He was the one who eventually pulled back. He looked at her with hazy eyes and a gentle smile. "Thank you."

"For what? A kiss?"

"No. For coming back for me," Gael said. "For pushing forward. For ... for what you're about to do."

Lena turned away from him and grabbed her pack. It held a few essential supplies they had requisitioned from the Myrtons—food, water, poison pills—in case she didn't make it back. She also activated the bomb they had planted underneath her seat. It was enough to take out the entire wing of the docks where they were stationed and take out any fighter ships and transports in port when it went off.

Lena had given them a vote of confidence. In activating the bomb, she'd given them all exactly twenty minutes to execute their plan. It should be enough.

"I'm doing exactly what I have to do. And so are you," Lena said. She had no illusions. As much as she could, she was going to take care of things. She only hoped she wasn't destroying any hope of a future as she severed ties with her past.

Gael seemed to understand that Lena didn't have any more to say. He certainly understood that their countdown had begun. They had a job to do. He turned around and grabbed his own pack from the bench behind him and headed for the door. He stopped and looked back one last time.

"Good luck, Helena Lomasky." Funny. In his mouth, her full name didn't seem so bad. "You're one of the good ones."

And with that, he was gone to his own mission.

Lena spared herself a full ten seconds alone to just breathe.

She could do this. She was the best pilot she knew. She could thread a luxury liner through an asteroid belt. She could certainly navigate the multiple branches of a shipyard with a single fighter. She could get to *Aspasia* before the Pyrrhens even knew what was headed their way.

And then, she would blow them away. Plans and all.

CHAPTER THIRTY-TWO

Lena ran down the hallway to the fighter ship Chandra had indicated on the map. Three down on the left. A single-pilot fighter with long-range ballistics. Designed to deliver large missiles and heavy explosives over extensive spaces with incredible accuracy while the pilot of the craft watched from a safe distance and got away clean.

Today, she would not be delivering anything at an extensive distance. She'd be up close and personal.

Still, Lena didn't hesitate. She slipped aboard her bird and closed her flight cage.

She should have a flight suit. If anything went wrong, she had no alternative source of air.

No room for error.

She switched a toggle and felt the air pressure change as she strapped herself in. No artificial gravity here. Just a single pod for a single passenger. The harness was a bit loose, so she adjusted as she let the bird power-up.

The hum of electronics and the glow of the control screen brought her a tiny bit of comfort. She'd flown a few of these when she was in training. The tight confines, the solitude, the oneness of her and the ship. It made her feel secure in her purpose.

Fifteen minutes.

She could do this.

She followed the menu on the screen to the launch sequence. Streamlined launch tubes on a ship this big. Minimal clearance needed because the launch trajectories did not cross in any way.

There would, of course, be some safety mechanisms to prevent her leaving the tubes, but she could assume that they would not be re-engaged before she could override and exit.

Lena submitted a request to the auto-launcher at the same time she triggered the gate open. Move fast. Prevent response.

She hated tube launches. Under normal protocols, the fighter would be pulled out through the tube with a mechanical apparatus, designed to slingshot her out in a straight line. It was supposed to both save initial propellant fuel as the fighter fought the artificial gravity of the station, but it also helped make sure that concurrent launches were controlled by the flight deck manager. No autonomy meant little room for screwups.

She would ignore all the protocols. She had no need to preserve fuel, and she didn't think any fighters would be launching immediately beyond the ones that she, Gael, and Chandra were stealing.

So long as the tube door opened by the time she got to the end, the launch sequence was irrelevant to her.

She pulled up the field screens for manual pilot, disengaged the launch hook, and made sure her wheels were down. She would need them to help get some speed out of the tube. She would be relying on friction for at least a few seconds before she got beyond the grav field of the docks, and that would take as much speed as she could generate out the elongated tube.

It was crude, and much trickier piloting than she was used to.

As soon as she received confirmation the tube was clear, she powered up the engines. It took less than a minute, but those seconds were agonizing as she imagined the timer on her bomb ticking away. Propellant fuel and chehon alike cycled through her plane's engines, as she confirmed her flight controls. The propellant engine heated up to degrees that would burn through her delicate skin as the grav engines irradiated the chehon, exciting the gravitons while holding them in reserve. She'd use them soon enough.

First, she punched the propellants, expelling hot exhaust out her back and surging her craft forward out the tube. She didn't need to steer. Just hold it steady. Forward. Onward. Outward. And into space she shot.

As soon as she cleared the tube, she flipped off the propellants. She didn't think she'd need the fuel, but best keep the option.

She engaged the chehon, flipping a toggle to switch the control systems. From here, it was instinct as she tugged on the edge of the shipyard to her left. It was massive enough to allow her to navigate around and through it. A push here, a tug there, and she was soon whipping back past the military sections of the yards at speeds that would have been unseemly in a high gravitational field. But here, just outside the pull of the artificial gravity of the Halten yards, she was free to move about as she needed.

She put as much space between her and the military section as she could and then headed straight for the civilian docks. Straight for *Aspasia*.

There. There she was. Her beautiful ship.

Her hull was scarred and scraped from the usual debris of close-body dockings. Lena hadn't had a chance to have her buffed in the past year. She had meant to dock her and have a full detailing when she met up with Clara for their spa date in Cygnus. She wondered if she'd ever see Clara again.

And *Aspasia*. Lena might never restore her to her beautiful gleaming self. She'd not have the chance to treat her ship the way she deserved.

Aspasia really was beautiful, no matter what anyone said. The clean lines of her sleek body, like a bird about to take flight. Her bridge lifted with a haughty tilt. Even with her gangway extended out to the Pyrrhen shipyard, she looked composed, capable. She wasn't grand or elegant or fancy by any stretch. But she was strong. She was steady. She was enough.

Lena approached quickly. She was close enough to see in through the bridge, to see whoever skulked about inside.

She couldn't bear to look.

She circled once.

Twice.

On the third pass, she targeted the gangway, the point that connected her home to the enemy, and she let her missile fire.

Before she could even see if she made contact, Lena had circled past and directed herself away from the shipyards, back toward the Myrton outpost.

She couldn't see, couldn't hear, couldn't feel the impact of the blast as it severed her home from the Halten shipyards and sent *Aspasia* hurtling out to empty space, leaving her insides and whoever was in there open to the vacuum of space.

She couldn't see the blast moments later as her bomb exploded through the military wing of the Halten shipyards and destroyed ships and supplies and killed dozens, maybe hundreds of soldiers and civilians stationed throughout.

She couldn't know how many of the remaining fighter ships immediately deployed after her fighter or the two stolen fighters that followed her, but she knew it would be the majority of the ships still capable of flight.

She did know that Gael and Chandra in the two fighters on her flank would follow her and that as they approached the Myrton outpost, her crew would open fire on the Myrtons. Even as they themselves were fired upon by the Pyrrhens behind them. She knew that the Myrtons would rationally assume the blasts that were shot in their direction were all from Pyrrhen forces.

And that would be enough for Myrto to mount her much-awaited aggressive defense.

The war had spread to the edges of the Sinopean system.

CHAPTER THIRTY-THREE

It took several hours for Lena and the others to rendezvous on the Myrton warship *Bretagne* just beyond the outpost. It was hidden amongst a field of debris on the edge of the Bellows' Belt, just beyond the orbits of Pyrrhos and her shadow outposts. They would have docked back at the Myrton outpost and cut their trip in half, but no one felt like dodging through the heavy exchange of fire they had instigated.

Besides Royer was already waiting for them at the *Bretagne*.

He greeted them warmly as they climbed down from their individual fighters, nodding at Chandra, shaking Lena's hand, and warmly embracing Gael. "Well done! Oh, what a show! Now we won't have any choice but to fight back. Well done. I've been waiting for weeks for things to get started. Someone should have shot Domonkos long ago!"

Gael stepped forward before Lena could say anything. "Jules, any word back from our other team yet?"

Royer shook his head. "Not yet. Your ace pilot here," he jerked his head toward Lena, "sent your ship into a bit of a spin with her missile. It took almost half an hour for your crew's shuttle to even catch up with the thing. Another hour to get anyone on board."

"Is she okay? *Aspasia?* Is my ship okay?" Lena asked. She would never forgive herself if she had done irreparable damage to *Aspasia*.

"Far as I know, she's fine," Royer confirmed. "Your gangway is shot, though. No pun intended. Not going to be able to dock with anyone that can't take the ship in whole. Not any time soon."

Aspasia was going to be fine. Lena released the tension she had been holding since she had fired on her home. "And Raines? Cat?" It's not that they were an afterthought. It's just she never doubted that Raines would take care of things on his end.

"Raines got them on safely" Royer beamed with pride. "But apparently he had to take out a few stragglers. Seems there were a few guys still on your bridge when you attacked. They were able to seal off the inner bay doors. Restore pressure. Whole place was oxygenated, and stable time Raines got on board."

That was a stroke of luck. Raines and Cat would have had trouble getting from the walk-out behind the shuttle bays all the way to the bridge without gravity or air. They could have stabilized themselves in the shuttle bays, though that assumed she didn't blow the hull containment completely. They'd then have to seal the cargo area before they could make it anywhere to the rest of the ship. Lena wondered if she could rig a safety mechanism to automatically seal and stabilize the upper levels of the ship if the gangway were to be damaged again.

What was she thinking? She was never ever going to intentionally damage *Aspasia* again. Hell, she was never leaving *Aspasia* again. They were going to get out of this damned system and never look back. She had had enough excitement for one lifetime. She didn't have to go to Rien. She just wanted to be anywhere but here in the middle of this war.

"Are they on their way here?" she pressed.

"'Bout an hour. Maybe less. Autopilot took a straight shot from where they stabilized. Seems your missile got them clear of the entire battle."

That was good news, too. If the Pyrrhens had realized the ship was still viable, that the plans were likely still on board, and that the crew had taken back control, they probably would have given chase.

"It should be an easy transition. Get you back on board. Get that intel from you. Get you on your way."

That's right. They had promised Pyrrhen intel and cryptography on their communications; the same thing Mason had told her was on the datastick. She really hoped that information was on there somewhere. In everything that had happened, she still had yet to personally access the information and confirm what she was carrying. If there weren't any blueprints or troop descriptions or movement plans for either military or even plans for the elusive Lomasky weapon, they might have nothing to give to the Myrtons.

Would that be such a bad thing? Lena wondered. If they had the plans and could develop the weapon, the Myrtons could resist anything the Pyrrhens came up with. They could quickly gain the upper hand in this war, despite the greater numbers of the opposition. They could defend the peoples of Aegea and Aella. They could keep the system free and independent.

Or they could seize control themselves.

A weapon of this capacity, was that the sort of thing one just handed over?

Lena didn't know if she could empower any single government like that. Whether it was the Myrtons or Aegea's Black Hand, she didn't know if she could trust any authority or government to do the right thing with a weapon so powerful as this was rumored to be. She should just destroy it all.

But the knowledge was out there. Someone had already discovered how to harness the great destructive powers of gravitons. Someone had already weaponized the brilliant discoveries of her grandfather.

Not someone. Her own family. Her father's company. And maybe the Pyrrhens.

And if they had figured out how to do it, someone else would eventually.

She couldn't destroy the plans. They might hold the key to fighting back against such a weapon.

She had to get them to someone who could figure that out.

"You'll get your intel," Lena assured Royer. "As soon as we get back on our ship, we'll have Gael retrieve the plans and beam everything directly to you. Shouldn't take more than an hour after they dock."

Gael gave Lena a brief look, but he quickly nodded in agreement. "It's the least we can do. We would have never gotten our ship back if it wasn't for the cover your navy provided."

"Your navy, too," Royer wrapped his arm across Gael's back and clapped a hand over his shoulder. "Sure is good to have you back, *mon ami*. Raines, too. Like the good old days. And looks like we're going to have some interesting times ahead. Could sure use your help. Your expertise. Sure we could make it worthwhile."

Gael smiled but shook his head. "I appreciate it, Jules. But I can't. My place is with Lena and Raines and *Aspasia*. This, all of this, just isn't part of my world anymore."

"Weren't you the one who told us it's part of everyone's world right now? That this war is going to affect this whole system?"

"That's the reason I'm going to get everyone I care about out of this system. Well, everyone who is willing to leave." He patted the hand Royer still had draped over his shoulder. "I surmise from your enthusiasm for the fight that you're going to stay."

Royer laughed. "Wouldn't miss it, *mon ami*. Wouldn't miss it."

"Then I wish you all the luck," Gael said. "Now, if you would be kind enough to show us somewhere we can collect ourselves, I believe we would all appreciate a moment to ourselves before our ship gets here."

"Of course," Royer gasped. "Was so caught I almost forgot how much you have been up to. Please, this way."

Royer led them down a series of halls to a small lounge area. He murmured a quick apology and told Gael how he could be reached if they needed anything before he left them to the silence of the inner parts of the warship.

Chandra sank into a plump leather chair and almost instantly fell asleep. Gael likewise sank into the edge of a long leather couch and closed his eyes. Just when Lena thought he had fallen asleep, though, he held out his arm. "Stop pacing and come sit down," he said without opening his eyes. "Raines won't get here any faster whether you fret or not."

Lena obeyed and sank down into the crook of Gael's arm. She nestled in and rested the back of her head on his shoulder. She couldn't stop worrying entirely, though. "Gae?" she asked after a few minutes.

"Hmm?" He said, fully alert but relaxed.

"Can the Myrtons be trusted?"

His body tensed so slightly that if she hadn't been nestled so completely against him, she might have missed it. "What do you mean?"

"I don't know," she demurred. "I just, these plans. This weapon. We can't keep it hidden. And we can't just keep running with it. Too many people know we have it. And before long, they'll all know we have our ship back. And if this weapon can do everything it's advertised to do, we'll have every power in the systems after it. And even if they don't ever catch us, which is a big if, they're bound to develop their own weapons that do the same thing eventually."

"Okay," he said as she paused to catch her breath.

"So, we have to do something with it," she continued. "We have to give these plans to someone, right? Someone that can actually develop it, the weapon, or develop countermeasures, or both, because if it *can* be developed, it *will* be developed. And ultimately we want the right people to develop it because if the wrong people develop it, it could mean terrible things for innocent people. But, and this is the problem, how do we know who are the right people? Is it the Myrtons? Because they are here, and they're not the Pyrrhens, and they seem willing to help right now, and that would be incredibly convenient. But of course, I could be blinded by the need to just get rid of this damn thing, even though I have yet to put my hands on it, because it seems to be burning a hole right through the middle of my life."

Gael pulled her closer. "I know. It's a heavy burden. We all feel it. But keep going. Who else? What are our other options? Talk it out."

She didn't need much prompting. "I guess we could take it farther. Out of the system. To the Judanese? Maybe? They have the bigger military and engineering capacity. They certainly have the capability of building something like this. And they are allied with both the Aegeans and Myrtons. They could defend against the Pyrrhens. They're motivated to develop the weapon quickly. But, they lack the raw materials, the chehon to power a weapon like this. They're already relying on imports for their fuel consumption. Or maybe that's a point in their favor? If they can't really mass produce it, then the weapon isn't so much of a threat. But then, what if someone else develops it? Then the Judanese can't provide a strong enough opposition. They could maybe develop counter-measures against the weapon. But if the foundation of the weapon is chehon and graviton based, then a counter-measure would likely have to be as well. And, now that I think about, a strong motivation to develop a weapon of such mass destruction is not a great reason to give it to them. We don't want it to actually be used on anyone. Just to have the threat of it. So not Judan."

She sat up straighter as she continued to work out the problem. Gael sat straighter, too. "We need someone who can produce the weapon and counter-measures independently. Someone who has demonstrated the technological capacity but is politically neutral enough to not use it except in the most necessary circumstances. We need someone outside of this system. We need..." She couldn't bring herself to say it.

Gael said it for her. "We need the Lomasky Corporation."

CHAPTER THIRTY-FOUR

Aspasia arrived as promised, within the hour. Royer was apparently occupied with other things, but he sent a lower sergeant to escort Lena, Gael, and Chandra to the ship. She was a pretty brunette that looked like she hadn't smiled in years. She marched them down to the lower full-ship ports in silence, and Lena was relieved when she tapped out a code on a door, barked out an order to wire the plans to Liviani and left.

Lena only had eyes for what she had done.

Aspasia was here. She was still here. Her huge, beautiful ship was here, towering over them in the cavernous full-entry port. But the damage was substantial.

"Oh my darling, what have I done?" Lena whispered as she saw the front gangway.

The entire thing was destroyed. A smooth hull should have fallen away beneath the protruding nose of the bridge, with two doors that slid back to allow the telescoped tunnel gangway to extend outward and seal against any other ship or dock for easy entry and departure. Instead, Lena was looking at a gaping hole in the hull with the gangway mechanisms visible and obviously destroyed. Only the interior bulkhead was left to keep *Aspasia* from venting air in flight. She could only imagine what would happen if they tried to take *Aspasia* through atmospheric entries with her so exposed. Surely the bulkhead would hold, but the forces of entry on any planet or moon would tear at the exposed mechanisms, further damaging the hull. It could even affect the chehonic field generators that gave the ship gravity.

It was going to cost a fortune to fix her.

Thankfully the ship was still space-worthy. Raines and Cat had made it here after all. Lena was already headed to the walk-out at the ship's stern.

They'd have to use the airlock walk-outs and the shuttles for docking for a while.

She could be okay with that. She had *Aspasia* back. She could deal with anything right now.

Up the dropped ladder. Code entered. In through the walk-out. Secure exterior door behind her. Wait for the beep and alert light to go off as the air locks engaged. In through the interior door. Through the hall between the engine rooms. Past the shuttle bays. Into the cargo hold.

From inside she couldn't see any damage from the blasted gangway. The interior bulkhead was completely intact. No evidence that anything had happened.

She let that happy news float her up the stairs, all the way to the top, to her bridge.

Raines was waiting in her chair, his back to her, but at the sound of her footsteps, he spun and leapt toward her in one solid motion. He was on her in a second, sweeping her into his arms. "You beautiful, wonderful, amazing woman!" He whirled, lifting her around the waist before setting her down and laying a deep kiss on her astonished lips. "You are incredible. You got her back. You did it."

"I shot her," Lena protested, dizzy and lightheaded, though whether it was from the spinning or the kiss she wasn't sure.

"You freed her. And I cannot thank you enough." He kissed her again lightly on the lips.

"Well," Lena said, pushing him away gently. "I didn't do it for you."

Raines chuckled. "Of course not." He stepped aside and let Lena walk onto her bridge.

She walked straight to her chair, sank into it, and ran her hands along her console. "I am so sorry," she whispered as she stroked the screens, caressed the buttons, soothed the controls. "I am so sorry I let them touch you. But I'm here now." She turned to Raines. "How bad is it?"

Raines considered her carefully before answering. "All of our rooms are trashed. Everything is torn apart or destroyed. Gael's books, Cat's souvenirs —"

"Is the ship okay?" Lena didn't care about anything in her room. If the ship was okay, she was okay.

"No structural or mechanical damage."

Lena heaved a sigh of relief. "And the plans?"

"Right where Gae said they'd be. Though, if I'd known he was such a teenager and still hid his valuables under his mattress, I'd have thought twice about making him my right-hand man."

"The classics work for a reason," Gael said, entering the bridge with Chandra behind him. "And what teenager do you know who has a hidden compartment worked into the bed frame for contraband?"

"Contraband? Action I can get in on?" Chandra said from the doorway. She stepped aside as Cat came up to the bridge as well. Cat stumbled up the last step, and Lena noticed Chandra's hand as it shot out to the small of her back to steady her and help Cat up.

"What are we smuggling this time?" Cat asked. "Last time it was supposed to be illegal fish! That didn't work out so well."

Lena brought her hand to her face and pinched the bridge of her nose until she could see stars. "Can we at least get our bearings before we start any further crimes?"

"Lena's right," Raines said. "I want to know where this whole thing," he gestured to Cat and Chandra, "is going before I agree to you staying on long-term. On-board romances can be quite complicated." He leaned up against Lena and kissed her lightly on the cheek.

Lena shoved him away. Hard. "Are you fucking serious right now? My ship is in pieces. Our friends are dead. We've just started a war! And to top it all off, we possibly have the blueprints to the biggest weapon the systems have ever seen, and we're supposed to hand them over to the Myrtons and potentially be responsible for ending millions of lives. And you want to flirt?!" She then let off a scream that had been building for days, letting the shrill, harsh panic of it ricochet off the metal walls around them and echo until it almost matched the cacophony in her head.

For a moment, the crew stood shocked into silence. Gael started to walk toward her in his calm, non-threatening manner.

"Back off, Gae. I'm not in the mood to be talked down."

"What are you in the mood for, then?" he asked, keeping his voice low and even.

"I'm ready to get this ship back in the air and get out of here."

"And the plans?" Raines asked, equally cautious.

"I don't even know what's on them. But if it's half of what I think it is, I'm destroying them before I give them to anyone."

Cat and Chandra exchanged glances. "Um," Cat said. "I thought they were part of our payment for getting back the ship? The Myrtons fight the Pyrrhens in exchange for the data Gael was hiding, right?"

"If the plans are what we've been told they are, no," said Gael. "They're too dangerous to hand over to any government."

"Liviani won't like it," Raines said, but Lena could tell by the way he settled back on the console behind him, that he was accepting what Lena suggested.

Cat was more reticent. "Wait, what?" she protested, stepping forward. "You can't be serious. We can't just run off with these plans or blueprints or whatever. We promised them to the Myrtons. We made a deal."

Lena turned her back on Cat and her reasonable arguments. "No. Until we know exactly what we have, really, it's a moot point. We're not giving up our only leverage to anyone."

Cat started to protest again but was pulled back by Chandra. She guided Cat from the bridge, recognizing the close to the conversation, even if Cat didn't.

Raines and Gael however, moved closer to Lena. Gael took the seat beside her, while Raines remained perched, as ever, on the console beside her. Lena didn't even bother pushing him aside. She just looked up wearily. "So? Where are the plans?"

Raines reached over to his shoulder and took the datastick out of the pocket there. He handed it to Lena. It was so small. This little thing, no bigger than her thumb, was the cause of all they had suffered these past few days. This was it.

Lena laughed a little. It just slipped out. A small chuckle. And then another. And then they were falling out of her. Gasps, tears, sobs. She dropped her head onto the console as she gripped that tiny datastick. She squeezed as if she could squeeze out the final drops of blood this damned piece of technology would wring from her, from her friends. She wanted to burn it. To destroy it and all the knowledge it held.

But she couldn't. She knew she couldn't. She had to do something.

It was her responsibility.

She was a Lomasky. This was her mess.

She slowly came back to herself. She stopped the gasping sobs, the hysterical noises she had let slip from her. She swallowed it all back.

Whatever else, she was still a Lomasky.

She could handle this.

She sat up to find Raines holding her left hand and Gael to her right slowly stroking her back. She set the datastick down and wiped her eyes with her free right hand and rolled her shoulders back, forcing Gael to drop his hand away. Then she gave Raines a small squeeze and reclaimed her left hand.

"I'm sorry. I'm okay," she assured them.

"Yeah," Gael smiled. "We know. You always are."

"Okay," Raines clapped his hands together and rubbed them eagerly. "If everyone is okay, then we can fire this bad boy up, right? Find out what's on it?"

"Only on an un-networked computer," Gael reminded him. "If we access it and a security program finds a network, it could send out a signal. Let everyone who's looking for it know where it is."

"And that would be bad," Raines agreed. "Got it. Lena? Remote device?"

Lena nodded and reached down under the console. She input a code into a hidden safe and pulled out a computer. "This old thing is just for personal use."

"Diary?" Raines teased.

"Something like that," Lena smiled. It was actually a backup device that she kept turned off and in a lead-lined cabinet. It held all *Aspasia's* programming, logs, and support systems as well as all the backed-up data from everyone's personal networked devices. She ran backups once a month, just in case they ever ran into a situation where *Aspasia's* security protocols were overrun, and any of their data got erased. She kept a secondary backup in her room. And a third in the shuttles. And she rotated each of the devices three times a year. It never hurt to be careful. Or paranoid. Same thing.

Lena inserted the 'stick into her device and accessed the file menu. She quickly scanned the contents: blueprints, both video and photo recordings, maps with locating tech, and dozens of data files. She opened a few of the files as both Gael and Raines looked on. There were the blueprints she had seen at Evan's office, more complete, but similar enough that she recognized them. Photos of the completed device with closeups and diagrams of each component. Files titled "Potential Buyers," "Expected Revenue," "Production Estimates." Videos of the device in action. She queued one of those up.

"We're here at the Strunken White Chasms on the Yager moon of Faizura," a woman said amongst a team of other scientists. "We have chosen this location for both its remoteness and for its diverse topography. Note the heights of the nearby bluffs and the depths of the canyon." She turned the camera to face down toward the canyon. "We're going to cut now as we establish a safe distance from the blast site, but for our purposes, what you see below is our ground zero." There was a cut, and then you could see the woman again, sitting in an open-air vehicle, her back to the horizon. "We are now about three miles from the blast site. You can see," and she gestured behind her, "the same bluff I highlighted earlier. That will be your marker. Now we're doing an aerial delivery, with the marksman aiming downward and at an angle. He does not want to be directly above, nor really in any close radius to the delivery site when the weapon detonates."

She then panned the camera up to a craft speeding past them overhead. It had to be at least a klick up, maybe more. Lena didn't even have time to identify the type of ship as it flew beyond the crew and toward the target site. It passed over, and in seconds, it was gone. Not the aircraft. It was still moving farther away. But the bluff, the cliffs, the canyon was gone. Lena hadn't even had time to register the event. There was no flash, no explosion, nothing that she could see to indicate that anything had happened. One second there had been an amazing vista, and then there was nothing. It was if someone had taken an ice cream scoop to the horizon.

Lena watched as the science team rode forward in their vehicles, right up to the edge of the crater. "Gone," the woman beamed. "Collapsed in on itself and eliminated with the force of a planet's center of gravity. We estimate that the payload came to its ignition point about 500 meters above the edge of the chasms, so just above the highest bluff. If I'd have to guess," she aimed the camera down into the gulf below them, "I'd say we've reached a depth of about the same. And to judge the distance across," she panned out to the edge of the crater, "we have about the same. We're looking at a complete destruction diameter of 1 kilometer. Enough to provide a sufficient deterrent in any situation. What's notable is the absolute edge of the damage." She panned down again to the edge of the chasm, jumping out of the vehicle and focusing on the outer edge of the crater. "The edge is clean, and there seems to be no damage outside of the blast radius. Previous tests have indicated there is no radioactive fallout, no disturbance whatsoever to the area outside of the immediate blast radius. That evidence marks this as an optimal precision weapon for ultimate annihilation within a given sphere. However, I should note that though we can deliver much larger effects, we have yet to establish an amount of chehonic isotopes small enough to deliver a payload smaller than about a kilometer. The agitation of the matter at any quantity sufficient to establish an explosive response will obtain a blast radius of at least 987 to 1007 meters. Further exploration of —"

Lena didn't even realize she'd shut off the video until the woman stopped talking. She couldn't watch the Lomasky logo on the woman's labcoat any longer.

"I think we can assume we have the full plans for the weapon, then." Raines said it matter-of-factly. "Anything other than this we can give the Myrtons in here? Because I'm sure as hell not handing over blueprints for something like that."

Lena looked through the rest of the files. She found some lists of names and some maps, but they seemed to be mostly of the Aegean rebels' underground tunnels. They might help the Myrtons know where not to attack, but they were nothing close to the intel they had promised. No cryptography. No Pyrrhen plans.

"Nothing else," Lena admitted.

Then, deep in the blueprints folder, she saw a hidden file. She tapped it, and a message "For Lena" popped up.

A voice filled the room.

"Mason," Lena whispered. Her old schoolmate. Her friend. She hadn't even appreciated him as such. But he'd remembered her. He'd remembered her when she was cast out of Rienen society. And when things got bad for him, he'd reached out to her. He'd remembered her. He'd trusted her.

And now he was gone.

Except for his voice now filling her bridge.

"Lena, let me begin by saying how sorry I am to bring you into this. I know perfectly well how hard you have worked to get away. From your family, from their machinations, from the politics of home. I know what it means to drag you back in. I regret that. And yet, you're the only one I can turn to. You're the only one I can trust. And I know I lied to you. I know I didn't tell you the truth about the data you hold. If you've found this folder, you've seen. You've seen what you carry and you know the full extent of what it can do. And you have no doubt seen your family's logo on every single page of the blueprints. I'm sorry to lay their sins on you. Especially after what they did to you. But you're the only one who would truly understand what has to be done.

"The Pyrrhens have been monitoring my actions for months. They know I have the complete plans for the weapon, or they must suspect. And I can't let them get their hands on it. I cannot be responsible for what they will use the weapon for. I cannot be responsible for the loss of thousands, millions of lives. I won't be. I know you will understand this. I know you will do what you have to get these plans back to Rien, into the hands of those who can fight back against the development of this weapon. Those who can develop countermeasures.

"At the very least, you can keep these plans out of the hands of the Pyrrhens. These are the only complete plans that I know of, but the Pyrrhens have seized hold of the idea of a gravity bomb and are actively working on their own prototype. It's a matter of time before they have their own weapon. Get these plans home. My contacts, if they're still alive, will help you. I've included a file with their names and any last known contact info. They'll know what to do. They can also get the Rienen military to help end this rapidly degenerating political situation here. And they can win this war for the right people."

He paused, and Lena thought it was the end of the message. Just as she went to turn it off, Mason's voice returned, softer. "Lena, if I could have kept you from this mess, I would have. If I could have gotten these plans back to Rien in any other way, I would have. If I could have spared you this journey, I would have. But the stakes are too high. You're the only one I know I can trust to get these plans where they need to go. I hope someday you can forgive me. And if I make it through this war, I promise I will make it up to you. Good luck. And thank you."

The message ended.

CHAPTER THIRTY-FIVE

The bridge was silent for a few moments. Then, Raines spoke. "Lena, there's another message." She looked up at the screen but saw nothing in the files that stood out. "Not on the datastick. On our networked-comms. It was sent a few days ago."

Her entire self seemed to contract. "Who?" she asked. Mason, Cedo? She couldn't hear any more dead voices.

"It's your fiancé." Raines said.

"Ex," she said automatically.

Evan had sent her a message.

Of course. He had known exactly where her ship was. He had no way of knowing that Chandra had told her the truth of what he was. That he had been manipulating her this whole time. That he had been after the plans.

"Play it," Lena said. She turned away from the console. If there was a video component, a holograph, anything she could look at, she didn't want to see it. If she could have shut off his voice and read a transcript instead, she'd have chosen that. But in a second, there it was. His voice. His warm, comfortable tenor. Despite everything, she sank into it like a warm bath.

"Lena, if you are listening to this, then you are safe back on your ship. I could not be happier for you. In fact, my only regret is that I could not accompany you back to your *Aspasia*. I am sorry things got complicated, as they always do. If there was any way I could be there with you, if there was any way I could go with you back home, I would. I would bear your burden with you. I hate that you are there without me, without the strength that I could offer you. No doubt you will face temptations along your way. When people know what you hold, they will stop at nothing to get it. I am doing all I can at my end to keep your way clean. I hope one day that you can understand what I am doing for you. And that one day, you can forgive me and see me for what I truly am. Good luck, my love. Great speed."

And the message cut out.

It was such a straightforward, good-hearted message. Whatever his intentions, whatever his hidden motives, his actions had been what had freed her crew. Surely that was worth something.

There was a beep.

"Another message?" Raines said, looking to Lena. Then he turned back to the console. "Same source. Not...three minutes ago. It's Evan."

The voice flooded her bridge once again. This time, though, he didn't give her the same act of the concerned ex-fiancé. He had shed the voice she knew. Gone was the level tone, the understanding, and measured pace. Lena had the feeling that this was the first time she had ever heard his true voice.

"Well, I guess some congratulations are in order," the voice spat. "Great job getting it back. Your precious *Aspasia*. I knew you couldn't do it. You couldn't destroy your damn ship. But guess, what, bitch? You may have your ship back, but you're not getting away. I don't care where you go. You can't hide, you can't jump far enough away. I will find you. I will hunt you down. I will get back what you took from me, and then I will deal with you personally." He paused, releasing the initial blast of wrath with a deep sigh. She could picture him shaking his head, his brow knit in a tight furrow over his green eyes. "Lena, it doesn't have to be like this. We can work with you. We, the Pyrrhens, we can keep you safe. We can give you all the security you need. We can work with you, make it worth your while. Just give us the plans. Give us the plans and come back to me. It can be like it was. We can have everything we've ever wanted. Lee, just come back. Things can be good again. You can be respectable again. Hold your head high, be part of a real world again. Just come back. Come home to me. I still love you. And I need you."

The message cut off, and everyone was silent. Both Raines and Gael seemed to be watching Lena. She gave them nothing and began to type into the console in front of her.

"Uh, Lee," Raines said. "You good?"

She didn't look up as she continued to enter data. "Great," she said without reaction.

"Lena," Gael tried. "Are you okay?"

"If either of you ask me one more time if I am okay, if I am happy, if I am at all at peace with whatever desperate decision I am having to make, I swear to whatever gods you swear allegiance to, I will take Chandra's gun, and I will shoot off one finger at a time until you realize that, no, I am not okay."

Gael stepped back with his hands in the air. "That seems fairly straight forward. I withdraw my question."

She pulled up the last message's metadata. Its path was a direct stream from a ship emerging from the battle at the Pyrrhen outpost. Lena focused the screen on the ship. It was advancing.

"Dammit."

"Evan?" Gael asked.

"Who else? Should have known they'd put a tracking device on the ship. I should have done a sweep. Dammit."

"We haven't really had the time," Raines assured her. "It's okay. Chandra always assumed they'd follow. As soon as they realized *Aspasia* was still flying. It's why she arranged for the Myrtons to get involved."

"She just thinks of everything, doesn't she?" Lena muttered.

She turned and shut out both Raines, Gael, and any lingering disgust, anger, or guilt over Evan. Myrton was out. They couldn't protect against a full onslaught if the Pyrrhens decided to come after the plans.

Rien, it was. *Aspasia* might still be able to outrun the Pyrrhens coming for her, but it would take some solid flying. And they had to go now.

"Go get settled," she told the men behind her. "We're in the air in five."

"Um, correct me if I'm wrong," Gael said, looking to Raines for confirmation. "But don't we have to give the Myrtons something?"

"What would you have me give them? We agreed the weapon plans stay with us. And there's really nothing else. We looked at the files. There's no cryptography. No maps. No military plans. We have nothing they want. Except the weapon." She shook her head and started powering up the ship. "No, we run."

"But we're docked inside their station," Gael said.

"Then we either make them open the door," Lena smiled. "Or we blow a hole."

CHAPTER THIRTY-SIX

"*Aspasia*, I repeat, you are not cleared for departure. Power down."

The voice on the other end of the comms was growing impatient, and Lena thought she detected a hint of fear.

"Or else, what?" Lena challenged. "You have no internal controls to access my ship, so you can't override me. And you have no weapons inside this bay."

"We can deploy fighters to await you outside in moments, Ms. Lomasky. Please do not try us." That voice was new.

"Colonel Liviani. I was wondering when you'd reach this standoff. I must say, I'm disappointed it took a full five minutes," Lena said idly. "Now would you kindly order your subordinates to open my bay doors, or shall I make good on my promises?"

There was a moment or two of silence on the other end of the comms.

"You're going to get us all killed," Cat hissed. "Just give them the plans." Chandra, who was holding her arm and keeping her back near the door, tried to hush her. "Lena, it's not worth us getting killed over this."

"You're right," Lena said. "It's worth so much more. Now, dear friend, shut up, or leave my bridge."

She didn't wait for a response, but she heard the protestations as Chandra once again escorted her out. That pairing really could be good for them both.

"Well," Lena said into the comms, prompting a response. "I'm not going to wait for your fighters to reroute. They really have a more pressing battle to engage in, don't they?"

Liviani laughed lightly into the speaker. "I have to admire your bravado, here, but your threats are all empty, Ms. Lomasky. I hear that you have threatened to blow your way out of our bay and destroy our docking components? Is that correct?" She laughed again. "Your ship has been docked for a bit of time, now. We have clearly been able to ascertain that you not only lack a functional gangway, but you also lack any sort of external weapon on your ship. I assume you didn't also blow those off your own ship back at the Pyrrhen station?"

"No," Lena agreed. "*Aspasia* has never had external weapons."

"So how do you expect to accomplish what you have threatened? Give us the plans you promised us, and you can leave freely. Stop the theatrics."

Lena responded calmly and clearly. "These are not theatrics, Colonel. Allow me to explain the physics of the matter. Unless you open those doors in the next five minutes, I plan to expand each of my push vectors at once, in all directions. I will direct all my ship's energy to chehonic outputs. I will push all the energy that I can in a continuous stream until I blast through these small doors that you refuse to open. But I'm afraid that such an all-directions push will naturally expand past this bay into the connecting bays and passageways surrounding us. And since I'm not entirely sure the amount of energy it will take to bypass both your walls and your anti-grav, I can't be entirely sure how much damage I will inflict beyond this particular bay."

Liviani was silent. Then she gave another forced laugh. "You can't do that. Vectors are mono-directional."

"Says who?"

"Says physics. The technology doesn't allow for you to exert multiple vectors at once. Especially not in all directions at once."

"You're only saying that because no one's ever done it before."

"You're talking about turning chehon power into a weapon."

"Exactly," Lena said.

"But," Liviani protested. "The technology doesn't work that way."

"Ma'am, I'm a Lomasky. Don't you tell me what MY technology can and cannot do. Now open my door. You have two minutes."

With that, she cut the feed.

"Is that true?" Raines asked from his perch at the console.

"Is *what* true?" Lena asked, tensely watching her screen.

"Can you make chehon work to push out like that?"

"Technically, yes. That's the principle the gravity bomb works under. If I understand it correctly. It forces so much chehonic energy outward that it collapses on itself and creates a temporary black hole before the gravity collapses under its own weight and disappears."

"So, we'd kill ourselves," Gael concluded.

"Yeah." Lena grinned. "But Liviani doesn't know that."

Before either of them could say more, Liviani's voice responded. "Take your damned ship and go." She cut off the feed without a word more, and the doors behind *Aspasia* began to slide open.

Lena turned on her anti-grav, dropped her landing gear, and got ready to push out.

"How do you know she doesn't have fighters waiting right outside?" Gael asked.

"She doesn't." Raines said, grinning like a fool, his hand on Lena's shoulder. "Let's do it."

And with that, Lena pushed *Aspasia* out of the Myrton station.

CHAPTER THIRTY-SEVEN

They were several million kilometers above the Belt before Lena finally accepted that Myrtons were not following. Raines assured her a dozen times there was no one else behind them before heading off for food and a nap. Still, she kept running scans trying to find some ship that was discretely tailing them.

Only the one. Evan was closing in.

"Is there no way we can increase our speed?" Gael asked from the seat beside her.

"Against what?" Lena asked gesturing to the vast blackness ahead and behind them. "We're not close to anything. No planets, no asteroids, nothing. I'm going off the strongest push I could manage against the warship without spending too much of our fuel. And if I'd had to blow our way out of there, we wouldn't even be going this fast."

"I thought that was a bluff?" Gael said.

"It was!" She turned on Gael. With little to no sleep in the past few days, she was feeling a bit edgy. And without Chandra to hate on, Gael was the next target. "There's nothing I can do at this point. The ship behind us obviously had a stronger initial push vector. And they, no doubt, have longer range than we do, so they may have even been able to increase their speed against the station when they veered up toward us. Whereas I have to conserve as much as possible to get us through our jump to the Samaran system, and then still slingshot us toward Rien. So no, we can't increase our fucking speed."

Gael wasn't affected by her outburst. "The good news is, though, that they're far bigger than us, right?"

"Oh, yeah. They're bigger. With more fuel, more reserves, better tech. Great news for us. Yay."

"What I mean is, that as they approach, we can use their own mass to fuel our own vector. Can't we? Gain speed against theirs?"

Lena shook her head. "Their range is still longer than ours. And more powerful. Even if we wanted to try that, they'd have us in their reach before we had them in ours. They'll start pulling on us before we could even touch them. They'll gain on us no matter what."

"How long until they reach us?" Raines asked from the door.

"I thought you went to sleep," Gael said.

"Had an idea. How long?" he asked Lena stifling a yawn. "Estimate?"

Lena consulted her charts. "They should catch up to us just short of the jump stations."

"How short?"

"Under a hundred clicks."

"So, we'd be in range of the station?" Raines said as he approached and pulled up the charts to look for himself.

"Close enough, yeah," Lena said. "But if you're wondering if the stations might help us, they won't. They're required to be unarmed. Neutral. Jumps are protected space, and even an interplanetary war won't stop that." Any attack on the jump stations at the edges of each system or any attempt to seize control would be sure to bring the full military strength of each of the three systems in response. It would be the most surefire way to end the war in a single self-destructive move. "Raines, you aren't thinking...?"

Raines snorted as he stepped away again. "I don't think even the Pyrrhens are stupid enough to attempt to attack the stations. No, I was thinking we might be able to use the station itself as a pull point to gain some extra speed at the last minute."

Lena considered. "It's possible. We'd be cutting it really close. Our range would just reach the stations as we slid into Evan's. We still have hours before we know either way."

Raines turned to her, meeting her eyes. He looked for a moment or two before his lip quirked, and he nodded. "You can do it." He left.

She closed her eyes and let her head drop to her chest. "I hate when he does that."

"What? Has faith in you?" Gael asked.

"What if I can't do it?"

"Then you can't do it," Gael said matter-of-factly. "And we'll figure something else out."

"If I fail, then the Pyrrhens take us. Evan takes us. He gets the plans."

"We won't let him take you, Lena."

"You can't stop him!" she shouted. He was so calm, so assured, so wrong! "I can't stop him. Raines and his precious pet mercenary can't stop him. I'm not sure if the entirety of Yoddha's force was here that they could stop him!"

"Evan is not invincible."

"He will be if he gets his hands on this weapon. Gael, you saw what it can do."

"I did. It doesn't matter. He's not going to get it. He'll have to blow us out of the sky before Raines or I or, yes, Chandra, let him board this ship. We're not going to let anything happen to you. I'm not going to let anything happen to you."

Lena closed her eyes as she turned away from Gael. "I hate that, too."

"What?"

"That you keep trying to prove how much you love me."

Gael sighed. "Would you rather me keep it quiet? Keep it inside?"

"Yes!" Lena reeled on him, throwing her hands up in the air before clenching them into fists so hard she could feel her nails cutting into her palms. "I know. I would be stupid not to know how you feel about me. And yeah. It would make sense. You and me. We'd work well together. We **do** work well together. But not like that. Gael, I am sorry. But I just can't. I've got this, whatever I have with Raines. I don't love you."

"I know," he said honestly.

"Then why keep trying?"

He stood and walked to the glass wall in front of them, looking at the stars. He didn't respond for a few seconds, but then he turned to look at her. "It doesn't matter, Lena. I love you. And it doesn't matter if you don't love me back. Whether you want to be with me or not, I'm still going to do what I can to keep you safe, to make you smile, to let you know in whatever way I can that I love you. Because you deserve to know, that no matter what you've done, no matter what others may think of you, no matter what you may think of yourself, I think you are worthy of love. And even if you never love me back, then you should at least know that."

He didn't wait for a response but walked past her and toward the door.

"Wait."

Lena didn't mean to say it. The words escaped her before she realized she'd even thought them.

Gael stopped. He waited.

He turned to her.

She walked right up to him, right beneath those warm, chestnut brown eyes, and let him just look at her. The whole, unvarnished mess of her.

He didn't waver. He truly did love her.

She didn't deserve it. She knew he saw her in a way that wasn't real. He thought she was brave and kind and warm and whatever it was that men looked for in broken women. He thought she had something special inside of her, and he was willing to look past everything she did to contradict all that. He didn't care that she was distant; she was just deliberate, he'd reason. He didn't mind that she was brusque; she was defensive. He ignored that she was careless and dismissive of people; she was independent and strong.

The way he looked at her right now. It made her want to be better. It made her want to be what he saw. She reached up and grabbed the back of his neck and pulled him down into a hard and desperate kiss.

She wanted to be what he saw. She wanted to be better. Someone that deserved to be looked at that way.

She wasn't that person, but some part of her wanted to be.

She kissed him harder. Maybe, maybe if she kissed him hard enough, his ideals would pass into her. She could be what he saw, and all of the pain and hurt of her current reality could disappear.

She clung to him, wrapping her arms around him, as he eagerly wrapped himself around her. He reached to the wall behind himself and jammed the button to close the door to the bridge.

Lena stumbled back, still holding him close, dragging him with her. She let the moment envelope her.

His eager mouth told her that she was worth loving. That she was worth whatever they were doing here. And she was desperate to feel like that was true.

Never breaking contact with his lips, she spun him around, until she wasn't pulling on him, but was pushing him back to her console. She took control.

He wanted her. He could have her. She would give that to him, and maybe erase some of his pain and hers. They could lose themselves in this moment and forget everything else. She could be perfect for a few moments.

She pushed him back into her pilot's chair. He fell back with a gasp, and she stood over him for a moment, drinking in the sight of him. The deep umber of his skin was lean and lithe under his clothes. Full sensuous lips were swollen with kissing. His deep brown eyes were wide as she lifted her simple black shirt over her head and let drop it somewhere behind her. She stepped forward and perched over him, one foot planted on the ground and the other knee nestled in between the edge of the seat and him.

She reached for his face and brought his full attention to her. "This doesn't mean anything, Gael. I'm not your girlfriend. I'm not in love with you, and I'm not going to come to your bed every night you feel like a cuddle."

He nodded. "I know that."

"What do you want out of this?" She had to know. Before she got at all involved.

He reached out a hand to touch the side of her face. The heel of his palm rested on her chin as his fingers brushed along her hairline and the edges of her ear. Her skin tingled, and for once, she let herself feel the full sensation of it. The pads of his fingers stroked gently, just a millimeter, like a whisper, a feather tracing along her face. "I just want you to know."

She reached up a hand and pressed his hand firmly to her face, eager for his warmth, his strength, the weight of him. She wanted to feel him, not wonder at him. "Know what?"

He leaned in, using the pressure of his fingers to pull her face toward his lips. "To know what you deserve."

She was breathless. "What do I deserve?"

"To be loved."

And with that, he removed his gentle hand from her face and wrapped his arms around her, easily lifting her off her feet. He spun her around and placed her up on the console.

She gasped with the sudden and unexpected movement. But she wrapped her arms around him and pulled his mouth into hers. After a breathless moment, she pulled away. "Then show me."

CHAPTER THIRTY-EIGHT

"How close?"

Raines paced back and forth before the console.

"Raines, I've already kicked everyone else out. If you don't sit down or be still or get out of my line of sight, I'm going to miss our window."

Lena watched her console closely. They were closing in on the jump station, and within a few hundred kilometers she'd be able to initiate a pull on the relatively tiny station. What she wouldn't give for a moon or a massive asteroid! Anything with a wider grav range. The mass on this thing was hardly enough to give her any real pull, and she had to be so close to even attempt it.

What was much closer was the Pyrrhen ship on her tail, and it was gaining fast. The only thing that was keeping her out of their pull range was *Aspasia*'s light mass. The Pyrrhen ship would have to be right on top of them to do anything, and Lena was hoping that by the time that happened, *Aspasia* would be flinging themselves away, using the larger mass of the station to slingshot them toward the jump point and away into another system.

But the margin of opportunity was miniscule.

She literally had a window of a few thousand, maybe a few hundred kilometers to begin pulling hard on the station's mass before she fell into the Pyrrhen ship's range. At the speeds they were currently traveling, that meant she had seconds at most to transfer as much energy as possible to the pull while retaining enough chehon to get them through the jump and to Rien on the other side.

She'd run the calculations a hundred times. She could do this.

She had to do this.

If they got taken, she couldn't let the weapon fall into Pyrrhen hands. If she failed, the Lomasky Corp couldn't develop a countermeasure. The Aegeans wouldn't be able to defend themselves. Myrto would fall. She had no choice. If they were taken, she had to jettison the plans. Destroy them.

And if the plans were gone when the Pyrrhens boarded, she could only imagine what the Pyrrhens would do to her crew.

She could do this.

She watched the vectors.

Closer.

Closer.

Almost there.

It was going to be a razor-thin margin. The Pyrrhens seemed to be gaining speed.

That was impossible.

Unless.

"No," she breathed.

Raines whirled. "What?"

"They anticipated our pull. They have a wider range." She pulled up the vectors. Confirmed it.

"What does that mean, Lee?"

"They stole our move. They can reach farther than we can. They started pulling on the station before we got in range of it. They're going to be on us before we can even start pulling." She looked for anything. Could she start pushing against them before they started on her? No, their mass was stronger. She would be fighting their mass and their energy. And they had more of both. She'd be wasting fuel. Was there any chance they could reach the station? "No, no, no. There has to be something."

"Lena, talk to me," Raines said, kneeling beside her. "Tell me there's something we can do."

She started shaking her head. There was nothing else. There were no other bodies out here. No other large masses. That was the whole point of jump stations. They were located far above the solar system, above the planets, moons, asteroids, above the surprisingly monodirectional rotational pull of the star that kept all the LIBs of the system in their relative orbital plane. There was only one point that could be used as a system's jump point, and it was straight up and at that exact distance away from the star where its gravity and the combined gravity of its orbiting masses stopped working against you. Where you could finally reorient your drives to twist space against itself and fold yourself into another solar system. Where you could bridge the gap, and tesseract or wrinkle space-time or jump into another part of the universe. She never understood it, she hated the physical effects, and she dreaded every single jump. But it was a foundational part of any traveler's life.

Lena was doing everything she could to get to that point, but nothing was working.

"It's too late," she choked out. "They've already got us."

"The Pyrrhens? They've got us?" Raines stood again, staring at the station still slowly growing in their view. "But we're so close."

"I'm sorry, Raines. I'm sorry." Lena couldn't quite catch her breath. She had failed. The Pyrrhens may not have outflown her, but they'd out-thought her. It didn't matter. They were caught all the same. She wiped away tears that were stinging the inside of her eyes. "We have to dump the plans."

"No," he said.

"We can't let them get a hold of them," Lena insisted. "We have to. It's okay. If the Lomasky Corp developed the weapon, then they have to be able to replicate the plans on their own. They had the weapon itself at some point. These can't be the only plans in existence. There have to be copies somewhere. It'll be fine. *We* might not be, but everything else will be."

"Lena, no. We're going to get to Rien. We're going to get you home, and we're going to rally an army. The Aegeans can't fight this war alone. Even with my people behind them, they're going to lose this thing. And my people are going to suffer incredible losses. Myrto doesn't have a strong enough navy to stand against Pyrrhos. We never have. And Judan will never get her parliament organized in time to make a difference." He grabbed her by the shoulders and gave her a shake. "Lena, we need to get to Rien. Your people have a navy that can rival the Pyrrhens'. And if we get the Naftish involved, even better. Samara united might make a difference. But if we give up, if we let the Pyrrhens develop this weapon, if we don't do all we can to stop them, they'll destroy Aegea. They'll destroy Aella. And then they'll destroy Myrto. And Iphito. And then they'll jump systems. They'll take Samara or Pandia. They won't stop. We have to stop them."

"And how do we do that?" Lena said.

"We still have a trump card." Raines stood up and looked out the front view at the approaching station.

"What are those?" Lena looked away from the visual in front of her to focus on her console. There. Multiple dots emerging from the station. Ships. Big ships. Tiny in real-view, but prominent in her scanners.

What were dozens of ships doing at a jump station? There weren't enough accommodations for layovers or tourists. The station was just a core containment around a variable mass unit. Only enough personnel to keep the station running and the chehon stable.

Yet, these ships seemed to blossom from behind the station out of nowhere.

"Myrton fighters," Raines said. "The warship is farther out past the jump point so as not to tip anyone off."

"You knew this was here?" Lena demanded.

"I had hoped not to call in the reinforcements, but I never wanted to be without a contingency plan. The warship has been lurking out here for a few months. I just asked them to route a few fighters in toward the station. Thought it might be worth their while."

Of course, Raines had a backup. He always had a plan. He would never have left things up to chance. Or to her. She should have known. "You never really thought I could do it, did you? You didn't think I could save us."

Raines turned, confused. "What? What are you talking about? This isn't about you. It's about the mission."

"Right," Lena said, swallowing her hurt pride. "Right. Yeah. The mission."

The mission. Get the plans away. Get to Rien. Get to Lomasky Corp.

Focus on the job.

An alert pinged through on the comms. The Myrtons. They were close enough by now that they could establish a direct connection. Lena opened the comms. "This is *Aspasia*. We sure are glad to see you."

"*Aspasia*, this is Fighter 6-89. On behalf of the Myrton government, I order you to power down your ship and surrender. We will be commandeering your ship and seizing your contents."

"What?" Lena looked at Raines. "This was your plan?"

"No," Raines said to her before raising his voice to the comms. "Fighter 6-89, this is former Captain Sebastian Rainier of Myrto's Naval Unit 1274. We were told you'd help us get through our jump without incident. Who authorized you to seize our ship?"

"Apologies, Captain, but I am acting under orders of Colonel Liviani. Your ship is hereby seized by the Myrton Navy, and your contents forfeit."

"Bitch," Lena swore. "I knew she let us go too easily. She double-crossed you." She had to still be after the plans. And if she couldn't get them consensually, she'd take them by force.

Raines waved at her to keep her quiet. They were still connected on comms. Raines paused for a beat, his eyes rapidly shifting from the visuals out the window and back down to the scanners below. A wide smile spread across his face, and he replied with confidence. "Well, you can tell your superior that she is welcome to come and claim what she feels is due her. But I should warn you, our grav field has already been claimed by the Pyrrhen ship on our tail."

The line was silent as the fighter pilot digested this and likely radioed back to his ship for further instructions. Then he came back on the line, a little less confident in his demands. "You will disengage from the Pyrrhen ship immediately."

Raines laughed. "Oh, son, if that were an option, we would have done that already. I'm afraid the Pyrrhens have engaged us without our consent. We haven't heard a word from them yet. But if you want to pass along a message for us? Tell them we'd love to give them the plans they so desire, but that we've already promised the goods to you."

Lena clicked off the comms on their end. "What are you doing?" she hissed.

"New plan," he said quietly. He winked and clicked back on the comms. "And if you could let them know, also, that we're flattered by their offer of such a generous payment, but that honor and our word carries more weight. We'd much rather do business with our own people anyway."

The line went dead again as Raines cut the comms, his jovial manner gone. "*Ma petite*, I'm going to sell this for all I have, but this is all going to be on you. As soon as the Pyrrhens drop their pull, and I think they will, I am going to need you to pull as hard as you can on the station and institute a strong push against the Pyrrhen ship. We need as much speed as we can manage. Are they in range?"

She consulted the console. "Yes, but..."

"No. No buts. You can do this."

Enacting a simultaneous push and pull in opposite directions wasn't impossible, as it was a single trajectory for the ship, but it was still difficult. Usually, a vector in a single direction could be tempered by alternating pushes or pulls in short bursts in different directions to alter course, but to enact two engagements at the same time with the appropriate amounts of energy extended to each? The calculations, the checks? She wouldn't have time for the math. She'd be acting on instinct alone.

"What makes you think the Pyrrhens will drop their pull?"

"That."

Raines gestured at the console, and she could see the Myrton fighters pulling into a formation as both the *Aspasia* and the Pyrrhen ship approached. They were going to attack the Pyrrhen ship.

"Wait! They can't attack. We're in the middle. We'll be hit."

"No," Raines said, calm as ever. "They won't risk us. We're the toy they're both fighting over." He leaned forward, watching out of the real-view screen as Lena leaned over the console. He was right. The fighters were fanning out, going wide, giving them straight shots past *Aspasia*. They were aiming for the Pyrrhens. But if the Pyrrhens were taken out, the almost completely unarmed crew of the *Aspasia* would still have to deal with the armed Myrton fighters. And if the Pyrrhens returned fire?

"Be ready."

CHAPTER THIRTY-NINE

He didn't have to tell her again. She readied her vectors. With the formation of the Myrton fighters, there was no one between her and the jump station. She'd be able to enact a direct pull. She zeroed in on the center of the station. Then she located the secondary anchor: the small stable mass beyond the station. The anchor wasn't large enough or massive enough to act as a primary pull or push point, but it was enough to allow ships to alter course and direct themselves around the station.

Her hands were poised over the controls, ready to move when the comms beeped.

"The Pyrrhens," Raines announced. He'd been waiting patiently as she focused, and now he connected the call without even looking at her. He knew she was ready. They were going to face this one together.

That familiar voice came over again. "Lee, stand down."

Raines tensed beside her, but before he could say anything, Lena grabbed his arm and squeezed a warning. This one was her fight. "What do you want Evan?"

"You know what I want. I want you."

"And the weapon," Lena finished.

"I'd be foolish to not want the plans for the weapon. It could make my career. It could turn history. But without you—"

"You'd have a cleaner shot?"

He paused. "Lena, you know how I feel about you."

She did. She'd heard his voice on the last message. His true voice. He'd let it slip in his anger. She wasn't going to forget it. He didn't care about her any more than he cared about Cedomir or Dejan or any of the rest of the bodies that got in his way.

"Go to hell, Evan."

With that, she cut the transmission.

She looked over in the silence that followed to find Raines smiling over at her. "What?"

"Nothing," he said, but his grin grew even wider.

"Shut up," she said and turned back to her console. She knew they only had one shot at this. If she hesitated, if she gave either the Pyrrhens or the Myrtons a chance to seize the upper hand, she would lose their opportunity. They would be claimed.

Lena saw the shot in real-time before it showed up on her console. The blinding flash came from the ship most directly in front of them, and it took her a moment to remember that she wasn't the one being fired upon. The Myrton ship at the center of the formation had taken its shot, signaling to the other fighters that the engagement was on. That bright a flash meant they were using light-delivery explosives. The targeting was incredibly exact, though the damage inflicted from a single shot was typically minimal. They were hoping for surface damage at this point. They were still just sending a message to the Pyrrhens to back off. It worked. Whether the LDEs achieved maximum damage by hitting a vital system or whether the threat of a full array of Myrton ships against a single Pyrrhen transport was enough to cow them, the Pyrrhens dropped their pull on *Aspasia*.

A half-second later, Lena put a hard pull directly on the jump station, using a significant portion of their chehon to accelerate them far beyond what she should have done in such conditions. They were less than a hundred kilometers at this point. Such an intense pull could set them up for collision in mere seconds. No one sane would have pulled at such strength on a stable target at this close a range.

Which made her sudden forward propulsion a surprise to both the Pyrrhens and the Myrtons.

She gave neither time to consider her movements.

She half expected to feel the acceleration as they hurtled toward the station, but beyond the alerts from her screens and the quickly approaching station in her foreground, there was nothing to convey her speed.

The station grew and grew until it filled their forward screen.

They were coming on fast. Too fast.

They were going to hit.

Raines pushed himself back into his chair as if that would save him.

Lena smiled. Doubt her, would he?

She waited until the last possible millisecond to throw their vector in a new direction. She threw out a sudden chehon burst toward the anchor. That small pulse yanked the ship outwards, toward the anchor, before Lena dropped the pull and let them follow their sudden new vector on residual speed. Most of her inertia was preserved as *Aspasia* suddenly swept right and flew past the jump station.

Raines gasped as he could make out the individual ports along the station's starward wall.

It was close.

Too close.

But Lena exulted. This was her ship. Her element. Nothing could touch her out here.

In just another minute, she would be far enough away to escape the gravitational pull of the entire Sinopean system and escape all this. She pushed harder against the station that was now behind her to gain the extra speed needed for her jump. The station would then take her cue and alternate its boson field flows, dropping its artificial mass as she executed the jump. That would eliminate any residual gravitational influence as she dropped her own push and allowed her jump drive to fold her and her ship into a whole new star system.

Just a few more seconds and they would be away, safe in Samara. They could breathe, complete their mission, and be free of this war.

Still, she couldn't help but look back at what mess she was leaving behind.

She looked down at her console. The Pyrrhen warship was facing down the Myrton fighters. *Aspasia* might be getting away with the plans, but the Myrtons still saw the Pyrrhen ship as a threat. A threat they would eliminate.

Lena watched as the Myrtons opened full fire on Evan's ship. The Pyrrhens quickly returned the volley, but they were outnumbered. They'd take heavy hits if they didn't try to get out of there.

A light on the console told Lena that someone was trying to get through on the comms. She didn't even have to guess who it was.

"What's the matter, Evan? This war getting a little too real for you?"

"Lena," he said. "You have to stop this. Please. You can stop all of this." Gone was the unshakable scientist who thought to leverage her family's work, to manipulate her feelings for him. All that was left was the scared, small man he had become. "Lena, please. You owe me."

"And what exactly do I owe you? You lied to me, you stole from my family, you put me and my ship in danger, got my friends killed, and you started a war. So please tell me how I owe you anything more than my complete disgust."

"I saved your life," he said. "My people would have killed your entire crew if I hadn't intervened on your behalf."

"Your people never would have caught us in the first place if you hadn't been following me."

"I need you, Lena. And I love you."

Raines guffawed beside her but had enough sense to keep his mouth shut.

"You love me?" Lena asked. "You expect me to believe that."

"After all this time, I never gave up on you. On us. Please, Lena. We can work something out."

"Evan, darling. Let me tell you something about us. We were done when you abandoned me on Rien. We were done before you ever thought to drag me into this mess. So why don't you work something out with the Myrtons?"

"Lee, you can't do this," Evan protested, his voice growing shrill.

"Watch me." She cut the comms and jumped away.

CHAPTER FORTY

Lena felt her insides unfold as they came out of the jump. A brief wave of nausea rolled through her stomach as she got her bearings in an entirely new system. A familiar small star beckoned them from across millions of cold kilometers.

Samara.

She was home.

Well, she was still a long way from home. But she had arrived in the familiar system for the first time in years.

They were somewhere in the empty space far below the star Samara and the orbits of her many planets, stars, and assorted other bodies. There was nothing to encounter out here. No LIBs, no stations, nothing to suddenly arrive upon or crash into. Just a single anchor point they could use to push themselves toward the star above them. Most ships carried a fair bit of inertia from their jump, and they could rely on that alone, or use a burst from the anchor to send them in their desired direction. At the speed Lena had approached her jump, they were already on a good track for home. They could reach Rien in a matter of days. They were so close.

Lena prepared to plot a course directly for Rien.

Home.

The coordinates were already in her system. There was nothing she had to do. Her inertia, any push points, her destination, and its rotation: all were accounted for in her systems. She put in where she wanted to go, and there was her route. There was everything she needed to arrive at Lomasky Corporation's headquarters on the Palerm Coast of Rien, outside the city of Maritown.

Less than two days. How could it be possible?

"Lena?" A voice spoke from the back of the bridge. Gael. He didn't step forward. Didn't come onto the bridge. Instead, he lingered by the door. "Can we — Can I do anything?"

"Nothing to do, *ami*. She did it all," Raines said, clapping Lena on the back of her shoulder. "We're here."

"Can I just— I mean, do you need anything?" Gael was hesitant, afraid to approach her.

Just as well. She didn't want to look at him. Didn't want to face what happened between them earlier. Didn't want to acknowledge that their relationship had likely irrevocably changed. "No," she said, not turning around. "We'll arrive in a few days. Raines will have a plan then."

She didn't have to hear him disappear. Raines watched, though. "Right. Want to tell me what that was?"

She confirmed the course and the lack of obstacles between *Aspasia* and Rien. They'd be fine for hours. She closed down the flight menus. "I'm going for a run," she said, standing.

"Don't you think you've run enough?"

She gave him a withering look. "Not cute," she said as she pushed past him and went straight to her room. Raines followed closely on her heels.

"Lena. Hey. Lena." The insistence in his voice grew.

She tried to shut the door on him, but he stepped inside before it could slide shut. "What is going on?"

"Leave me alone, Raines." She turned her back on him and faced her dresser drawers, opening one and grabbing her running shorts. Keeping her back to Raines, she began to shimmy out of her pants.

"No," he said. Stepping closer to her. She grabbed a t-shirt and stepped away, trying to dance past him as she shrugged out of the black shirt that still smelled of Gael. "What was that?"

"What was what?" She lifted the clean t-shirt to pull it over her head, but he grabbed it out of her hands. "Hey!"

"What happened between you and Gael?" He demanded, standing between her and the door.

She crossed her arms across her exposed midsection and glared at him. "Nothing is between us."

He took a deep breath. "I'm not going to play games. I've flown with you for seven years. I've known Gael for over twenty. What happened?"

"We fucked on the bridge. Jealous?" She didn't know why she said it. She wasn't trying to hurt him; she wasn't trying to protect Gael. It just came out.

He closed his eyes and took another deep breath before looking at her. "Please don't hurt him."

The words hit her like a pulse blast to her sternum. That hadn't been the reaction she'd expected. It took all the fight out of her. She braced herself back against her drawers. "I wouldn't hurt Gael." The words felt hollow, so she leaned into them. "I wouldn't."

"I know you wouldn't mean to," Raines said, offering her shirt to her. "Just. Be careful."

She accepted the shirt. Instead of putting it on, she sat back on the bed, holding it limply in her hand. "I don't want to hurt anyone." She looked down to the limp, black fabric. Cheap, synthetic nothing. "Least of all Gael." She twisted the shirt, back and forth, knotting and creasing it in between her hands. "Least of all you."

Raines sat down beside her. He didn't look at her. "Lena." He stopped. Looked at her. Then back down at his feet. "I know you. And I love you. But I don't harbor any illusions about you. I don't harbor any illusions about who or what you are. You don't need to be...I don't know. Any of those silly ideas about what you think you should have been. An heiress, a pilot, a Lomasky. You're you. That's... enough." He reached over and placed a hand over her clenched fist, encompassing the fabric of her knotted shirt and all of her panic. "You're perfect the way you are." He squeezed and let her hand go, letting his own hand fall limply to his side. "But I can see where ..." He stopped. Clenched his own fists and released them. "I understand why you might want someone who ... someone who sees you for what you could be."

Raines stood then without turning to look at Lena. She looked up and stared at the outline of his shoulder blades on the back of his shirt. "Just don't hurt him," Raines said, before turning back to the door.

He reached for the button, but Lena grabbed his arm. He turned back to her. It was rare to see any vulnerability in his eyes, but it was there. For half a second, it was there. And it was enough to confirm Lena's decision.

"I don't want Gael," she said. She didn't know it for sure until she said it. But it was true. She didn't want someone who loved her like he did. Who saw her only for her potential. Who believed in what she could be.

She needed someone who knew who she was. Who accepted that she was flawed and wrong and selfish and broken. She wanted to be with someone who saw exactly who she was; not some idealized version of herself, but the stripped-down, raw, dirty truth of a damaged and flawed woman.

What had happened on the bridge, what she'd done with Gael, it had been because he saw the fantasy version of her, and she'd needed that in that moment. She had needed someone to push her through the hurt and the pain of the last several days. She'd used his adoration to get through her grief.

But she looked at Raines now.

This arrogant, insecure, blustering man knew what it was to be lost in the black. He knew how it felt to be stripped of moorings and cast adrift. He knew her, and he came to her without any illusions.

"I want you." She stepped up to him and kissed him. It felt right. Never mind the assurances and comfort she found anywhere else. Raines's embrace didn't shelter her from the panic she felt. She didn't forget where she was going, what she had to do. She didn't lose track of where she was in the grand scheme of things: a small thread in a rapidly fraying tapestry.

But in Raines's arms, she felt real. Whatever her faults, whatever her misgivings, he accepted them.

He kissed her back and gave her everything she asked, everything she needed of him.

CHAPTER FORTY-ONE

Two days went faster than Lena wanted.

Too soon, she could see Rien looming. At first, the planet was just a small glittering dot in the distance; then as they approached, she took on a blue glow. The atmosphere glittered around the large planet like a halo, with Samara lighting half of her face. As they came closer, Lena began to see landmarks on the southern hemisphere. It was early morning where they were headed, the electric lights just beginning to fade away as Samara dawned, bright and unyielding. The eastern edge of Palerm on the Oreta continent was stark against the sea, Gendar a glittering metropolis to the north and Monticello along the southern border. Meadon was the large central city with long spokes of cities and towns extending out from her center to connect the people of her nation. And there, the largest city along the western coast, the lights of Maritown seemed the brightest of all as she waited for the sun to wake her.

Lena couldn't help the tears that came unbidden to her eyes, but she kept them mostly to herself. Cat, who had come to see the final approach, had no such hesitation about her home planet. She leaned into Chandra's arms and wept openly. "She's so beautiful."

"Quite beautiful," Chandra agreed, though she seemed uneasy with this sudden display of emotion. She rubbed Cat's arms but kept looking to Lena for help. She was out of luck. Lena was focused on the planet below.

She focused on the Palerm space station orbiting over the continent. The station had ports that could easily take in *Aspasia* whole for docking, so Lena wouldn't have to worry about the lack of a gangway. Then they could take a shuttle to the surface. With luck, they'd be at the Lomasky Corporation headquarters within the next twenty-six hours.

From there, Lena wasn't sure what would happen. Tadashi Lomasky was not a warm man, but he might welcome her back after all this time. She was his only heir, his last living child. Surely, he would be glad to see her.

And if not, well, she had leverage. She had the plans. He would want those back.

She contacted the station and arranged a port for *Aspasia*. The cost was exorbitant, extortionate, but Lean accepted the charges. It's not like she could take *Aspasia* to the surface of Rien in her current state. The atmospheric pressure of reentry would rip a hole in her hull.

She reached over to announce their approach when the ship shook violently. Cat and Chandra were thrown to the ground as an alarm blared through the bridge.

Lena clambered to her feet and saw alerts across all her systems. "We've been shot?"

Raines burst onto the bridge within seconds, followed closely by Gael.

"Rien?" Gael asked, pulling himself up to one side of the console.

"Systems?" Raines asked simultaneously, throwing himself into the co-pilot's chair and pulling up the life-support and hull systems. Lena had assessed those immediately and seen nothing to concern them. She had already moved on to finding out where the shots were coming from.

She pulled up her LIB view and found a ship bearing down on them. She focused her scan on that ship.

It couldn't be.

Pyrrhen.

Evan.

But how? How had he caught up?

It didn't matter. He was here. A few thousand kilometers out, but closing quickly. And his ship was firing on hers.

"Hold on, everybody," Lena said. Before Evan's ship could react, Lena pulled on Rien below, ushering in speeds that were, once again, unsafe at this distance. When she should have been decelerating, she was hurtling toward the planet faster and faster.

"Lee?" Raines said, eying her uneasily.

"Shut up," Lena said. She had to concentrate.

"We're landing planet-side?" Raines was incredulous.

"Right in the middle of Lomasky Campus. It's summer. Most of the outer lecture halls and buildings will be empty." Lena tried to assure them, to assure herself. "We don't have another choice. Everyone, find somewhere safe to bunk down. We're on a hard approach."

Cat and Chandra quickly fled the bridge, but Raines and Gael stood where they were.

"I'm serious," Lena said. "This is going to hurt."

"We're staying here," Gael said.

"And uh," Raines said. "We've got a comm waiting." He indicated a flashing light.

"Ignore it," Lena said. "It's Evan."

Raines snorted. "Yeah, I figured that much." But he obliged and stayed quiet.

Lena looked down at her console. They had a few minutes before they hit atmo, but after that, it would be hard burn down to the surface. She wasn't going to be able to mitigate the effects from that, but the direct route through would help them get through it all faster. They'd be approaching as the Palermian continent turned away. So they'd have to enter at the turning edge of the planet. If they hit it correctly, they could have the planet's spin help slow down their approach. Not much, but at the margins she'd be working with, the angle of descent might make the difference between them maintaining hull security as they entered the atmosphere.

"Safest place is Shuttle 1," Lena announced through the intercoms. "You want safe passage, head there." She turned to her two shadows. "You, too."

"Not unless you're going with us," Gael said.

"I've got to manually set course," Lena protested.

"And why is that? Some particular martyr complex?" Raines pressed.

"I've come too far to give up now," Lena said. "No, I'm not trying to get myself killed. But I can't program in our coordinates and expect *Aspasia* to land herself. If Evan comes after us, if the hull breaches, if anything happens, I have to take care of it."

"Lena, we can't let you take that risk with your life," Gael said.

She cocked an eyebrow at him. "I'm not risking anything. I was planning to strap in and close every bulkhead doors leading up here. If you want to stay on the bridge, it should be as safe as the shuttles."

"Oh," Raines said abashed. He and Gael exchanged a look. "Okay, we'll stay."

"All right, then. You still might want to buckle down. This won't be a smooth landing."

She ignored them as they went to batten down the hatches as it were. She had a spaceship to crash.

She didn't even bother to look at the ship behind her. Evan didn't matter. The Pyrrhens didn't matter. Nothing behind her mattered. She only had one mission. Land this damaged craft without killing everyone on board.

Easy.

She checked to make sure Cat and Chandra were settled in the shuttle before closing all the bulkhead doors in the ship. It might be a futile measure, but if any one compartment was compromised, especially the cargo hold with the damaged gangway, the sealed doors along each compartment could help the crew hold onto enough air until she got the ship on the grounds of the Lomasky Corporation headquarters.

Lena retrieved the coordinates from memory and then wired them into her navigation systems. An automated path was immediately returned. The path took a smooth slope into the planet's atmosphere and allowed for slowing at an easy pace to preserve fuel and minimize the impacts of increasing atmospheric pressure. It was the safest course.

Lena didn't have time for safe. She upped the pull to increase her speed.

The most logical pull center would be the center of gravity for the planet, but since her destination wasn't directly below her, the move would throw her off course at the speeds she was planning to use. She'd have to use something else to pull her back on course. The sun was coming up on the eastern edge of Palerm. And the moon was cresting the far edge of the planet; Palerm would be enjoying a waxing moon face. Perfect.

Three vectors. She could handle that. She was a Lomasky.

Though the ship was already headed toward the planet, she tugged harder on Rien's center of gravity. That would increase their speed and get them clear of Evan's ship. It would also set them on a collision course if she didn't react fast enough.

Though she couldn't feel the actual physical sensation of the tug, Lena felt her stomach flip in the direction of the planet. Everything told her she was going too fast, but she knew what her ship could handle. When she wasn't damaged.

She ignored that last thought.

Faster, faster, they hurtled toward the planet. The blue of the sphere grew more complex. She could make out clouds, bays, inlets along the coastlines. A storm was brewing off Monticello. There'd be flooding over the weekend.

There. The first shakes as the ship met the edges of the protective sphere that surrounded her planet. Hydrogen, helium, nitrogen, and the thinnest edges of oxygen were attacking the outside of her ship as she passed through. Too much matter here. Too many molecules hitting her as she moved at speeds she should never attempt this close to the planet.

Soon she would hit the thermosphere. That's when things would get really exciting.

She pulled tight on her own restraints. The small fabric straps over her torso would do little if they crashed onto the surface of the planet, but they could help a lot to keep her in one place as they were jostled by the journey there. Small consolations. The ship lurched.

"Are we hit?" Gael asked.

"No, that was normal," Lena said. That was the thermosphere.

Soon. Soon.

Now.

She threw out a push on Samara, nearly a hundred million kilometers away. Just a small pulse. It was enough. *Aspasia* jerked away from a direct shot toward the heart of Rien, to a vector that set her more on a parallel with the planet's horizon. This close, though, the gravitational pull of the planet was enough to keep her from veering too far away. She was still hurtling at incredible speeds through the outer edges of the planet's atmosphere.

"Lee? Um, Lee?" Raines said. "Should we, shouldn't we, aren't we going a bit fast?"

She ignored him. *Aspasia* was beginning to shake in earnest. She could feel it in her bones. Every moment, closer to ground.

Clunk.

Best case scenario, that was a piece of her ship being ripped away. Best case.

Ignore it.

The view outside was growing hazy. The particles they were traveling through were catching fire, but also slowing them down.

Good, she thought as the edges of her hull began to glow red with friction and pressure.

She let go of her pull on the planet. This close, the pull of normal gravity would do enough.

She wasn't slowing down. Not yet.

There. The pop.

They'd crossed the Karman line. They were almost to the mesophere.

She then aligned her sights on the moon, just cresting over the far edge of the planet. She couldn't see it with the sun coming up, but her screens all said it was there.

Target locked.

Just a few more seconds, and there. A quick tug. The ship lurched into a new vector.

The move barely reoriented them into a partial parabolic thrust. Just a few thousand kilometers of crest, and then back to Rien's gravitational influence.

Lena let *Aspasia* back into freefall.

As the atmosphere grew thicker, the pressure began to tear away at the ship. The hull began to heat up, and those jagged, unprotected edges and what was left of the gangway began to strain to break free. Lena watched as a flaming panel flew past the bridge.

"Was that important?" Raines asked from his strapped in seat beside her. He attempted a bemused tone, but Lena could hear the strain in his voice. He was scared.

She wasn't.

Everything was going the way it should. Lena stopped pulling on everything. Bosonic power was not going to be much help at this point. She did push once back at the planet's center, not enough to send them back into the upper reaches of the atmosphere, but enough to slow them down and give them a more graduated descent.

Now was the hard part.

Lena powered up thrust engines and grabbed hold of the flight stick. They were coming in too hot.

There was still time. She could pull them back up and orbit once for a safer approach.

No. That would give Evan time to catch them.

They had to land now.

She threw on the hard brakes. Side panels along the entire hull expanded out to slow her speed. She hoped they held. *Aspasia* was already starting to groan. The shaking that had started as they entered the outer edges intensified as the ship opened herself up to the full brunt of the air. Lena could feel her teeth banging together.

It was working. They were slowing. Now to find her landing site.

She scanned her readouts of the Lomasky Research Campus. The shuttle port was too small to handle a ship of her size, and there were no large fields to land in. There were too many buildings, too close together. But the administration buildings ringed a large natural lake.

It was deep enough, and if she approached from the south, she could take it at the deepest part as she moved toward the heart of the Lomasky campus.

If a ship is space-worthy, she's definitely lake-worthy, Lena assured herself as she pulled hard on the flight controls.

She pulled right and circled the campus in as wide an arc as she dared before aiming the ship down and forward. She spread the panels wider and lowered her landing gear.

"Hold on," she told anyone who would listen.

Down, down, down. Then at the last possible minute, Lena yanked hard to bring *Aspasia*'s nose up, letting the bottom skid down into the water. She anticipated the initial smack, but not the skip that followed. Her jaw clamped hard on her tongue, and she tasted blood as water exploded around them, washing the world away.

Were they underwater?

No, it streamed away. They were slowing down. They were alive, skidding through the water.

They weren't stopping.

Aspasia felt as though she would shake apart as she skidded along the bottom of the lake, spraying water out into the forest around them. Lena felt as the braking panels were ripped away along the bottom of the lake.

"I'm sorry," Lena murmured under her breath. "Oh, baby. I'm so sorry. Hang on. Hang on. Hang on." She pulled hard on the brakes. She had no idea if the landing gear would even work under the water, but she had no other options.

She felt something catch, and they started to slow.

It wasn't going to be enough. The buildings along the edge of the lake. The huge glass buildings looking out over the lake. They were going to hit.

There was nothing she could do but brace for impact. Instinctively, Lena tried to throw her head down under the console, but her restraints held her fast. She could only throw her hands up over her face.

The ship skidded through the front of the building finding far less resistance than they had faced when they hit the water. But finally, the steel and glass structure or the hard ground they slid along finally did what nothing else could.

Aspasia came to a stop in the middle of the Lomasky Corporation Research Campus.

She'd made it.

She'd come home.

CHAPTER FORTY-TWO

"We've got to move," Lena said pulling at her straps. "Evan will be here any minute, and we've got to get out without a gangway." She tugged again at her restraints. "Why won't this let go?!"

Raines grabbed her hands. She hadn't even known she was shaking so hard until he stilled her. "I got it." He let go with one hand and pressed the strap release. Her restraints fell off as she took a deep breath.

"Thanks," she whispered.

Raines nodded. He looked up. Gael was already waiting at the open door. "Walk out?"

"It'll be a drop, at this angle," Gael said, "but at least we cleared the lake. And most of the building."

Lena only hoped no one had been in the building they demolished.

"Let the others know?" Raines asked as he pulled Lena to her unsteady feet.

Gael was already out the door.

"Come on," Raines said. He supported her under her elbow as her knees threatened to give out. "Almost there. You've done the hard part."

"You sure?" Lena laughed. Now she just had to find her father in the central building and get him to agree to help develop countermeasures to a weapon he had commissioned in the first place. Was that supposed to be the easy part?

"Yeah," Raines said, smiling. Still smiling. He had that much confidence? "You've got this." In her? He had to have another plan waiting. "Now where are we headed?"

Lena sucked in a deep breath and thought for a second. "It's summer, so the executives are engaged in planning and strategy meetings. My father is most likely in his personal offices to the east. Two buildings away from the lake and to the right."

"Let's go." Raines steered her off the bridge and down through the cargo stairs toward the shuttle bays. They passed the shuttles and found Cat and Gael waiting.

"Chandra?" Lena asked.

"Grabbing some extra guns," Cat said. "In case."

Lena hoped they wouldn't need an arsenal. They were just going to meet with her father. And if they had to face down Evan between here and there, well, okay, then an arsenal might be worth having. She'd left her own pistol in her room, but she wasn't about to turn back now. If she turned back, if she stopped moving forward, she'd never make it.

So, she kept going. Raines led the way and was the first through the walkout door. He went in alone and let the airsafe door automatically shut behind him. Then apparently he let himself out the other side, letting the auto-close shut the outer door behind him. Even now, the life-support systems wouldn't allow for an override of the walkout protocols.

As soon as they had the go-ahead, Lena and Gael entered the walkout safe-space. The inner door shut behind them and gave them clearance to open the outer door. Gael swung it out and revealed the ladder had broken away, and there was a six-meter drop to Raines who was waiting below.

"Okay, you first," Gael said.

Lena looked down. "Do I just let myself dangle, and then drop?"

"That's the idea."

Lena looked down again. Six meters wasn't that much, but it was enough.

She got down on her hands and knees and began to back out the door, feeling her feet exposed to empty air. She let herself out slowly over the edge, holding herself up by her torso, her chest, and then just her elbows. She could do this. She pushed herself out, holding on by her forearms, and then, Gael grabbed her hands. "I got you." He grabbed her by the wrists and leaned over to dangle her as far down as he could manage. "Okay, you have to drop. Raines will catch you."

She nodded and let him count to three. They each let their hands release, and Lena fell to Raines's waiting arms below. She came down, feet first, and he barely had a chance to catch her about the waist to absorb her fall. She felt the ground with a thud that reverberated through her knees. But she was down.

She looked up to Gael. He already had let the door close and was waiting on Cat.

Within moments he had lowered her and landed beside her absorbing the fall with a crouch, and they all looked up as they watched the door close cleanly behind them. Chandra would follow on her own.

"Where to?" Gael asked.

"This way." Lena turned and began walking east, to her father's office.

She tried to keep her head high, to breathe normally. She belonged here. This was her domain, her legacy.

Every step forward threatened to send her to her knees.

Security crews ran past them headed toward the ruined conference building and *Aspasia*, calling into their comm devices. Dozens more people had run out to see what had caused such a terrible noise in the commons and were standing around gawking at the crew as they limped forward toward the executive building. Lena thought she heard her name amongst the voices, and she swore there were screens aimed at her, taking her picture already. Sirens approached in the distance. So much for a quiet homecoming.

The grand entrance to her father's personal office building grew larger and larger. He was in there.

She wasn't sure how she knew it, but she was certain. It was like she could feel him inside. She could see the scene play out in her head as she made her way across the green space. She could imagine his face as she met his eyes for the first time. His steely brown eyes under heavy-lidded eyes. His dark hair cut sharp above straight-edged eyebrows. He would look at her with disappointment as he asked her why she destroyed his beautiful campus.

No. That was absurd.

He'd welcome her home warmly. "My long-lost daughter. My only heart. Welcome home," he'd say with open arms and a smile.

That was even more absurd.

She walked through the open archway of the executive building, into the large sunlit entryway, and blinking in the refracted light found herself face-to-face with Evan.

"You have got to be kidding me. How?" she asked.

He stood there with an exultant grin on his face. He'd beaten her. He'd gotten there before her.

And he had a gun trained directly on her.

"If you reach for your guns, I shoot her now," Evan said as Gael, Raines, and Cat walked in behind her. "And my friends shoot you." He gestured behind him to two bodyguards with their own pistols aimed at the crew.

"We outnumber you," Raines said.

"Are you fast enough to move before I shoot your girlfriend?" Evan smiled. "I didn't think so. Gunter." He nodded to one of his guards who stepped forward to disarm the crew, claiming over six weapons in all. Raines and Gael had been more prepared than she had thought.

"How did you get here before us?" Lena asked. It was impossible he had beat her after that flight.

"I've been waiting here for days. Enjoying the hospitality of my former boss. Your father has quite the extensive wine collection."

Lena scoffed. He was lying. Her father hated him. "We just talked in the Sinope System. There's no way you beat us here."

He beamed. "Recorded responses. My techs came up with a variety of phrases that would answer anything you asked or said. All of my ships have them. I didn't think they'd manage to convince you to roll over, but my superior insisted we try to take you peacefully." He shrugged. "I did tell her you were a bit too headstrong for that. The only place you'd be sure to go, though, was here. Hell of an entrance, by the way."

"Thanks." She gritted her teeth. Maybe if she stalled, her father's security would happen on them. They couldn't all be investigating the crash site. "So, it's all been an act? The declarations of love, the engineered escape attempt—"

"The courtship, the engagement, yes, yes, yes." He rolled his eyes at her. "Look, you're a sweet girl, Lena. Really. I'm sure you make your little captain there very happy. But can we cut this short? I have a shuttle to catch." He held out his hand. "The plans."

Lena clutched at the left pocket on her hip. It was a feint. She didn't have the plans. Gael did. But if she could keep Evan guessing, looking for the plans, that could buy them more time. Raines would come up with something.

Lena shook her head sadly. "What happened to you, Evan? You aren't the man I remember. You are a scientist. An engineer. You don't believe in using violence like this."

"And your family doesn't develop weapons, does it?" Scorn dropped from his lips and thudded heavily in her ears. "Wake up, princess. Your father would do anything if it would help him cling to his pathetic legacy a few more years. And he'll probably get what he wants because he has more money than the entire Pandian system. Which is about half of what I'm going to get when I develop this weapon for the Pyrrhens. Now, give me the damn plans."

"I'm not giving you anything."

Evan sighed. "Then I'll start shooting your friends." He signaled to one of his guards who trained a gun on Raines. "Do you think your captain will be as handsome without a face?"

"Wait!" Lean said. "You can't shoot him. Lomasky security will be on us in seconds."

Evan chuckled as he shook his head. "You weren't listening, *liebschien.* I told you. I've been here for days. Headed straight here after the *Scharnhorst.* You were always going to come running to daddy. His personal sanctuary. His office. The executive building has been cleared for decontamination this week. Seems they had a problem with pests." He now trained his gun on Raines as well. "Now, give me my damn plans, or your sweetheart gets it."

"Stop! I'll give you the plans. I just don't have them."

Evan gestured with his free hand. "Your pocket."

She reached into her pockets and pulled out the lining. "Nothing. It was a bluff. I left the plans on *Aspasia.*"

"I'm not an idiot, LeeLee. You just crash-landed in the middle of Lomasky-ville. Security is crawling over your precious ship by now. You wouldn't take the chance." He retrained the gun on her. "I'm through with the games. Now. Hand them over."

"He is right, Helena," a voice said from above. "We've had enough games. Where are the plans?"

Lena looked up to the balcony overlooking the entry lobby. There he was.

Tadashi Lomasky.

Her father.

And his dozen armed guards with weapons aimed directly at her.

CHAPTER FORTY-THREE

"Hello, Father," Lena said. Her voice was steadier than she anticipated. She sounded the way she wanted: cold, collected, professional. The best way to approach Tadashi Lomasky. Inside, though, she was liquid fear poured into a frozen basin of anger and resentment. She would hold her icy exterior as long as she could.

She gave herself about five minutes.

"Helena," Tadashi nodded just as coolly as he made his way to the stairs along the edge of the lobby. He stalked down, seemingly oblivious of the guns defending him to his back and the two weapons now aimed up at him from Evan's guard. He wouldn't give them more than a minute's thought. He had his security, and he trusted them because he had handpicked them. The guns were their responsibility, their job. Therefore, he could attend to other matters. Compartmentalized. Everything filed away in its proper place.

And at this moment, his daughter took up all his attention.

She remembered what it was to be looked at like that. Like you were his entire world. Sometimes it was good—recitals, big games, bringing home that award. And other times it could be terrifying—when you forgot your solo, when you swung and missed, when you brought home a failing grade. She wasn't sure what to file this under.

"You have recovered our plans?" he asked.

Our. Yours and mine. Ours.

"I have them," she replied just as evenly, falling into their once familiar rhythm. "I'm disappointed, though, to hear that there was only one copy. You always taught me the importance of redundancy. What happened to your backups?"

He sighed and waved his hands as he reached the bottom of the stairs. "This and that. Theft mostly. Drive corruption, hard copies burned, an entire lab of developers and researchers blown up with all that information locked away in their brains. And then the assassinations of those responsible? I must say it was quite the cleanup."

She didn't know how to interpret that.

"Sounds like an ordeal," she said. "But it seems you handled it."

"Indeed," her father confirmed, walking up beside her. He gave her a good looking over, from head to toe, taking in her appearance as well as her companions'. "You look well." And that was it. No tear-stained welcome. No heartfelt acknowledgment of her seven-year absence. Nothing. He turned instead to glance back at Evan to give him the same appraisal before turning back to Lena. "I thought you got rid of this one?"

Evan seethed. "I'm sorry to interrupt this little family reunion." This was clearly not going according to his carefully laid plans. She understood the feeling. "But I have things I have to do. A war to return to. Can we get this whole thing moving?"

Tadashi cocked a perfectly manicured eyebrow at him and turned back to Lena. "Do you have an explanation for this?"

"Sorry, Father," she said. "He just won't leave me alone."

"Mind if I—?" he gestured to Evan.

"Mind if you what?" Evan barked.

"Not at all," Lena said.

Tadashi turned to his head guard. He nodded once. Shots rang out from up above as Evan's men collapsed, each one taking a bullet to the head. Evan was left standing, his arms crossed over his head.

Tadashi walked up to Evan. "I told you once before: you do not deserve my daughter. And you certainly don't deserve the fruits of my labor. There is no deal between myself and your pathetic excuse for an empire. There never was and never will be. You have exactly ten seconds to exit this building, an hour to leave my planet, and precisely one week to have your ship and all Pyrrhen ships gone from this system before I eliminate you completely." He turned his back and nodded to his guard again. The head of Tadashi Lomasky's guard lifted his gun and pointed it at Evan. Lena didn't doubt that he had already started counting.

Evan apparently didn't doubt it either. He was gone without a single glance spared for Lena.

"I always did tell you he was a waste of resources," Tadashi said. She could almost detect a smile in his almond eyes. Almost. He did so love being proved right. "Now, about my plans?" So, it was back to **his** plans.

And his guns.

Now that Evan was gone, Lena noticed all the guns—from the snipers on the balconies above to the bodyguards here on the ground—were aimed at her and her crew. "Father? Could you ask your men to lower their weapons? We're not a threat."

"The plans," he repeated, ignoring her comments. "I entertained your boyfriend for most of a week waiting on you. He promised you were coming with the plans. Where are they?"

She hesitated. She had brought the plans here with every intention of handing the plans over and letting her father take control of the situation. She had felt certain that he would know what to do, who to contact in the Rienen government to get things moving, how to put countermeasures into place to help defend the innocent people of Aegea should Pyrrhos develop anything like this. He would take care of things.

Now she doubted that.

"We don't have them on us," she said. She was acting on instinct here and really hoped her crew followed her lead. "They're hidden back on our ship."

Tadashi half turned his head to his guard but kept his eyes on Lena. "Search them."

"It's true, Mr. Lomasky," Gael said, clenching his hands at his side to keep from fingering his jacket pocket. "They're hidden in the frame of my bed, in a hidden compartment. It's where they've been for the past few weeks. The lead frame protects it from external scans, but also protects the contents against any electromagnetic weapons."

"We didn't want to risk bringing them off-board until things were secure, sir," Raines continued seamlessly. "We have had, shall we say, several security incidents recently."

"We also left behind a senior Yoddha agent, to protect the ship against attack," Cat added to Lena's surprise.

Tadashi wasn't buying it. He nodded again to his guard, who waved forward a woman who was going to search them. She started toward Lena, who threw up her hands and stepped back. Lena reacted in fear, but she tried to pass it off as indignation. "You will not touch me," she spat, summoning as much aristocratic outrage and disgust as she could. It was scary how quickly it came back to her. She turned on her father feigning more indignation to hide the hurt. "This is really how you're going to welcome me home? After everything? After all these years?" She advanced on him, doing her best to ignore every gun that immediately trained on her. "Haven't I sacrificed enough for this family? What more do I have to do to show you I'm sorry?"

"You're sorry?" Tadashi asked.

"Of course, I'm sorry!" She wanted to scream, but she swallowed hard against it. "I never meant to hurt anyone." She was not going to cry. She would not show him weakness. But those people. Her baby sister. "I never wanted — I never meant for Mariko to get hurt."

"Do not speak her name." The look he gave her. The pain, the hopelessness. Then he softened. For just a second. She saw a weakness in her father. But it was gone as he took a deep breath. "She was never supposed to be a part of it."

"Mariko? Part of what?" Had she misunderstood him?

"She was supposed to be back with us, your mother and me. In the docks, waiting for your triumphant arrival. I didn't even know she had gone until it was too late. If I had known. If I had realized she was on that loading arm..."

"But you couldn't have known what was going to happen," Lena protested. "You can't blame yourself. It was an accident. It was my accident. And there was nothing you could have done...but I...I could have...it's done. It's still done. And we have to move forward." She stepped forward to offer him comfort.

He recoiled as the guards behind him shuffled, uncertain.

He laughed then. Unexpected and cold. "It is done. You are right, my daughter. My only daughter. The last Lomasky. It is done." He reached his hand out. "Now give me the plans.'

"We already told you—"

"You are lying to me." Gone was the emotional man who had embraced her. Gone was the man who mourned the death of one daughter and the loss of the other. He was all business once again. "Your ship is empty. You have no agent on board. No plans in bed frames. Your ship has already been searched. You have hidden them somewhere, and I will know where. Now tell me where the plans are, or I will finish what your feckless fiancé started. Your friends will die here."

CHAPTER FORTY-FOUR

Lena didn't doubt her father was capable of ordering them all killed and then mopping away their existence if it would get him what he wanted.

"Okay," Lena said, holding up her hands. "No one has to die. We'll give you the plans. I just want to know something first."

Tadashi sighed deeply and gestured at her to continue as if he was indulging a small child in some inane whimsy instead of granting his only child a last request.

She wouldn't be put off. "Why? Why would you ever commission something like this weapon? You had to have known what something like this would mean. That once it was thought up that someone would build it. And once it was built, someone would use it."

"One only hopes that one's ideas will find usefulness in the world," her father conceded.

"But a weapon? It's one thing to develop new means of travel, of revolutionizing the way we conduct our lives, our businesses. But weapons? Why would you even think to use our legacy for something like this?"

"I secured our legacy," he said. "Helena, a legacy is nothing but history if it doesn't have a future. And without this weapon, we had nothing to offer the future. We had no power. Prestige? Money? They have been watered down, democratized. Science and innovation are the tools for the small man to elevate himself. But for those of us on the top, we need to find ways to stay there. We needed strength."

"You developed a super-weapon as a power grab?" Lena sputtered, disgusted.

Tadashi frowned. "I had this weapon developed as way to give us a voice in the future. I have ensured that the Lomaskys will always help to direct the path of history. We will mold the universe into the shape we desire, and no one will tell a Lomasky 'no' ever again."

"If only you had someone to pass that legacy onto." She was being childish. She didn't care. She was buying time, hoping that Raines and Gael worked out some way to get them out of there and keep the plans from her father. There was no way she was handing over this super-weapon to him if this was his motivation. He had no ultimate plans. He just wanted to stay on top, keep power in his own hands. No matter what else he said, this innovation was about power. His power, and no one else's.

"Do not be petulant, Helena. You were never entitled to anything I built. To what your grandfather built. You have always been expected to pave your own way."

"And I would have, if not—"

"For the accident?" he finished. He sneered. "You still think the accident was what held you back. Oh, my dear, you were never going to amount to much. A pilot?" He laughed. "Your family creates things. We solve problems. We change the world. You would have done what? Chauffeured your betters? You never deserved what was coming your way."

Raines started to step forward in Lena's defense, but he was quickly stilled by a redirection of a few laser sights.

Lena was on her own. In so many ways.

"But I was the best," Lena protested weakly.

"Of the pilots, yes," Tadashi placated. "A real knack for skilled labor." His words dripped with disdain. He turned his back to her. He held his hands clasped, but she could see the blood draining from them, and his shoulders begin to droop as his head fell forward. "It should have been you that died that day," he whispered.

Lena couldn't find her breath. Her vision spotted with dark stars that danced around her head. "What?" She needed him to say it again, or she'd never believe she heard him correctly.

Tadashi straightened and turned to look her in the eye as he delivered his indictment again. "It should have been you that died in that accident."

Lena felt the statement like a punch to her gut. It left her winded and gasping. She wanted to protest, to ask him to explain himself, to tell her why. But she couldn't find the words.

Her father didn't have that problem.

"Your sister was never meant to be on that loading arm. She was supposed to be safe with me. She was going to take your place. Carry on after you were gone. She was my legacy. A scientist, an inventor. She was brilliant, capable, ambitious. Everything you were not." He advanced on Lena, staring down at her, filled with hatred she never imagined he would feel for her. "And you killed her."

"It was an accident," Lena whispered, cowering before her father.

"It was carefully planned." He shook his head. "You stupid, stupid girl. The whole thing was designed."

"But," Lena protested. "I pulled on the dock. I miscalculated and used the wrong force."

"No," he shook his head. "Or maybe you did. Wouldn't that have been convenient? But it didn't matter. My engineers installed a subprogram that would have made that move regardless. You were supposed to recognize that the arm wasn't approaching correctly and reach out to it, guide the ship in instead of letting the dock come to you. It's what you did in every landing you ever made. The subprogram was going to make sure you came in too hard and crushed the loading arm. It was going to be a horrible tragedy, and we'd all mourn the lives lost. But you'd take the fall, die in ignominy, and leave the company blameless."

It was planned? She hadn't been responsible. All these years, all these years she'd found herself wracked with guilt over that her stupid mistake, and it had never been her mistake. She'd done nothing wrong. Relief, anger, confusion warred in her.

"But why?" she asked. "Why would you do that to me?"

"We needed someone to fall from grace. And you were never going to amount to anything, anyway."

She waited for the impact of those words to hit her like all the other betrayals, the disappointments and hurts. She waited for the punch in her gut, the breathless desperation of losing her ground, of setting adrift in a world where even her own father didn't care about her. She waited for the lump in the throat, the tears in her eyes, and the clenched knot in her chest.

But none of it came.

Not this time.

Maybe it was the realization that all that guilt she'd been holding had been for nothing. That the pain she'd held onto for seven years was based on a lie. That she wasn't to blame.

Maybe it was the pattern of betrayal and deception. First Evan and now her father. Two of the men she had most trusted had turned on her, but she'd survived anyway.

Maybe it was that of all he had said, the idea that she was never going to amount to anything was so obviously a lie that even she could see through it.

Whatever the reason, for once, the hurtful things he said didn't strike her as deeply.

They just made her angry.

"What do you mean, 'you needed someone to fall'?"

"Your potential was always so pedestrian, Lena, you must know that," he continued.

"No," she said. "No. Stop." His eyebrows raised at her ordering him, but he waited. "I get why you chose me to set up. I'm the expendable daughter. I get that part." She was over that part. "Why did you need to set someone up in the first place?"

He hesitated, and the revulsion in his eyes was replaced by fear as he dropped his gaze for a half-second before returning to her. "You had to be removed for your sister to thrive."

"Bullshit," she said. "This is about the damned weapon." She made a noise that was halfway between a strangled laugh and an exasperated sigh. "It's all about the weapon. You needed to redirect attention away from what you were developing."

Her father gave her a look. "You're smarter than that. If I had my hands on the greatest technology our race has ever developed, beyond even the advances we've made in space travel and normalized gravity manipulation, why would I attempt to hide that fact? I'd make billions on stock speculation alone."

"You had already lost the plans by then," Raines concluded.

Tadashi nodded to him. "He is as smart as your last boyfriend, Helena. I hope he has better character."

"After everything, you're going to try and play father?" Lena narrowed her eyes at him. "No. You lost that privilege." She crossed her arms and stared him down. "But he's right. You lost the plans, didn't you?"

"They were stolen, yes. By one of our scientists, we believe. And they were planning to sell it to the highest bidder. The Pyrrhens most likely. But the plans they took were incomplete."

He didn't know that it was Mason and his team that had stolen the plans, then.

"Regardless, they took the plans, deleted the backups, burned half my lab down, and half of the team that knew of the damned thing disappeared."

"So, you cleaned up the mess," Gael spat.

"I would have been ruined. The weapon only matters if I control who has access. If it's out there, in the hands of just anyone? Lomasky Corp would have been destroyed. I panicked. I admit it. It was beneath me. But I couldn't risk it getting out that I had created and then lost something of this importance. Stocks would plummet. I couldn't afford it. So, I eliminated any unsecured trace of it. I, of course, kept copies of what we had left for myself. But the equations were incomplete. We— my scientists still haven't been able to recreate the exact circumstances that made the weapon possible."

"And that's why you need the plans."

"It's been seven years. If they haven't figured it out on their own, then the technology may be lost to us. So, you see, I need that data. Now, Lena. I'm done explaining myself. Your time is up. Give me the plans."

She closed her eyes and clenched her teeth to hold back the anger, the disgust that was welling up inside her. He didn't care about what this weapon really meant. He only cared about the profit he could wring out of it, the influence, the power he could gain from controlling it.

Suddenly Tadashi's tone softened. "Helena. Lena. I need you tell me where the plans are." She opened her eyes and watched as he reached out to her but drew back before he ever touched her. "This technology is dangerous. If you've seen what it can do, you know that. We have to keep this sort of thing safe. If this thing gets into the wrong hands, it could mean destruction like we've never seen. Helena, if I don't control it, who will? Someone without my moral grounding could use this technology for evil. I need it to keep my planet safe."

He meant it. He truly meant and believed what he was saying. He was so sincere, so vulnerable in that moment, that she almost gave it to him. "For the sake of our family, Helena, tell me where it is."

Family?

He had cast her aside, framed her for the death of hundreds to keep his precious company safe.

To preserve his own name.

To keep his pocket sufficiently lined.

Family?

He'd disowned her, his own daughter, for something he'd done.

Family?

Mariko, her baby sister, was dead because of him.

Lena stood tall and looked him directly in the eye. "Father?" she said with a smile. "Go to hell."

He straightened, his lips a thin line and his eyes steeled. "Very well." He then turned around, took a gun from one of his guards, aimed it directly at Gael and fired.

Gael's face went slack with shock as he collapsed.

CHAPTER FORTY-FIVE

Tadashi turned back to his guard and handed him the gun. "Kill one more every minute she withholds her information. I have a press conference to run." He turned then, and walked past the crew, stepping over Gael's bleeding body, and out the front door. Two of his guards accompanied him.

Lena wanted to run to Gael, but the waiting guards still had guns trained on them. She opened her mouth to tell them that Gael had the plans, but before she could make a sound, one of the guards staggered back, the top of his head blown away.

A quick glance straight up revealed Chandra on a higher balcony.

Lena didn't wait to see the other five guards drop one by one as Chandra took them out from her position on the balcony above. She rushed to Gael's side. She knelt beside him and lifted his head up into her lap. "Gae? Gael? Talk to me."

He opened his eyes. "Ow." He pressed a hand to his side. "That bastard shot me."

"Raines!" she shouted, but he was already there, tearing Gael's shirt open to see the wound. The bullet had passed clean through the right side of Gael's torso. Blood pooled around the gaping wound, but it was so far to the side that Lena didn't think any vital organs were hit.

"You're okay, *mon ami*. Her old man is a terrible shot," Raines said. "I just need to stop the bleeding and get you stitched up." He pulled off his own shirt and wadded it into the wound. Then he looked up and scanned the room. Chandra had taken out the guards and was now going to each wounded and dead one of them, removing weapons, while Cat stood wide-eyed and terrified beside them. "Cat! Cat!" He snapped his fingers. "I need you. Find a med."

Cat seemed to come to herself all at once. She nodded, then turned on her heel and ran out the door.

"Where—?" Chandra asked.

"She's going to the crash site. There'll be med techs for any casualties. Follow her," Raines commanded. Chandra obeyed, and Raines turned his attention back to his friend. Gael tried to reach for his jacket pocket, but couldn't get to it. Raines understood and got the datastick himself. He pressed into Lena's hand. "You have to go."

"What? I'm not leaving Gael like this. He could die."

"Not today," Gael said, though his voice was strained. He was still losing a lot of blood. "I wouldn't do that to you."

"You don't know!" Lena insisted. "I'm not going anywhere."

"You have to," Raines said. "Your father said he's going to a press conference. Probably about *Aspasia*'s crash. Lena, you can end this. With reporters there? With publicity? You can expose him."

He was right. She looked to Gael. He nodded. He knew the job wasn't done.

Lena looked to the two men. They had stood by her when the universe turned its back. When she had no family, they had taken her in. They'd given her a home. And they believed she could do this.

She carefully lifted Gael's head and slipped out from under him, but before she could stand, Gael grabbed her hand. "He's wrong. Your father. You are worthy of so much love."

Lena squeezed his hand and brought it carefully to her lips. "Thank you. I'm sorry for ... for what happened between us. I'll be back. I'll make it right."

"I'll be here."

"You better be." She looked to Raines. "I'm holding you responsible for him."

"Stop stalling and go," he said, but he smiled at her. "We've got this." He looked over her shoulder as Cat and Chandra came running back with a bewildered med-tech fast on their heels. "Chan, go with Lena."

"Right," she said.

Lena didn't even try to fight it. She had more important things to worry about.

The datastick hot in her hands, she stood and followed after the path her father had taken.

She knew where the press room was in the next building. First floor, left theater after the entrance hall. She'd played in the staging cove behind the curtain when she was a child. She'd listen to her father give some announcement and wait to be paraded out with her brother, sister, and mother for the cameras afterward. One happy family. One brilliant, prosperous family. She'd supported the illusion, defended her family, even after they cast her out.

Now she came bearing truth.

And her father would pay for what he'd done to her.

CHAPTER FORTY-SIX

Lena took the back entrance to the press room, hurried past the handlers and PR crew, and pushed through the curtain at the center of the stage, emerging directly behind her father who was in the middle of addressing a roomful of cameras and reporters. She expected some sort of reaction to her arrival, some sort of gasping, murmuring, shouted questions. There was nothing but silence.

It could have been because she was Lena Lomasky, the long-lost daughter finally returned. Or it could have been because she was bloodstained from the waist down.

Or maybe her father just commanded that much respect in his press room.

Either way, her father stepped away from his lectern to give her the mic.

His acquiescence at least, she was pretty sure, was because offstage Chandra was holding a gun on him, and the guards at each of the entrances were nowhere to be seen. Lena took her place before the waiting cameras. Every face watched her expectantly.

She took a deep breath.

"My name is Lena Lomasky. Some of you may have heard of me." That earned her a few chuckles. Good. She needed them on her side. She was entering this as the villain in most people's minds. "I don't know what this particular press conference is supposed to be about. I assume it's about the ship I just crashed into my father's compound. It's okay. He can afford it. Or maybe not. Your perspective on Lomasky Corporation is going to change today." She took a steadying breath and continued. "Most of you know me as the 'lost daughter of Lomasky.' I was blamed for the tragedy at Larissan Yards and the crash of the Nereid that claimed 1,267 lives. I have shouldered that blame for seven years because I thought the accident was my fault. I was led to believe it was my error, and my error alone, that destroyed so much for so many. Today, I learned the truth."

Some of the reporters began to react. They turned to one another, while some began to whisper frantically into their personal comms.

Lena shut them out and continued. "The crash of the Nereid was orchestrated by Tadashi Lomasky in an attempt to distract from a dangerous research project his company had undertaken and subsequently lost. The Lomasky Corp has developed and built a weapon using gravity-based technology. The weapon they developed has the ability to annihilate everything within at least a kilometer radius with no lingering radiation or fallout of any kind. This weapon, as I understand it, would revolutionize warfare as it eliminates the messiness of killing, even as it greatly expands the ability to take lives. Actually, I don't need to tell you. Let me show you."

She took the datastick and inserted it into the port on the front of the lectern. She quickly navigated through the files to the video. The room fell silent as the pretty scientist came to report her findings and eliminated an entire canyon.

As the scene showed the canyon disappear, a murmur began through the room. A voice called out, "It could be faked."

"Indeed, it could," Lena admitted. "But it is not. And I have the complete plans for the weapon as well as further evidence of its destructive capability, its intended buyers, and more. These plans were stolen from my father's labs seven years ago by researchers who found the project to be unethical with potentially catastrophic repercussions for the three systems. I have the only complete set of plans that we know of. My father, Tadashi Lomasky, arranged the crash of the Nereid to distract from its existence and its subsequent theft. His goal was to use this weapon to secure his own legacy and his own power. I will not allow this to happen."

She pulled the datastick from the port and held it up. "This weapon has the potential to change the course of history. It can destroy cities and lives in an instant. The Pyrrhen government has expressed interest in owning this information. I imagine there are others who gladly pay to get their hands on this information. I haven't yet decided what to do with these plans, but I hold the only viable and complete copy of the original blueprints. My own hope is that interested governments and corporations will be willing to work with me to develop countermeasures and protections against this weapon's power. If that isn't feasible or practical given my own circumstances at the moment, well, then, I am willing to hear ideas."

She looked out at the press. Mouths hung open, disgust read clearly, and greedy journalists' eyes sparkled at this turn of events. Lena Lomasky, the most hated woman in Samara, had just planted an even bigger target on her shoulders. She knew what they were thinking: she was either the most naive and greedy woman on the planet or the most brilliant and devious woman in the universe.

Neither were true.

She knew her options. She could destroy the plans, knowing that the Pyrrhens were close to solving the problem of the weapon on their own, giving them the full power of the weapon until someone else solved it independently. She could give or even sell the plans to the Samaran government or some other great power in the universe in the hopes that they would use the weapon's power for good and develop countermeasures. She could publicize the information indiscriminately, knowing that multiple entities could then develop the weapon and use that knowledge as a deterrent against mutually assured destruction.

Or she could control the information herself and measure out who knew what and when. Parceling out the science and the engineering to competing parties could prolong the development of the weapon, and let her either come up with a better plan or find a way to deal with the consequences later.

It also gave her the power her father sought so desperately to deny her.

She turned now to look at her father. He was diminished. He still stood tall and defiant, but he seemed smaller, without anything to say against her. "And finally, I have a message to give to my father. Forgive my using public time for a personal matter, but given that he has conducted so much of his own life in the public eye, I feel it appropriate to do this here." She turned to look at Tadashi Lomasky directly. "Father, you have disgraced your name, dishonored your family, and destroyed any legacy you may have hoped to preserve. The Lomasky name was once synonymous with brilliance, innovation, genius, and potential. Now, it will mean nothing but death and destruction. Your legacy is a cancer, and it will destroy all the good that came before it. Therefore, I renounce my name and any connection to you or your actions. Lena Lomasky is dead."

Lena turned off the mic and walked over to Tadashi Lomasky, the failure. "Goodbye, father." She reached up and kissed him on the cheek. "Good luck." And she turned and walked away from him forever.

CHAPTER FORTY-SEVEN

Lena walked off the Lomasky Campus without a name and with no idea what she was going to do.

Gael and the rest of the crew had relocated to a hotel on the Palerm Coast with a med crew, and messaged Lena and Chandra there were rooms under the name "Pierce Mason." Lena and Chandra hurried there before anyone could follow them.

After a long shower and a much-earned room service meal, Lena sat quietly in a plush hotel robe, sipping a glass of wine staring out at the Bacchan Sea. She slipped her hand in her pocket to touch the datastick. She hadn't let it out of her reach since the press conference and didn't plan to do so anytime soon. She had, however, made multiple hard copies, given them to each of her crewmates, and mailed them to secure holdings in her own personal and anonymous mailboxes in no less than three time zones and two different star systems.

She wasn't ready to leave, though. She had to find a new ship. *Aspasia* would be in no shape to fly for the next several weeks as repairs were made, and even then, by now, everyone knew that Lena Loman flew the *Aspasia*. She was no longer anonymous in the black. Infamy had found her, along with a new price on her head.

She briefly considered taking Chandra's suggestion to send a copy of her files to Yoddha. The mercenary company would certainly have the security to keep the plans safe, but Lena worried they might be willing to sell the plans to someone if they came with a high enough offer.

She wasn't sure exactly what she was going to do at this point.

Raines came out onto the balcony, interrupting her thoughts. He wore an identical robe, and he carried the bottle of wine. "More?" he asked.

She waved him away. "No, I think I want to keep my head clear for a bit longer." She smiled as he sank into the chair beside her. "How's Gael doing?"

"Chandra says he's healing nicely. The hotel doctor got him some salve for the puckering around the stitches that should minimize scarring, and there's no infection."

"We got lucky," Lena said, not willing to let the good news stand in the way of her brooding.

"We did." He smirked. "You know things are going to get more complicated now?"

She rolled her eyes. "Wasn't aware. Gee, I guess I should have chosen the easy way out back there. And what would you have done, oh Captain Wonderful?"

He laughed, not willing to rise to her bait. "Honestly? I don't know. Destroy the plans and light dear old dad on fire on live TV?"

It would have solved some of her problems. Tadashi Lomasky was finished. She'd watched the news coverage as he fled his campus on a private shuttle. He could be halfway to Pyrrhos by now, willing to cut a deal. Or he could be in any of the dozens of mansions he owned across Rien. She didn't know, and frankly, didn't care.

"I like the idea of him living with his shame for a little while," Lena said. Now everyone knew what he had done, that he was deliberately responsible for those lives at Larissan Yards, and that he had orchestrated it all to protect his own hide. Even if no one blamed him for engineering the most dangerous weapon known to man, at least let him shoulder the blame for those lost lives.

"He certainly earned it," Raines agreed, sipping at his own glass of wine. "Let him hide as long as he can. He can't run from that guilt."

"And us? When do we start running? And where?"

Raines gestured out to the open sea before them. "As soon as you're ready. Name a place, we'll go there."

"You have a ship?" Lena was impressed.

"I have a ship. Or rather, Cat has a ship. She and Chandra have been making calls, pulling on some of Cat's old Rienen connections, some Yoddha people. They've got a ship and a mechanic ready to go as soon as you give us the word."

A mechanic. Someone to replace Cedomir. Lena fell quiet again.

Gravity had shifted under her feet once again, and she was just struggling to find the bottom. But as soon as she found ground, as soon as the dust settled, and the world stopped shifting, she could start climbing her way back up. She'd done it before, she could do it again.

This time, though, she was unburdened.

She was free of her past. She wasn't weighed down with the guilt of lives, of her family's disappointment, of potential unfulfilled.

Of course, I have all new burdens to shoulder, she thought wryly.

But that wasn't entirely true. She had renounced her family's crimes, given up the guilt of their failures and misdeeds. She was her own woman.

A woman with a responsibility, true, but for now, it was all hers. Her choice.

Lena laughed, her chest light and head clear for the first time in years. "Can we leave tomorrow?"

"Absolutely. Just name the direction."

Lena pointed up and out beyond the horizon, away from Lomasky Corp, and away from Rien. "Anywhere but here."

NOTE FROM THE ÆUTHOR

Word-of-mouth is crucial for any author to succeed. If you enjoyed the book, please leave a review online—anywhere you are able. Even if it's just a sentence or two. It would make all the difference and would be very much appreciated.

Thanks!
Sara

ABOUT THE AUTHOR

Born and raised in Atlanta, Sara Bond is a southern tall-tale teller with a terrible poker face. So, she writes fiction to better conceal the difference between truth and imagination. After dabbling in careers in academia, politics, and even a lucrative job in high-end fashion, she always found her way back to writing.

Sara lives with her husband and two children who think communication is best achieved through volume, repetition, and pure conviction.

Thank you so much for reading one of our **Sci-Fi** novels.

If you enjoyed our book, please check out our recommended for your next great read!

People of Metal by Robert Snyder

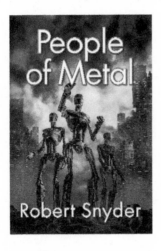

The well-intentioned leaders of China and the U.S. form a grand partnership to create human robots for every human vocation in every country in the world. The human robots proliferate, economic output soars, and the entire world prospers. It's a new Golden Age. But there are unintended consequences—consequences that will place biological humanity on a road to extinction. Ultimately, it will fall to the human robots themselves to rescue biological humanity and restore its civilization.

Made in the USA
Las Vegas, NV
05 December 2021

36134262R00163